All Saints, Murder on the Mersey

All Saints, Murder on the Mersey

Mersey Murder Mysteries Book II

Brian L. Porter

Published 2015 by Creativia
Paperback design by Creativia (www.creativia.org)
ISBN: 978-1530037377
Cover art by http://www.thecovercollection.com/

Dedicated to the memory of John Gill, 1945 – 2015

Former Karting and lawn mower racing champion John Gill was the husband of a dear friend. Just two weeks before his sudden and tragic death, John wrote a glowing review of the first book in this series, *A Mersey Killing*. It turned out to be the last review the book received before his untimely death. With the permission of his widow, Carole, I have dedicated All Saints, Murder on the Mersey to John's memory, in the firm belief he would have enjoyed this second instalment of the Mersey Mysteries series.

John's review of *A Mersey Killing:*
A MERSEY KILLING IS FAB
A Mersey Killing, as well as being a great story, succeeded in taking me back to the days of my own youth. The hopes, dreams and aspirations of a generation were perfectly summed up here by young Brendan Kane who simply wanted 'something more than his Mum and Dad had, maybe one of those new colour television sets'. Few of us had them back then unless you had plenty of money. Nothing too grand in his ambitions then, and that's the great thing about the book. It recreates the sixties just as it was for those of us who lived through those heady days of The Beatles, Gerry and the Pacemakers, et al. The author's descriptions of sixties life were bang on, right down to the washing drying on the old wooden clothes horse in front of the coal fire, which had to be kept going in the summer to heat the water!

As we moved to the nineties, the investigation into the skeletal remains found in the old disused Cole Brothers wharf sets in train an investigation that leads the detectives right back to those early years of the Merseybeat, with murder, betrayal and a missing woman thrown into the equation. As D.I. Ross and Sergeant Drake delve into the past, we eventually learn the tragic secret of A Mersey Killing... simply fab!

Other Books by the Author

The Mersey Mystery Series

- A Mersey Killing
  Coming soon

  - A Mersey Maiden
  - A Mersey Mariner
  - A Mersey Ferry Tale

Thrillers by Brian L Porter

- A Study in Red - The Secret Journal of Jack the Ripper

- Legacy of the Ripper

- Requiem for the Ripper

- Pestilence

- Purple Death

- Behind Closed Doors

- Avenue of the Dead

- The Nemesis Cell

- Kiss of Life

Short Story Collection

- After Armageddon

Remembrance Poetry

- Lest We Forget

Children's books as Harry Porter

- Wolf

- Alistair the Alligator, (Illustrated by Sharon Lewis)
  Coming soon

  - Tilly's Tale
  - Dylan's Tale
  - Charlie the Caterpillar, (Illustrated by Bonnie Pelton)
  - Hazel the Honeybee, Saving the World, (Illustrated by Bonnie Pelton)
  - Percy the Pigeon, (Illustrated by Sharon Lewis)

As Juan Pablo Jalisco

- Of Aztecs and Conquistadors

Acknowledgements

All Saints, Murder on the Mersey is the second book in my Mersey Mysteries series and owes its existence to a number of people who were invaluable to me in bringing the book to life.

First and foremost, my thanks must go to Miika Hannila at Creativia Publishing, whose faith in, and enthusiasm for the first book in this series, A Mersey Killing, inspired me to decide to create a series of books based on the cases of Detective Inspector Andy Ross and Sergeant Clarissa, (Izzie) Drake.

Thanks also to Debbie Poole of Liverpool, who so enjoyed A Mersey Killing that she contacted me to volunteer her services as a beta reader for All Saints. She has done a fantastic job and she has earned my gratitude for her diligence and attention to detail, not to mention the laughter we've enjoyed along the way at one or two hilarious typos she's picked up during the process, e.g. 'hysterical window,' where I of course meant 'hysterical widow'. Thank you, Debbie.

As always I have to thank my dear wife for her patience and her patient checking of each chapter as it was written, and also a big thank you to fellow author, Carole Gill, who helped me enormously during a potentially catastrophic computer breakdown, and provided her usual support at times when my muse threatened to desert me.

Finally, my thanks go to the members of my family, mostly and very sadly no longer with us, in the great city of Liverpool, upon whom many of the characters in the book are based. I should also say a thank you to the people of Liverpool, my ancestral home town. It took me many years to finally get around to setting one of my books in the city, but since writing A Mersey Killing, I've received so much wonderful feedback from the people of Liverpool by way of reviews and messages that I wish I'd done it years ago.

Contents

Introduction

All Saints, Murder on the Mersey is the second book in my Mersey Mysteries series, featuring Detective Inspector Andy Ross, Sergeant Izzie Drake and the fictional Merseyside Police Murder Investigation Team, following on from the so far successful, *A Mersey Killing*.

Though set in my ancestral home of the city of Liverpool, this is a work of fiction and though many of the places mentioned in the book are of necessity, real locations in the city, many of the places are in fact fictitious, the creations of my own mind. This is particularly true of the churches mentioned in the book. Liverpool is blessed with many churches of differing faiths, but it would not have been fair or respectful to use any of them as locations for this story. The churches mentioned in *All Saints, Murder on the Mersey* should therefore not be assumed to bear any reference to actual churches in the city that bear the same names.

Look out for the forthcoming books in the series, *A Mersey Maiden, A Mersey Mariner, and A Mersey Ferry Tale.*

Prologue

Speke Hill Orphanage, Liverpool

Strictly speaking, Speke Hill Orphanage was something of a conundrum. First of all, it wasn't in Speke, the area of Liverpool that today is possibly best known as the location of Liverpool's John Lennon airport. Secondly, there wasn't a hill in sight, and in point of fact it had never been designed to be used for its current purpose. There probably wasn't a living soul who could rightly recall how or why the former Mental Asylum had been given its original name other than those who assumed it was perhaps an attempt to give the old place a touch of the grandiose with a name bearing a similarity to Speke Hall, the Tudor mansion once owned by the wealthy Norris family, and now in the care of The National Trust, a few miles away. Though, bearing in mind the 'clientele' of the old asylum, it would have been debatable whether any of the inmates would have appreciated the pleasant rural-sounding name of their place of incarceration.

For most of those held within the grim walls of the old Victorian buildings that comprised the asylum, Speke Hill would have been the last place on earth they wanted to be, and for the worst afflicted, it may also have been the last place on earth they would see, many being confined without limit of time behind the locked doors and corridors of the bleak, forbidding red-brick buildings.

Set back from Woolton Road, in its own deceptively pleasant land-scaped grounds, a sweeping, curved gravel driveway, bordered by an avenue of fir trees, the asylum employed all the horrors of early Victorian psychiatric 'treatments' to those in its care, including dousing with freezing cold water from high-pressured hoses, to beatings, long periods of solitary confinement and worst of all, the enforced use of frontal lobotomy in a madly useless attempt to cure the sufferers of perceived insanity.

Thankfully, the suffering of those held behind the walls of Speke Hill ended when the asylum was closed in the 1930s, and its inhabitants transferred to other establishments, though whether their treatment improved or deteriorated in their new 'homes' was hardly a subject considered worthy of recording by the chroniclers of the time.

After standing empty for five years, it was decided that, rather than the council going to the expense of demolishing the three buildings that comprised Speke Hill, the old place could be utilised, following a cheap and cheerful programme of renovation, as an orphanage, there being an ever growing proliferation of parentless children in the city and its environs during the austere and barren industrially sterile years following the Great War of 1914-18. Often, children whose fathers were away at sea and whose mothers simply couldn't cope would be placed in orphanages. Hunger, general deprivation and homelessness had taken a bitter toll on the great port city.

The project gained more popularity with cost-conscious council-lors when the local diocese of the Roman Catholic Church offered to contribute a sizeable portion of the cost of renovation, provided they were given the rights to run the orphanage, placing a strong emphasis on discipline and religious instruction, with the stated aim of turn-ing out useful members of society by the time their charges were old enough to leave full time education, usually at the age of fifteen, which would be provided in the school which would be run in one of the three old asylum buildings. There had been some opposition in the council chamber at this development.

It was felt by some that the orphanage should be run on secular lines, as not all the children who would populate the orphanage would be of the Catholic faith, but the voices of dissent were over-ridden, probably for reasons more to do with cost than matters of faith. It was, however, written into the constitution of the new Speke Hill Orphanage that no child should be forced to follow the Catholic faith if they held strong beliefs of an opposite faith. Of course, this tended to be easier to say than to execute, as most children of tender years would find it difficult to argue such a point with those in charge of their everyday lives, and so catholic or protestant, the children who first moved into the dormitories of the newly renovated buildings found themselves being taught as though they were all of the Roman Catholic faith. Most of them, being children of the poorer inner city areas and rather wise to such things, tended to take the religious instruction with a pinch of salt, and most people thought at the time that the new orphanage was initially a great success. What many failed to realise at the time was that by allowing Speke Hill to effectively become a closed community, many of the children accommodated in the new orphanage felt as though they were in an environment that almost amounted to being incarcerated in much the same way as the previous inhabitants of the old asylum must have felt.

The well-meaning diocese of the church provided plenty of areas within the grounds for the children's recreational needs, a football pitch and netball court, two separate playground areas containing various implements of play, slides, swings, etc, and the children were allowed out of the grounds on certain days so they could interact with the local population, but those youngsters who were forced to call Speke Hill home found they would never be fully integrated or accepted by those who lived in the surrounding areas along Woolton Road.

And so, life went on at the new orphanage, the old wards gradually being modernised and the large open dormitories eventually becoming partitioned so that groups of four children could have their own shared 'rooms' and a modicum of privacy. The school, taught by well qualified Catholic priests, and at first thought of as providing nothing more than basic education to the children of Speke Hill, surprised everyone by establishing a good reputation for turning out young teenagers with a higher than average standard of education for the time, and even bred a little resentment among the children and parents of some children at other schools in the area.

With the coming of World War Two, things changed at Speke Hill, as they did almost everywhere in the country. Though those in charge attempted to carry on normally, by the time the blitz arrived, with regular bombing of the city of Liverpool, the docks being seen as a prime target by the Luftwaffe, it had become apparent that even one stray bomb, dropped on the buildings of Speke Hill, could result in devastating loss of life, and the children were added to those who would be evacuated out of the cities to temporary homes well out of reach of the Luftwaffe's bombs.

Speke Hill closed temporarily, and didn't reopen its doors, unscathed by the attentions of the Luftwaffe, until after the end of hostilities in 1946. Most of the staff who had worked hard to build the reputation of the orphanage and its school, both ecclesiastical and civilian, in its early days had moved on to other things during the war years, and indeed, many of the children who had been evacuated had reached an age where they were ready to leave school and begin their working lives, and for the most part, Speke Hill was virtually reborn in the post war years with new staff and a mostly new population of poor and needy children from the poorest housing estates of Liverpool.

* * *

The nineteen sixties arrived with little having changed in the running of Speke Hill during the post-war years, apart from the fact that the new Local Education Authority exercised more control over the educational standards required of pupils in the United Kingdom than in pre-war years. As such the school at Speke Hill was overseen in greater detail than before and the priests charged with the children's education were now all required to hold relevant teaching qualifications in the subjects they taught. For the most part the orphanage had grown to be a reasonably happy place for those living there, with educational standards once again rising, and very little trouble caused by those very children who might at one time have been deemed 'troublemakers' if left to roam the streets from whence they originated.

In an effort to add a touch of 'class' to the educational side of things, the teaching staff copied the 'house' system, as used in many secondary schools at the time, to help instil a sense of pride, belonging and competition among the children, and so Molyneux, Norris, Stanley and Sefton, all names historically associated with the city, were chosen by a Diocesan committee as the names for the four Houses of the Speke Hill School.

By the time the 'Swinging Sixties' hit the United Kingdom in general and the city of Liverpool in particular, Speke Hill had expanded its sports facilities to include a second football pitch, a rugby pitch, the netball court remained of course, and the school now boasted an indoor gymnasium, with sport and recreation having been deemed as being good not only for the body, but for the soul as well, by those with responsibility for the youngsters in care in the orphanage.

As Cilla Black's *You're My World* became her second UK number one chart hit at the end of May, 1964, the staff and children of Speke Hill prepared for their forthcoming school sports day with all the usual enthusiasm that went hand-in-hand with a day spent out of the classrooms and buildings of the orphanage. An air of excitement spread through the halls and dorms of the orphanage, and the children felt a slight lessening in the usual strictness of the regime enforced by the priests and nuns who held control over their everyday lives. An extra hour was allowed for all the boys and girls in the communal TV room, a privilege extended to allow a similar additional allowance to radio time, for those lucky enough to possess a transistor radio and the batteries to power it. Only a few lucky children owned such treasures, saved for out of their meagre weekly allowances, pocket money that most would quickly spend in a few days at the local sweet shop or

Brian L. Porter

on cheap throwaway toys, perhaps from Woolworths, on rare visits to town, under supervision by an ever watchful priest and nun.

And of course, in case you were wondering, due to its former incarnation as an asylum it was almost inevitable that over the years certain stories of a more fanciful nature began to attach themselves to the orphanage, spread no doubt by boys or girls with lively imaginations and too much time on their hands in their spare time to allow such thoughts to manifest themselves, and so, as with many such institutions, Speke Hill is reputed to possess its very own resident ghost...

7

Chapter 1

Homecoming, Liverpool, 2002

Gerald Byrne stood at the ship's railing, his eyes stinging slightly, his hair damp from the salt spray of the voyage across the Irish Sea. He would not, however, have missed the sight of the ferry's arrival in Liverpool for the entire world. As the ship neared the great sea port, the city of his birth, he smiled as the iconic view of the world-famous Liverpool waterfront came into view, dominated by the three majestic buildings that had come to be known as 'The Three Graces'. The Royal Liver Building, The Cunard Building and the Port of Liverpool Building had dominated the Liverpool waterfront for almost a century, defining the city's skyline for locals and visitors alike. The sun was already quite high and played upon the waterfront buildings, making them gleam and reflect almost perfectly in the waters of the River Mersey. Byrne could make out movement on shore as the people of the city went about their daily business, pedestrians, buses and cars clearly visible from his ship-board vantage point as the ferry drew nearer and nearer to Liverpool's ferry port.

The priest sighed as the ship swung towards the ferry terminal, and his view was temporarily obscured by the change in the ferry's orientation. The eight hour crossing had been boring and uneventful, the Irish Sea not too violent in its treatment of the ship and its passengers. Father Byrne had spent most of the trip in one of the aircraft-like seats that P &O Ferries supplied in lieu of cabins on the service, his mind alternating between his reading of the Bible and thoughts of returning to the city of his childhood after so many years.

Life had been good to Gerald Byrne over the years. Born in a back-to-back terraced house on Scotland Road, one of the poorest areas of the city in nineteen fifty four, he and his sister ended up in Speke Hill after their mother died of pneumonia in nineteen sixty-one, their father having died four years earlier, having eventually succumbed to ill health as a result of disease and deprivation suffered during his time as a prisoner-of-war, working on the notorious 'railway of death' in Burma under the brutal regime of the Japanese guards.

Against all odds, young Gerald thrived in his new environment and impressed his teachers and the caring staff at the orphanage with his capacity for learning and exemplary behaviour. He developed a deep interest in theology and the Catholic Church and from an early age, he knew the direction he expected his future to take.

Following his chosen path by living his life in the Roman Catholic Church, he'd left Liverpool in nineteen seventy five, at the age of twenty-one, and following his eventual ordination in Rome, of all places, he'd led a good life, serving the church in various locales around the world, expanding his knowledge of the diverse people and races that went to make up the vast worldwide congregation of Catholicism. Gerald had witnessed life and death in all its forms, having served in war zones, areas of famine relief, and in disease-ridden areas of some of the poorest nations of the world, ministering to the poor and the sick. He'd managed to learn to speak four languages, apart from English, quite fluently, and had learned from his experiences that quite often the rich were in as much spiritual need, if not more in some cases, than the downtrodden masses of the third-world nations so often in the news headlines around the world.

Now at the age of forty-eight, the church had agreed to his request to return to his home town, following a diagnosis of severe unstable angina by his doctor. If anything were to happen to bring him ever closer to his eventual meeting with his maker, Byrne wanted to be in his home city when it occurred. Five feet ten, hair still a dark brown with only a few flecks of grey, Byrne looked far fitter then he really was, his physique built over many years of enjoying various sporting activities.

Having spent five years teaching at a seminary just outside the village of Enniskerry in County Wicklow, Byrne had moved on to become a parish priest once again, and now, his congregation at the small church of St Clement in a small town in County Cork had been upset and saddened to see their priest of these past ten years leave them. Gerald Byrne had become part of the fabric of their lives, a fixture in their religious and devotional faith, and in truth, it saddened him to be leaving them also, but, as he explained to a full church at the end of his final mass at St. Clement's, God, his conscience, and the lure of his home meant it was time to leave, to go back to his roots, and to be at peace with God, with himself and with his past before finally leaving this earthly plane.

* * *

Father Byrne found himself jolted out of his reverie by the sound of the ship's hooter as the *Port Erin* swung beam-on to the dockside and crewmen ran to the port side of the ship, where they heaved the thick hawsers over the side to be caught by the dock workers on shore, who proceeded to wrap the ropes around the capstans on the dock, until the ship was made fast and the throbbing of the powerful diesel engines died away, and the vibration of the deck beneath the passengers' feet ceased as the eight hour voyage came to its end. For a few seconds, the silence was palpable until, as if as one, passengers and crew seemed to come to life and there began a mass exodus from the ship, as the city of Liverpool beckoned those on board.

Within a short time, Father Byrne found himself being carried along in a wave of humanity down the gangplank, and he said a silent prayer of thanks as his feet touched the ground on the dockside. He was home again.

Carrying his single suitcase into the ferry terminal building, and wearing his charcoal grey suit, black shirt and white clerical collar, Gerald Byrne's calling was evident to anyone who cared to look at the tall handsome man with the dark brown hair, only slightly greying at the edges. Within seconds of his arrival in the terminal, a diminutive figure, at least six inches shorter in height, and dressed in similar fashion to the priest, came scurrying up to him, addressing Byrne in a breathless voice as he held out his right hand in greeting.

"You must be Father Byrne," said the new arrival. "Please say you are. I'd hate to be speaking to the wrong priest after being delayed in a traffic jam on the way and then finding hardly a space to park the car."

Gerald Byrne smiled as he shook hands with the little priest, whose words spilled out in a hurry, as though he was recently qualified in speed-speaking.

"I am indeed Father Byrne, have no worries, and you, I presume, are Father Willis?"

"Yes, yes, that's right, Father. David Willis, your Deacon, praise God, and pleased to be so."

Still grinning, Byrne placed a hand on the young priest's shoulder as he spoke again.

"Father Willis, David, if I may?" Willis nodded emphatically. "Good, now David, calm yourself, dear boy. There's no harm done. The Good Lord saw fit to aid you through the traffic jam and the car park just in time to meet me here, without you having to wait for ages and perhaps having to sit and drink some terrible potion masquerading as tea or coffee out of that infernal machine over there."

Willis looked behind him to where Byrne indicated a hot drinks machine, beloved of railway stations, ferry terminals and bus stations the world over

"Well of course, Father Byrne, you're quite correct in that respect. I was just so afraid you'd arrive and there'd be no-one here to meet you and you'd have thought me so terribly remiss."

"So, there's no harm done, now, is there?"

"No, Father, as you say, no harm done at all."

"In which case, I suggest you take a moment to calm yourself and then we'll take a walk to your car and you can drive me to my new church, and my new home, and we can become better acquainted along the way, eh, David?"

"Oh, yes, of course. The car park's not far away and we'll soon have you at St. Luke's, Father."

Byrne placed another steadying hand on Willis's shoulder.

"And tell me, David, do you always speak so quickly, as if the words are likely to go out of fashion if you don't get them out fast enough?"

"Oh dear, that is a rather bad habit of mine, when I'm stressed or nervous. Father O'Hanlon used to say the same thing to me, you know, bless his soul."

"Well, please, David, there's no call for you to be stressed or nervous around me, that's for sure. Did you work under Father O'Hanlon for long?"

"I came to St. Luke's exactly a year ago this month, Father. It was a real shock when poor Father O'Hanlon passed away so suddenly."

"I'm sure it was, David. A heart attack I believe?"

"Yes, indeed it was, Father."

"Well, he's with our Lord in Heaven now, David and it's my job, and yours, to ensure we carry on the Lord's work at St. Luke's, and so, let's go."

David Willis nodded, took up Byrne's suitcase, and led Gerald Byrne to the car park, where the older priest couldn't help but smile as Willis stopped at a rather battered looking Ford Escort, that had obviously seen better days, opened the boot and deposited the suitcase within. The young priest then rushed to open the passenger door for the new parish priest of St. Luke's, Woolton, and within minutes they were clear of the ferry terminal and heading to Byrne's new parish, and new home.

Chapter 2

Norris Green, Liverpool, 3 Months Later

Detective Inspector Andy Ross pulled the unmarked police Mondeo to a halt, its right side wheels pulled up on the pavement outside St. Matthew's Church in Norris Green in an effort to avoid restricting the traffic flow along Brewer Street. The Norris Green housing estate, built on land donated to the council by the Norris family, was unusual in that the original bequest of the land included the stipulation that no public house be built on the land. To this day, that instruction has been adhered to, meaning residents of Norris Green have to venture further afield to obtain whatever alcoholic stimulation they require.

There were already two police patrol cars parked on the street, together with another pool car identical to his own which he knew would have brought his assistant, Sergeant Clarissa, (Izzie) Drake and Detective Constable Derek McLennan to the scene as well as an ambulance and the green Volvo he recognised as that belonging to Dr. William (Fat Willy, but don't tell him that) Nugent, the overly rotund but eminently brilliant pathologist who served as the city's senior medical examiner. Blue and white police crime scene tape had already been strategically placed across the wide double gated entrance to the churchyard, with an attendant uniformed constable on guard to prevent unwanted sightseers trying to gatecrash the crime scene.

Ross silently cursed the court case that had demanded his appearance at nine a.m that morning. The trial of a serial mugger who had almost killed his twelfth and last victim before being almost comically apprehended by the off-duty Andy Ross had been suddenly curtailed when the accused changed his plea from not-guilty to guilty, thus relieving Ross of the need to hang around the court building waiting to give evidence. As soon as he exited the court and turned on his mobile phone, Ross received word of the 'incident' involving a body being discovered in St. Matthew's churchyard from his squad's collator, D.C Paul Ferris. The fact that he would now probably be the last to arrive on the scene did little to improve his humour after what he considered a wasted and fruitless start to his day.

Luckily for him, the uniformed constable on duty at the gates recognised the detective inspector and with a brief, "Good morning, sir," waved Ross through after lifting the crime scene tape for the detective to pass beneath. Ross had no need to ask the constable where to go. He simply followed his nose along the path that led around the church itself, in the direction of the noise of voices and activity in the graveyard that stood to the rear of the church.

As he neared the scene, Ross could see Dr. Nugent on his knees, his assistant, Francis Lees beside him, both men obviously intent on carrying out their initial examination of the body of the unfortunate victim. Sergeant Drake and Constable McLennan were in attendance, standing just behind the doctor and Lees, while three uniformed constables stood further back from the scene, each man bearing what Ross could only describe as a disturbed look upon their faces.

Seeing him drawing near, Izzie Drake broke away from her position and walked briskly towards him.

"Morning, sir. I'm afraid we've got a bad one today."

"Hmm, well, there are never any good ones when it comes to murder, are there, Sergeant?"

"I know sir, I'm sorry, I just meant..."

"Forget it, Izzie. My apologies. I'm just in a foul temper after wasting my time at the damn court this morning."

"I know, sir. Ferris told me when he called to let me know you were on the way. Damn shame, wasting your time like that, but, at least Phillip Downes won't be troubling the courts again for a few years after he's sentenced."

"Very true," Ross replied. "Now, come on, what have we got here?"

"It's bloody gruesome, sir, and that's the truth. Poor Derek threw up almost as soon as we got here, as well as one of the uniformed lads. Bet they both wish they hadn't eaten a hearty breakfast this morning. Come on, sir, best you see for yourself."

Ross nodded and the two detectives walked slowly towards the location of the body that had necessitated the appearance of the Murder Investigation Team at the scene.

Sensing their approach, William Nugent turned and looked up from his kneeling position as he greeted Ross in his variable Glaswegian accent. Ross always thought of the word 'variable' when it came to Nugent's speech as the more upset or irate he became, the more guttural and broad his accent became, even after spending most of his working life in the city of Liverpool.

"A late start this morning, eh, Detective Inspector?" he chided, though Ross knew the pathologist would have been made well aware of the circumstances surrounding his delay in attending the death scene. Ignoring Nugent's obvious attempt at a witty remark, Ross replied, in a total business-like tone.

"Yes, indeed, Doctor. I take it you've been here long enough to carry out at least a cursory examination of the victim?"

"Aye, well, you could say that, I suppose. Ye'd best come and take a look for yourself, but I'm warning ye, it's not a pretty site. Francis, please step away and allow the Inspector and the Sergeant to get a good look at the poor soul, would ye?" he said to his tall, thin assistant, whom many of Ross's team though of as being almost as cadaverous in his appearance as some of the bodies they were forced to deal with in the commission of their jobs.

"Oh, my God," Ross exclaimed as he drew closer to the scene, Drake slightly behind and to the side of him.

"I told you, sir," his sergeant said, quietly.

"Yes, but this...this is, well, nothing short of bloody monstrous. What the hell happened to the poor bastard?"

William Nugent spoke up in reply from behind the inspector.

"Well, at first glance," he spoke almost reverently, "the victim, a man I'd put in his mid-to late fifties by the way, has been almost totally eviscerated. As you can see, the poor sod's intestines have been removed and draped across the headstone of the grave on which his body lies, and his other major organs, liver, kidneys, spleen and heart are neatly arranged around the body, almost as though the killer had laid them out for us in readiness for a post-mortem examination. But, and if you look closely, you'll see the worst part of all this, Inspector, your killer removed the victim's penis, and then stuffed it down the poor bugger's throat. Oh yes, one more thing, he also removed the victim's tongue, though I cannae find it anywhere up to this point in time. The killer may have taken it with him, a trophy of his handiwork, perhaps. Of course, that's more in your pervue than mine, I'm simply surmising."

Ross couldn't help himself. He visibly gagged as he took in the blood-drenched scene that lay before him. The naked body of the unfortunate victim lay across the gravelled top of a grave, and as Nugent had indicated, the intestines had been draped across the headstone that stood at the head of the grave, the internal organs dripping blood as they lay in the gradually warming sunshine around the sides of the grave. From what he could make out, the look on the dead man's face was one of total fear and horror.

Ross gulped hard, and turned his face from the scene. Hardened detective he may have been, but this definitely was 'a bad one', as Izzie Drake had called it, and he was hardly surprised that the uniformed constable and his own detective constable had felt the urge to be sick at the sight that they'd stumbled onto when they'd arrived at the scene.

"Tell me Doctor, can you say whether these... er, these mutilations were carried out while the victim was alive or dead, and what may have been the actual cause of death? I know that sounds stupid, but would one particular injury the victim sustained have been enough to cause death, or was this a prolonged and sadistic attack by some kind of pervert, perhaps?"

"Ah wish I could tell ye, Inspector, but, it's too early for me to say and you know I dinna like to speculate on these matters. We'll have to wait until we get what's left of yon laddie to the morgue and I can carry out a detailed examination. For now, I think we can say without much doubt that the cause of death was exsanguination, though which wound, or wounds were the fatal blow, well, I just cannae say."

"Any identification, his clothes, any personal items, were they found?"

"Not a thing," Nugent replied. "As far as I can tell, he was left here naked as he is now. Whoever did this, and he's a sadistic bastard I can tell you for free, made sure he took the poor man's clothes and any identification he was carrying with him when he dumped the poor sod here."

"Thank you Doc," said Ross, turning to his sergeant who was by now visibly pale at being in close proximity to the remains of the victim for so long.

"Who found him, Izzie?"

"The poor bloody priest, Father Michael Donovan. He entered the churchyard through the rear gate and was making his way along the path towards the church when he almost literally stumbled over the body. Apparently, he threw up too, over there."

Izzie pointed to a grave two places along from where the victim lay. At least the priest hadn't contaminated the crime scene.

"I'm not surprised," Ross grimaced. "And where is the good Father now, may I ask?"

"Last seen in his church, praying as though his life depended upon it, sir"

"Right then, let's go and have a word with Father Donovan."

* * *

"Terrible, simply terrible, that poor, poor man," Father Donovan wept openly, his head in his hands as he sat in one of the pews at the front of his church, five minutes later, speaking to Ross and Drake who sat either side of the visibly shaking priest.

"It must have been an awful shock for you, Father," said Ross, sympathetically.

"It was indeed, Detective Inspector. I mean, there I was, enjoying this beautiful sunny morning, whistling to myself, *All Things Bright and Beautiful* of all things, and then, all of a sudden he was there, lying on that grave, virtually in pieces, I tell you, in pieces."

Izzie Drake placed a comforting hand on the priest's right arm in an effort to calm him.

"Father, you need to calm down a little," she said, quietly. "Just take your time and try to recall everything that happened as you walked along the path from the time you passed through the gate until the moment you found the victim."

"Please, Father, it's very important," Ross added, grateful to his sergeant for using her feminine compassion to reach out to the shaking priest.

Michael Donovan took a couple of deep breaths, closing his eyes as he attempted to compose himself and recall the terrible events of earlier that morning. Finally, opening his eyes, he spoke in a faltering voice.

"Well, Inspector, it was just after eight o'clock. I'm sure of the time because I always leave the manse which is just behind the church, at eight precisely. I like to come to church when it's peaceful and quiet and pray for a while in solitude. I hold a morning mass at nine, you see, and, oh, it was just awful seeing your officers turning my parishioners away as they arrived for the service," he rambled for a moment.

"It's alright, Father. I know you're in shock, so just take your time. Now, it was just gone eight o'clock, you say?"

The priest gathered himself together again and went on with his statement.

"The sun was shining and it was already quite warm. I heard a blackbird singing and looked up and saw him perched on the wall that runs along the north side of the churchyard. I remember smiling to my self and began whistling the tune of *All things bright and beautiful.* I didn't stop to watch the bird as I wanted those few precious minutes of contemplative prayer to myself, you see."

Ross nodded but didn't interrupt.

"The path winds its way around the church as you've probably seen, in a sort of S pattern, I suppose you'd call it and as I came round the corner of the church onto the straightish part of the path that leads to the main doors, I saw something ahead of me on one of the graves. At first I thought it might be the work of vandals, the Lord knows we get enough of that sort of thing round here, or maybe someone had dumped a load of old rubbish on the grave, in an act of blatant sacrilege. I slowed down as I got closer and it was then, when I was just a couple of yards away that I realised what I was seeing. I know it sounds stupid, but the first thing I did was wonder if I might be of some help to the man but when I got even closer I saw the terrible, monstrous things that had been done to him and I'm ashamed to say I...I...well, I'd just finished breakfast before I came out, you see, and I couldn't help myself. I staggered over to one of the adjacent graves and was awfully sick, I'm afraid. I've never in all my life seen anything like it, you see, and I pray to God I'll never see the likes again as long as I live."

"You've nothing to apologise for, Father," said Ross. "Two experienced police officers have been sick out there as well. We're all human and none of us should ever have to see such things."

"But sadly, you do, don't you Inspector Ross?"

Ross nodded, but still remained silent, allowing the priest to speak and hopefully recall any small details he may have noticed when he discovered the body.

"There was blood everywhere, Inspector, so much blood. And then, I saw the other things, you know the, the..."

"It's alright, Father, I know what you saw, but tell me, from the time you entered the churchyard until you found the victim, did you see or hear anything else, or any other people, perhaps?"

"Not a soul, no. To be honest, if there had been anyone lurking around, I might not have seen them. I was so focussed on the sunny morning and the birdsong. But I'm still pretty certain there was nobody else around."

"Now, and perhaps most importantly, I know you probably only got a quick look at the victim, Father, but did you recognise him? Is he known to you at all, either as a parishioner or maybe just someone you've seen in the area at all?"

"Yes, it was only a quick look, Inspector. Nobody could possibly have stood staring at that poor man, but I saw enough to know he wasn't anyone I know. I'm sorry. I can't help you there."

Father Donovan's face paled again at the thought of the sight he'd witnessed in his churchyard and he fell silent for a few seconds. Izzie Drake spoke in her quiet voice again.

"I know this is pretty much a rhetorical question, Father, but we have to ask...er, you didn't touch anything at all before calling the police did you?"

Donovan looked aghast at the mere thought of having done so as he replied.

"Sergeant, I most certainly did not. What kind of man do you think I am? A person would have to be very sick in the head to want to mess around with what I saw out there. I simply tried to compose myself and then ran as fast as I could into the church where I rang 999 from my little office in there. Then I waited at the church gates for the police to arrive and to keep anyone from entering the grounds until your people got here."

"And a very good thing you did, Father," said Ross. "It wouldn't have done for anyone else to come wandering in and be confronted with the sight of the poor man out there."

There being little else the priest could tell them, the two detectives left the church, with Father Donovan again on his knees praying before the altar, and moved back into the daylight, where by now the forensic experts of the Crime Scenes Unit had arrived and were busy searching and examining the crime scene and surrounding area.

Ross spoke briefly with Constables Knight and Riley, the first officers to respond to the emergency call, who confirmed they'd arrived on the scene, assessed the situation and immediately called for C.I.D. assistance, and a second squad car of officers to help secure the area, realising the gravity of the situation they'd found. Ross commended both men and then returned to speak to William Nugent, who, together with his assistant, Lees, was packing up his instruments and accoutrements as the body and associated parts were being carefully loaded into a body bag ready for transportation to the morgue, having been fingerprinted where it lay in the hope of identifying the victim, and once at the morgue, he'd carry out a full post-mortem in an effort to determine exactly what had happened to the deceased.

"Anything else to report, Doc?" Ross asked as he drew closer to the pathologist.

"Nothing that I can tell you at present, Inspector. Ye'll get ma full report as soon as possible, like always. Let me get back to the mortuary with the poor man and I can get on with ma job."

There was that strange and for some, disconcerting comingling of accents again, part Glaswegian, part Liverpudlian, that always rather amused Ross.

"A preliminary report will suffice for now, Doc, as soon as you can. This case is likely to generate some nasty headlines if the press gets hold of it, so I'd like to move as fast as I can to find the sick bastard who did this."

"Aye, well, I'll give you a call later today, if I can, and if you and your sergeant care to come along in the morning, I'll schedule the full post mortem examination for nine a.m. if that'll suit you, Inspector?"

"Perfect, thank you Doc." Ross replied, standing aside to let the Doctor and his assistant pass. Ross next spent five minutes talking to Miles Booker, the senior Crime Scenes Officer who was leading the examination of the area around the body. Booker would ensure his team combed every blade of overgrown grass, every sliver of granite chips, every nook or cranny where a minute piece of trace evidence might have been deposited. As he broke away from Booker, Detective Constable McLennan walked up to Ross. McLennan shared the same post-vomiting complexion as the uniformed constable and Father Donovan.

"You alright, Derek?" asked Ross.

"Yes, thank you sir," McLennan replied. "It was just a bit more then my stomach could stand, seeing what the killer did to that poor man."

"No need to apologise, Derek. We're all human, after all. None of us should have to see things like that. Sadly, it's our job when some bastard decides to make a mess of someone in that way. Now, do you have anything for me, anything we can use?"

"Not really, sir. I've spoken at length to the two constables who were the first attenders. They're both adamant there was no one around in the churchyard when they arrived, and neither of them saw anyone acting furtively or suspicious out on the streets as they arrived in response to the emergency call from Father Donovan."

"Alright Derek, Sergeant Drake and I will be heading back to headquarters soon. I'll arrange for Sam to join you out here in a minute. Then I want the two of you to take charge of the scene, until the crime scene boys have done their thing, and then, make a quick sweep of the area, talk to some of the nearest residents in the hope someone may have seen or heard something. I'm going to organise a team of uniforms to carry out a house to house inquiry in a half-mile radius of the church, but something tells me we're going to come up empty handed. And, Derek?"

"Sir?"

"Get one of those constables at the gate to arrange to seal off the back gate too. We're lucky nobody's blundered through there so far."

"Right, sir. I'll get on it right away."

As they spoke, Miles Booker walked up to the detectives with a small cellophane evidence bag in his hand.

"Got something for me, Miles? Ross asked.

"Not sure," said the Crime Scene Investigator. "One of my lads came up with this," and he held the bag up, close enough for Ross and Drake to see a small silver coloured key inside.

"A key," said Drake.

"Hey, ten out of ten, Sergeant," Booker grinned.

"But a key to what?" Drake persisted, "and how do we know it belonged to the victim?"

"That's just it, you see," said the C.S.I. "We don't, at least not yet. Maybe, once we have his fingerprints, we may get lucky and find they match the print we found on the key." He smiled.

"Ah, so you do have a print?" Ross asked.

"Yes, and a pretty good one, looks like most of a thumb print, you know, from when someone held the key to insert it into a lock."

"Looks like the sort of key that fits a safety deposit box, or maybe an airport or railway left luggage locker," said Drake.

"Can I see it, please?" asked Derek McLennan. Booker passed the bag containing the key to the detective constable who scrutinised it carefully for a few seconds before passing it back to him.

"Sir," said McLennan, turning to Ross, "I think we'll find that it is a locker key but not for a left luggage locker at the airport or from a station."

"Alright Derek, let's have it. What's your theory?"

"I think it's from the Halewood Plant, sir."

"The car factory? What makes you think that?"

"Well sir, the cellophane makes it hard to see, but there are a series of four numbers on one side of the key. My brother-in-law works at Halewood, sir and he has a key just like that on his car key ring. The anglar shape is quite distinctive. I've seen it when he's let me use his car once or twice. The way the numbers are etched into the key looks just like this one."

"So, we may have a clue after all. Well done, young Derek," said Ross.

"Thanks, sir," McLennan replied.

"Yes, well, that's assuming the key belonged to the victim, isn't it?" said Miles Booker.

"Very true, Miles," Ross agreed. "Any way you can tell us more that might help?"

"Sorry, Andy, not a thing. If the fingerprint matches your man over there, okay; if not, you're going to be hard pressed to discover if it belonged to him or not."

"We can show his photo to employees at Halewood, see if anyone recognises him," said Izzie Drake.

"Yes, well, bearing in mind what he's got stuffed in his mouth, I wish you luck with that one."

"I'm sure Doctor Nugent can make him look presentable enough for us to get a photo likeness we can show around," Drake responded.

"Of course, just me joking around, Sergeant."

"Could be easier than that, sir, Sarge," McLennan interjected again.

"How's that, then Derek?" asked Drake.

"The numbers on the key," he replied. If it is from Halewood, they'll refer to a specific numbered locker, and that locker will be allocated to an equally specific employee. Simple logic really."

"Yes, of course, well done Derek," said Ross.

Andy Ross had learned to come to rely on young Derek McLennan in the three years he'd served with him. The young man had developed from a hesitant, awkward young D.C. into a clever, confident and reliable member of Ross's team, with a quick mind and an even temperament when working under pressure, not a bad thing when faced with some of the cases the team was called upon to handle. Ross recalled the first major case the young detective had worked on with him, when the skeleton of a long time dead pop guitarist had surfaced in the mud of an old dried up dock in the city, sparking one of Ross's strangest and perhaps most tragic cases to date, which resulted in the ultimate suicide of a woman who'd spent over thirty years of her life officially listed as 'missing'. That case had been the foundation on which Derek McLennan had gradually forged his career and now, Ross knew he could rely on the man's intuitive skills as well as his quick, intelligent mind.

Ross and Drake left soon afterwards, and made their way to the city mortuary, where they knew William Nugent would by now be carrying out an initial examination of the victim's remains. Ross had questions that needed answers and for the moment the only man who could help him was the rather obese but professionally superb pathologist.

Chapter 3

Speke Hill Orphanage, Woolton

Charles Hopkirk, Senior Child-Care Officer in charge of the latter-day orphanage rose from his leather chair and stepped out from behind his desk to greet the newcomer to his office. Five feet nine, already turned grey, and with a slight stoop as he stood, Hopkirk looked every bit as worn down as his slightly crumpled dark blue suit with its shiny elbows, and his black shoes with attendant scuff marks, betrayed the lack of a Mrs. Hopkirk. No one would believe a good wife would allow her husband to leave home each day looking quite so dishevelled. Doing his best to look the opposite of his actual appearance and putting on an air of assumed authority, he held his hand out as he spoke and shook hands with his visitor.

"Father Byrne, welcome to Speke Hill. We're delighted to have you here as our new chaplain to the pupils."

"It's a pleasure, Mr. Hopkirk, I assure you, and you must call me Gerald, please, unless we're in formal circumstances, of course."

"Well in that case, you must call me Charles. I insist. And, it seems rather appropriate to have you here as part of our community, don't you agree?"

"It does?"

"Oh come now, you must know we'd soon find out you were once one of our boys here at Speke Hill, and to have you return as the Parish

Priest at St. Luke's and our chaplain here is wonderful, a great example to hold up before the children."

"I wouldn't go so far as to say that, Charles. It's a tradition that the priest at St. Luke's takes the role of chaplain here at Speke Hill, and yes, I may have been an orphan myself, raised here, as you say, but I wouldn't want to be held up as an example of something I'm not. Not everyone at Speke Hill aspires to grow up to be a Roman Catholic Priest."

"You're too modest, Father, er, sorry, Gerald, I'm sure, but let's not dwell on it. I imagine you'd like a quick tour? Many things have changed since the days when the Catholic Church ran the place. Now that Liverpool Council, together with the Local Education Authority have control over Speke Hill, there've been many improvements and changes to the place, as you'll see."

"And some things never change, eh, Charles?"

"I'm sorry?"

"The entrance gates and the driveway, with those rowan trees and elms lining the gravel drive. It still gives the false impression of arriving at some old Victoria country mansion. It was just the same when I was a boy here"

"Oh, I see," said Hopkirk, who'd wondered for a moment just where Father Byrne was heading with his previous remark.

"Yes, I suppose like the original incumbents of Speke Hill, those in authority long ago decided to maintain the sweeping curve of the driveway and the grandly ornate gates at the entrance. It does after all give the place a touch of the grandiose, don't you think? Nice for those who live here, Father, I think. Not just some grey concrete monstrosity in the middle of an inner city sink estate. At least the boys and girls who live here and are schooled here can feel proud of the place, which does of course, have an excellent academic record and a long list of former pupils at the school who have gone on to achieve good things in life. Rather like yourself, Father Byrne."

"Yes, well thank you, Charles, and please, my name, again is Gerald. I did well, as have quite a few former orphans and pupils from here.

It's a pleasure to be able to come back and perhaps contribute a little to the spiritual welfare of the boys and girls."

"I looked you up, Gerald," said Hopkirk, looking pleased with himself.

"Did you now?" asked the priest. "And just what did you discover, I wonder?"

"Only that you arrived here, together with your ten year old sister, Angela, as a seven year old after your mother died, in nineteen sixty-one, with no other relatives left to look after you. Your father had died a few years earlier, finally succumbing to illness following years of ill treatment during the war in a Japanese Prisoner-of-War Camp and the two of you then lived in the orphanage and attended the church school here until you were both old enough to leave and make your way in the world. One particular note on your records really stood out, Gerald."

"And what, I wonder, would that be?"

"Well, it was two things really. It said you were an outstanding sportsman, having represented the school, and Stanley House, at football, rugby and cricket, and that you also, even then, possessed a strong sense of spirituality, and had professed your intention of entering the priesthood as soon as you were old enough. It's nice to know you were successful in your ambition, Gerald."

"Thank you, Charles. My life has indeed been one of enrichment and service to God, and I'm happy to be home again after so many years away."

"And your sister, Angela? How has she fared in the big wide world since leaving us?"

A cloud momentarily seemed to pass before the priest's eyes and his shoulders appeared to droop as his demeanour changed for a few seconds, until he pulled himself together before replying.

"I'm afraid Angela died at a young age, Charles. I'd prefer it if we don't discuss the details. It was a painful time for me and remains so to this day."

A look of genuine concern appeared on Charles Hopkirk's face. He'd looked up the original records of their new priest as soon as he'd heard that he was an 'old boy' of Speke Hill. Those records showed his sister Angela to have been a resident of the orphanage at the same time as Gerald Byrne, but obviously, those records ended when each of the children reached the age of maturity and passed out of the local council's care. He now felt he may have committed something of a 'faux pas' in mentioning what was obviously a painful subject for the priest.

"I'm so sorry, Father Byrne," he said, returning to a veneer of formality. "I didn't mean to upset you."

"It's okay, Charles, really. It's just that it all happened a long time ago and isn't something I care to talk about any more. My sister dwells with the Lord now, and I'd like to leave it at that, and, my name is Gerald, remember?"

Byrne smiled now, and Charles Hopkirk felt an instant forgiveness in that smile. Here indeed, he thought, is a good man.

"Right, well, I suppose you'd like to take a brief look around the old place eh?"

"That would be nice, thank you."

"I hope you won't mind, Gerald, but, knowing you were coming today, I asked one of our teachers to give you a guided tour of the modern version of Speke Hill. A lot of things have changed since you were here, as I've said, but many things are still the same. It just so happens that we have another 'old boy' on our staff at the senior school, another lad from your own age group during your time here. You might remember Mark Proctor?"

Byrne's face almost betrayed an emotion he wouldn't have wanted the senior care officer to witness at the mention of Proctor's name. Mark Proctor, who the other children back then used to call 'Garibaldi' due to his lack of hair, even at such a tender age, had never been a particular friend to Gerald Byrne, who recalled him as something of a bully, always picking on those younger or smaller than himself and unable to defend themselves against his aggressive tendencies. He'd always felt that Mr. Pugh, the senior housemaster for Stanley House knew just what Proctor was like, but could never actually catch him in the act of bullying, so had tried to channel some of his aggression into boxing training, a sport at which Proctor excelled and in due course won a number of trophies for the school in local competitions. Byrne doubted very much that boxing would feature on the modern day sports curriculum, far too violent for today's passive and non-confrontational educational system. Keeping his dislike of the man, well, in fact the boy he'd known decades earlier, hidden for now, he replied politely to Hopkirk's minor bombshell of information.

"Mark Proctor? Yes, I do kind of remember the boy, Charles. What subject is he teaching?"

"Physical Education."

"That makes sense. Proctor the boy was always involved in all things physical."

Byrne tried hard not to let the sarcasm of his words transmit themselves to Hopkirk, who barely seemed to register the priest's reply as a knock on the door heralded the arrival of the former bully, now respected teacher of P.E at Speke Hill, and Byrne's thoughts turned to buried memories.

Chapter 4

Mortuary Matters

Andy Ross exited the car, leaving Izzie Drake to lock up and he was first to the entrance to the mortuary building. He'd just pressed the intercom button as Drake arrived at his side, and a familiar voice came through the little box on the wall.

"Please identify yourself and state your business today."

"Peter, it's D.I. Ross and Sergeant Drake. Dr. Nugent is expecting us."

"Ah, hello Inspector. You know the routine, please come in."

The speaker pressed a button inside the building and Ross waited until he heard a 'click' and then pushed and the door swung open to admit the detectives. Ross and Drake soon arrived at the office, (Ross thought it more of a cubicle really, but politeness precluded him mentioning it), where Peter Foster, the senior mortuary receptionist was seated behind a small desk, protected by plate glass. A circular speaking outlet allowed visitors to speak through the glass, and a small slot at the bottom allowed Foster to pass the appropriate 'Visitor' badges to those authorised to progress into the main mortuary building. Ross could clearly remember when a younger Peter Foster had first begun working here, just before a complex case relating to the long deceased singer, Brendan Kane had reared its head some three years earlier. Foster had become a real asset to the department and had been promoted to the senior position some months earlier, much to the delight of Izzie

Drake, who Ross had been surprised to discover had been dating the younger man for a few months by then.

"Good morning, Inspector, Izzie," Foster said as the detectives smiled in greeting.

"Everything okay, Peter?" Ross asked.

"Fine, thanks," Foster replied.

"Hello, Peter," said Izzie Drake,

"You're looking good, Izzie," he replied.

"Considering what we've seen this morning, I'll assume you're being very nice to me, Peter. I feel like shit after being in that churchyard."

"Oh well, you know me. I know nothing about the cases when they first come in so I have to assume it was a bad one?"

"Very bad, Peter," Ross interrupted, "and if you two lovebirds don't mind, I'd rather we didn't keep Dr. Nugent waiting while you discuss my sergeant's appearance."

"Oh God, yeah, sorry, Inspector, he's in Autopsy One," a flustered Peter Foster responded, pushing two visitor badges through the slot at the base of the window and pressing the entry button that allowed the detectives into the main corridor. Ross grinned at the man, who smiled sheepishly back at him. Ross still found it strange that his sergeant had found herself attracted to the younger man, though only by a couple of years, and he'd been surprised when she'd told him in his office one day that she'd met Foster in a pub one night, quite accidentally, and that they'd shared a drink or two and found they shared a number of common interests. Soon after, they'd begun dating on a regular basis and six months down the line, it seemed the couple were growing closer with the passage of time. Ross was pleased for Izzie who'd always seemed to be beset by bad luck in her personal relationships in the past. Perhaps Peter Foster might be her 'Mr. Right' at last.

Izzie blew Foster a kiss as she and Ross disappeared along the corridor, and a minute later they found themselves in Autopsy Room Number One, in the company of William Nugent and his assistant, the ever-present Francis Lees.

* * *

The cadaver on the stainless steel autopsy table bore little resemblance to the living, breathing human being he had been up until a few short hours ago. By the time Ross and Drake had arrived, Dr. Nugent had already made a start, the customary Y incision not really necessary after the killer had virtually opened up the entire upper torso of the victim and he and Lees had clearly been hard at work on the remains of the as yet unidentified victim.

"Ah, Inspector Ross and Sergeant Drake, welcome. As ye can see, Mr. Lees and I have made a start without you. I thought you'd appreciate not having to watch the really grisly parts, as usual."

The pathologist had a wry and at times wicked sense of humour. He'd long ago learned of Ross's aversion to the procedures of a postmortem examination and he loved to occasionally wind-up the inspector a little. It was all part of a strange but mutual admiration that existed between the doctor and the policeman; not quite friends, but respected colleagues would be an apt description.

"Your thoughtfulness is amazing, Doc," said Ross, a smile on his face. "Anything to tell me yet?"

"Quite a bit to tell the truth, Inspector. Look here," he indicated the deceased's throat, and now, with the blood washed away, it was clear to Ross and Drake that the killer had not only cut the throat of the victim but had done it so viciously that the cut had almost gone through to the man's spinal cord.

"Bloody hell, sir," Drake exclaimed.

"Bloody hell indeed, Sergeant," Ross agreed.

"Cause of death, I presume, Doc?"

"In all likelihood, yes," Nugent replied. "However, I have to admit that with the massive amount of 'work' your killer has carried out on this poor soul, any of the wounds to his lower abdomen could have led to death from shock and blood loss. If I had to hazard an informed opinion though, I'd say he cut the victim's throat first and then swiftly got to work on the evisceration of the body."

"I thought the heart stopped pumping blood at the moment of death, Doctor," said Drake. "So why was there so much blood at the scene if the first cut to the throat led to the man's death?"

"Quite simply, ma dear girl, because the killer didn't just stab or inflict wounds on the body he literally cut the man open, gutting him, to all intents and purposes, so all the blood contained in the abdomen and chest cavity simply flowed out onto the ground around the body. You and the inspector have attended enough autopsies here to know how much blood leaks from a body when cut open, hence the channels in the tables here for the blood to drain from. Don't forget, he also cut out virtually every major organ from the torso too, leading to even more blood being dumped rather than bleeding out onto the ground."

"Yes, of course, sorry Doctor. I should have known that."

"Don't you go beating yourself up about it, Sergeant. You had a real shock seeing that murder site this morning. Police officer or not, it had to have an effect on you, so it's no surprise if you're nae thinking straight right now."

Drake nodded her thanks to the pathologist, though inwardly cursing herself. She'd seen enough bodies and attended enough post-mortems over the years and she really did think she should have been a little more 'on the ball' over the subject of the blood loss. It was Ross's turn to question Nugent.

"Doc, the other, er…mutilations? Can you tell us if they were carried out using the same weapon as the killer used on the man's throat? If not, we have to assume our killer used more than one weapon and as yet, we haven't located any weapons at or near the graveyard. I'm presuming at this stage that the murderer took the weapons away with him."

William Nugent, used to seeing some of the worst that man can inflict on his fellow being over his many years as a pathologist, shook his head slowly before replying to Ross's question. He looked across the room to where his assistant, Francis Lees, was busily weighing the various organs removed from the victim by the killer, before placing them in sealed jars of preservative.

"Francis," Nugent said, and Lees turned and waited for his boss to speak again. Bring me your clipboard will you, please?"

Lees nodded, and stepped across the room and handed the clipboard, containing various sheets of paper, including the notes he was making on the victim's organs, to the senior pathologist, who flicked Lees' notes over until he arrived at what he was looking for.

"Right, Inspector," he began, "all I can say is that whoever perpetrated this damnable atrocity on the victim certainly wasn't medically trained. The poor man was systematically hacked open by what I estimate to be an extremely sharp blade of around nine to ten inches in length, almost certainly the same implement used to cut the poor man's throat. There are enough tell-tale signs on the body to show where he literally chopped at the torso in order to open the man up, almost using the blade like a saw, but, without a serrated blade, it got very messy. Look at the abdomen."

Ross and Drake leaned over to see what Nugent was indicating.

"See, the flesh is hanging in shards around the cuts, and from the depth of penetration, I think you can assume great rage existed within the mind of your killer. There was no need to go as deep as he did to reach the organs, which were then almost chopped out of the body cavity."

"Sounds as if this was very personal Doc."

"Aye, well, that's for you and your people to determine, I'm pleased to say. My job is simply to tell you what killed the poor chap and I still have to determine that for certain."

Izzie Drake rejoined the conversation.

"But, I thought you said the wound to the throat..."

"Aye, Sergeant, but I did qualify that statement by adding the words, 'in all probability' ye may recall."

"So you're not certain?"

"Look, detectives, with the massive amount of damage the killer inflicted on this poor man, it's safe to say that any one of the wounds inflicted on the body could have been fatal, but in my opinion, I am leaning towards the belief that it would have been easier for the killer to ensure the man was dead by slitting his throat first before carrying out his series of atrocities upon the body."

"So you don't think the poor sod was alive while he was being disembowelled?" Ross asked.

"Correct, Inspector," said Nugent, who then hesitated before going on, "but, there is a possibility that one of the injuries was inflicted ante-mortem."

Ross had a feeling he knew what the pathologist was about to say, and he felt a sinking feeling in his stomach as he waited for Nugent to continue.

"With the amount of trauma, and copious blood loss in the genital region, I have to hypothesise that your killer removed the victim's penis while he was still alive."

"Oh, God," said Drake,

"That's fucking sick," Ross added.

"Indeed it is," Nugent agreed, "but it is highly likely."

"And that would almost certainly confirm a highly personal motive," said Ross.

"Aye well, that's your job to determine, not mine, as I said," Nugent replied, "but one thing's pretty certain. You are, without doubt, seeking an individual filled with severe rage and also with sufficient strength to have somehow overpowered and subdued the victim in order to carry out this heinous attack."

"Would he have placed it, his, penis I mean, in the mouth before or after killing the man?" Drake asked.

"I cannae be sure, Sergeant, but I'd say after if you wanted to pin me down. The way it was located so far down the throat, I doubt he'd have managed that with a living, struggling victim, as this poor bugger must have been doing at the time."

"Right, I see. Thanks, Doc. I think we'll leave you to conclude your examination in peace," said Ross. "If you find anything else you think may be helpful..."

"I'll let you know, right away, Inspector, as always. Hopefully, that clever young detective of yours at headquarters may have a name for you by the time you get back."

"You mean D.C. Ferris?"

"Yes, that's him. I had Mr. Lees here send a copy of the victim's fingerprints over there as soon as we'd taken them. I remembered the detective constable was your team's collator and you'd be anxious to try and make a rapid identification, so yes, he has them and if the victim is in the system, you may have a name for him very soon."

"That's great, Doc, thanks" said Ross as he and Drake prepared to head back to police headquarters. Ross wouldn't wait to get back before contacting Ferris though. Once outside the building, he'd turn his phone on again and call Paul Ferris to ascertain what, if any progress he'd made with the fingerprints.

"I'll be in touch if I find anything else of interest," Nugent called, as the two detectives were just about to exit the autopsy room, adding, as Ross's hand closed on the handle to open the door, "Oh yes, and how's your love life, Sergeant Drake?"

Izzie Drake blushed; having been unaware that word of her relationship with Peter Foster had reached the ears of the city's chief pathologist"

"It's, erm, it's fine. Thank you, Doctor," she said, quietly.

"Aye well, I'm glad to hear it. Just go gentle on my poor receptionist, you hear me, Sergeant"

Nugent had a grin like a Cheshire cat on his face, enjoying his small moment of managing to embarrass Izzie in such a jocular way.

"Goodbye, Doctor," she said, as she and Ross exited the room, her boss also grinning at her momentary discomfiture.

Chapter 5

Memories

In the few seconds it took for the door to Charles Hopkirk's office to open, admitting Mark Proctor, Gerald Byrne experienced one of those strange, almost out-of-body experiences, whereby his memory took him back in time and an entire scene seemed to play out in his mind, a reminder of one particular episode from his youth.

The sun was shining, and an air of excitement permeated every dormitory and school classroom of Speke Hill. As was the custom, classes had been suspended and all thoughts, of both pupils/residents and staff turned to the afternoon's events. Sports Day had arrived and each House wanted to emerge victorious from the proceedings. The winning House Captain would then assume the honour of receiving the 'Bishops Cup,' a beautiful engraved silver trophy awarded each year to the victorious House.

The morning had begun like any other, with breakfast, followed by prayers in the school chapel. Prayers over, normal routine was suspended as everyone returned to their dormitories to prepare for the big event. One of the responsibilities of the senior girls in the school was to make sure all sports kit was clean and ironed. All pupils had chores to perform, from juniors to seniors, and this was one of the tasks never allotted to junior school members due to the dangers of using a hot iron. In fact, the words 'senior' and 'junior' were rarely used at Speke Hill as the younger children attended what was termed the 'lower' school and seniors the 'upper' school. So they became 'lowers' and 'uppers' within the terminology of the school.

Gerald Byrne made sure his kit was ready for use. His shirt, like all the sports shirts at the school was reversible. The fronts of the shirts were green with cream coloured collars and cuffs, while the reverse side was the same green with a large, broad hoop across the chest area in the various house colours, yellow for Molyneux, red for Norris, blue for Stanley and white for Sefton.

Most of the boys thought the shirts would make people think they were playing for Liverpool Corporation Transport, whose buses were a similar green to the school's. Gerald's shirt had a blue hoop, showing he represented Stanley house, and he laid it out, together with his white shorts and green socks, on his bed and made sure his running plimsolls were clean of mud before placing them under his bed, ready to change into soon before the afternoon's events began. Gerald excelled at most sports, but athletics, track and field were far from his favourite sporting activities. He preferred football, rugby and cricket, team games, rather than the individual competition he'd be involved in today. He'd been selected to run in the 100 yard sprint for his year group, and later in the afternoon, he'd take part in the relay race at the same distance. Between the two events, he had an hour and a half of free time to watch the rest of the day's events or just do whatever he liked if he chose not to watch his fellow school mates toiling in the afternoon heat, and anyway, he hardly knew any of the uppers who'd be competing in their events in the latter half of the day's events, apart from his sister, Angela, who was taking part in the upper girls' long jump competition, not the most riveting of events to watch for a spirited ten year old boy.

As the other boys in his dorm also prepared themselves for later in the day, Peter Forester, a friend of Gerald's, switched on his little transistor radio, and the sounds of Radio Caroline filled the room. The pirate radio station had begun broadcasting in March of that year from a ship anchored just outside British territorial waters off the coast of

Felixstowe. The kids of Speke Hill thought the idea of a 'pirate' radio station was great fun and loved tuning in at every opportunity they got. Thanks to the relaxing of the usual school regime for the day, they were able to listen to the radio while they enjoyed the morning's relief from the usual routine of their lessons.

They all wanted to hear the Beatles of course, as only that month, the group's movie, *A Hard Day's Night* had been released in cinemas, and though most of the children would eventually get to see their idols at the cinema, only a few lucky ones had so far saved up enough pocket money to see the film. Some of the boys and girls from Speke Hill had asked the teachers if they could go into the city on the day the Beatles returned in triumph from their latest tour, but wisely the staff refused, as over three hundred people were hurt in the crush that accompanied their return. As Father O'Reardon, headmaster of the school had said, "School not scream is the order of the day," a reference to the screaming fans who always accompanied any public appearance by the Fab Four.

Gerald, known to his school friends and fellow orphans as Gerry, meanwhile teamed up with his two friends, Tim Gregson and Frank Jessop to complete the one task they had to carry out that morning. Usually, the lower school pupils had certain chores that would be carried out between the close of school at three-thirty p.m and their evening meal at five p.m but today, due to the extended time taken up by the sorting activities the pupils were instructed to carry out such tasks during their free time in the morning.

So, the three boys set about cleaning the dormitory's shower room and toilets, while others attended to such jobs as cleaning windows, polishing the tiled floor and vacuuming and dusting, all designed to engender not only a sense of cleanliness and domesticity in the boys, but to foster a spirit of teamwork,

With the job finished the boys returned to the main dormitory, where it took Gerry no more than a minute to realise something was wrong. His plimsolls were missing from their place under his bed. Someone was quite clearly playing a prank on young Gerry and he wasn't in the least bit amused by it.

"Okay, you bunch of scallys, who's taken my plimsolls?" he called at the top of his voice to the room in general.

All eyes turned to look at him, but not one reply was forthcoming.

"I said, who's taken them?" he tried again, receiving the same negative result.

"One of youse lot has had me pumps," he shouted, getting louder as his frustration boiled over, "and whoever it is had better own up and give' em back, right now."

As silence pervaded the room once more, Gerry Byrne looked intently at each of the boys in turn. Most looked genuinely innocent but one or two seemed to be doing their best not to break out into mischievous grins.

"Well, ain't any of you got owt to say?" he asked yet again.

"Gerry, honest, none of us saw anyone take 'em. If we had, we'd tell you, wouldn't we?" said Billy Ryan as he joined Gerry in trying to look for the missing footwear.

"Some of you would, and some wouldn't," Gerry replied in an accusing tone.

There weren't many places in the dorm where a pair of shoes might be hidden and Gerry and Billy had soon checked under all the beds in the room, the broom closet, where Gerry, Tim and Frank had already returned the cleaning materials from their shower cleaning, making it an unlikely place to find them, and behind all the boys' individual lockers and small wardrobes that stood either side of each bed. Leaving the main dormitory, and being joined by Tim and Frank, the small group now went from dormitory to dormitory, checking and asking all the other boys in their accommodation about the missing plimsolls.

Almost on the verge of tears, and knowing he wouldn't be able to compete that afternoon without his pumps, Gerry now realised that whoever had taken them must have them hidden in his own bedside locker or wardrobe.

"If someone doesn't tell me where me pumps are in one minute, I'm going to report it to Father Mullaney," said Gerry, referring to the priest in charge of the orphan boys' accommodation blocks.

As he spoke he looked around at the others in the room once again and this time he saw that one boy just couldn't seem to hide a knowing smirk from appearing on his face.

Gerry Byrne now fixed a look of realisation on young Mark Proctor. As he did so, Proctor tried to switch off the tell tale look, covering his mouth with one hand and affecting a false cough to hide the knowing grin that now began to appear on his face. Proctor was taller and heavier than Gerry and already earning something of a reputation as a minor bully amongst the lower school boys, but, not one to back down in the face of what he now felt sure of, young Gerry Byrne now stomped across the room to where Bolton sat on his own bed, obviously enjoying the smaller boy's discomfiture.

"It was you, Mark Proctor. Give 'em back, right now, you rotten thief," he shouted at the other boy.

"Aw, listen to little Gerry," Mark Proctor smirked. "Lost yer pumps, 'ave yer, little boy?"

"Give 'em to me, you thieving little git," said Byrne. "You've got 'em in your locker. I know you have"

"Yeah, right, if you say so, and who's going to make me open up my own private locker, eh, Gerry boy?"

"I'll tell Father Mullaney, and he'll make you open it and then you'll be in real trouble, you scally, Proctor."

"Watch who you're calling a scally, you little bastard, Byrne"

"I'm no bastard, Proctor, not like you. You don't even know who your dad is."

"Liar! My Dad was a famous American soldier."

"Famous my arse," Gerry Byrne laughed. "Everyone knows he was an American soldier alright, one of them stationed out at Haydock after the war, until they all went home and he left your Mam with a snivelling little brat to look after. No wonder she killed herself, Mark Proctor. Who'd want to look after you for the rest of their life?"

Quite clearly, the piety of his later calling had not yet had time to mature in the young Gerald Byrne and his telling remarks now led to Mark Proctor springing up from his bed and the fight that ensued saw both boys throwing punches at each other's face, and letting loose with a few well-aimed kicks. Mark Proctor landed the most telling punches, his future success in the boxing ring giving him the upper hand in close combat, while young Gerry Byrne, the footballer, was ahead on points in the kicking department as the other boys in the room cheered the fight on, until a loud voice boomed out from the doorway.

"And what in the name of all that's Holy is going on here, might I ask?"

The look on the face of Father Mullaney was enough to halt the cheering in less than a second and as the hubbub surrounding them died a death, so the two combatants sensed more than saw the six foot three inch priest as he marched down the centre aisle of the dormitory, and grabbing both boys by their shirt collars and dragging them apart, feet off the floor, he slowly deposited them back on the ground.

"I want the truth, now, no lies, and I'm only asking once. Who started this unholy scene?"

"He stole my pumps, Father, and then he attacked me when I told the truth about his Dad," said Gerry Byrne.

"Is this true, Mark?" asked the priest, and Mark Proctor's face turned even redder than it was already from his exertions in the fight. He remained silent however, forcing Father Mullaney to ask again, "I said, did you steal this boy's plimsolls?"

Shamefacedly, Mark Proctor looked up at the towering figure of the priest and, trying his best to sound contrite and innocent, replied,

"It was a joke, Father, just a prank. I was going to let him have them back before Sports Day started."

"I see, and just where are they now, young Proctor?"

"In my locker, Father."

"Go and get them and return them to young Mr. Byrne, right now, if you please."

Mark Proctor ran the few feet to his locker, and quickly opened it and removed Gerry Byrne's plimsolls, and quickly handed them over.

"Here they are, Gerry. Sorry, honest. It won't happen again."

Gerry Byrne scowled at his adversary, saying nothing as he grabbed his plimsolls and gathered them against his chest.

Father Mullaney next turned to Gerry.

"And as for you, Byrne, what gave you the right to insult this boy's dead father, if that is indeed what you did?"

"Because he wouldn't give them back, Father and he called me a bastard, too."

The priest sighed, before speaking again.

"I can see that you two boys have a lot to learn about the ways of the world and about learning to get along together. Now, you'll shake hands with each other and as it's Sports Day and things have been allowed to be a little too relaxed, to my way of thinking, I'll be lenient with the pair of you. You, Mark Proctor, for stealing the plimsolls in the first place, and for compounding your crime by then starting a fight, will be confined to the dormitory after evening meal for one month, and you will attend chapel both morning and evening every day during that time, where you will pray on your knees to our Lord Jesus Christ for forgiveness for your sins, for one hour in the evening session, and for ten minutes in the morning, which should leave you time to get back to your dorm after chapel and gather your books in time for school."

Mark Proctor gulped, looking totally crestfallen as he saw his freedom being seriously restricted for the coming four weeks. Father Mullaney next turned to Gerry Byrne.

"Now, as for you, Gerald Byrne. I thought better of you than this. Fighting in the dorm, indeed, and making accusations against another boy's father is not the Christian way of handling a dispute. You are all unfortunate enough to be without your parents, which is why you have all ended up at Speke Hill Orphanage, and no matter the reason for your loss of your parents, I will not have you using the circumstances surrounding that loss to be used in such a way. You'll be confined to the orphanage grounds for the next four weekends. No walks into the village or trips to town with Father Hunter, do you understand?"

"Yes, Father. I'm sorry, Father, it won't ever happen again."

"And, you'll say ten Hail Mary's before and after every lesson in school for the next week, is that clear?"

"Very clear, Father," Gerry said, quietly.

"Very well," the priest went on, "I've a mind to stop you both taking part in this afternoon's events but that would unfairly penalise your fellow house-members, so I suggest you both stay well away from each other until this afternoon, and don't you ever let me see or hear of such behaviour taking place ever again, or, in the name of our Lord, I'll personally take my cane to the pair of you, and you'll not be able to sit down for a week. Is that clear?"

Both boys nodded and looked totally abashed at Father Mullaney's words. As the priest turned on his heel and stormed out of the dormitory, the two of them shared a look of pure hatred at each other, and an enmity was born that would last far beyond Sports Day, until both boys were well into their teens.

* * *

Mark Proctor walked confidently in to the room, his hand extended in friendship.

"Gerry Byrne, as I live and breathe, it *is* you. I'm sorry, it's Father Byrne now of course, isn't it? Welcome home, Father, it's good to see you again after so many years. How are you?"

Gerald Byrne was almost taken aback by Mark Proctor's effusive welcome, but he thought the P.E. teacher could do nothing else under the circumstances. It would hardly be fitting for his old adversary to greet the new chaplain of the orphanage and school with a roundhouse punch to the head, now would it?

Quickly recovering his composure, Byrne reached out and took the proffered hand, and the two men shook hands vigorously, like two old friends, reunited after so many long years.

"I'm well, thank you, Mark. It's good to see you again, too. I see the wheel has turned full circle for you too, ending up back here again. I take it you haven't always taught here?"

"Quite right, Father Byrne. I've taught at a few schools over the years, but when I heard of the vacancy for this job, I just felt I had to apply for it, and, well, as you can see, here I am."

"Yes, indeed, and I hear you're to be my guide around the 'new' Speke Hill, too."

"Yes, that's right. When he realised we were both old boys from the same year at Speke Hill, Charles here asked if I'd be happy to show you the changes that have taken place since you last saw the old place. I was delighted to be able to help."

I'll just bet you were, Byrne thought to himself, sarcastically, but kept such uncharitable thoughts to himself and instead replied, "Excellent. So, I've taken up enough of Mr. Hopkirk's time this morning, shall we get on with the guided tour?"

"It's nice to have met you and had our little talk," Hopkirk said as Father Byrne stood, and the two men shook hands.

"Yes, indeed Charles," Byrne replied as he moved to follow Bolton out of the office. "We'll doubtless meet in the future, I'm sure."

"Oh yes, I look forward to it. I don't attend the services in the chapel as a rule but we'll bump into each other during your visits, without doubt," Hopkirk said as the two former residents of the orphanage left the room and the door closed behind them.

Mark Proctor appeared not to harbour any ill-will towards Gerald Byrne as he took pleasure in showing the priest around. Whether his attitude was a true reflection of his thoughts, or a clever cover-up, Father Byrne couldn't ascertain at that point.

Surely he can't believe the past is totally buried, that all his bullying and cruelty towards those weaker than himself can be put down to childish pranks as he used to call them, thought Byrne, as he followed Bolton around, trying to be polite and showing interest where he felt it was called for.

In truth, there hadn't been too many drastic changes to the old place. The trees lining the approach drive had grown substantially of course, and the dormitories had undergone quite a radical upgrading, with those living at Speke Hill now being housed in rooms that held just four people, rather than the open dorms of the past which held up to thirty boys or girls. Such a change had inevitably meant that over-all numbers had been reduced, with Speke Hill now being 'home' to twenty-five percent fewer boys and girls than in Byrne's days as an orphan.

The biggest changes had been effected in the school, with the class-rooms having been totally modernised. Gone were the old chemistry lab, and art room, both being replaced by modern versions of the same, which bore little resemblance to the originals. Each classroom now had state of the art computers installed to enable the children to be taught about, and using, the latest technology. Gerald Byrne managed to keep conversation to a minimum, for the most part managing to make the appropriate noises and speak the expected words in response to Proctor's enthusiastic showing off of the facilities.

Quite naturally, he lingered for a little longer than necessary in the chapel, kneeling in prayer for a couple of minutes, during which time he prayed for forgiveness for his feelings of antipathy towards his old nemesis and Mark Proctor waited patiently in the doorway, not intruding upon the priest's solitude while at prayer.

A visit to the staff room followed where Proctor introduced him to the few teachers who were present at the time, and then he was led to the headmaster's office where, unfortunately, Mrs. Davis, the head's secretary informed them that Mr. Machin was teaching and wouldn't be free until after lunch, and would be sad to have missed Father Byrne, but she was sure he'd look forward to seeing him on his next visit. Gerald Byrne replied that he understood how busy the head must be and he too would look forward to a future meeting, though inwardly he felt the headmaster might have made time to meet him, as he'd known in advance of his visit. He concluded this was a sign of the times, the church no longer wielding the strings of power at

Speke Hill as it used to, and his part, therefore, in the overall scheme of school life, would be far les than he'd perhaps imagined.

Not until they exited the main school building towards the end of his visit did the two men find themselves speaking of anything attached to their joint past at Speke Hill.

As they walked down the sweeping arc of steps that led from the main doors down into what was now a much larger car park than used to exist there, Proctor suddenly stopped and pointed to a point to the left of the low wall that stood along the length of the steps.

"Do you remember when old Father Loony used to park his old motor cycle just there every day?"

Gerald Byrne couldn't help but smile at the sudden recollection.

'Father Loony' had in reality been Father Rooney, who taught both geography and history. The name 'Loony' had been affectionately applied to him by pupils who found it quite incongruous that a priest of the Roman Catholic Church, and a serious teacher of stuffy old geography and history would finish teaching for the day and then change into full motorcycle 'leathers' before mounting his gleaming, powerful Norton Commando motorcycle, revving the engine in a display of power, and then zooming off, in a cloud of exhaust smoke, down the drive and out onto Woolton Road, destination unknown.

The boys who'd drooled over Father William Rooney's superb Norton machine would have been surprised to know the priest was a member of the Liverpool Motor club, a long established group catering for both motorcycles and motor car enthusiasts, and often rode his bike in various road trials and shows. Likewise, many of the club members would have been astounded to know that the rider of the red and black Norton was a Roman Catholic Priest, and not a rather well-turned out 'rocker'.

Gerald Byrne smiled as he recalled the motorcycling priest.

"Yes, I remember him well. He used to help me quite often with history projects, and he also helped to fuel my thirst for knowledge of life in the priesthood. He made me realise you could be a Catholic priest and still have a life that included outside interests, as he had with his motor bike. He was a great Rugby League fan too, and used to travel to watch Wigan's matches whenever he could."

"I didn't know that, about the Rugby, I mean," Proctor replied.

"He told me he used to play the game himself for an amateur club in his teens, and even had trials for Liverpool City, at the old Knotty Ash Stadium but never quite made it. Most people have forgotten them now of course. They moved and changed their name to Huyton and then slowly slid into oblivion I seem to recall."

"I remember them," said Proctor. "Never very good, were they?"

"Maybe not, but they played the game because they loved it, a bit like Doncaster and Batley in those days, always bottom of the league but still turned out every week and their small band of supporters would follow them around the North of England in the hope of an occasional win to talk about."

"You played rugger for the school, didn't you, Gerry?"

"That was Rugby Union," Byrne nodded in reply. "The good Fathers of Speke Hill preferred us to play according to the amateur code, which most schools did in those days."

"Who'd have thought you'd have ended up as a rugby player though? You were a bit weedy as a lower, if you don't mind me saying."

Gerald Byrne inwardly seethed at Proctor's obvious reference to their days in the lower school, when he'd been small enough to be on the receiving end of Proctor's 'pranks'. It was only when he'd attained his teens that his muscular development had kicked in and Gerry Byrne had grown into a strapping rugby winger and footballer. Not wanting to rise to the bait, he instead took a deep breath before replying, diplomatically,

"We all developed at different times and in different ways in those days, Mark. I recall you suddenly putting a few pounds on in your teens, after all that boxing you did."

This was a clear reference to the fact that Mark Proctor gradually went from well built to rather flabby, and by the time he reached school leaving age, his boxing days were already behind him.

"Yes, well, I managed to lose some of that weight in later years so I could qualify as a P.E teacher," Proctor responded.

It was now becoming clear that the atmosphere between the two men was growing strained and Father Gerald Byrne quickly made his excuses and walked away from Mark Proctor, wishing in a very non-Christian way for God to send a thunderbolt to strike the man down, to the car where young Father Willis had patiently waited for him while he'd 'enjoyed' his visit to Speke Hill. Willis turned the car radio off as Byrne opened the car door and they were soon on their way, back to the sanctuary of St. Luke's, where Byrne later insisted on Father Willis hearing his confession

What the young priest thought when he heard Father Byrne confess to wishing Mark Proctor some kind of harm, only he could know, thanks to the sanctity of the confessional, but, on hearing Byrne's words, Father Willis couldn't help raising an eyebrow in surprise at the thought that the new Parish Priest might not be as pure and Godly as he'd initially thought him to be. But then, he comforted himself with the thought that it was only a silly wish, brought about by some reference to an event that had taken place a long time ago...wasn't it?

Chapter 6

'Razor'

"Any luck with the victim's fingerprints, Paul?" Ross spoke into his mobile phone as soon as he and Drake walked out of the doors of the mortuary building. Detective Constable Paul Ferris, his team's collator and expert on all things of a computer based nature had received the prints only an hour or so earlier but had achieved success already.

"Got a hit right away, sir. The victim is in the system. His name's Matthew Remington, aged forty-eight, known to his friends as 'Razor', for obvious reasons. Not very original I must say, naming someone after a brand of shaving products. Seems our Matthew had a record going back quite a few years, mostly minor stuff, petty theft, taking a vehicle without consent, a couple of assault charges, but, get this, sir, his most recent conviction though it was a few years ago, was for a sexual assault offence."

At that, Ross's mind immediately switched on to the hacking off of the victim's sexual organ. Could this murder be a simple case of revenge by someone connected to Remington's victim?

"Good work, Paul. We'll be back in a few minutes. Get me all the information you can on this 'Razor' Remington. Let's see if someone decided to exact a brutal revenge for his last offence."

"I'm on it already, sir," Ferris replied, as Ross pressed the red 'end call' button on his phone.

"I take it Ferris came through quickly," said Drake as she drove towards headquarters.

"He did, Izzie. The guy was a sex offender by the name of Matthew Remington"

"A ha," Drake replied, her thoughts immediately echoing those of the inspector. One of the reasons the two worked so well together was their uncanny way of thinking along parallel lines at times.

"Exactly," said Ross. "It looked bad, but the solution may be simpler than we thought."

Drake fell silent for a few seconds, and Andy Ross knew her brain was ticking over, an idea forming in his sergeant's thoughts.

"You're thinking of something, Sergeant, I can tell. Come on, out with it."

"Well, it might be nothing, but I wonder if there's any significance in the fact that the victim's name was Matthew and his body was found in St. Matthew's churchyard?"

"Good point," Ross conceded. "Let's see what Ferris has got for us when we get back before we begin jumping to any conclusions, though"

An hour later, having taken time to study the information D.C. Ferris had unearthed on the victim, Andy Ross and Izzie Drake sat in the small 'murder room', a small conference room used by the murder investigation team for the purpose of team meetings and where Ferris had already begun composing his 'murder board', a large whiteboard that would hold all the information on the case, and where all the team's planning and strategy meeting were held.

As well as Ross, Drake and Ferris, also present were D.C's Samantha Gable and Lennie Curtis, the newest member of the team. For some reason, despite his real name being Leonard, his colleagues had chosen to address the young D.C. as 'Tony', naming him after the famed American Film Actor. Ross guessed it was probably due to Curtis and the actor having similar looks and hairstyles that made the detective look like the actor in his *Vikings* days. Sam Gable had initially been seconded to Ross's team three years previously and had since been made a permanent member of the murder squad, after spending years working in vice. Gable and Derek McLennan had only just returned from their initial sweep of the vicinity of St. Matthew's, with none of the residents having reported seeing or hearing anything out of the ordinary in the hours preceding the discovery of Matthew Remington's body. McLennan was conspicuous by his absence, a fact not unnoticed by Andy Ross.

"Where's Derek, Sam?" he asked Gable.

"He won't be long, sir. He was rather embarrassed about throwing up at the murder scene, and felt a bit, well, you know, unclean. He's in the gents now, changing into a shirt he managed to borrow from one of the uniform boys who had a spare in his locker."

As though on cue, the door to the conference room opened and Derek McLennan walked in, looking a darn sight better than when Ross had last seen him at the murder scene, or body dump. Ross still wasn't certain which description could be best applied to the churchyard. Dr. Nugent thought the man had been killed on site, there being enough blood to qualify the churchyard as the location of the murder, but, there was still a chance the man had his throat cut elsewhere and the blood at the scene was a result of the multiple mutilations carried out on the victim.

"Sorry I'm a bit late, sir," said McLennan as he ran his fingers through his tousled hair, still wet from his attempts to tidy himself up in the gents' toilets. His borrowed shirt hung on him a little, being at least a size too big for him, but at least he'd regained some of his natural colour again. "I was...you know, just..."

"Don't worry about it, Derek. We know it was bloody awful back at the churchyard. You're only human, so nobody's going to hold it against you. Come on in and sit down, while Paul brings us up to date regarding our victim. All yours, Paul."

D.C. Ferris stood and moved to stand in front of the whiteboard. He'd already appended photos of Matthew Remington's body, provided in double-quick time by the forensics team as well as a copy of his prison mugshot which had already caused one or two raised eyebrows as the team members realised their victim was an ex-con. Ferris had also added comprehensive crime scene photos, a picture of the Parish Priest, Father Donovan, where he got it from, Ross wondered in admiration, and finally a photograph of a young woman, who looked to be in her early twenties, and as yet unknown to anyone other than Ferris himself. As the rest of the team fell silent, Paul Ferris began.

"Thank you, sir. Okay everyone, it's confirmed that our victim is one Matthew 'Razor' Remington. I'm sure I don't need to explain the source of his nickname."

A short chorus of laughs and groans followed, before Ferris continued.

"Remington was 58 years old, locally born, lived on Hazel Avenue in Norris Green and worked at the Motor Vehicle Factory at Halewood."

"I knew it," exclaimed Derek McLennan, now feeling a little more like his usual self.

"Eh, what's that, Derek?" Ferris sounded a little annoyed at the early interruption.

"Oh, sorry Paul. It's just that we found a key at the scene that I thought looked like a locker key from Halewood. I've seen one before."

"Right, okay, thanks, Derek. Now, where was I? Yes, right, looks like our victim was a bit of a scally in his youth, always in trouble for one thing and another. Nothing serious, just a long string of petty crimes, though he gradually worked his way up to a couple of assault charges in his thirties. He was married for a short time, God bless the poor woman who fell for his particular charms, and his wife, Margaret, known as Maggie, left him after he was jailed for the second assault charge. The marriage had lasted eight years apparently, but only because he spent four of those years in prison. She still lives locally, in Norris Green.

Anyway, our friend would probably have remained under the radar if he'd stuck to the petty stuff, but not long after his wife did a runner on him, he really messed up. A young woman called Claire Morris," he pointed at the picture of the young woman on the whiteboard, "was raped after leaving a pub in Croxteth. I'm not going to go into all the details, as they're all in the files I'll pass out before we leave the room, but her assailant grabbed her from behind, dragged her onto a building site, and made her strip her skirt and underwear off in front of him before raping and sodomizing the poor girl."

"So he was a right bloody sadist as well," said Izzie Drake.

"Sounds like it," Ferris replied, "Claire stated later that she felt he wanted to humiliate her, as well as doing what he did. When he'd done with her, he gave her the skirt back but kept her underwear."

"The bastard wanted a trophy," Lennie 'Tony' Curtis snapped. "Sounds to me as if the low-life scumbag got what he deserved."

Ross felt it wise to interject at that point.

"D.C. Curtis. I'd be grateful if you kept those thoughts to yourself. Whoever or whatever he may have been, Remington was a human being, and one who's been murdered in a particularly brutal way. It's our job to catch his killer, and we'll do our job to the best of our ability. I will not have anyone in this city taking the law into their own hands, besides which, whatever we may think of Matthew Remington, he was caught, tried and convicted and served his sentence, so technically, he'd paid his debt to society. He didn't deserve to die like that. If any of you are uncomfortable investigating his death, speak up now and I'll have you removed from the case."

A deathly silence filled the room for a few seconds. Although Ross felt pretty much the same as his young detective constable, he had to maintain his own position as head of the unit and at the same time make sure his team didn't lose sight of their duty to uphold the law. After what seemed an interminable silence, Curtis spoke up.

"I'm sorry, boss. I spoke without thinking. It won't happen again."

"Good," Ross replied. "Anyone else got anything to say?"

Silence.

"Right then, please continue with the briefing, Paul."

Paul Ferris cleared his throat loudly, and took up the reins of the briefing again.

"Right,sir. Where was I? Oh yes, Claire Morris managed to stagger a few hundred yards until, as luck would have it, she spotted a passing patrol car and literally stepped out into the road right in front of it. The driver only just managed to stop in time without hitting her. The two officers in the car ascertained what had happened and called the incident in. One of them stayed in the car with Claire, waiting for the ambulance and back-up while the other officer made an examination of the building site in a search for clues.

Thanks to them coming on the scene so quickly, forensics were on the scene in no time and Claire was examined at the hospital within an hour of the rape taking place.

Remington was soon picked up and Claire picked him out of an identity parade, and the case became what the Americans call a 'slam dunk.' He got eight years, was released in five, placed on the sex offenders register, and nothing more was heard of him until his body was found this morning. Seems he'd kept his head down and had been working at Halewood for the last three years. That's it, folks."

Ross took over once again.

"Thanks, Paul. Now listen up everyone. I want this killer caught quickly. Don't ask me why, but I've got a bad feeling about this case. The way Remington was killed was so brutal that I feel we haven't heard the last of this killer. Whether he's someone seeking revenge for what happened to Claire, or some kind of vigilante, he's got to be found before he does anything else."

"You think he could strike again, sir?" asked Derek McLennan.

"I don't know, Derek, but he virtually butchered Matthew Remington and I sure as hell don't want to think he might do the same to someone else. Sergeant Drake has a short list of assignments for you. Listen carefully, and let's move fast, people, but also, let's not miss a thing. Be professional, understand?"

Murmurs of assent circulated round the room as Izzie Drake stood up.

"Okay, everyone, here goes," she began. "Derek and Sam, I want you to take the Claire Morris file and go through it with a fine tooth comb. Then, go and talk to everyone involved, her family, friends, whoever gave statements at the time. If they're in that file, talk to them, got it?"

"Okay, Sarge," said Sam Gable. "What about Claire Morris? Do you want us to speak to her as well?"

"No Sam, you two stick to the other witnesses and family members. The boss and I will talk to Claire. She'll need very careful handling. Tony", she said, referring to Lennie Curtis, "I want you to go out to the factory at Halewood. Talk to Remington's boss, supervisor, co-workers. See if anyone knows if he had anything on his mind recently, whether he told anyone about any threats he might have received, you know the type of things to ask."

"Right, Sarge," Curtis replied.

"Anything else you want me to do?" Paul Ferris asked.

Before Drake could reply, a knock at the door heralded the arrival of George Thompson, the force's senior Press Liaison Officer. Unlike some P.L.Os from other constabularies, Thomson was held in pretty high regard by the officer of the Merseyside Police. He always consulted with the officers in charge of a case before releasing any information to the media, and was quite happy to allow those officers to work with him on ensuring the accuracy of the information released to the news hounds. As he walked quietly into the room, dressed as he always seemed to be in a grey pin-striped suit, blue silk tie and pristine white shirt, Ross groaned inwardly. It was obvious to the inspector that Thompson's presence meant the press had got hold of the story and would be clamouring for the details of the gruesome killing of Matthew Remington. Ross also allowed himself a moment to wonder why George Thompson never appeared to look any older. In the years he'd known him, Thompson managed to look no older than about thirty-five or thereabouts, though he must be in his late forties by now. One day, he'd ask him how he kept looking so youthful, but now wasn't the time for such thoughts.

"Am I interrupting your briefing, Andy?" asked the PLO, knowing full well that he was.

"Hello, George. Yes, you are, but don't let that worry you. Your presence here makes me think that news of the murder has somehow leaked to the press?"

"I'm afraid so, Andy. D.C.I Porteous just called me into his office and asked me to come and see you and your people. Seems someone tipped the press off about the murder. Whether it was the priest at St. Matthew's or one of the uniforms on the scene perhaps, I don't know, but the Chief wants me to try and cap the lid on the story before the sensationalist element of the media takes over and blows it up into something like the modern embodiment of bloody Jack the Ripper."

Detective Chief Inspector Harry Porteous was Ross's immediate superior and the overall head of the Murder Investigation Unit. An old-school police officer, Porteous was happy to leave the day to day running of the unit's investigations in the capable hands of his officers, while at the same time maintaining close contact and overall control of the team.

"It sounds as if it might be a bit late for that," Ross said, ruefully. "I'm sure the press hounds will already be making up their own sensationalist stories before you've breathed a word to them."

"Yes, well, that's precisely why I'm here. I know you're incredibly busy with the investigation and need to be out in the field pursuing leads and so on, so whatever you can give me to help put a short statement together will do for now, as long as I can give them something that will allow you and your team a little breathing space."

Ross fell quiet as he thought of the best way to give Thompson what he needed without compromising the need to get out and track down a particularly vicious killer.

"Tell you what, George. We need to hit the streets, as you rightly point out, so why don't you sit down with D.C. Ferris and he can fill you in on what new have so far, little though it may be. I presume you'll want to give the local press in particular something to make the evening edition?"

"That's what I'm hoping for," said Thompson, referring to the *Liverpool Echo*, the major local newspaper.

"Right, Paul, you make sure George gets what he needs, and then you can go to St. Matthew's. I want you to talk to the priest, Father Donovan. Now that we have a name, address and place of work for the victim, it might mean something to him. He only got a quick look at the dead man this morning and went into shock almost immediately so he might have remembered something that could be helpful by now."

Ferris nodded.

"Okay, sir."

Ross turned to Thompson again.

"George, I hope that helps and I'd like you to run anything you intend to release to the press by me before you give it to them."

"No problem, Andy. Where will you be if I need to contact you?"

"Sergeant Drake and me are going to talk to the girl Remington was convicted of raping, either at home or at work, if we can track her down quickly. Then we'll be back here in time for any press briefing I hope. If we're delayed, you can call me on my mobile."

"Okay," Thompson replied. "Shall we get to work, D.C. Ferris?"

With that, Ross and the rest of the team left them to it as they left the conference room, each detective intent on playing their part in the hunt for Matthew Remington's Killer.

Chapter 7

Claire Morris

"Did you really mean all that crap you said in there about Remington being a human being, paid his debt to society etc. etc? Sorry if I'm speaking out of turn, sir, but well, it wasn't like you to sound so conciliatory about a low-life like Remington obviously was."

Izzie Drake was talking as she drove Ross and herself to Claire Morris's home. Information obtained by Paul Ferris had told them that the rape victim had moved from her address at the time of the attack, understandably in everyone's mind, and that she now lived in a terraced house in Seaforth, which she apparently shared with her boyfriend. She knew how her boss thought, the pair usually sharing an almost telepathic understanding of each other's thought patterns, and she'd been a little taken aback by Ross's words to young D.C Curtis back at headquarters.

"Course I didn't really mean it, Izzie. What d'you take me for? But, young Curtis had to be put in his place. It's okay to think these things, and believe me I sympathized with the lad's feelings, but we have to make sure everyone is focussed on the job. If they thought for one minute that I endorsed what he said, we'd have the whole team thinking it was okay for some bastard to do what he did to Remington. I thought you'd have realised that."

"Yes, I suppose I did really, but just wanted to hear you say it. Didn't want to think you were suddenly going soft in your old age," she said with a grin on her face.

"We'll have less of that, Sergeant Drake," Ross said, grinning back at her. "Old age indeed! I'm not quite in my dotage yet, young lady"

"No, I must say you're not looking bad for your age, sir. Maria looks after you well, I'd say," Izzie replied, referring to Ross's wife.

"What makes you think it's all Maria's doing? I know how to take care of myself, you know."

"Of course you do, sir," Drake said with a hint of sarcasm. "Last I heard, Maria had banned you from all those juicy burgers you enjoy so much when we're out on a job."

"Oh yeah, and who told you that?"

"You did, as a matter of fact, sir, about a month ago."

"Oh, right, well, she may have a little to do with it, I agree."

The pair continued their cheerful and relaxed banter as the Mondeo ate up the final couple of miles to Seaforth, one of the older parts of the city, mostly made up of old Victorian terraced houses, and home to Seaforth Dock, the largest dock facility in the modern port of Liverpool. Drake took her foot off the peal as they slowly drove along Garstang Road, looking for the home of Claire Morris.

"There it is, sir, number twenty-four," she said as she pulled in to park the car behind a battered looking old Ford Transit van. "What do we do if there's nobody home? Don't you think we should have got her phone number and checked first to se if she was at work or at home?"

"I didn't want to phone in advance and give her the opportunity to decline to talk to us, Izzie. Rape is such a delicate subject and she may have done her best to put it all behind her. I know it'll be difficult for her to talk to us, but at least just showing up like this will make it harder for her to refuse to speak to us. It's also why I wanted you with me, a woman's touch and all that, you know? We may have to have a rethink if she's not at home, of course, but we'll soon find out."

Drake and Ross exited and locked the unmarked pool car, and walked the few yards to number twenty-four, where Ross stood back and allowed Drake to knock on what appeared to be the recently painted dark green front door. He wanted the first face Claire Morris saw on opening her door to be that of a woman, rather than of a man totally unknown to her.

A few seconds later the door opened, and the detectives were surprised to find themselves confronted not by the woman they were expecting, but a man, whom Ross estimated to be in his late twenties, wearing a white shirt and black trousers, somewhat reminiscent of a uniform of some kind.

"Hello, can I help you?" the man asked with a puzzled expression on his face.

"I'm Detective Inspector Ross and this is Sergeant Drake, from Merseyside Police," said the inspector, as he and Drake both held up their warrant cards to identify themselves. "We're looking for a Miss Claire Morris and we were led to understand this is her home?"

"Claire? Well, yes, it is, but she's not at home right now. I'm her fiancé. Won't you come in, please? She'll be home very soon."

A minute later the two of them were seated in a neat sitting room, furnished in a modern style, with a two-seater sofa, a single matching armchair, and a large wall-mounted television above the old original Victorian fireplace. In one corner of the room stood a state of the art hi-fi system and a new looking laptop computer sat in the middle of a glass topped coffee table in front of the armchair. In truth, there wasn't room for much more in the room and Ross found himself wondering whether the couple ate their meals on trays on their laps, or perhaps had another downstairs room, an old-fashioned dining room maybe. These old Victorian terraced homes could, he knew, be deceptively large inside.

"I'm Lee Denton," the man said, introducing himself. "Can I ask why you're here, Inspector?"

"Well, we'd rather discuss that with Miss Morris, if you don't mind?"

"Is it connected with the rape?" Denton asked, bluntly.

"As I said, it's a private matter, Mr. Denton. You said Miss Morris would be home soon?"

Denton smiled.

"Yes, in the next few minutes, I'd say. She finished work not long ago, and is usually home within half an hour. She works as an input clerk for a computer services company not far away."

"And you, Mr. Denton, what do you do for a living?" asked Ross, still feeling the man had an air of authoritative confidence about him.

"Me? I'm a customs officer, Inspector Ross."

Ross smiled to himself. He knew it had to be something like that.

"I see, at the port?"

"No, at John Lennon," he replied, referring to John Lennon Airport, renamed after the former Beatle from the original name of Speke Airport. "I'm home because I'm on night shift this week. We don't get many flights late at night but we have to maintain a customs presence on the site twenty four hours a day. Listen, can I get you both some tea or coffee while you wait for Claire?"

"I'd love a coffee," Izzie spoke up, before Ross could refuse.

"Right, well, yes please, Mr. Denton. Coffee would be nice, thank you."

"Great," said Denton as he rose from his chair, and moved to the door, quickly making his way to the kitchen from where he called loudly.

"Milk and sugar for everyone, is it?"

"Milk and no sugar for both of us, please," Drake called back.

"Oy, I like a spoon of sugar in my coffee if you don't mind," he complained quietly to his sergeant.

"Think of your waistline, sir, and your cholesterol levels. I could be adding years onto your life."

"Yeah, or driving me into a mental home," he laughed.

Almost simultaneously, Lee Denton walked back into the living room, carrying a tray loaded with three mugs of steaming coffee, a sugar bowl, much to Ross's delight, and a plate of digestive biscuits, and the front door opened and Claire Morris arrived home.

"Hi, Lee, you there?" she called as the front door closed and before Denton could reply, she walked into the room, just as he placed the tray on the coffee table. Claire stood looking at the two visitors, smiling tentatively at the unknown newcomers to her home, The attractive young woman was smartly dressed in a dark blue pantsuit with low heeled black shoes, her shoulder length blonde hair cut in a fashionable bob, exuding an air of professional respectability.

"Oh, you've got visitors," she said, making an obvious assumption.

Andy Ross rose from his seat and took out his warrant card as he identified himself and Izzie Drake. After he'd corrected her assumption, informing her it was herself he and Drake wanted to talk to, she sat down and asked him the obvious question.

"And how can I help you, Inspector Ross?" she asked as Lee Denton hurried out to the kitchen again to make another coffee, this time for his fiancée. Before Ross could answer her question, Denton returned with Claire's coffee and asked if the detectives would rather speak to Claire on her own but she insisted he stay with her. He sat on the arm of the sofa next to her and Ross began.

"I'm sorry to have to bring this up after all this time, Miss Morris, but we need to speak to you about the man who raped you."

"Matthew Remington?" she snapped the name out as if it was a swear word. "Why, Inspector? Has he done it again to some other poor girl? I always said his sentence was too bloody short, and please, call me Claire. Miss Morris makes me feel like some middle-aged school teacher."

"No, Claire, he hasn't re-offended," Ross replied, instantly feeling stupid at his use of the police jargon, "he's dead. Matthew Pennington was murdered sometime in the early hours of this morning."

A look of what Ross saw as genuine shock appeared on the young woman's face on hearing the news of Remington's demise.

"Murdered? How? Where?"

"He was found in a churchyard. I'm not at liberty to reveal any details yet, I'm afraid."

"I see," Claire responded and then, as realisation struck her she said, "But, what has it to do with me? I can't pretend I feel sorry for him,

Inspector Ross, but you can't think I had anything to so with his murder, surely?"

"Not directly, no, Claire. But it's theoretically possible that someone may have attacked Remington in revenge for what he did to you."

"You can't be serious, Inspector. I know that Remington was released from prison years ago. Don't you think if I, or someone I know was going to do something like that, it would have happened back then?"

Izzie Drake spoke before Ross could answer.

"Ever hear the phrase, 'revenge is a dish best served cold', Claire? In other words, wait until your target is least expecting it and then strike."

Claire Morris, far from becoming angry, looked aghast at Drake and then burst out laughing.

"Sergeant, that's funny. Really, it is. All the revenge in the world could never make me feel better about what that man did to me. Do you know how I felt when I was in the hospital, being examined after the rape?"

"No, Claire. I can't begin to know how you felt," Drake answered honestly.

"Then let me tell you," said Claire." First of all, I was scared in case my rapist had given me AIDS. Secondly, I was afraid of being pregnant. The thought of carrying a rapist's child filled me with more dread than you can imagine. I'm Catholic, Sergeant, so the possibility of abortion could never have been an option if I was expecting, and then thirdly, I was afraid in case the man came back and did it again. I only relaxed a little bit eventually when first the AIDS test came back negative, then I found out I wasn't pregnant, and eventually my rapist was sent to prison. When I saw him in court at his trial, I suddenly realised he was nothing to be afraid of. He was such an insignificant and pathetic excuse for a human being. I knew I'd be ready for him if he came back again after his release, and I took martial arts classes until I graduated with a black belt in Tai Kwan Do, and also in Judo, so slowly the fears went away. No amount of revenge in the world could pay me back for what he put me through that night. Listen, when I was told how rapists got treated in prison, that made me feel good, and then I knew he'd have to go through his life always looking over his shoulder just in case someone did go after him, just like what's happened, and that was better than any thoughts of actually harming him, just knowing he'd never really be free, even though he'd been let out."

"Wow, that was some speech, Claire," said Ross. "I admire your resilience and your strength in getting your life back together, but we do have to investigate Remington's murder and find his killer. Whoever did this, they had a powerful motive, I can tell you that much."

Ross turned to Lee Denton.

"How long have you and Claire been together, Lee?"

Lee looked a little surprised that Ross had addressed him directly.

"Oh, must be about three years, Inspector. We got engaged when we bought this place together two years ago."

"I assume you were aware of what happened to Claire?"

"She told me all about it once we found ourselves growing close. I admired her for the way she'd fought to put her life back together after such a terrible experience. As it happens, my own sister was the victim of an indecent assault some years ago, so I found I could relate in a small way with Claire's emotional turmoil. Anyway, don't look at me for your killer, Inspector. I have too much respect for the law in the first place, and in the second place, you said the murder tool place in the early hours of the morning, right?"

"That's right, and you were on duty all night I presume?"

"From ten last night until eight this morning, Inspector. I should have finished work at six, but we were short staffed as usual so I ended up doing a couple of hours of overtime. By the time I got out of work and drove home, it was about nine fifteen when I got home. I put my feet up and watched the breakfast news programmes for a while, had some breakfast and then dozed off for a while. I was about to go up for a shower and a shave when you and the sergeant came knocking on the door."

"And you, Claire?" Drake asked.

"Me? I left for work just before eight, after Lee phoned to say he'd be late home, started at eight thirty and finished about an hour ago. I stopped for a few bits of shopping at Khan's Deli on the corner before coming home. The bags are still in the hall. I dropped them when I came in. I should get them and put the stuff in the fridge."

"We won't keep you much longer, Claire," said Ross. "Just tell me, honestly, if you think anyone in your family or circle of friends could have hated Matthew Remington enough to kill him?"

Claire laughed again, then replied.

"All of them, Inspector, obviously. They all had a motive, didn't they? But I doubt either me Mam or Dad would have the strength or the real inclination to do it, and as for my brother Steve, I doubt he made a trip up here last night to knock Remington off and then zoomed back down to Devon in time for lectures. As for my friends, they're all female, but as much as the ones who know about my rape might have wanted Remington dead, I doubt they'd have gone so far as to murder him. You still haven't told me how he was killed, Inspector. Was he shot, stabbed?"

"As the inspector said, Claire," Izzie stepped in, "we can't reveal that, yet, but believe me, it wasn't something you'd care to think about, unless you feel like having nightmares for a month."

Claire Morris seemed to stop in her tracks, drawing a deep breath and then said just the one word, "Oh."

"That bad, was it?" Lee Denton asked.

"That bad, yes," said Drake.

The mood in the room seemed to deteriorate further at that point, and Ross felt it was time he and Drake made their exit. He could always come back if he needed to talk to Claire Morris again.

"Right, well thanks for your time, Claire," he said, rising from his seat as he spoke. Drake followed his lead and stood also.

"We'll be in touch if we need any further information."

Claire and Lee both stood also and Lee Denton shook hands with both detectives as he saw them out at the front door, Claire remaining in the sitting room.

"I know you had to come and talk to her, Inspector," Denton spoke very quietly, "but believe me, Claire's spent her time since that man was jailed doing all she can to put the rape behind her as best she can and has built a new life for herself, happily with me, She would never have had anything to do with something like this. It's not in her nature."

"I understand what you're saying, Lee," said Ross, "but we have to explore every possibility in a case like this. The chance that someone saw a chance for some kind of retribution against Matthew Remington has to be investigated, and..."

"Lee," Claire called from the sitting room. "Are you coming in or what?"

"I'd better get back inside," said Denton, quietly.

"We'll be in touch again if we need to," Ross replied and the two men shook hands, before the two detectives walked away and the front door of Claire Morris's home closed almost silently behind them.

* * *

"Well, what d'you think of her?" Ross asked Izzie Drake as they motored back across the city towards headquarters.

"I think she's done remarkably well to rebuild her life, sir," Drake responded. "A lot of rape victims tend to withdraw into themselves after such experiences, at least from what I've heard and read. Claire Morris seems to have been something of an exception, not letting it ruin her life and trying to just get on with things as normally as possible. Having Lee Denton around obviously helps."

"Yes, I liked him, too" said Ross. "He's the stability, the rock she probably needed to enable her to rebuild her life. I also think he's in the clear as far as the murder goes. I know he could have been part of some sort of conspiracy to get rid of Remington, but this crime feels more like a personal one, a single perpetrator with a strong motive for doing away with Remington."

"I agree," Drake concurred. "What do you think the others will find when they interview Claire's family?"

"We'll find out soon enough, Izzie. The others should be back around the same time as us, I think, but I doubt they'll find anything."

"Are you saying you don't think her family or friends are involved at all, sir?"

"It's too early to say, but we have to consider the possibility this case has nothing at all to do with Claire and what happened to her. Who's to say that Remington hasn't had other victims, and they've not reported the attacks and then taken their own revenge on him, without ever bringing us on board?"

"Good God, I never even thought of that," Drake exclaimed. "But you're right sir, a large proportion of rapes do go unreported. Remington could have carried out any number of attacks since his release."

"But we have no proof, Izzie, and we also need to keep an open mind. This could have absolutely nothing to do with his crime, or crimes. What if he upset someone during his time in prison, someone who's only recently been released and who saved up a whole lot of rage while he was inside?"

"You want me to look into that angle, sir?"

"No, but get Ferris on it. Tell him to contact the prison, find out who Remington was paired with, if at all. He'd probably have been on a segregated wing, being a sex offender, so he'd either have been kept in solitary or banged up with another rapist or molester of some kind. We need to know if he managed to upset anyone during his time inside, and if so, who."

"OK, sir. Looks like this case could turn out to be a bloody complicated one, doesn't it?"

"With the amount of rage the killer displayed in the way he killed Remington, I think you're right, Izzie. I've got a bad feeling in my gut about this one."

* * *

Back at headquarters, the rest of the team had indeed returned from their various assignments and were gathered around the incident board in the conference room as Paul Ferris updated it with the results of their findings when Ross and Drake walked in to the room.

"Hello, boss," said Ferris as he turned to greet the pair.

"Paul, everyone," Ross acknowledged the team collectively.

"Do we have anything useful?"

"Not really, sir," Ferris replied on behalf of the team. "I'm just listing the fact that we've visited and to a degree, eliminated the family of Claire Morris from the list of potential suspects. How about you and Sergeant Drake, anything for me to add here?"

"Just another elimination, I'd say, Paul," Ross replied. "Claire Morris has a new life, a new fiancé, and was genuinely surprised to hear of Remington's death, not that she shed any tears for him, mind."

"Same here sir," said Sam Gable. "Her parents were positively delighted that Remington had finally got his 'comeuppance' as they called it. When Derek here said he thought murder was a bit over the top in terms of a comeuppance they were quite vehement about it, saying they were glad it had happened, and that they could never forgive Remington for what he did to their daughter. Having said that, I don't think either of them has the gall or the strength to have murdered Remington. The mother is about five feet nothing and has arthritis in her hands and feet and anyway, together, she and the father have a solid alibi. He was at the hospital most of the night. He suffered a serious angina attack yesterday evening, was taken in by ambulance and then was kept in overnight for observation. Lots of nurses and so on to confirm he was on the observation ward until Mrs. Morris came to pick him up at about nine thirty this morning."

"And the son?" Drake asked.

Derek McLennan took up the reins as he answered Izzie's question.

"He's in the clear too. Steven Andrew Morris, aged twenty, currently studying computer sciences at Exeter University. We contacted the uni, and asked the administrator to check if Morris was on campus today. Turns out he was in a lecture at the time we called, so we asked the administrator to get someone to interrupt the lecture and bring him to a phone. The lady," he consulted his notes at that point, "er...a Mrs. Davenport, wasn't too happy about helping us out there, but relented when I told her it was a murder inquiry, involving his sister. Whether she thought his sister had been murdered, I can't say, but she suddenly seemed very helpful."

"You can be as sly as a Scottie Road scally when you want to be, Derek McLennan," Drake grinned as she spoke. "You worded that so that she'd think just that, you clever little detective, you. Well done."

The rest of the team, Ross included, laughed aloud at McLennan's display of resourcefulness, a display of initiative that would have been beyond the rather green and ineffectual McLennan who'd first joined the team three years previously.

"Yes, very well done, Derek," Ross agreed, as the young detective blushed at the unexpected praise.

"Yeah, well, I've been learning from the best, haven't I, sir?"

"Well said, Derek. Please go on," Drake encouraged him.

"Oh yes, where was I? Right, of course, so a few minutes went by and I thought the old bag, I mean, Mrs. Davenport, had left me in the lurch, but then she picked up the phone again. She said she'd sent a messenger to the lecture theatre where Morris should be and said she'd summoned him as a matter of urgency to her office. Due to the urgency, she asked for my mobile number and said she'd get him to call me back as soon as he got there. So, about fifteen minutes later he called me, and confirmed the fact that he'd been in the halls of residence all night, and his room-mate would confirm it if we needed him to. Either way, there's no way he could have got from Exeter to Liverpool and back in time to have killed Remington some time this morning and been back there in time for his first lecture. He was right relieved though when I told him his sister hadn't been murdered."

Spontaneous laughter broke out once again among the team, everyone grateful for the brief moment of levity in the midst of a horrific murder investigation.

"Oh yes, he's turning into a right good joker is our Derek," Sam Gable giggled, with a broad smile on her face.

"Alright, you two, calm down a bit," said Ross. "Anything from Claire's friends, if you managed to contact them after all that?"

"Nothing at all, sorry, sir," said Gable. "There were two witnesses, if you could call them that, listed in the file. One was Lisa Owen, a friend of Claire's. She wasn't at home, but her mother directed us to the florist's shop where she works. She confirmed her original statement, that she'd been with Claire in the pub that night and got into a taxi and said goodnight to Claire at the end of the night. She said Claire wanted to walk home to clear her head, it wasn't too far, and the next she heard, was when the police came to her door the next day, and she learned about the rape. She said she hasn't seen or heard from Claire since around the time she moved into her new house with her boyfriend. Told us Claire's built a new life and let most of her old friends and reminders of the past behind her."

"Yes, that last bit gels with what Claire told us herself," said Ross. "Anything else?"

D.C. McLennan looked up from his notebook, his composure fully returned after the previous levity.

"The only other witness was Martin Riley, sir. He was the neighbour who told of Remington coming home late that night. He told us again what he'd told the police at the time: that he was letting his dog out for a wee last thing at night, when he saw Remington arrive home, looking dishevelled and 'aggravated' as he put it. There's a street light right outside their houses and he clearly saw scratch marks down the left side of Remington's face and neck. He asked Remington if he was okay but Remington just grunted something at him that sounded like "stupid bitch," and almost staggered into his home. He wasn't surprised when the police came knocking at his door and he heard of his neighbour's arrest. Of course, the scratches he testified to matched exactly with what Claire Morris said she'd done as she fought with her attacker. He said he never much liked Remington who kept himself to himself but was never very friendly with anyone in the street. I can't see him as being involved, sir. He's almost sixty, and lives alone with his dog, Rex, and uses a walking stick to get around. There's no way he could have overpowered a man like Remington, even if he'd wanted to. Oh, yes, he also told us he hoped Remington's soul would burn in hell for all eternity after what he'd done to Claire Morris."

"Humph," said Izzie Drake. "Sounds like the only person so far not to have wished him dead was Lisa Owen."

"Oh but she did, Sarge," Sam Gable piped up. "She actually said she'd often wished him dead, and, get this for a coincidence, she said she'd often wished that someone would cut 'that bastards cock off and turn him into a fucking eunuch, so he couldn't hurt any more innocent young girls or women,' and I promise you we never said a word about what had happened to Remington. I was going to add that bit at the end, when Derek finished."

"Oh right, saving the best till last, eh?" said Drake, while Ross added,

"But you didn't think she could have been involved, Sam?"

"Oh, no sir, She was just spouting the kind of rhetoric that women often do when talking about scumbag rapists like Remington, erm, sorry, like our victim, sir."

"Yes, right, I think we all know the team's estimations of Mr. Remington's character, thanks Sam, but remember everyone, a crime has been committed, a bloody brutal and vicious murder, and whatever we may think of the victim, I'm reiterating for you all, our job is to catch his killer, so do not lose sight of that objective, not even for a second."

Grunts of assent and agreement mumbled their way from the lips of those in the room.

"Right then, how about you Tony?" Drake said, turning to D.C. Curtis, who'd been sent to speak with Remington's employers.

"Drew a blank there as well, Sarge. None of his co-workers knew of his past. The personnel department, who, by the way, they like to call 'Human Resources' now, knew about it, but their records are confidential, and his line supervisor knew, but that was all. Seems they have a policy of employing a limited number of 'rehabilitated' offenders at Halewood, only a small quota of the total workforce. Anyway, unless someone found out about his record from somebody outside work there's little chance any of his fellow workers would have known he was a convicted rapist. Makes you feel sick really, when you think of the women who work there, not knowing who they were sitting with in the canteen at lunchtime, for example."

"Yes, well, we've been through all that before, Curtis," said Ross, so let's all drop the references to what we'd all have liked to do with Matthew Remington, or what we think should have been done with him."

A few more low frequency grumbles ran round the room as Ross turned finally to Paul Ferris.

"What about you, Paul? Did the good Reverend Donovan have anything else to tell us?"

"No sir. He was still in a state of shock if you ask me. I took a picture of Remington as he was in life to show him and he said he'd never seen him before. He might have come to his church at some time for all he knew, but he certainly wasn't a regular. If you ask me, sir, the churchyard was our killer's choice for the murder and had nothing to do with Remington, or whether he attended St. Matthew's or not."

"I think you're right, Paul," Ross agreed. "And listen, everybody. I want this bastard caught sooner rather than later, because, if what you've all told me today, backed up by what Sergeant Drake and I learned from talking to Claire Morris is correct, then it's my strong suspicion that Matthew Remington's murder had nothing to do with the rape of Claire Morris. If that's the case we're not only back to square one, but we now have a crime without an apparent motive. That, as we all know, is bollocks. A crime as violent as this had to have been caused by a very strong motive, and we have to start again and try to find out just what that motive is.

I want everyone to start digging into Mathew Remington's past. Go back to his childhood if you have to. Someone in this city hated him enough to virtually butcher him and then cut off his manhood and stick it down his throat. It takes real hatred, and real rage to do all that to a man. I want to know what Remington did, no matter how long ago to make someone feel they had to do what we saw the results of today. Any questions?"

Silence filled the room, accompanied by a chorus of shaking heads.

"Okay, listen, people, it's too late to do much more today. Go home, all of you, get some rest and be here bright and early in the morning. I'll be holding the morning briefing at eight a.m. sharp.

With that, the working day ended for Ross's team, and within minutes, all were on their way to their homes. Ross couldn't wait to see his wife, Maria. He felt somehow soiled and sullied by the day's events and he needed to feel a semblance of normality and humdrum home life, even if only for a few hours. His neat suburban detached home in Prescot might only be a few miles from the city, but right now, as he left the headquarters building, it felt like it was a million miles from the smells of blood and death that had followed him around all day.

Chapter 8

Respite

"You look absolutely shattered," Maria Ross exclaimed as she looked at her husband, who'd just walked in to the kitchen, his sagging shoulders and downcast expression betraying the effects of a stressful day at work. Andy always used the back door as a rule when coming home from work. Nine times out of ten, his shoes would be dirty and soiled from his exposure to the 'wild side of life, as Maria described his job. Today was no exception.

"Been a rough day, sweetheart," he replied as he dropped exhaustedly into an armchair that looked out of place in its surroundings. The old, blue velour upholstered fireside chair had moved with them from their previous house and had previously belonged to Ross's father, where it had held pride of place in his parents' kitchen. It was probably the most comfortable chair Ross had ever sat in and Maria would never dream of asking her husband to get rid of it.

"Want to talk about it?" she asked.

"You won't like it," he replied.

"Try me."

"We had a bad one, Maria. A man's body was found in a churchyard in Woolton. He'd been virtually butchered and..." he hesitated.

"Go on, Andy, and what?"

"Well, the killer opened up his body and cut out and sort of scattered all his major organs around the grave he'd been dumped on, but the worst part was the other thing he did. He cut off the guy's bloody penis, Maria, and stuffed it down his throat."

"Before or after he was killed?" Maria asked, calmly.

"Doc Nugent thinks the mutilations were all carried out post-mortem, apart from the penis, maybe. The man's throat had been slashed, cut almost through to the spine, and he was almost definitely dead before the killer hacked him to bits."

Maria's face registered a mixture of shock and sympathy at Ross's gruesome revelation.

"That must have been a terrible thing to see, my darling. I'm sorry you had to be there."

"That's my job, isn't it? Clearing up the mess the criminal fraternity leave behind themselves. It then turned out the victim was a convicted rapist. We thought at first he might have been killed by someone connected to his victim but we moved fast to interview her and her friends and relatives and there's no way I can see them being involved. So, we're back to square one."

Maria moved to her husband and, standing behind him, placed her hands on the back of his neck and slowly began to massage his tense and taut muscles. It was something she always did when he was stressed from a hard day at work and gradually, he began to relax a little.

"I love you, Maria Ross," he spoke quietly as her hands gently eased away the tension in his neck muscles.

"I love you too, Andy Ross," she whispered as she bent down and kissed the top of his head gently.

"Better stop before I nod off," Ross said as he felt his eyes beginning to droop.

"Why don't you go and take a shower and freshen up while I cook us something?"

"Good idea," he agreed, as he heaved himself up from his chair, kissed Maria tenderly on the lips he loved so much and walked from the room. As she heard him walk up the stairs to the bathroom, Maria thought, not for the first time, of how lucky she considered herself to have Andy Ross as a husband. She'd fallen for him almost from the first time she'd met him, and that love had never diminished. She loved his olive tinted skin, the result of his distant Anglo-Indian-Portuguese ancestry, and his intense dark brown eyes, with a head of luxuriant dark brown hair that was only just beginning to show a hint of grey as he approached his late forties. Equally, she knew Andy cared just as much for her. He never ceased to compliment her on her long, blonde hair, blue eyes, and her lips, always a prime target for his kisses. She'd kept herself in shape and still had a figure that many women half her age would have craved.

Daydream over, Maria set to work and quickly prepared a meal of spaghetti bolognaise for the two of them. After dinner, the pair snuggled up together on the large four-seater sofa in their lounge, her head resting on his chest as they relaxed together, watching TV for a while, and then listening to music for an hour until tiredness began to summon them both to bed.

"Doctor Ross prescribes an early night, Inspector," she whispered quietly in his ear.

"I'm happy to go along with your prescription, Doctor," he replied.

"You lock up down here, then go and get into bed, Andy. I'll grab a quick shower and be with you in ten minutes. If you're a good boy, the doctor might prescribe a spot of intimate massage, if you follow my meaning," she grinned at him.

"Mmm, sounds good to me. Don't be long in the shower. I'll be waiting."

They rose from the sofa, Maria quickly heading upstairs for her shower. Andy went round each room ensuring all the windows were locked, and then finally making sure the front and back doors were locked and the security alarm switched on, finally following his wife up the stairs.

"Don't be long, darling," he shouted, as he quickly undressed and jumped into bed.

"Two minutes," Maria shouted from the en-suite bathroom. Shower over; Maria quickly removed the shower cap that had kept her hair dry, shaking her hair loose, allowing to cascade down, creating a look of wilful abandon. *Pefect,* she thought. Now wasn't the time for washing her hair and spending fifteen minutes with the hair dryer, certainly not for what she had in mind. Although she and Andy slept in the nude, she reached up and took a slinky, narrow strapped satin negligee from a hook behind the bathroom door. She knew her husband enjoyed the feel of the satin against her skin and removing it was one of his special sensual pleasures. A quick look in the mirror, a brush through her hair and Maria was ready. After the kind of day he'd endured, Andy deserved a little pleasure, and she was intent on providing it.

She exited the bathroom and softly padded, barefoot across the bedroom to where Andy lay, on his side, facing away from her. She smoothed the chemise down as she moved closer and lifted the edge of the duvet. Sliding in beside and behind him, Maria softly whispered in his ear, "I've got something special for you, big boy"

Receiving no reply and no response, she reached her right arm across her husband's body, allowing her hand to gently stroke his manhood.

"Are you kidding me?" she asked, and then realised he wasn't. Andy Ross was fast asleep.

* * *

"Don't stop, Oh god, please, don't stop."

Izzie Drake lay beneath Peter Foster, her legs apart and wrapped tightly round him as he approached his own climax. Izzie could feel the beginnings of her own orgasm as she urged him on, until he gasped, grunted and cried out a loud *"Yes,"* as he spilled his seed deep within her. Feeling his penis throb and swell within her as he came, Izzie's own orgasm burst through the barriers of her own expectant passion and she herself cried out in ecstasy as the strength of the orgasm overwhelmed her, shutting out all other feelings and sensations until, slowly, as Peter sighed loudly, she released him from the intense leg lock she held his body in and allowed her legs to fall languidly and lewdly apart, knees slightly raised, as the lovers allowed themselves a few moments of breathless respite.

"Bloody hell, Izzie. You're amazing!" Peter exclaimed, having finally got his breath back enough to speak.

"You're not so bad yourself," she grinned up at him, before pulling his face down and planting a long, lingering kiss on his lips.

The pair had spent the evening at Peter's two-bedroomed apartment in a fairly new mid-priced development overlooking the docks. He'd bought it the previous year after inheriting a reasonably generous legacy from his always doting grandmother, who'd brought him up herself after his parents had died in a car crash when the young Paul Foster was ten years old. Her death from liver disease had hit him hard at the time, and his relationship with the pretty police sergeant had helped him greatly in his recovery from the initial grief at her passing. He and Izzie had enjoyed a takeaway from the local Indian restaurant before falling into bed together, Izzie virtually ripping his clothes off as she pulled him to into the bedroom.

"You're not usually quite so...intense," he observed, tactfully, as Izzie eventually eased herself out from beneath him, pulling herself up to a sitting position beside him.

"Not complaining, are you?"

"Hey, no way. Just wondering what I've done to deserve such a treat, that's all."

Izzie sighed before replying.

"I think it was just such a shit day at work today, Paul. I've never seen a body mutilated in that way. I mean, come on, you might not have seen it when it was brought in, but you must have heard what the killer did to Remington."

"Oh, yes, it was quite the talk of the office when we heard the details. I was glad I'm only employed on the admin side of things, so I can imagine a little bit of what you're getting at. I don't know how you can look at stuff like that every day and not be physically sick," he said.

"I felt like being sick, for sure, but I held on, I'm glad to say. We don't get to see that kind of thing often to be honest. Most murders are nothing like that, maybe a simple gunshot, or sometimes a stabbing or strangulation, but this was different, and to be honest, when we found out just what Remington had done in the past, I found it hard to feel too much sympathy for him."

"That's only natural, Izzie. You're only human, after all, and a gorgeous young woman too. You must feel a certain empathy with the girl he attacked."

"That's true, and Peter?"

"Yes?"

"Thanks for being so kind and understanding."

"Come here," he said and as she turned to face him, he kissed her long and hard, the kiss carrying a welter of emotion that carried Izzie back from her thoughts of work and once again turned her on to the romantic and erotic feelings they'd been sharing up until a few moments ago.

"Peter?" she gasped as she pulled her lips away long enough to talk.

"Uh huh?"

"Take me to the moon again."

"My pleasure," he grinned, pushing her down onto her back once more.

Izzie Drake needed no prompting as she opened her legs to welcome her lover into her body and into her very soul once again. As Peter Foster began to make love to her for the second time, a thought entered her mind, and for the first time, she realised…she was in love.

The couple soon fell asleep, though they woke twice in the night and indulged in repeats of their earlier lovemaking. Whatever the following day might bring, for now, at least, Izzie Drake was at peace with herself and with the world, the Matthew Remingtons of the world banished to the tiniest corner of her consciousness.

* * *

Sweat poured from every pore of Father Gerald Byrne's body. The sight of Mark Proctor, screaming in terror, and the sight of his blood, flowing in a torrent from a vicious head wound filled his mind until he thought his brain would swell and burst from his skull. Even then, his arm acted as though independent of his body, rising and falling in an arc of destruction as he wielded the heavy sword, one of two that usually hung in a display at the bishop's palace, the crossed swords being relics from the days of the crusades, so it was said. If this was indeed a crusader's weapon, it was enjoying a vicious renaissance in the hands of this twenty-first century warrior-priest.

As his arm finally tired, and the weight of the sword caused it to fall limply at his side, the bloodied blade pointing at the blood-soaked ground, Byrne finally allowed himself to stop, his chest heaving, and he surveyed his work. Little remained of Proctor's skull, his chest a gaping maw and the blood seeping from under the corpse until it appeared to be floating on a miniature lake of deep crimson.

That Proctor was dead, there could be no doubt, so, when the cadaver suddenly sat up, the bloodied, shattered head turning towards him, Gerald Byrne recoiled in abject fear. The hideously torn lips, the toothless mouth began to move and Proctor, impossibly, spoke,

"Gerry, oh Gerry, what on earth have you done? You'll be in trouble for this, you know you will."

Byrne screamed, a scream so loud it reverberated from the walls of his bedroom, so loud in fact that it woke him from his dream, or was it a nightmare? He really was sweating as he sat upright in bed, looked around him, recognising the familiar fixtures and fittings of his own bedroom, the dressing table, the wardrobe, the paisley-patterned quilt on his bed. Gerald Byrne forced himself out of the bed, and padded across the room to the dressing table, where he paused to view his reflection in the mirror. "Holy Mother of God, Gerald," he spoke to himself, "you truly look like shit, my friend."

Byrne almost staggered from his bedroom, making his way to the bathroom at the end of the landing, where he splashed cold water on his face and neck until he began to feel less wretched and more like his self again.

As he prepared to walk out of the bathroom, he became aware of an urgent knocking on his bedroom door, and he heard David Willis's voice calling out to him.

"Father Byrne, are you alright in there? Father, please open the door."

"I'm here, David," he said as he exited the bathroom, stepping out onto the landing. He realised his shouting must have woken the young priest, whose own bedroom was just along the landing from his own.

"Oh, thank the good Lord," Willis exclaimed, standing at the bedroom door in his red tartan dressing gown and matching carpet slippers, his blue striped pyjama bottoms protruding from the hem of the robe. "Was it a nightmare, Father? I was worried when I woke to hear you screaming so loudly. At first I thought someone had broken in and was attacking you."

Byrne walked up to Willis and placed a reassuring hand on the younger man's shoulder.

"Yes, David, it was just a nightmare, nothing to worry about. I probably shouldn't have enjoyed the biscuits and cheese so much after dinner. I've often heard that cheese can be the cause of bad dreams if eaten in excess before bedtime."

"Well, if you're sure you're alright, Father?"

"I'm fine, really, David. I'm sorry to have disturbed your sleep. You go and get yourself back to bed."

"Right, okay then, Father. I'll say good night again, then."

"Yes, goodnight, David, sleep well, and I'm sorry, once again."

Father Willis smiled a slightly worried smile as he headed back to his room, and turned round just before entering the bedroom but Father Byrne had already disappeared into his own bedroom, closing the door virtually silently.

Back in bed again a few minutes later, Gerald Byrne laid his head back on his pillows, closing his eyes, and allowed himself to slowly drift back to sleep. Just before sleep claimed him however, he found himself thinking,

Couldn't have happened to a more deserving case.

Chapter 9

Escalation

Every member of the investigation team was on time for the morning briefing, so much so that Andy Ross was the last to arrive, and he was ten minutes early! Acknowledging the greetings of his fellow officers, Ross felt good about himself this morning. Although he'd fallen into a deep sleep the previous night, depriving himself of the immense pleasure of a steamy lovemaking session with Maria, she'd made sure he was wide awake at five-thirty a.m. as Ross felt himself being gently coaxed into the mood by the tender ministrations of his wife's nimble fingers. What he'd missed last night, Maria was determined to make up for that morning. The sex was steamy alright, as his wife made sure they both extracted maximum pleasure from the thirty minutes they dared devote to each other before rising to begin the day. He hoped he could hide the self-satisfied grin that he felt was a sure giveaway to his team, but nobody appeared to notice, he thought.

Izzie Drake was at the front of the room, in conversation with collator, Paul Ferris, the pair of them standing in front of the whiteboard.

"Morning, sir," Izzie said as she turned to him. *My God, she looks like the cat that got the cream,* Ross thought as he looked at his sergeant's face and recognised the gleam in her eye as a sure-fire tell-tale sign.

"Good night, last night, Izzie?" he asked, looking straight in the eye, and Izzie instantly knew that he knew exactly what she and Peter Foster were doing the previous night.

"Very good, sir, thank you. And you?"

"Oh yes, very good, thank you, Sergeant. Very good indeed."

That was enough. The almost telepathic connection between Ross and his Sergeant meant that he realised she could read him as well as he read her. Seems like both master and apprentice had found the ideal outlet to release the tension and the stress of the previous day's gruesome discovery.

"Right then, that's good, so, let's get this show on the road, shall we?"

Within five minutes, Ross had summarised the efforts of the previous day, ending by thanking everyone for their hard work and professionalism in managing to complete a major slice of investigative procedure in one day. He praised Paul Ferris for helping George Thompson put together a Press Release that said very little, just enough to keep the press hounds at bay for a day or two while they attempted to press forward with the investigation, and then moved on to the orders for the day.

"We might not have unearthed a viable suspect as yet, but I think it's safe to say we've eliminated any connection between Remington's murder and the rape of Claire Morris. So, as I said yesterday, we go back into his past, and we dig, dig deep into anything and everything that man did in his life that might have some bearing on what happened yesterday. Someone held a pathological hatred for Mathew Remington. They must have done to have killed him and mutilated him as they did. We have to find out what he did to bring about such hatred."

"Any ideas where to start, sir?" asked 'Tony' Curtis.

"At the beginning of course, Tony," Ross replied. "D.C. Ferris will start the ball rolling by digging up his birth certificate. Paul, I want you to trace his early years, find out where he went to school, if he had any reported problems with other kids, or his teachers, that kind of thing."

"Okay, sir. I'll get to work right away, though I do know from the file on his arrest that he was an orphan with no known relatives, so we can eliminate the family angle right away," Ferris replied.

"Fair enough," said Ross, "concentrate on the rest. Sam, Derek, you two work together and go back to Remington's time in the nick. Speak to the prison governor, any of the prison offices who were there at the time. Bear in mind I don't know what we're looking for, but it's possible he upset someone badly while he was banged up. We know he was segregated from the general prison population because of the nature of his offence, but we haven't yet considered the fact he may have done something to upset someone who wasn't a prisoner."

"Bloody hell, sir. You think a prison officer might have done it?"

"I don't know, Derek, but I'm not discounting anything at this time." What about me, sir?" Izzie asked.

Before Ross could reply, the door of the conference room was opened and the figure of D.C.I. Harry Porteous stood there, framed by the doorway. His words sent an immediate chill down the spine of everyone in the room.

"We've had another one, and it's even worse than Remington."

* * *

Andy Ross's mouth fell open in shock, Izzie Drake looked as though someone had smacked her across the face and rest of the team froze where they sat or stood, unable to quite comprehend this latest shocking news.

The detective chief inspector strode to the front of the room and stood beside Ross before speaking again.

"I just received a call to say a body's been discovered in the churchyard at St. Mark's in Croxteth. It's another shocking mutilation scenario I'm afraid. According to the officers who responded to the 999 call, they've never seen anything this bad in their lives, and Sergeant

Donaldson has been on the force for over twenty years and has seen most things it's possible to come across in that time. If he says it's bad, believe me, it is. He's aware of the Remington murder but he assured me, when he was put through to me, that this is much worse. I want you there as soon as possible Andy. Take as many of the team as you can spare from here, if they're not actively pursuing any leads on the Remington case."

"Right, sir. Paul, you stay here and work on those records. With any luck, we may find a connection between Remington and the latest victim once we know who it is. Did the sergeant tell you if he'd managed to I.D the victim, sir?"

"No, he didn't. There was too much confusion at the scene he said, and he didn't want to disturb anything before C.I.D arrived on site. He's had the wherewithal to ask for forensic back-up and the duty pathologist is already on his way to Croxteth. You'll be pleased to hear it's your old friend, Dr. Nugent," Porteous informed them.

"It would be," said Ross, "but at least Fat Willy knows what he's doing and understands the urgency of what we need."

"Right then, you'd better get going, Andy," Porteous urged him.

"Consider us gone, sir," Ross replied as he motioned for the team to follow him and Drake as they led the way from the conference room.

* * *

Located virtually next door to Norris Green, Croxteth, 'Crocky' to most of its inhabitants is a fairly modern addition to the suburbs of Liverpool, despite being located close to Croxteth Hall and Country Park, once the home of the Earls of Sefton. Just prior to World War Two, large areas of housing were built there to house skilled workers from the English Electric and Napier factories who had moved to the area from the towns of Slough and Rugby. Later, families who had lost their homes during the bombings of the second world war moved into the area, which gradually grew over the years until it became what it is today, a large urban housing estate, which together with its neighbour, Norris Green, is one of Europe's largest housing developments.

St. Mark's church stood on the edge of the estate, close to the road leading to the country park, making it slightly isolated from the main housing areas of Croxteth. It was a small church, with a graveyard to the rear, and a small and continually dwindling congregation. The events of that morning would surely serve to reduce it still further.

Sergeant Vince Donaldson had taken charge of the situation as soon as he'd realised the importance of the crime scene. His partner, Constable Tim Mallory had quickly surrounded the entire church grounds with crime scene tape, making the whole of St. Marks an island of police and forensic activity. Donaldson had also requested additional uniformed officers from the local station and a total of six constables now stood ready to assist the detectives in any way necessary.

Ross and Drake led the way into the churchyard, where they were met by Donaldson, who'd had Constable Mallory on lookout for their arrival. Followed by Sam Gable, Derek McLennan and 'Tony' Curtis, they followed the sergeant along the narrow path that led round the church itself to the graveyard at the rear.

As soon as they turned the corner that gave them visual access to the graveyard, Ross saw just why Porteous had said this was worse than the previous day's crime scene.

"Bloody hell," he exclaimed.

"Oh...my...God," Izzie Drake choked the words out.

"Holy Mother of God," came from Sam Gable, who held her hand to her mouth in shock.

"Oh, fuck," was D.C Curtis's reaction, and whatever Derek McLennan was about to say never actually came out as he lurched off the path into the grassed area between two graves and for the second time in two days, was violently sick.

The scene before them was, Ross thought, surely something from a 'B' grade Hollywood slasher movie. About twenty yards ahead stood a grave, decorated as graves often are with the statue of a winged angel that Ross estimated to be around six to seven feet tall, the deceased obviously having been from a family able to afford an expensive funeral and the aforementioned grave statuary.

Far from appearing as a symbol of God's love, or of peace and benevolence, the angel instead presented them with a vision straight from hell. Tied to the outstretched wings of the angel with what looked like barbed wire, were the arms of the victim, crucifixion-style. The man's naked body hung in place across the front of the angel, his waist again secured by more wire, with his feet tied similarly, his legs bent unnaturally backwards to bring them into contact with the base of the statue.

Even without the benefit of Dr. Nugent's examination, Ross felt sure the victim had been alive when his murderer had fastened him to the angel. The amount of blood that had fallen to the ground from the man's wrists, his torso and feet surely indicated he'd been breathing at the time and must have endured interminable agony. Far worse however, were the additional wounds inflicted on the naked man. Whoever had perpetrated this horror had literally slashed the man's lower torso wide open and the detectives were faced with the horror of seeing the man's intestines and entrails literally dripping from the open gut. The victim's blood obscenely stained the consecrated ground red, both the grass and the once white surface of the grave stone itself. As with Matthew Remington, once again the man's penis was missing, a bloody void in its place and Ross held no illusions as to where they'd find it. Again, at first glance Ross could see no sign of the victim's clothes or belongings

"Who the hell could do this to another human being?" Izzie Drake was the first to break the shocked silence that had befallen the group.

Before anyone could proffer an answer, the sound of horrified gasps and exclamations from behind them announced the arrival of medical examiner William Nugent and his assistant, Francis Lees, accompanied by two obviously unnecessary paramedics. They were closely followed by Miles Booker and his team of four Crime Scenes Officers who had arrived simultaneously with the M.E.

"Och, man, ye've really got a doozy for me this morning, Inspector Ross. The poor soul. Ah cannae imagine any human being doing this to his fellow man."

"Sergeant Drake said virtually the same thing just as you arrived, Doc. This is just about the worst thing I've seen in all my years as a copper."

"Aye, well, standing here talking about it isn't going to help us find his killer is it? Come on, Francis, we've work to do."

Francis Lees followed the doctor, and as they began their initial examination of the body, to establish that the victim was in fact dead, though no one could be in any doubt as to the fact, Miles Booker walked up beside Ross.

"Jesus Christ, Andy. This is bloody grotesque."

"Tell me about it, Miles. I'm not sure my team can take much more of sights like this."

"Yeah, I can see young McLennan has lost his breakfast again."

Both men looked towards the death scene as Nugent beckoned to them. He and Lees, dressed in their white forensic suits and matching boots, resembled a pair of rather deformed wingless angels themselves as they tentatively examined the corpse.

Ross and Booker walked slowly towards the two men, stopping a few yards away, conscious not to disturb any trace evidence.

"Got something, Doc?" Ross called to him.

"Just confirmation your man is dead, Inspector. Mr Booker, does your team have a ladder in your van? I need to get up there and take a closer look at the victim. It's a good six feet to the top. We've tried not to disturb anything in the immediate vicinity, but I need to examine him in place before we take him down."

"Sure, Doc, give me a minute."

Booker sent a member of his team to fetch the ladder and in the meantime, Ross made an observation.

"Miles, I don't understand how the killer got him up there, or how he's overpowering his victims. Remington was no weakling, by appearances, and this poor sod looks quite well-built and muscular."

"Have you had the toxicology report back on number one yet? Maybe he's drugging them first"

"Ha, give the Doc a chance, Miles. Even Nugent can't quite work miracles. You know as well as I do it can take up to forty-eight hours to get the tox report, and let's face it, he didn't have a whole body to work with did he?"

Just then, one of Booker's crime scene techs arrived with a lightweight collapsible aluminium ladder and within a minute, despite his bulk, Nugent had ascended the angel and was carrying out a close-up examination of the victim. Meanwhile, one of Booker's men had identified a number of unidentified footprints in the immediate vicinity of the grave on which the victim had been displayed and was taking casts of the imprints, being careful to eliminate the prints left by Nugent and Lees in their need to carry out their initial examination. As everyone carried out their allotted tasks and with Ross's team pretty much idle for the moment, he sent Izzie to bring Sergeant Donaldson to him.

"Who found the body, Sergeant?"

"The vicar, sir, a Reverend Blake."

"Shouldn't that be Father Blake?"

"No sir, this is a Church of England church."

"So, our killer isn't just targeting Catholic churches as his kill sites. Either he doesn't really care about the religious aspect or he wants to take it out on all religions by leaving his victims in churchyards. Hard to fathom really. Ross looked at the gravestone again and at the incumbent angel, noting the family name on the long, horizontal slab of marble. I doubt the Seagrove family ever envisaged anything like this taking place on their last resting place," he mused, and turned to Drake. "Make a note of the family name, Izzie. We may find some significance in the killer's choice of gravestones by the time we're done with this bloody case. We might even have to investigate the families buried here and at St. Matthew's"

Drake nodded and dutifully noted the Seagrove name in her notebook.

William Nugent, his initial examination concluded, had descended from his position on the ladder and now walked across to Ross and Booker.

"Right then, Mr. Booker. Your people can carry on and do whatever needs to be done. As for your victim, Inspector, I believe your murderer has escalated his level of violence in terms of his means of execution."

"In what way, Doc?"

"Once we get him back to the mortuary I'll be able to tell you more, but for now, I think I can safely say that this poor man was still alive when he was hauled up and secured to the statue."

"Hauled?" Ross asked.

"Yes. There are marks under his arms and around his chest to suggest the killer tied a rope of some sort around the body and then literally hauled him up there. I found footprints some yards to the rear of the statue where he probably stood and heaved on the rope to slowly lift the body into place. You can see the indents where he dug his heels into the ground to gain purchase. Also, the amount of blood loss around the wrists, torso and ankles indicate he bled profusely from those wounds, which he wouldn't have done if he'd been dead at the time he received them. I can see numerous scratches all over the back too, where the dead weight of the body has caused it to sag forward, where he scraped against the angel as he was hauled up."

This information confirmed what Ross had initially thought.

"So, he knew what he was going to do before he got here and came prepared."

"I think so," said Nugent.

"There's not much more I can do here. Let's get him back to the mortuary and I can get to work," said Nugent, beckoning to the paramedics who would have the unenviable task of transporting the body, and its associated entrails and organs to Nugent's own domain, where a full post-mortem examination could be conducted.

"Perhaps, if they've got all the photos they need and your initial search for trace evidence is completed, Mr. Booker, you can get your crime scene people to take the body down and bag the organs so the ambulance crew can move everything back to the morgue for me?"

Booker nodded and moved off to organise his crime scene team.

"Oh, one more point, Inspector."

"Go on, Doc. What is it?"

"You're going to have the unenviable task of notifying a widow, I believe. Yonder laddie is wearing a wedding ring, so either he's married, or divorced and just hasn't bothered removing the ring. Some men do that, don't they?"

"Yes, they do, Doc, thanks. Don't suppose you took it off to see if there's any engraving inside the ring?"

"Perched on a ladder? Do me a favour, Inspector Ross. I'm nae stupid enough to try that. I'll make it a priority when I get him to the lab."

"Right, thanks Doc."

* * *

Leaving the specialists to handle the removal of the body, Ross and Drake stood looking at each other for a few seconds as they contemplated what they'd seen in the last hour or so. It was Drake who broke the silence.

"Sir? Are you with me? We need to move on this. What do you want the others to do?

"Yes, sorry, Izzie. I was just trying to think this through. There seems no way the two killings can be connected to Claire Morris so it's now totally safe to conclude her rape isn't part of our killer's overall scenario."

"Unless this victim is connected to Claire, sir?"

Ross nodded, thoughtful.

"A possibility, Izzie but somehow I doubt that. We do need to identify this man though, the sooner the better. Come on, we'd better go talk to the priest, sorry, the vicar. Get the others to start an immediate search of the area. Have Donaldson leave two men on duty here to secure the scene along with McLennan, if he's stopped throwing his guts up all over the churchyard and then team his officers up with our people. There aren't many houses in the immediate vicinity of the church so it's possible someone may have noticed something out of the ordinary."

"Such as?"

"I don't know, Izzie, but this bastard came prepared. I suspect he brought the victim here in a van or truck of some kind. He'd have needed a vehicle that could carry a ladder and whatever tools he needed to pull this off. He had to have had a roll of barbed wire with him and some pretty heavy duty gloves with which to apply it to the poor sod. He'd have needed cutters, God knows what else. This took time to execute, Izzie. If he did this in the dark or half-light of dawn, he'd have needed a powerful torch. He must have been supremely confident he wasn't going to be disturbed while he did this. Once we get an approximate time of death from Doctor Nugent we'll have a better idea of the timeline. I want to know exactly what time sunrise occurred. He needed light to see what he was doing, so may have strung the victim up to the statue and completed his killing ritual as the sun rose."

"Right, sir. When you said ritual, does that mean you think...?"

"I don't know what to think yet, Izzie. Let's not discount anything until we know more."

"I understand, sir," she replied as another thought struck the D.I.

"And another thing. If he was awake, the victim must have screamed his head off. Someone in one of those nearby houses just might have heard something."

With the team quickly allocated to their various tasks, Ross and Drake prepared themselves for an interview with the Reverend Blake, whom Donaldson had sent back to the vicarage, accompanied by one of his uniformed officers, to await the arrival of the C.I.D detectives.

Chapter 10

Confession

The fourth confession of the morning at St. Luke's Parish Church sent shivers down the spine of Father Gerald Byrne. As the voice, quite clearly that of a young woman, a teenager perhaps, on the other side of the confessional screen described her inner torment, it brought back memories to the priest, painful memories that he'd rather remain locked away in the deepest part of his soul. But, even as the young woman divested herself of sin before God, hoping for an absolution, Byrne knew that those memories, now resurfaced, could never be put back in the convenient mental box where he'd managed to store them for so many years.

As the woman/girl eventually fell silent, waiting for his response, a new and terrible burden came to rest on the shoulders of the Catholic priest. Bound as he was by the sanctity of the confessional, Byrne knew he could never reveal any of what the young woman had just imparted to him, no matter what the eventual outcome may be, a fact that troubled him deeply, far more than it should do, given his priestly status.

Byrne rushed through the next stage of the confessional, the young woman probably being surprised at the priest's response and lenient penitence he demanded of her. As he heard her footsteps recede towards the church exit, Byrne slumped against the wall of his side of the confessional, his head resting on the cold, hard wood as his mind filled with recollections of those things and events he'd much rather remain locked away.

"Forgive me, Father, for I have sinned. It has been one week since my last confession."

Byrne was suddenly brought back to reality by the voice of the next occupant of the confessional box. For now, he needed to concentrate on the here and now, put the past aside, and yet, the priest knew now that the past could never be totally put to one side, locked away out of harm's way, and, after hearing the previous occupant of the confessional's story, Father Gerald Byrne was now a worried man, afraid the past and the present were about to collide, and there was little, if anything he could do to prevent the events that were to unfold.

Confession finally over, Byrne virtually staggered from the church and on arrival at the manse, he almost collapsed into a softly upholstered, welcoming armchair in the living room. Hearing his entry through the front door, David Willis, who'd been carrying out visits to sick parishioners that morning came into the room, ready to offer Father Byrne a refreshing cup of tea. One look at the Father's face however, made Willis stop in his tracks, a worried look upon his face.

"Father, are you alright? You look pale. Are you ill?"

Byrne failed to answer right away, and Willis would swear to it that the priest looked as though his mind was a million miles away at that moment, his eyes seemingly focussed on a point in time and space that had little to do with the here and now.

Willis now walked up to Byrne and placed a hand on his shoulder as he said again,

"Father, are you alright?"

Byrne suddenly appeared to return to life, as though he had indeed been in another time and place. He looked up and seemed surprised to see the worried face of David Willis staring down at him, his face a mask of concern. Byrne quickly attempted to pull himself together.

"Oh dear, David, hello. I'm sorry if I frightened you, but I must have been miles away. I'm afraid daydreaming is almost a pastime of mine these days. So many faces, so many events over the years. Sometimes I remember and recall those events through harmless little daydreams, especially on warm sunny days like this. I'm sure you understand me, David, yes?"

Although he didn't really understand what Byrne meant, and though he honestly believed something was deeply troubling Father Byrne, Willis just smiled and replied,

"Of course Father. You've had a long and interesting life within the church and must have many happy memories. It's nice to be able to recall them I'm sure."

"Happy memories? Yes, David, I suppose most of them are."

Byrne said no more and David Willis diplomatically felt he should press no further, though he was certain something was on the older man's mind.

"I'll go and make us a nice cup of tea, shall I Father?" he said instead and Byrne smiled up at him from his chair.

"Yes, David, you do that. That would be nice. Yes, a cup of tea, very nice indeed."

* * *

Lisa Kelly alighted from the bus and stood watching as it pulled away and disappeared into the distance. She began walking slowly but determinedly, knowing exactly where she was going. Soon afterwards, she arrived at her destination, the dunes at Formby Beach. Lisa had always loved coming here. Her mother had been taking her to the beach at Formby since she was a little girl, often taking a picnic with them and enjoying afternoons together walking along the beach, watching the red squirrels that frequented the 'squirrel walk', before catching the bus home as evening fell. After visiting the church that morning, Lisa had sat on a bench in the churchyard for ten minutes, contemplating her next move. Finally, knowing there was no other way, she checked her purse, making sure she had enough change for the bus fare, and set off for Formby. Lisa sat for a while, listening to the sound of the breeze as it played a soft concerto among and around the dunes. Taking her mobile phone from her purse, she turned it on, and over the next two minutes, recorded a message on its voice recorder that she hoped would explain her actions to her Mum and her priest, the nice new man, Father Byrne. Satisfied, she rose and began walking towards the beach. Being a weekday, there weren't too many people around and Lisa made sure she headed for the most isolated section of beach she could find.

Arriving at the water's edge, she kicked off her shoes, and without hesitation, began slowly walking into the cold water, her eyes filled with tears as the waves grew taller the further out she walked, until her feet began to lose their purchase on the soft sand beneath. A sudden shout from behind her came from a man walking his dog, obviously aware of what she was doing, but Lisa simply ignored him and allowed the waves to take her, finally succumbing to the power of wind and wave as she sank below the waves, the weight of her clothes helping to carry her down, until finally, her head disappeared as the man and his dog stood helplessly looking on as witnesses to the final living moments of Lisa Kelly, just seventeen years old.

Chapter 11

Tea at the vicarage

"Please come in, Inspector Ross, Sergeant Drake. I'm Simon, Simon Blake."

Ross and Drake followed the Vicar of St. Mark's church into a neat and tidy parlour, furnished as Ross would have expected a churchman's home to be, with a red leather three-piece suite taking centre stage in the room, a mahogany coffee table strategically placed in the middle of the room. Beneath the bay window, which overlooked an expansive lawn, planted with well established shrubs and trees of varying species, stood a desk, also in mahogany, on which stood a modern laptop computer and printer, an open invitation to a thief, Drake thought to herself, but also typical of the trusting nature of a man of the cloth. Along the adjacent wall a bookcase held a fairly eclectic collection of reading material, from religious tomes to crime thrillers and romantic fiction, quite clearly the reading material of the vicar's wife, Ross presumed. What immediately caught Ross's interest however, was a photograph of the man who stood before him in the typical dress of a Church of England Priest, black shirt and white 'dog collar,' that stood to one side of the mantlepiece across the rather old-fashioned granite fireplace. The photograph showed the Reverend Simon Blake, some years younger dressed in the uniform of a British Army officer. Ross would ask about that in due course.

For now, he and Drake sat side by side on the sofa, at the vicar's invitation. Before Ross could ask anything, Blake took the initiative and asked the first and perhaps predictable question,

"Would you both like a cup of tea? I imagine you could both use one after seeing that poor man out there."

"Yes please, Vicar," Ross replied. I think you're right, that's kind of you."

"Just a moment and I'll ask my wife to prepare the tea, and then I'll answer whatever questions you may have for me."

"Right, yes, thank you," said Ross, who noticed Izzie Drake smiling at him in a way he took to mean she was amused at seeing the vicar apparently taking charge. It was usually the other way round, and she knew Ross well enough to know he'd feel a little strange, being 'organised' by the man in the clerical collar.

Blake walked to the door and called to his wife, who Ross assumed must be in the kitchen or dining room perhaps.

"Darling, would you mind popping in here for a moment please?"

"Be right there, Simon," a disembodied voice replied from another room, followed seconds later by the entry into the parlour of a striking brunette, probably in her late thirties, with a figure that wouldn't have looked out of place on a woman half her age. Her hair was neatly styled in a fashionable bob, and her skirt fell invitingly just above the knee. Ross found himself thinking that if all vicars' wives looked like Mrs. Blake, the churches might be a little fuller each week.

Blake immediately crossed the room and stood beside his wife as he made the introductions.

"Darling, this is Detective Inspector Ross and Detective Sergeant Drake. Inspector, may I introduce my wife, Cilla?"

Both detectives looked at one another with a shared look. Ross was glad when Drake spoke first.

"Er, Cilla Blake?" she asked with a hint of levity in her voice.

"I'm afraid so," Mrs. Blake replied, smiling as she spoke. "It's quite alright to react as you have. You must remember though, that Blake is my married name. I was born Cilla Marianne Prentice, Inspector. My

Dad, bless his soul, was a fanatical fan of 60s pop music and loved Cilla Black and Marianne Faithfull. He had all their records, and so when I came along he named me after them. It was a big decision to make for me, when Simon proposed as I realised right away how people would react to my married name."

"Hey," Simon Blake began, but Cilla intervened.

"Of course, he knows I'm only joking, don't you darling?" She reached up and kissed her husband on the cheek. "After all, it's only a name isn't it? Now, I suppose you'll be wanting me to make the tea, Simon, while you discuss the awful business outside?"

"Would you, please, darling?"

"Of course. Won't be long, and do make yourselves at home, Inspector, Sergeant. You've both had a terrible experience, I imagine. I haven't seen that poor man of course, but from what Simon has told me…"

She left it there and quickly withdrew to carry out what she obviously saw as her duty as a good vicar's wife.

"Your wife seems a very capable woman, Reverend Blake," Ross observed, after Cilla had left the room."

"Oh yes, she certainly is, and please, Inspector, call me Simon."

"Very well, Simon. Now, you found the body, I believe?"

"Yes, I did. Terrible, just terrible."

"Tell me how it came about, please."

"Well, as you can see, the vicarage is immediately across the road from the church. Every morning, I cross the road and make a quick tour of the church, whether we have a service or not that day, just to make sure everything's alright, if you know what I mean?"

Ross knew only too well what Blake meant. So many churches had become easy targets for thieves, either for the lead from their roofs, or the communion plate or other valuable items stored within church buildings.

"Anyway, I came through the front gate, walked up the path, unlocked the church and spent five minutes making sure everything was okay. I left through the front door, locked up and then noticed the side gate on the north side was open. I always make sure it's closed at night, and I thought perhaps we'd had vandals in the graveyard again. It wouldn't be the first time we've had graves desecrated, Inspector. No criticism intended but I'm afraid the police have been singularly impotent when it comes to catching whoever is committing such acts."

"I'm sorry we…"

"No, please, forget it. It's not important right now. Of course, I followed the path round the church and saw…well, you know what I saw, Inspector. That poor man was just hanging, sort of suspended, I'd call it, from the statue of the angel on the Renton's family grave. What suffering he went through, I'd hate to imagine, and I've seen a few appalling acts of cruelty in my time, I can tell you."

Ross looked again at the photograph.

"You were in the Army?" he asked.

"I was in the Army Chaplain's Branch, Inspector. I held the honorary rank of Captain, but was universally known by all and sundry as 'Padre' as I'm sure you're aware if you know anything about the military."

"Yes, of course," Ross nodded. "I was wondering about the photo on your mantelpiece."

"Yes, you were probably wondering how a soldier became a vicar. Most people who don't know my past ask that same question. It's not always possible to make out the crosses on the uniform unless you look closely at the photo, and even then, some folk probably wouldn't know what they signify. Anyway, I served in a few trouble spots, ministering to the troops, and saw the results of men being blown apart by land mines, gunfire, air-to-ground missiles and cannon fire. All of it was horrendous, but to be honest, what happened out there in my churchyard this morning is on a par with the worst excesses I've witnessed of man's ability to cause pain and suffering to his fellow beings, Inspector."

The door was pushed open and Cilla Blake walked into the room carrying a tray, complete with teapot, cups and saucers and the almost obligatory plate of assorted biscuits. Izzie Drake jumped up to help her and held the door back as the vicar's wife placed the tray on the coffee table in the centre of the room.

"Thanks, darling," Blake smiled at her.

"You're welcome. Would you like me to stay and pour, or would you rather speak to my husband on his own, Inspector?"

Ross smiled warmly at Cilla Blake.

"Please stay, Mrs. Blake. You may be able to help us."

"Oh, I doubt that very much," she replied. "I was at home here while Simon was making his gruesome discovery."

"Even so, please stay," said Ross. "You may help your husband in remembering something."

Cilla nodded her agreement and sat on the arm of her husband's chair, smoothing her skirt in an attempt to appear demure as she did so. Ross thought it made her look even more attractive.

"So," Ross went on, "You saw the body and, then what, Simon?"

Blake paused for thought before replying.

"The first thing I did on seeing the man on the angel, realising he was dead, was to offer up a prayer to God. Then I approached the grave and stood some yards away. I knew the police wouldn't want anyone disturbing the scene, but I felt I needed to get a closer look, to see if perhaps I recognised the poor man."

"And did you recognise him?"

"No, Inspector. I did not."

"Could he have visited your church, perhaps as a member of the congregation?" Drake added.

"If he did, I can honestly say he never made himself known to me, Sergeant. As I said, I didn't recognise him at all."

Blake's reaction was just the same as Father Donovan's the previous day. Again, an unknown man had been murdered and left on display in his churchyard. Why? Ross needed to solve that one before he could go further.

"Okay, now please think carefully, you too Mrs. Blake."

"Oh, please call me Cilla, inspector."

"Right, yes, well, you too Cilla. As I said, take your time, think very carefully. Have either of you seen any strangers hanging around the church or its grounds in recent days, or weeks even? Whoever did this must have had a reason for choosing your church. It's possible they reconnoitred the area first, before picking St. Mark's. Maybe you noticed a strange van or car that was parked nearby more then once perhaps, or someone on foot watching the church, that kind of thing."

"I'm sorry, Inspector," Blake replied. "If I'm not sitting here writing my next sermon on the laptop over by the window, I'm usually out and about taking care of the work of the parish. I don't exactly spend all my time at the church. If I'd noticed anything out of the ordinary I'd tell you about it, without a doubt."

Izzie Drake suddenly noticed an odd look on the face of the vicar's wife.

"Cilla, you saw something didn't you?" she hazarded a guess.

"Well, now I come to think of it, yes. Last week I was dusting in here when a van pulled up just outside the church gates. I half expected it to be a delivery for Simon. He often receives parcels of books or garden plants that are usually delivered by courier. Then I dismissed that thought because there was no writing on the van."

"What colour was it?" Drake prompted her.

"White, definitely white," she answered.

"Did you see the driver at all, "Ross asked.

"I'm afraid not. I did hear a door slam as though someone had got out of the van but I never saw who it was."

Ross thought of something.

"Do you recall which way the van was pointing?"

"Oh yes, it was on the correct side of the road, so it would have been pointing that way," she pointed in the direction she was indicating, which would have placed the vehicle on the far side of the road from the vicarage, with the passenger door closest to the gate into the churchyard.

"Clever bugger," said Ross, then, "Sorry about the language, Simon."

"No problem, Inspector. I'm a vicar, not a member of the language police. We all slip up now and then, even me, and you have good reason today, I think."

"What are you getting at, sir?" Drake asked.

"Well, if he was pointing that way, in order not to be seen from here, he'd get out of the passenger door. That way, Cilla here would have heard the van door shut, but even if she'd tried she'd not have seen him and he'd have been through the gate and into the churchyard in a couple of seconds."

"So you think that van contained the killer?" Cilla Blake asked. "Oh, my, that's positively scary."

"I'm sure he wouldn't have bothered you, Darling," said Simon Blake, reassuring his wife. "If he really was reconnoitring the church and churchyard he'd have remained as unobtrusive as possible. Even if you'd walked out there to him, he'd probably have made up some valid excuse for being there."

"Your husband is quite right, Cilla," Drake said to the worried-looking woman. "He'd probably have just said he was looking for the grave of a dead relative of friend and I would think you'd have been quite satisfied with an answer like that. After all, you would have had no reason to suspect anything, would you?"

Cilla Blake looked a little relieved as she realised her husband and the sergeant were both, in all probability quite correct in their assumption. She felt a little better as she picked up her willow-pattern tea cup, sipping the contents, and then reaching out to the still warm teapot to pour herself a refill, automatically doing the same for everyone else.

"So, if we assume that the occupant of that van *was* the killer," Ross re-entered the conversation, "we know that he owns, or perhaps borrowed or rented a white van in advance of the murders, though I'd plump for it being his own van. It would be difficult to erase any forensic trace evidence as it is, and he wouldn't want to risk a rental company or even a friend coming across anything incriminating if he'd slipped up somewhere."

"Er, Inspector Ross, can I say something, please?"

"Of course, Simon," Ross replied as the vicar looked at him with a look of deep intensity on his face.

"I'm not a police officer of course, and far be it from me to tell you or Sergeant Drake your jobs, but, well a thought just came to me and I hope you won't me mentioning it."

"If it's a helpful thought, I don't mind in the slightest," Ross replied, wondering just what Blake might have thought of that he could have missed. The answer that followed really did stop him in his tracks, making him wonder why he hadn't thought of it in the first place.

Simon Blake paused before replying, sipping from his cup, much as his wife had just done. The great British stress reliever at work before his eyes, Ross thought to himself. When all else fails, 'Put the kettle on, Mother.'

"Well, Inspector, if you don't mind me saying, and I don't mean to sound critical, but you and the sergeant are both talking as if you believe you're only dealing with an individual killer here. Believe me, having been in the Army, the Royal Engineers in particular, I've witnessed plenty of scenes where it was necessary to haul heavy objects around and it's not always a simple task. Heaving that poor man out there up and into position on the statue of the angel took some doing, is all I'm saying. My question therefore is this. Have you at any time, since that poor man turned up yesterday at St. Matthew's which was on the news this morning, and that I knew about through the ecclesiastical grapevine within hours yesterday by the way, considered the fact that there could be two people involved in these murders?"

Andy Ross could have slapped himself across the face. When the vicar, of all people, albeit one with a military background, put it like that, it almost became obvious. Two killers, or at the very least one killer and a helper, would have been able to haul the current victim up and fastened him to the statue of the angel with far greater ease than a single perpetrator.

"Vicar, you're a bloody genius," Ross said, oblivious to his language, which only served to make Blake smile. "Why the heck didn't we think of that, Izzie?"

Blake answered before Izzie could reply.

"Don't beat yourself up, Inspector. I could be wrong anyway, and from what I hear, yesterday's attack could have been the work of one man, or woman, God forbid, and you've only just got here and your mind hasn't had a chance to process all the information yet."

"Maybe not, but you have, Simon."

"Only because I've been thinking about it since I first saw the body, over an hour before you did, and because my time with the military taught me to look at things a little differently, that's all. I may have only been a padre, but I learned a lot about the ways of the world, Inspector."

"Even so, we may owe you one, for this theory. It's worthy of serious consideration, wouldn't you agree, Sergeant?"

"It certainly is, sir," Drake replied, knowing her boss well enough to know he'd never reject positive or practical suggestions regarding a case, no matter what the source.

After asking a few more routine questions, similar to those they'd directed at Father Donovan the previous day, they ascertained that regular services took place at St. Mark's twice on Sundays, and just once during the week, on Wednesday mornings. Weddings, funerals and baptisms were different of course and could be arranged to suit individual requirements. A final check that Blake had never seen the victim before and with a promise that they may be back to show a photo of the dead man to Cilla Blake to see if she recognised him from anywhere, which didn't seem to faze her at all, and the two detectives said their farewells to the couple for the time being and rejoined those still working the scene in the graveyard.

* * *

Miles Booker's team was hard at work by the time Ross and Drake returned to the scene of human carnage in the graveyard. The victim's body had been slowly and very carefully removed from its position adorning the angel, and was now being respectfully placed in a black body bag, almost ready for transport to the morgue. William Nugent had completed his initial examination of the remains to the best of his ability, considering it still had yards of barbed wire wrapped round it, and was packing up his own instruments as he and Lees prepared to follow the ambulance back to the mortuary where they could commence a full and proper examination. Even Fat Willy was aware how urgent this matter had now become. Two gruesome murders in two days were enough to move this case to the top of everyone's priority list.

"The reverend gentleman should have been a detective, sir. That was a quick piece of incisive thinking back there, don't you think?" said Izzie Drake as they walked towards Derek McLennan, who looked pale, but brighter than when they'd last seen him.

"I have to agree, Izzie. Wish I'd thought of it first though."

"You would have done soon enough, sir. We'd only been here a few minutes, and first thing we did really was go talk to the vicar. He's very sharp though, thinking of that the way he did."

"It opens up a whole new ball game though, Izzie. Yesterday we thought we were looking for a lone killer, and today it looks like we may possibly be seeking a pair working together."

"What about the footprints, sir?"

"Eh?"

"There were footprints behind the angel, where it looks like someone hauled the dead man up but shouldn't there be footprints in front too if there were two of them?"

"Bloody hell, you're right. Let's go have that talk with Booker."

"You okay now, Derek?" Drake asked as they drew level with D.C. McLennan.

Derek McLennan looked shamefacedly at the inspector and sergeant as he replied.

"I think so, thanks, Sarge. Sorry, sir. Did it again, didn't I? Can't believe it, two days running."

"Not your fault, Derek. I felt like throwing up myself to be truthful," Ross answered with a sympathetic look towards the young detective.

"Really sir?"

"Really, Derek, I'm only human too you know. Now come with us. We need a word with the SOCO."

Miles Booker, the Scene of Crimes Officer waved as he saw them approaching, then held a hand up to prevent them approaching any closer to the blood soaked grave and its accompanying angelic statuary.

"Stay there, would you, please Andy? We might have something here."

"It wouldn't by any chance be a set of footprints would it, Miles?"

"Fucking hell, Andy, you turned psychic all of a sudden? How did you know we were going to find them?"

"To be honest, I didn't until the vicar suggested the possibility."

"The vicar suggested it? What is he, a modern day Brother Cadfael or something?"

"No, but he's ex-Army, a padre in the Royal Engineers and understands the business of heavy lifting better than most. He thought it unlikely anyone would be able to haul the body up single-handedly from the rear as we thought at first."

"Clever man, eh? Well, you'd better come and take a look. Just walk carefully and follow my footsteps, keeping to this side of the gravestone."

"They're small," Izzie Drake observed as Miles Booker indicated the indentations in the blood pools that had gathered at the base of the statue. Almost like…"

"A woman's," said Ross.

"I concur," Booker agreed. "We didn't see the prints right away because they'd been partially filled in by the blood that had pooled around the base of the statue and on the stone itself, and with this side of the churchyard being in deep shade until the sun rose fully, it was almost impossible to make them out. As the blood settled and began to dry and the sun rose higher and the shadows lifted, well, there they were."

"So, it is a pair," Drake exclaimed.

"Looks like it, "said Ross. "That means our job just got a damn sight more difficult, and do *not* tell me to mind my bloody language. I'm well aware we're in a churchyard, but doubt that the inhabitants are likely to complain, are they?"

"Sir?" Derek McLennan spoke up from his position behind Ross and Drake.

"Yes, Derek, what is it?"

"Just a thought, sir. If the second perpetrator is a woman, do you think it means this victim could also be a sex offender and that we are looking for someone seeking revenge? I know we decided that Remington's murder wasn't about Claire Morris, but what if we have a pair of vigilantes at work, targeting known sex offenders who've been released from prison. Maybe they think the rapists or whatever they are haven't been punished enough by the courts."

"You could be on to something, Derek, well done lad. We're going to have our work cut out with this case if you're correct though. Where the bloody hell are we going to start looking, and who the heck is this second guy? We need to I.D. him, and fast."

As the ambulance carrying victim number two rolled away, taking the bloody corpse towards its appointment with the scalpels and bone saws of Doctor William Nugent, Ross left McLennan to co-ordinate the police presence at the scene until the others returned from their house to house inquiries, with instructions to bring everyone back to headquarters as soon as they reassembled at the churchyard. Miles Booker's forensic team would complete the examination of the death scene and report back to him as soon as they had something to tell.

The inspector and Izzie Drake meanwhile, motored as fast as they could to headquarters, where Ross wanted Paul Ferris to begin setting up the murder room to include this latest victim, start the identification process and to report to D.C.I Porteous on the latest developments. Ross felt he might need more help on this case, and Porteous was the only one who could authorise the additional officers and resources he felt the case deserved.

Chapter 12

Mispers

"I want to know who he is, and fast"

D.C.I. Porteous rarely raised his voice when speaking to his own officers, but the frustration caused by the team's inability to identify the second victim with two days having passed since the discovery of the bloodied corpse in the churchyard of St. Mark's was clearly evident as his voice now reached hitherto unheard of decibel levels, causing those in the murder team's conference room to visibly wince, as he addressed their morning briefing.

"We're doing all we can to i.d. the victim sir," Ross replied in an attempt to placate his boss."

"Then all you're doing just isn't good enough, Detective Inspector. We've had two killings in two days, and so far you and your team don't appear to have made any progress whatsoever."

Allowing his voice to descend an octave or two, Porteous now opted for a less aggressive tone.

"Andy, you're the best we have in this kind of investigation. Please tell me you have something, anything, that I can report to the Chief Superintendent, who, I can tell you, is getting his ears burned by some very senior officers, not to mention the fact that the press are sniffing around, sensing a real sensationalist story. Word has somehow reached the *Echo* that the second victim was even more horribly mutilated than Remington. Only the fact that the editor is a good friend of the Chief Super is keeping them quiet for the moment, but they aren't going to fall for any weak and non-committal press release from George Thompson this time. They can sense blood, like sharks round a shipwreck. Now, talk to me, for God's sake."

Andy Ross knew things were bad when his boss adopted such a stance as this. Admittedly, they had made little progress since the discovery of the second body, but he knew also that no case could ever be as simple as the top brass might like. He took a deep breath before responding to Porteous, as his team waited with baited breath, wondering just what he could say to placate the boss.

"Sir, we're doing all we can to identify victim number two. So far, D.C. Ferris has been able to ascertain that the man's fingerprints do not show up in any relation to any criminal activity. That leads me to assume he either has no criminal record, or, if he has, he's never been apprehended for any of his crimes. Even if he'd been fingerprinted in relation to any investigation and later eliminated, as you well know, those prints would have been destroyed thanks to current legislation regarding storing such prints. I've asked all police stations in our own force and all neighbouring forces to inform us instantly if they receive any mispers reports of anyone fitting our victim's general description, but you know as well as I do, sir, that missing persons reports will generally only be accepted once someone has been gone for forty-eight hours. If our man was taken immediately prior to his murder, any such report may not even have been accepted by one of the smaller police stations in the area. They have enough to deal with in terms of everyday policing, as we all know. However, I have sent a flyer out to all stations that any report of anyone remotely resembling the victim must be reported to me, whether an official report has been filed or not. In other words, if anyone walks into any Merseyside Police station to try to report a missing person from now on, if it's a male and fits our victim's description, we're going to know about it."

"What about releasing a photograph?" Porteous asked.

Before Ross could answer, Izzie Drake, a horrified look on her face, took it upon herself to interject.

"Sir, you've seen what the victim looked like after the killer finished with him. D.C. Ferris has sent facial close-ups to the other forces and circulated them to other stations in the area, but I'm sure you'll agree it wouldn't be a good idea to allow the press access to such a gruesome sight. Can you imagine how that poor man's wife or family would feel if they saw that picture in the Echo or in a national daily? Bad enough for any family to know their loved one is missing, but I'd hate to think they found out about his death by seeing such a bloody gruesome picture plastered across a front page."

Porteous seemed to come down from his high horse in reaction to Izzie's words.

"Ah, yes, you're right of course, Sergeant Drake. Look, D.I. Ross, I'm not telling you how to run your investigation, but the pressure from on high is already building and it's going to get a damn sight worse before we solve this bloody case. You said the wife of the vicar at St. Mark's saw a van lurking around outside the church. Any chance of a lead arising from the sighting?"

"Yes, she did, sir, but you know what it's like, people see something briefly but they never quite see the whole picture. It's possible she might have noticed something but not been able to recall it yet."

"Hmm," Porteous mused. "I'm not interfering here, but I want to call in a spot of specialist help for you, Andy."

"What sort of help, sir" Ross wondered what was coming next.

"I've been instructed by the brass on high to bring in a profiler, and she's arriving later today."

"A profiler? What do we need a profiler for, sir?" Ross asked, having always been sceptical about the modern trend of using psychological aids to criminal detection.

"Because the Chief Super says so, and I say so, which gives you two powerful reasons to co-operate with her when she arrives."

"She?" Ross asked.

"Yes, 'she', unless you have some objections to bringing in a female to assist you."

"Not at all, sir. It's just that I didn't think we had any female profilers, or male ones come to that, employed on Merseyside."

"Quite correct," Porteous agreed. "We don't. Christine Bland is employed by the Home Office as a sort of roving profiler, going where she's needed, when she's needed. The Chief assures me she's one of the best there is and she may just be able to help us by pointing us in the right direction towards the type of people our killers might be, if indeed there are two of them operating together, and what their motives might be, and therefore where we might begin looking for them. Any objections, D.I. Ross?"

Faced with the inevitable, Ross shook his head.

"None at all, sir. If she can help us pinpoint what to look for it can only be helpful, I suppose."

"Good," said Porteous, forcefully. "In the meantime, I'll leave you to it. For crying out loud, try to find out at least who the second victim is before she arrives, and that means all of you."

Before anyone could reply, the D.C.I. performed a smart, almost military about-turn, and marched out of the room, leaving Ross and the team almost speechless. Andy Ross gathered his wits quickly, turned to the assembled team and said,

"Right you lot, you heard the boss, let's get to it!"

Chapter 13

Brief Encounter

Lime Street Station, Liverpool, is a main line terminus station, originally opened to the general public in 1836. In keeping with the grand designs being applied to their station buildings by the early railway companies, the station was fronted by a magnificent reproduction of a French Château, formerly the North Western Hotel and now serving as accommodation for students at Liverpool's John Moores University. The whole station edifice stands as a magnificent testament to the ingenuity and design of the Victorian age, with its vast iron and glass roofs sweeping in a graceful arch over the station's nine platforms.

Two days after the murders however, the Burger King on the station concourse found itself playing host to a couple with no thoughts whatsoever for the beauty of the architectural history that surrounded them. Sitting opposite each other at a table near a window looking out onto the main concourse of the station, slowly sipping coffee from Styrofoam mugs, the man and woman hunched over the table, selected by the man as being the most isolated from the numerous travellers seeking refreshment before during or after their journeys. Keeping their voices low, but not too afraid of being overheard against the general hubbub of the comings and goings around them, their conversation continued as another train thundered into the station with a squeal of brakes as it slowed to a halt against the buffers at the end of the platform, easily heard from where they sat.

"We have to wait a few days before the next one. The police aren't entirely stupid and we need to pull back, let them run around chasing their tails for a while before we carry on," the man said, glancing around at regular intervals surreptitiously in an effort to remain anonymous. His nondescript olive green padded waterproof jacket, dark blue faded jeans and cheap chain store trainers, topped off with a Liverpool F.C. baseball cap already made him appear as nondescript as any typical walker heading up to the Lake District for a weekend in the hills and lakes. His partner, a few years younger and similarly dressed, with a black cotton tracksuit under her hiking jacket, and a red woollen cap on her head, with her shoulder length hair tucked up underneath, almost exuding a masculine appearance. At her feet, sat a weather-worn rucksack, a recent purchase from a charity shop, blending perfectly with her weekend hiker image, but which in fact contained a single change of clothes and her make-up bag.

"But we planned to hit them fast, get it done and fade away into the background again," she replied. "Why stop now?"

"Because I say so, for one thing, and secondly, number three is away on holiday in Greece until next week."

"Oh, well, we don't have much choice do we?"

"No, we don't. Did you get rid of the clothes from this morning like I told you to?"

"Yes, I burned everything, including my trainers, like you said. Bloody shame that was. They cost me a lot of money."

"Sod the money. The bizzies aren't stupid you know. They're bound to have found mine and your footprints around the grave, and too many people have been caught over the years through stupidly hanging on to things like shoes and clothes that the cops can use to link them to whatever offence they're investigating."

"Okay, okay, I get the picture. So, what do we do in the meantime?"

"Go to work, carry on as normal. Express your horror when people talk about the murders. They're bound to feature number two on the news tonight, and it'll be in the evening edition of the *Echo*, for sure, and it's bound to make the national dailies too."

The woman nodded in agreement, sipping from her coffee mug, then grimacing as she realised the contents had gone cold as they'd sat talking.

"Ugh" she spluttered. "Stone cold. I need a refill. Want one?"

"Yes, please," the man answered politely.

She rose from the table and walked across to the servery, looking back once and smiling at her partner. To any casual observer they looked as innocent as any other travellers waiting for the arrival of their train. As he waited for her to return with the fresh drinks, the man drummed his fingers on the table top, a random tattoo that he performed in order to stop his hands from shaking. He'd felt repulsed by the sight of their latest victim's innards spilling out from his guts after he'd slit him open, and he hadn't been prepared for the immense gush of blood that had accompanied the outpouring of intestines and bodily fluids, not to mention the smell as the man's life ebbed away in front of him. He knew they were doing what had to be done, but that didn't mean to say he had to like it, though it wouldn't be wise to share that with the woman who now came striding back to the table, a plastic tray in her hands, bearing two fresh disposable mugs of steaming hot coffee.

"You look a bit pale. Are you alright?" she asked as she placed the tray in the centre of the table before taking each mug and placing one in front of him, the other on her side of the table, then placing the tray on the floor beside them, propped up against the table leg.

"I'm fine," he replied, forcing a smile on his face. "Just daydreaming for a minute, that's all."

"About number two?" she asked, receiving a non-committal nod in return. "Did you see the look of panic on that bastard's face when he realised what was about to happen? It was priceless, and then the look of pure terror and shock on his face when you slit his guts open? I just wish he'd have lasted a bit longer, suffered even more, before going to hell."

"Keep your voice down," the man ordered. "Someone might overhear you."

"Right, yeah, sorry," she whispered across the table. "Just can't believe it was so easy, and so bloody satisfying to see his blood pouring out onto the ground like that."

"Come on," the man replied. "Enough of that. We're doing what has to be done. Let's not revel in it too much, ok?"

He felt he had to say something, if only to shut her up, before she blabbed too loud and someone heard her and called the police.

"Drink your coffee and we'd better go."

"When will I hear from you again?" she asked.

"Not until I've got things sorted and in place for the next one," he replied. "Best if we're not see together too often. That way nobody will think of connecting the two of us. It has to be bloody obvious to the bizzies that there were two people involved in the last one by now. They'll know one person couldn't have got him up on the angel by himself and the footprints we must have left in the blood and on the ground will confirm there were two of us as well. Hopefully, they'll think they're looking for two men, which will also work to our advantage. They probably won't dream a woman could be involved in such gruesome killings."

"Ha," she exclaimed, being careful to keep her voice to a bare whisper. "That just shows how wrong they are, doesn't it?"

A few minutes later, the pair rose from the table, the woman picking up the tray and depositing it in the used tray rack at the end of the counter, then walked casually from the fast food restaurant and out of the station onto Lime Street.

The pair quickly separated, the man walking to the station car park where his own transport was parked waiting for him. He looked back just once, to see his partner in crime walking briskly away from the station in the direction of the city centre, where, he knew, she'd soon find a store with a ladies changing room where she'd quickly transform herself back to her usual everyday appearance. The 'hiker' from the railway station would disappear, never to be seen again.

As he pulled away and began the drive back to home and work, he allowed his mind to drift back in time, and to a reminder of just why he was following his current course of action. The mind pictures that played in his thoughts reassured him and he knew that despite what the police and the law might think, his actions were entirely justified. Soon, it would be time to venture out once more, and the hunt would begin anew.

Chapter 14

All I have to do is dream

Sunday evening Mass completed, Gerald Byrne was looking forward to a meal, a hot bath and perhaps relaxing in front of the television for a couple of hours, followed by a cup of cocoa and a little light reading in bed before sleep claimed him for the night. Father Willis was in his room, reading before dinner, and would join him when their house-keeper/cook, Mrs. Redding, informed them their evening meal was ready. Byrne enjoyed the company of the younger priest and had soon began to feel at home in his new parish, feeling particularly pampered by the wonderful cooking of Iris Redding, who kept the house spotless and seemed to enjoy mothering the two priests. Aged sixty-two, but trim and sprightly for her age, Iris had kept house for the priests of St. Luke's for almost twenty years, and couldn't imagine her life with-out the daily tasks of 'doing for' the Fathers, as she described her work. Her husband, Tom, younger than Iris at fifty-eight, had worked as a landscape gardener until a heart attack had restricted his activity, and now kept his hand in by taking care of the quite substantial gardens at the manse, as well as tending to the not insubstantial task of looking after the grounds of the church, keeping the grass cut and tending to the graves, keeping St. Luke's churchyard a neat and tidy oasis of calm for the relatives and friends of those buried there, and who came to pay their respects at their loved ones' gravesides. Tom worked in the churchyard three mornings a week, though what he'd think when he saw the blood-stained grave and desecrated angel statue of the Seagrove's joint grave on his next scheduled gardening visit the following day, Iris Redding didn't dare to imagine.

Mouth-watering smells were already emanating from the kitchen and wafting through the house by the time Byrne had changed into a comfortable pair of jeans and his favourite brown polo-neck sweater. He seated himself in one of the room's two armchairs and reached across to the nearby magazine rack to pick up the latest edition of the *Liverpool Echo*, delivered each day to the manse.

The local newspaper's banner headline read, GRUESOME DISOVERY – SECOND MUTILATED BODY IN CITY CHURCHYARD.

Byrne had heard of a second murder via the bishop's office earlier that afternoon but the way it was reported in the *Echo* was sensationalist to say the least. Byrne guessed that the reporter had made light of the truth in a lot of his article, the priest doubting the police would have provided the press with some of the more lurid details contained on the front page.

As he read, Mrs. Redding knocked quietly on the parlour door and walked in to the room to announce that dinner would be ready in five minutes, but seeing the priest reading the article she felt she had to say something.

"Oh, Father, that poor man. What could he have done to make someone do those terrible things to him?"

"Now, now, Mrs. Redding," Byrne replied, "We mustn't necessarily believe all we read in the newspapers. I'm pretty sure the journalist who wrote this article used an awful lot of speculation and half-truths in his composition. The police certainly don't usually give information like this to the press, especially as it says near the bottom that the police will be releasing further details when the victim has been identified and next-of-kin informed. The police would never release some of this stuff in the newspaper article if the nearest and dearest hadn't been informed yet. They're not that insensitive."

"Perhaps you're right, Father, but it does sound as if it's a horrific killing, doesn't it? And just a day after the other one, and both victims left on holy ground, in churchyards. What is the world coming to?"

"Indeed, Mrs. Redding. It makes one think, for sure."

"Does young Father Willis know," she asked.

"Oh yes, I spoke with him when I arrived home this afternoon. He was shocked of course and we both prayed for the victim together."

"That was kind of you," said the housekeeper, and then, satisfied that she'd fulfilled the need to show concern for the victim of the latest brutal murder to hit the city, she went on, "Anyway, Father, dinner will be ready in five minutes. Liver and bacon, with onions, served with mashed potatoes, carrots and peas. And gravy, of course. Perhaps you'd be kind enough to let Father Willis know while I'm serving it out, and you can both enjoy it and take your minds off horrible things like murder and mutilation."

"Yes, of course I'll tell him, Mrs. Redding. Five minutes in the dining room, right?"

"Right Father. Five minutes," and then almost as an afterthought, "and there's one of those 'Stop Press' boxes at the bottom of page three, Father. Some young girl, nothing more than a teenager apparently, drowned herself off the dunes at Formby. All it says is a man walking his dog witnessed it and police are investigating."

"Ah, poor, tortured soul," Gerald Byrne said, sadness evident in his voice.

"But suicide's a sin, Father, isn't it?" Iris Redding said, as though in condemnation of the girl's action.

"So the good book tells us, Mrs. Redding, but that doesn't preclude us praying for the poor girl's soul, now, does it? For one so young to take such drastic action must mean she was under intolerable pressure of some kind to have pushed her into making such a terrible decision. We mustn't be too quick to condemn in such cases. Perhaps, like I will, you'll say a prayer for that poor girl's immortal soul before going to bed tonight."

Feeling a little guilty, Iris Redding replied,

"Yes, of course, Father. I didn't mean anything bad about the girl, just well, you know, it does say in the Bible that..."

"Yes, I know, Mrs. Redding, but also, the Bible tells us it is not the pure in heart that Jesus came to save, but the sinners, who he called upon to repent and accept the love of God, does it not?"

"Yes of course, Father, you're right of course."

Gerald Byrne smiled at his well-meaning housekeeper as the tantalising smell of his evening meal assailed his nostrils as it wafted through the door.

"Always remember, Mrs. Redding, that without sinners, people like me and Father Willis would technically be redundant. Now, about that excellent meal you've prepared for us?"

"Of course, Father, forgive me waffling on like this when you must be starving hungry. I'll be away and getting it now for you."

With that, Mrs. Redding walked swiftly from the room to begin plating up the two priest's evening meal as Byrne quickly glanced at the Stop Press article before placing the paper back in the magazine rack, walking into the hall and calling upstairs to his young assistant priest.

"David, Father Willis, dinner will be on the table in five minutes. Are you coming to join me?"

A muffled reply was just audible as Willis acknowledged Byrne's call from his bedroom, and five minutes later joined Byrne in the dining room as Mrs. Redding, in a display of perfect timing, followed within seconds, a smile on her face, with two tantalising tasty meals steaming on their plates as she approached the dining table with her serving tray.

"That smells delicious," David Willis said as Iris Redding placed the dinner plates down in front of the two priests.

"Mmm, looks it too," Gerald Byrne agreed. "You always do us proud, Mrs. Redding, thank you."

Smiling, Iris Redding stepped back and tucked the now empty tray under her arm.

"Enjoy it Fathers," she urged, "and there's my home-made treacle sponge pudding for afters, too."

"Oh, she's spoiling us to death, David," Byrne enthused. "You treat us too well, Mrs. Redding."

"Nonsense, Father," she replied. "You deserve a good meal at the end of the day. Now, go ahead and eat. I'll be back in a while to see if you're ready for pudding."

The two priests tucked in to their meal with gusto, finishing off with the promised sponge pudding, with home-made custard, after which Mrs. Redding cleared the table, stacked the pots and cutlery in the dishwasher ready to attend to the next morning, said goodnight to the priests and then headed off home to her husband, who would be eagerly awaiting his own evening meal when she got there.

* * *

After a quiet and peaceful evening in the company of his younger assistant, having enjoyed watching the television together and spending a short time discussing the day's news, including the horrific murder at St. Mark's, both men expressing their disgust and horror, not just at the gruesome nature and cruelty of the murders, but also the acts of sacrilege committed on holy ground, Byrne and Willis bade one another goodnight and headed upstairs. Byrne made for the bathroom where he kept his earlier promise to himself and spent a half hour luxuriating in a hot bath, before towelling himself dry and heading off to bed, calling out his goodnight to Father Willis as he passed the younger priest's bedroom door. Receiving no reply, he assumed Willis was already asleep and was soon tucked up in his own bed where he first spent ten minutes at prayer before picking up his book from the nightstand beside the bed. Less than ten minutes later, with his eyes growing heavy and the words of the pages beginning to swim in front of them, he placed the book down, plumped up his pillows and fell into a deep sleep in seconds, the sleep that carries the mind far inside itself, leading the sleeper into dreams so vivid they become, for a time, the sleeping brain's reality...

Speke Hill Orphanage and School's Sports Day, 1964, proved to be a great success. Teachers, carers and pupils alike had all entered into the relaxed spirit of the day, with much cheering and applause greeting the winners, and indeed the losers of each event. The ethos of the Catholic priests and nuns in charge of the event was simple, taking part was ultimately its own reward and though prizes were awarded to the winning house, everyone was to be congratulated on giving their all in the cause of their team.

Earlier in the afternoon, young Gerry Byrne had received great applause as he finished first in the 100 yard sprint, the blue hoop on his shirt flashing past the finish line a good two yards ahead of the white hooped shirt worn by Mark Proctor, who finished second for Sefton House. Alan Prosser, a school prefect and the Upper's House Captain of Stanley House, even came across to young Byrne and slapped him on the back in congratulations as another ten points for first place were added to Stanley House's total for the day, taking them into a sizeable lead. Mark Proctor was angry with himself for failing to beat the smaller Gerry, who he'd fully expected to defeat in the race, and he promised himself there'd be no repeat of his defeat when the pair faced each other again later in the 4 X 100 yards relay race.

Gerry's sister Angela, meanwhile, did her bit for Stanley House by winning her long jump event and as proceedings drew to a close, only the two boys 100 yards relays remained, with Stanley being three points ahead of Sefton, the other two houses trailing some way behind. The Lower School race was first, and Proctor saw his chance. As the pair took up the baton within a half-second of each other both having been picked to run the last leg of the relay, he surreptitiously tripped Gerry Byrne with a sneaky tap on the ankle, enough to make Byrne stumble and lose enough ground to be unable to make up over such a short race distance. Mark Proctor snapped the finish tape ahead of Molyneux and Norris with Stanley, in the shape of Gerry Byrne in fourth place. Thinking his triumph complete, and that he'd put his house into the lead with one race to go, Proctor was ecstatic until Master of Ceremonies, Father Rooney, announced an inquiry into the running of the Lower Boys relay. As the Upper boys relay race took place, with a win for Stanley, Sefton finishing a distant third, Stanley House was once more just in the lead in the race for the Bishops Cup. Everything now depended on the result of the inquiry into the earlier race. Mark Proctor's trip on Gerry Byrne had been seen and he was disqualified and Sefton House placed last, with the other houses all being promoted a place. Stanley House were the winners of the Bishop's Cup for 1964, and Sefton were runners-up, with Molyneux third and Norris fourth.

Gerry Byrne's disappointment at being cheated out of the chance of a win in the relay was slightly assuaged by the sight of Proctor's fellow relay team members kicking and thumping and slapping him in disgust at his behaviour, out of sight of the priests of course, that had cost their house the opportunity of winning the Bishop's Cup.

* * *

Angela's screams broke into his dreams. Young Gerry was fast asleep, his mind reliving his win in the relay, and the later sight of Proctor being knocked about by his own team members, when the shrill sound of his sister's voice, in obvious distress brought him to full wakefulness in an instant. Jumping up from his bed, Gerry leapt to his feet, oblivious to the cold of the lino floor against his skin, and ran to the window. There, on the grassed area outside, he saw Mark Proctor and three other boys holding his sister down on the ground. Gerry didn't know what they were doing to his sister, but the fact she was screaming and trying to fight them off and in obvious distress spurred him to action. Gerry clambered through the window and ran the few yards to the group on the ground, leaping at Mark Proctor, who was immediately on top of his sister, trying it seemed to Gerry, to force her to open her legs by forcing a knee between them. Whatever it was he was doing, Gerry knew it was wrong and he flung himself on to Proctor's back shouting as many obscenities as he knew at his tender age, while lashing out with his fists and bare feet, scratching

Proctor's face as his nails clawed down the other's cheek, until the other three boys grabbed hold of Gerry and began pummelling him with their fists, until he fell back on to the grass, blood pouring from multiple cuts on his face and legs. As he lay there, sore and bleeding, he heard his sister scream again, and saw a look of terror on her face as Mark Proctor began to remove his trousers, and Gerry wondered why none of the boys, Proctor included, had spoken a word, why nobody else had heard her screams and why no-one had come to help, and even as his mind pondered these questions, everything turned black.

* * *

"Wake up, Father Byrne. Father, Gerald, please, wake up."

The voice of Father David Willis eventually penetrated into the dark world of Gerald Byrne's dream state and he felt himself being pulled back to reality. Slowly opening his eyes, Byrne felt the strong arms of David Willis on his shoulders, shaking him as the younger priest's words continued to implore him to escape the nightmare in which he'd become entrapped.

Byrne looked up and there was David Willis, his countenance one of deep concern, his words soft and soothing.

"Father Byrne, are you okay? I was so worried. You were screaming fit to bring the roof down, and woke me from a deep sleep, not an easy thing to do, I assure you."

"Screaming? I was screaming, David? I was…I saw…I was young again and…it's a bit hazy."

"Get off her. Leave her alone, you bastards. That's what you were screaming in your sleep, Father. Well, that and more, but all in similar vein."

"Oh, Holy Mother of God forgive me, David, for disturbing your sleep and frightening you half to death, I'm sure."

"It's alright, really. Here, take a drink of this," Willis lifted a glass of water from the bedside table and handed it to Byrne, who sipped from it gratefully, then gulped down the second half of the glassful.

"No, really, I apologise, David. I don't know what came over me."

"A nightmare, Father, for sure. Who were you trying to defend? Do you recall the details? Who was the girl? Was it something that maybe happened to you in the past?"

"A nightmare, yes, of course it was. No, I don't recall the details," he lied, "and I don't remember a girl in the dream," another lie, "but I guess I ought to thank you and let you get back to your bed, Father Willis. I'm certain I'll be okay now, really."

Willis thought Father Byrne was being evasive, but why would he lie about a dream of all things?

"God save me," Byrne prayed once Willis had been placated sufficiently and had returned to his own room. The truth was, he recalled every detail of his dream, wining the race, being tripped in the relay, Proctor's subsequent disqualification, all real-life events, but the attack by Proctor and his friends on Angela, his sister? Fact and fiction were somehow merging in his mind and if he wasn't careful, he was in danger of losing his grip on reality. That attack by Mark Proctor was just a terrible, nightmarish distortion of reality…wasn't it?

Sleep was a long time coming again for David Willis that night. Something, he felt, was seriously troubling the new parish priest. This was the second time Byrne's nightmares had encroached upon his sleep. Could Father Byrne be ill, perhaps some dread, nameless terror from the past had reared its head and was torturing the older priest? Willis knew something of the background of Gerald Byrne as told to him by the bishop when he'd told Willis of Byrne's appointment to St. Luke's, but was there something more, something no-one was telling him? David Willis eventually drifted off into a fitful sleep after first deciding to try and find out more about the new parish priest of St. Luke's.

Chapter 15

All in the mind

Andy Ross had grown tired of waiting for the Home Office Profiler to arrive. A visit to the mortuary had brought little new in the way of information that would help them find the killer or killers of the two graveyard victims. The 'immediate' post-mortem promised two days ago had been delayed as William Nugent had cut his hand badly on his return to the mortuary and had required medical attention himself, leading to the postponement of the examination for just over twenty four hours.

Doctor Nugent and Francis Lees had at last carried out the post-mortem on the 'angel of death' victim, a name given to the unfortunate man by one of Miles Booker's crime scene technicians. Nugent had, at length, given Ross a tentative cause of death.

Standing over the autopsy table, his left hand heavily stitched where the knife blade had slipped and bitten deep into his flesh, Nugent looked up from the cadaver and looked at Ross.

"This one seems a little different, Inspector. The throat has been cut, as before, but not as deeply and it's my professional opinion that this poor bugger was killed by disembowelment. The massive trauma to this area," he indicated the lower abdomen with a flourish of his right hand, "is massive and the blood loss would have been tremendous. I believe yon laddie was opened up and bled to death as he hung, attached to that bloody stone angel. The blood pooled on the grave back at the churchyard indicated such a massive blood loss and my examination confirms it."

Ross rarely felt ill during post-mortems or autopsies but found himself feeling quite nauseous as he looked at the dead man's remains on the table in front of him. Izzie Drake also felt her legs going weak as she looked at the butchered remains of what, not long ago had been a living, breathing human being. Both officers had seen the scene at St. Mark's, which had been bad enough, but to now stand over the remains as Nugent picked over them in his hunt for clues they might use to find the killer or killers, was almost too much for them.

"I'm also pretty sure now that ye'll be looking for two killers, Inspector. It's my opinion that the slash across the throat was inflicted by a different hand than the wound on Remington's throat. It's not so deep, and there's evidence that whoever did it almost used their blade in a sawing motion, totally different to the first murder. The two sets of footprints help to confirm it. I think you might be seeking a woman, and a man, who probably was the one who opened up the man's abdomen, letting the innards spill out as he died. Oh yes, and the tongue's missing as with the first case, so that gives you your confirmation that this murder was comitted by the same killer or killers as Matthew Remington?""

"A woman?" said Drake, surprised, who, since talking with Miles Booker, had denied to herself that a member of her sex could have been responsible for such savagery. Are you sure?"

"Aye, Sergeant, a woman. The Crime Scenes Officers will confirm it, but those footprints in the blood in front of the angel looked too small to be those of a man, and that neck wound would be consistent with a woman's hand being at work."

"That puts a new slant on things," Ross commented. "A man and woman working together would be unusual but not unheard of. If there's nothing else you can tell us right now, Doc, we'd better get back to Headquarters. We're expecting the arrival of a profiler."

"Och, a profiler is it now? Your bosses think you need some help, I take it?"

"I'll take any help I can get right now, Doc," Ross acknowledged as he and Drake took their leave of the autopsy room, Drake lingering in reception for a brief conversation with Peter Foster before joining Ross outside as he stood by the car.

"Lover boy alright, is he?" Ross asked as Drake unlocked the Mondeo and the pair climbed into the vehicle.

""Peter's fine thank you, sir," Drake replied.

Ross smiled as Drake squirmed a little at his 'lover boy remark'.

* * *

The squad room at headquarters was unusually quiet on their return. Most of the team were out pursuing inquiries to try to establish the identity of the latest victim, with Gable also trying to find more on the life and relationships involved in the life of Matthew 'Razor' Remington.

Paul Ferris looked a forlorn lone figure among the desks and computers of the room but he quickly rose to his feet as Ross and Drake walked in.

"Everything okay, Paul?" Ross asked.

"Yes, sir. I'm still working on the tracking the life of Matthew Remington, while Sam is on the streets trying to find anyone who can give us more intel on his recent activities. I'll have it all up on the murder board as soon as I can, and by the way, sir, you have a visitor."

"The profiler?"

"Yes, sir, waiting in your office."

"Been here long?"

"About half an hour sir. I wanted to call you at the mortuary but she told me not to, that she was happy to wait and didn't want to interrupt you in mid-investigation."

"Very considerate of her, I must say. Come on Izzie, let's go meet the woman who'd supposed to help us solve the case."

With that, Ross walked off towards his office, Drake following closely in his wake. As he opened the door to his inner sanctum, he caught his first sight of the Home Office Criminal Profiler.

Doctor Christine Bland rose from the visitor's chair in his office as he and Drake entered the office, immediately holding her hand out towards Ross. He took it and as they shook hands, she spoke first.

"Pleased to meet you, Inspector Ross. I'm Christine Bland. Sorry I'm late. I know you were expecting me hours ago, but there'd been a mega pile up on the M62, and the traffic delays were horrendous."

Ross looked at the woman standing before him. Christine Bland was, he guessed somewhere in her late thirties. Her long blonde hair was tied in a pony tail and the two piece black skirt suit accentuated a well formed figure and the pencil skirt helped to accentuate her slim legs, She was about as far from the look of a profiler as he could imagine, but then, she wouldn't be here if she couldn't to the job, he supposed.

"No apologies needed, Doctor. Bland," he replied. "We've had plenty to do in keeping the investigation moving forward." He nodded in the direction of Izzie Drake. "This is Sergeant Clarissa Drake, by the way. Anything I know about the case, she knows, so you can speak freely in front of her."

"Pleased to meet you, Doctor," Drake said to the profiler, "and most people call me Izzie. Clarissa sounds so formal."

"Hello, Sergeant, good to meet you too."

The woman turned again to face Ross.

"Inspector Ross, I'm aware you might be a little dubious about the value of what I do. A lot of officers are the first time they work with a profiler, but believe me when I say that there are many ways in which I can maybe help you identify the type of person or persons you may be seeking in this case. D.C. I. Porteous already told me it looks like you're looking for a man and woman team now."

Ross, trying to be welcoming despite his doubts about the value of Bland's potential help, smiled as he replied.

"Look, Doctor Bland, I have no doubts that you're good at what you do, but it's not as if we have a serial killer at work with a string of murders behind them already. I know the top brass feel you can help and on that basis I'm happy to work with you, but just don't see how much you can possibly read into what's taken place in the last few days."

"Perhaps you'll change your mind after I've had an opportunity to review the case files, Inspector?"

"What? Oh, yes, of course."

Turning to Izzie Drake, he asked her to go and bring all the case files and notes they had amassed to date for the profiler to look at. Two minutes later, she returned, with Paul Ferris in tow, the team's collator looking agitated and somehow excited at the same time.

"Sir, you need to listen to Paul, right now," Drake informed him.

"Okay, Paul, what have you got for us?"

Ferris looked at Christine Bland, a questioning look on his face. Ross reassured him.

"It's okay, Paul. Doctor Bland is here to help us."

"Oh, right sir. I just had a call from an Inspector Woodruff out at Bootle. He thinks he might have identified our second victim."

Ross's senses jumped to full alert.

"Go on Paul. Don't keep us in suspense."

Looking at a sheet of paper he held in his hand, Ferris read from the notes he'd made of his conversation with Inspector Woodruff.

"Well sir, seems they had a report of a missing person from a lady whose husband hadn't come home from work the previous day. She'd called the station the previous night and of course they'd told her to call back if he didn't turn up by morning, and anyway, he didn't come home and when she called his work, they told her he hadn't shown up that morning either. She called the station at Bootle immediately and they sent someone out to see her, a D.C Collins. Anyway, Collins seems to be a bright chap, and he took notes, and obtained a photograph of the husband.

When he returned to the station, Collins remembered seeing the flyer with our inquiry the previous day and when he compared it to the photo of the missing man he went straight in to report to his boss, Inspector Woodruff, who took one look and called us."

Ross, becoming impatient, urged Ferris on

"Alright Paul, come on, who the hell is he?"

"Well sir, this is where things begin to come together a bit, I think. The dead man appears to be Mark Proctor, a P.E teacher. The thing is, sir, he taught at Speke Hill School."

"That place with the orphanage combined, out on Woolton Road?" Drake asked.

"That's right, the old loony bin they turned into an orphanage and school years ago. Anyway, what made my brain cells go into overdrive sir is that Matthew Remington, victim number one, was a resident of the orphanage and pupil at Speke Hill when he was a boy. There has to be a connection, sir, surely."

"Bloody hell, Paul. You might be on to something. It has to be too much of a coincidence for an ex-pupil and a current teacher from the same place to meet with similar violent deaths like this," Ross replied.

"How old was Proctor?" Drake asked.

"Fifty seven," Ferris replied.

"Similar ages," said Ross. "Paul, I think we may have our connection, as you say. Please start a background check on this Mark Proctor. Let's find out how far back the two dead men could have been connected to each other."

"Consider it done sir. Anything else?"

"Not for the moment. Give it your highest priority, Paul. I want to know all there is to know about Mark Bolton. I'd better speak to Inspector Woodruff and then go and talk to the widow, if we're sure of the identification. Did Woodruff give you any indication of what they're doing about that?"

"He said he thought you'd want to see her yourself sir, and arrange for her to identify the body."

"Of course he did," Ross said with a wry smile. "Pass the buck as soon as possible. No one wants the task of dealing with a potentially hysterical widow at the best of times, and certainly not one with a victim as badly mutilated as this one. Do we have a copy of Mrs. Bolton's statement yet?"

Bootle are emailing it to me as we speak, sir. I'll have a copy printed out for you by the time you're ready to go and see her."

Ferris left the office and the two detectives and the profiler looked at one another. It was Christine Bland who broke the silence.

"Looks like you might have something I can work with here, Inspector Ross. Do you mind if I accompany you and Sergeant Drake when you go to speak to the widow?"

"Not at all, Doctor. As you say, you may be able to offer some helpful insights."

"How will you proceed without a formal identification?"

"At this point, I want to talk to Inspector Woodruff, see how much he can tell me, then we'll go and talk to the widow, and show her a photo of the dead man. She'll see enough to be able to tell us if it's her husband, I'm sure."

"Even the touched up versions of the photos, taken at the morgue, are pretty awful to look at sir," Drake pointed out to her boss.

"I know, but if we're to move fast in trying to find his killers, we have little choice, and anyway, a photo will be far less painful than the formal identification she'll have to make at the mortuary tomorrow. Sorry Izzie, you'll have to put off seeing lover boy tonight. Looks like we might be in for a spot of overtime. I'll phone Woodruff then let Maria know I'll be late home too.

Why don't you take Doctor Bland for a quick coffee while I'm talking to Woodruff then we'll head off to Bootle as soon as I'm finished in here. Is that okay with you, Doctor?"

"Coffee sounds good, Inspector, and please as we're going to be working together, don't you think Doctor Bland is a little cumbersome every time you talk to me? Chris will do fine as far as I'm concerned. It's what most people call me."

"Fine, Chris it is then," Ross replied. "Now, you two ladies go grab a coffee, let me talk to Woodruff and Maria."

The switchboard connected Ross to the police station at Copy Lane in Bootle. Ross had visited that station maybe once or twice over the years, the only memorable fact he could bring to mind about the place was the fact that it was located not far from a McDonalds on the nearby leisure park. He'd heard of, but never met Inspector Bob Woodruff, nothing bad, a sensible, level-headed copper as far as he knew.

"Woodruff here," a rather gruff voice answered after a couple of rings of the internal phone system.

"Inspector Woodruff, Andy Ross here from the Major Crimes Squad."

"Hello there, the specialist murder team, eh? Call me Bob. You must have got my message about Mark Proctor."

"Yes, thanks, Bob. Sounds as if you're pretty sure this Proctor chap is our victim?"

"Sure sounds like it. The photo his wife gave us looks very close to the one you guys circulated, minus the facial wounds of course. It's too close a match to be anyone else, really."

"Did you tell her you think we may have found him?"

"Er, no. I didn't think it wise at that point. Thought you guys might prefer to handle it, being as it's your case and all that."

And saved you the problem of dealing with a hysterical newly-widowed wife of a murder victim, Ross thought.

"Thanks a lot, Bob," he voiced instead.

"Hey, never say I don't leave all the fun to the big boys," Woodruff laughed down the phone.

"Okay, but thanks for getting in touch so quickly. Can you give me the Proctor's address?"

"Sure," said Woodruff, reading off the address, which Ross duly noted down on a pad of post-its on his desk. "You can't miss it," he added, "It's just off the main road, about a mile from the station, about a hundred yards past the Shell filling station."

After thanking Woodruff, Ross made his way out of his office to find Izzie Drake and Christine Bland, coming to the end of their coffees, talking with Sam Gable.

"Meeting of the Women's Institute?" he joked as he drew near.

"Ha-ha, very funny, Boss," Drake replied. "Sam here was just telling us she used to live not far from Speke Hill."

"Really?" Ross said, quizzically. "What's it like, Sam?"

"Creepy, sir," she answered. "Well, it was when I was eight years old. It used to be a mental asylum back in Victorian times, and was converted to an orphanage and school sometime in the early part of the twentieth century. It was a real old gothic pile, at least, that's how it looked to us kids when we were growing up, you know, a real haunted house look to it. In fact, there were lots of stories around at the time about the place having a resident ghost."

"Ah, well, it would have to have a ghost wouldn't it?" Ross laughed.

"The thing is, sir," Gable went on, "lots of the kids who lived there used to get out at weekends and hit the local shops and villages or the older ones could catch the bus into town, and me and my friends often knocked about with some of the girls from there. They used to tell us about strange goings on in the orphanage at night."

"What kind of 'goings on' were they talking about, Sam"

"They said that sometimes they'd hear screams in the night, like a child in pain, a girl, they thought, and some of them said they'd seen a dark figure prowling the corridors in the dead of night, moving silently as though it was floating along, not touching the floor."

"Oh, come on Sam. You don't expect me to believe in some ghost wandering around scaring girls shitless in the night do you?"

"I'm only telling you what they told us, sir. Oh yes, and they did say that girls sometimes disappeared and were never seen again."

Now Ross's interest was aroused.

"Do you remember the names of any of those girls you talked to," he asked.

"Oh God, no sir, sorry. It was years ago and they were only kids we met up with now and then at weekends. I don't think we even knew some of their names."

"Okay, well, try to think of anything you can while we're out. Write down any memories you have that might help give us some additional background on the place. We're going to have to visit Speke Hill very soon. You might as well join us when we head over there. Your knowledge might be useful."

"Right you are, sir," said Gable, pleased to have the opportunity to work alongside Ross and Drake when the time came.

Chapter 16

Melanie

Crossing the car park to reach the pool car, Ross noticed Christine Bland casting a long look at a gleaming maroon Vauxhall Carlton, parked in one of the visitor spaces.

"Yours?" he asked, pointing to the pristine looking car, the Registration plate indicating the car to be around ten years old.

"Yes, it is," Bland replied

"I thought you'd have owned something bang up to date and trendier than the Carlton," he observed.

"Sentimental value, Inspector," the profiler replied. "It belonged to my late father. He bought it brand new and it was his pride and joy. He looked after it as though it was his baby. When he died five years ago, I asked Mum if I could have it, and I've done my best to keep it as he'd have liked. Vauxhall ceased production of the Carlton a few years ago but the parts, if needed, are still cheap enough and in plentiful supply."

"Nice," Ross said. "Sorry about your Dad."

"Thanks," Bland responded. "He was a lovely man, my Dad. Supported me in everything I did as a girl, through uni, the lot. I miss him a lot."

A companionable silence fell over the small group as they entered the car, and Drake drove out of the car park and headed for Bootle.

On the way, Izzie decided to try and find out more about the new temporary addition to the team.

"If you don't mind me asking, Doctor," she began, "but how did you get into the business of criminal profiling? We didn't get much chance to talk back there, thanks to Paul Ferris and his new information."

"I don't mind at all, Sergeant. I always wanted to by a psychologist, from around the age of twelve or thirteen anyway. I was lucky, got the grades I needed to get into medical school, got my M.D. and then went up to Oxford and got a degree in Psychology, followed by another in Criminology. When I was suitably qualified, I applied to the Home Office to be included in their list of Criminal Psychologists, able to assist the police in difficult cases. I became fascinated by the actual science of exactly what made certain criminals tick, why they did the things they do and so on. An opportunity came along to spend a year studying with the F.B.I's specialist Criminal Behavioural Analysis Unit at their H.Q at Quantico in Virginia. I applied and was accepted, and the rest, as they say, is history. I came back and was employed as one of a small number of profilers working directly for the Home Office, on a full time basis, basically going wherever I'm needed when a force such as yours specifically asks for help with cases like this one."

Drake was impressed and said so in no uncertain terms.

"Wow. That's fascinating. You must have been really determined to have gone through all that studying and training."

"I wanted to make my parents proud of me," Bland replied. "I'm pleased to say I think I succeeded."

Ross, who'd listened intently to her reply to Drake's question, added.

"Well, Christine, with all that training and your obvious qualifications for the job in hand, I have to say I'm pleased you're here to give us the benefit of your expertise."

"Thanks," she replied. "I'm developing a few thoughts already. I'll know more after we've seen this poor lady and when I finally get to finish reading the case notes you gave me back at headquarters. I might need to talk to the pathologist too, a Doctor Nugent, I believe?"

"No problem. Maybe you can take Doctor Bland to meet our friend at the mortuary tomorrow, Sam, after she's had a chance to read up on the case?"

"Be glad to sir," Sam Gable replied from her place in the back of the car, seated next to Christine.

* * *

"This is it, number forty-five," Drake announced as she pulled the car to a halt on the street outside a fairly modern detached three bed-room house with a well kept lawn to the front, liberally planted with various hybrid tea roses in well kept borders. An almost new Toyota Corolla, in a fiery red, stood on the drive in front of a closed up-and-over garage door.

Ross hated the task that lay ahead of them in the next few minutes. Informing a loved one of the death of a spouse or other relative was about the worst job a police officer had to attend to in his career, and in a case like this, the thought of how the man's widow might react was almost too terrible to contemplate, but knowing there was no way to avoid what had to be done, he took a deep breath before grasping the door handle, ready to open the door, and then...

"Okay, let's get this over with. Izzie, in the front with me. You at the back with the Doctor, please, Sam."

The woman who answered the door in response to the ringing of the doorbell looked to be in her mid-fifties, slightly overweight though not obese, with auburn hair that fell to her shoulders and looked in need of washing and brushing. Ross assumed worry about her husband had brought about the temporary neglect of her otherwise neat and well turned out appearance. She wore a cream blouse, and brown trousers that ended at a pair of brown house shoes of a similar colour.

"You must be the police," she immediately stated as she took in the rather large contingent of people standing on her doorstep.

"Yes, and you must be Mrs. Melanie Proctor," Ross said as he held up his warrant card to identify himself, and sought confirmation they had the right woman in front of them.

"Yes, please come in. Do you have any news of Mark?"

"Let's go inside and sit down, Mrs. Proctor," Drake urged as the woman seemed to hesitate for a second before moving aside and admitting the four of them. "We can talk better indoors rather than on the doorstep."

"Oh yes, of course, I'm sorry, please come in."

Melanie led them into a spacious living room, neatly furnished with three-piece suite in deep red leather, good quality carpet with a soft, deep pile in a dark grey shadow design, and a large screen television in one corner. A bookcase stood against one wall and a standard lamp stood in the corner opposite the television. A chest of drawers stood under the window and Ross couldn't help but notice the wedding photograph proudly displayed on top of the chest, a younger and slightly slimmer version of Melanie Proctor smiling with happiness beside her husband, Mark.

"Sit down, please," she invited, and Drake, Gable and Christine Bland did as she suggested while Ross remained standing behind Drake's chair, while Melanie stood looking nervously at the officers from a position standing in front of the cream marble fireplace.

"Do you have any news of Mark, then?" she now asked again after Ross had introduced the others. "Has he been involved in an accident? It must be that. I told him not to buy that bloody Subaru, it was too fast for him, but I think he wanted to show off in front of the boys at school. Is he in the hospital, Inspector? Was someone else hurt? Is that why you're here?"

Ross knew she was babbling, her words flying from her mouth from a nervousness born of fear. He'd witnessed this type of behaviour previously over the years as a kind of 'advance denial' reflex that kicked in to protect the speaker from potentially hearing bad news. He tapped Izzie Drake on the shoulder, and the sergeant spoke.

"Mrs. Proctor, Melanie, please, calm down. Inspector Ross needs to tell you something."

It worked. Melanie Proctor fell silent for a few seconds, and then spoke once more.

"Forgive me Inspector, I'm sorry. It's just that I've been so worried. Please tell me if my husband's alright or has he been hurt in some way?"

Andy Ross took a deep breath and then said, as sympathetically as he could.

"Mrs. Proctor, I'm sorry to inform you that we believe your husband was the victim of a vicious assault that took place in St. Mark's churchyard..."

"What? Wait a minute, I heard about that on the news on Radio Merseyside. But, that poor man, was...he was..."

"Dead, I know, Mrs. Proctor. I'm sorry to tell you we have good reason to believe the body currently in the mortuary is that of your husband, Mark Proctor."

Melanie Proctor didn't shout, she didn't scream or become in any way hysterical. She stood staring directly into Ross's eyes for about twenty seconds as his words seemed to bore their way into the deepest recesses of her consciousness, and then, as all the colour in her face drained away, leaving her looking paler than a ghost, she simply fell to the floor in a dead faint, so fast, none of the officers could move to try and catch the poor woman.

"Oh shit," said Ross.

"She'll be fine sir," said Drake. "Sam, go and find the kitchen, bring her some water, and if you can find a towel or something, wet it and bring that too."

"Right you are, Sarge," said Gable, heading for the door.

"Can I help?" Christine Bland asked.

"She's only fainted," Ross replied. "We'll bring her round in a minute."

Eventually, they did just that and Drake and Gable gently laid Melanie Proctor on the sofa as she seemed to struggle for breath.

"Do you want us to call a doctor?" Ross asked, or maybe someone to come round and be with you?"

"No, thank you. Why do you think it's my Mark?"

"We sent a photo of the victim to all police stations in the area, Mrs. Proctor. Inspector Woodruff at Copy Lane recognised the man from the photo you'd given them at the station. I'm afraid I don't have much doubt that the victim in the churchyard is Mark."

Tears were now flowing copiously from the woman's eyes, which were becoming redder by the second. Ross hated moments like this. There was just no way to make such moments any easier for the bereaved.

"I'm so sorry, Mrs. Proctor, but if we're to find who did this we need to ask you a few questions, and eventually, we'll need you to come and identify the body officially."

"Oh my god, no. It can't be Mark, Inspector. Who could possibly have wanted to hurt him?"

"That's one of the questions we need to ask you. Do you know anyone who might have held a grudge of any kind against Mark, or perhaps someone he'd upset at work recently?"

"No, nobody at all. Mark is a teacher, Inspector. As far as I know he doesn't have an enemy in the world. He teaches P.E. at Speke Hill"

Melanie continued to speak of her husband in the present tense. Ross knew it might be a while before she used the past tense, accepting he'd gone.

"Alright, and I know this is hard for you, but we have to ask these things. When did you last see Mark, Mrs. Proctor?"

Melanie suddenly began shaking and her body almost convulsed as it became wracked with sobs and tears of pure grief.

Ross spoke quietly to Izzie Drake.

"I think we should give her some time. Izzie, you know what we need to find out from her. You and Sam stay here with Mrs. Proctor. Try and question her again when she's recovered slightly. I'll call Copy Lane, see if they can spare a patrol car to run me and the Doc here back to Headquarters, and also get them to send out a Families Liaison

Officer to sit with Mrs. Proctor after you leave. Hopefully by then she'll have given us the name of someone, a friend or relative who can be with her. She shouldn't be on her own at a time like this. Before you leave, fix a time for her to come and identify her husband's body."

"Okay, sir."

"And Izzie?"

"Sir?"

"Don't be all day about it, know what I mean?"

"I know exactly what you mean sir," Drake replied.

Ross turned again to Melanie Proctor.

"Mrs. Proctor, this is terrible news for you, I do appreciate that, but anything you can tell us may be helpful in finding whoever did this to your husband."

"I understand, Inspector," she sobbed.

"Let's make a nice fresh pot of tea, Melanie," Izzie said. "We'll talk again in a few minutes when Inspector Ross and Doctor Bland have gone, okay?"

Melanie Proctor nodded and allowed Sam Gable to lead her into the kitchen, leaving Izzie Drake to talk privately with Ross for a minute.

"She's in shock, Izzie, so go easy on her, but try to find out anything you can about her husband's day to day life and activities. We need to establish whatever links him and Matthew Remington as well, which is vital if we're to move this case forward."

"No problem sir. We'll use the gentle touch with her, see what we can prise out of her."

"I thought you'd be talking to her yourself," Bland said to Ross.

"Izzie knows exactly what she's doing, and she and D.C. Gable will probably get more from her than I will, being women and perhaps more empathic with Melanie."

"Ah, so you do employ a little psychology in your methodology," Bland smiled at him.

"Well yes, I'm not a total dinosaur, Doctor. We do try to be sensitive to victim's families as well."

A knock on the door was answered by Izzie, who admitted a uniformed constable to the hallway.

"Constable Holland, sir. I'm supposed to drive you to headquarters," the young man said to Ross.

"Excellent, let's go, then, constable."

On the way back to town, Ross took advantage of their time together to find out a little more about Christine Bland.

"So, where are staying while you're in Liverpool?" he asked.

"The Marriott," she replied.

"Very nice," said Ross.

"Yes, it is. The room's excellent and I can work in it if I need to."

"So, what do you think so far?"

"It's too early to draw any conclusions yet, but you've already established that there must be a link between the victims. Once I read through the case files I may be in a position to offer a suggestion or two."

"Well, I hope you can offer something that will help us identify who or what we should be looking for, and soon."

"I'll do my best, Inspector. I don't offer miracles, but if I can at least point you in the right direction, establish a motive, anything to help, I will."

* * *

Meanwhile, Izzie Drake, having questioned Melanie Proctor about her husband's friends, regular routine and more now sat back and allowed D.C. Sam Gable to ask the widow of Mark Proctor a number of questions based on Gable's own knowledge of Speke Hill, gleaned from her own friends who'd lived and been educated in the orphanage and school.

"So, Melanie, Mark was a P.E, teacher, right?"

"Yes, he was actually recently promoted to head of the P.E Department at the school. It made him very proud."

"I'm sure it did. Tell me, did Mark teach just the Upper or Lower School pupils, or did his job entail teaching both groups?"

"Oh, the whole age range, not just the younger or older children."

"Thanks, and did he teach just boys, or the girls as well?"

"Both. Speke Hill is a co-ed school, with mixed classes, although the children are accommodated separately of course."

"Yes, I see. Melanie, do you think any of the other teachers in the P.E. department might have been jealous of Mark's promotion?"

"Oh no. that's preposterous. The staff members are all very friendly. Mark said they were a great team to work with."

"Okay, but we have to ask these questions, you do understand?"

Melanie nodded, her eyes puffy and red with tears as she reached for another tissue from the box Gable had found in the downstairs bathroom not long ago.

"Did Mark ever become involved with the orphanage's weekend shopping trips into town?"

"Oh, you know about those?" Melanie sounded surprised. "No, he didn't. He was a teacher at the school, and the activities of the orphanage were organised and run by the care staff. Most of them are what Mark laughingly called 'civilians' though there are still couple of nuns teaching there. Once upon a time they were all priests and nuns you know, both the teachers and orphanage staff."

"Yes, until the place came under Council control," Gable replied.

"And was Mark particularly close to any of the other teachers, any of them special friends, maybe came round to dinner or you went to their homes?"

"No, I'm sorry, nothing like that. He just went to work and came home after school."

Another bout of crying took over at that point and Drake signalled with a sweep of her hand to Gable to bring things to an end.

"Well, I think that's all for now, Melanie. You've been really helpful, thank you."

The woman was clearly close to the verge of cracking up at that point and the two detectives where grateful when a knock on the front door heralded the arrival of the Families Liaison Officer promised by Andy Ross.

Police Constable Sally Akeroyd quickly introduced herself to the two detectives and Melanie Proctor. Sally seemed to form an immediate bond with Melanie and Drake thought how well suited she was to the role of Families Liaison Officer. The time was appropriate to take their leave and Izzie informed Melanie they would send someone at ten the following morning to collect her and take her to perform the official identification of Mark's body, and bring her home afterwards. Just as Izzie and Sam were about to leave, Melanie made a final comment that brought them up short.

"It's so unfair," she said. "Mark spent almost his whole life at Speke Hill, first as a child and then as a teacher. They'll miss him almost as much as I will."

"What do you mean, child *and* teacher, Melanie?" Drake asked her. "Are you telling us Mark was a resident of the orphanage when he was a boy?"

"Yes, didn't you know that?"

Drake shook her head.

"He told me all about it. His Mum died when he was young. His Dad, an American soldier, was sent back to the States when he was nothing but a baby. Don't ask me why his Mum didn't go with him. I've no idea. I do know that Mark never knew him or his name. Proctor was his Mum's name. Mark was sent to the orphanage because his Mum had no relatives that could or would take a baby into their homes."

Drake knew there and then that they'd found the connection between the two victims. Both had been orphans at Speke Hill, and from their ages, almost certainly at the same time. She knew they had to get back to headquarters as soon as possible to report the information to Ross.

Placing a comforting hand on Melanie Proctor's arm, she thanked the still gently sobbing woman and called to Sally Akeroyd.

"Take good care of her, Constable," she said.

"I will, Sergeant Drake, don't worry. I've done this for two years. She'll be fine with me."

Drake and Gable were soon motoring back across the city towards headquarters. From the passenger seat, Sam Gable turned and spoke to Drake.

"Bloody hell, Sarge. That was a real turn up, finding out about Proctor's childhood like that."

"Wasn't it just?" Drake agreed. "The way it just came out like that. We knew he was a teacher there. We'd never have thought to ask if he'd been an orphan in the home as well. The boss will be bloody gobsmacked. We've definitely found the link between the two dead men. You did well in there as well, Sam. I wouldn't have known what questions to ask about the way things worked at the school or kids home or whatever they want to call the damn place."

"Thanks, Sarge, I appreciate that."

A few minutes later, Izzie pulled into the car park at headquarters and she and Sam Gable almost ran from the car, into the building, and up the stairs, ignoring the lifts as they rushed to inform Ross of the latest development. Things were moving at last. Perhaps now they could begin to find a reason for the appalling murders in the churchyards, and if they had a reason, they might just have a chance of identifying and tracking down the killers.

A few minutes later, the two breathless women burst into Ross's office, as he sat talking with Christine Bland.

"Sir, we need to talk, right now!" Drake gasped as she almost collapsed into a visitor chair beside the profiler, and Gable stood panting against the office door.

"Er, sit down, Sergeant, why don't you?" Ross laughed. "Come on then. What's so important? Out with it, Izzie. I know that look, like the cat that got the cream. You've got something, I know you too well."

So she told him everything she and Sam Gable had learned from Melanie Proctor.

Chapter 17

Profile

Following the report from Izzie Drake and Sam Gable, revealing that Matthew Remington and Mark Proctor had attended Speke Hill Orphanage and School at what they believed to be the same time, Andy Ross knew they had the connection they were seeking. Now, he felt that if they could just 'join up the dots' of how the two men were connected together by their pasts, he'd be well on the way to solving the gruesome murders. Christine Bland also felt the new information would be helpful to her in producing at least a preliminary profile of the killers once she'd read the case files, which she'd taken back to her hotel room the previous night to study. Word had gone out for all officers to be on the lookout for Mark Proctor's silver Subaru. If they could locate the car, it might give them a clue as to where Proctor had been abducted, unless the killers had moved it from the abduction site and dumped it miles away. It would certainly give them the opportunity for locating any forensic trace evidence the killers may have left behind.

Now, as the early morning sun shone through the plate glass window of the murder room, highlighting Paul Ferris's murder board as well as illuminating rows of dust motes floating in streams across the room, Ross felt as if the case was about to witness a new beginning.

After a brief up-date from each of the team, with the only significant information being a report from 'Tony' Curtis that included the news that Remington had been to all intents and purposes a model prisoner during his incarceration for the rape of Claire Morris, but despite being kept on the isolation wing for his own safety, had nonetheless been the victim of two serious assaults during his time in prison.

"Maybe he was so weird even the other nonces couldn't stand him," said Derek McLennan.

"The impression I got from the governor was that Remington had something of a reputation on the wing for talking about what he called 'fantasies' though he wasn't able to tell me exactly what those fantasises were," Curtis went on.

"Hmm, wasn't or wouldn't maybe?" Drake interjected.

"But why would the governor stand up for a fucker like Remington?" asked Curtis.

"I don't know," Drake replied. "But you know what some of these modern prison governors can be like, glorified social workers who think it's their job to rehabilitate the offenders in their jails rather than punish them, so if he had no proof of Remington's fantasies actually taking place, he'd rather keep them quiet instead of telling us about them and sullying the dead man's reputation even more than it already has been."

"Are you serious, Sarge?" asked Curtis.

"Yep, she is," Ross spoke up. "You've a lot to learn yet, Tony."

"Fucking hell," said Curtis, not too loudly.

"Maybe we need to speak to the governor at Walton again," Ross added, ignoring Curtis's profanity. "We'll come back to that later. First, for those who didn't meet her yesterday, this is Doctor Christine Bland, a profiler from the Home Office, sent to try and help us identify the type of people we should be looking for if we're to stop these murders."

A murmur of greetings rippled through the assembled officers.

"Doctor Bland has formulated a preliminary profile overnight and she'd like to share it with us. It's all yours, Doc," he said, handing over to the profiler, dressed this morning in an immaculate grey pantsuit, with low heeled patent leather black shoes, her hair still tied in the same style as the previous day, obviously her working style, Ross decided.

Bland stood and faced the team, smiling as she did so.

"Good morning, everyone," she began. "I met some of you yesterday, and hope to get the chance to talk to you all individually later. I'm here to help and together, hopefully, we'll bring these vicious killers to justice. Please don't stand on ceremony with me. My name is Christine, forget the Doctor Bland bit. We're all on the same team, and now, if I may, I'll give you what I've got so far. I spent yesterday afternoon with Inspector Ross, visiting Melanie Proctor, then was present in his office when Sergeant Drake and D.C, Gable came back to tell us that Mark Proctor and Matthew Remington were both orphans and lived at Speke Hill Orphanage at the same time."

A general murmuring encompassed the room at this latest information. Derek McLennan spoke up.

"Er, Christine?" I'm D.C. Derek McLennan. "So you're telling us that as well as living and obviously studying there as a boy, he then went on to become a teacher there?"

"Exactly. Looks like his whole life, apart from a few years spent studying was tied up with Speke Hill. That place is going to bear some very close scrutiny in the next few days. I'm sure Inspector Ross will have more to say about that when I've finished."

She turned towards the desk behind her for a moment and picked up one of the case files, holding it up as she turned back to address the team.

"I spent last night going through every word of these files. From these, added to what Sergeant Drake and D.C. Gable learned yesterday and the minimal forensic evidence at the murder scenes, my immediate thoughts are as follows. We're looking for a team, a man and a woman working together who have implicit trust in one another. It's likely that the woman is older than the man by quite some years, as it's unlikely a younger female would have built up the type of rage we're seeing displayed here. Dr. Nugent has carried out a minute study of the wound patterns on both bodies and it's probable that the woman was responsible for most if not all of the shallower stab and slash wounds found on both victims. As to the man, he's younger, fit and strong enough to subdue the victims and carry out the actual killings. The grass behind the angel memorial at St. Mark's was quite long, so ascertaining his shoe size from the prints found in the grass is an approximation only, as many of the indentations came from the time he was obviously leaning back and pulling the body of Mark Proctor upward to harness him to the angel, so those prints are not perfect as they show greater heel indentations and less of the tread from normal walking. It's Doctor Nugent's belief that the man wears size 9 to 11 shoes and the tread marks at the scene indicated some kind of heavy-duty boots, perhaps hiking boots. Forget the woman's shoe size as the prints in the blood on the marble slab of the grave stone were so blurred as to be useless, but they were narrow enough to indicate a woman's foot. Any questions so far?"

She paused and D.C. Curtis raised a hand.

"Yes, detective?"

"Curtis, Tony, ma'am."

"Please, not ma'am, D.C. Curtis. Christine will do."

"Yeah, right, well, Christine, why can't they possibly be the same age? A younger woman might also be capable of making those shallow wounds, right?"

"It's possible, yes. Profiling isn't an exact science, but from previous experience of similar recorded partnerships, one side of the killing team is usually older than the other. You usually find that one of them will be the dominant side and the other more of a submissive partner. In this case it's not yet clear who the dominant one is, but my money at this point would be on the male."

"Why's that?" Curtis asked.

"The sheer savagery of these attacks indicates a hugely narcissistic personality, someone who has total belief in his own ability to carry out these killings, without showing any sign of mercy to his victims.

The fact that there were no hesitation marks on the victims, and I'm talking about the major wounds now, indicates a confident and well ordered mind. He knew what he was doing and he wanted to do it. This indicates a leader rather than a follower."

Moving on to the sexual mutilation, there are a couple of ways to look at this. One, the killer may be exacting revenge for an incident related to the victims' own sexual activity, either against his partner or some other perceived victim or, it may be connected with killer's own sexuality. Believe me, as gruesome as it seems, I've seen similar mutilations in the past in cases of homosexual killings."

Various comments swept the room as the gathered detectives speculated on the fact they now had to consider other motives for the murders.

Derek McLennan raised a hand.

"Go ahead, please," said Christine.

"Okay, if we accept what you're saying, why do you think the woman is involved with this man? Could she be a relative, his wife, or what?"

"I said there's trust between them so it is possible they are related, or, as seems likely, the large age difference, if I'm right in my estimation, means this case is probably rooted in something that happened a long time ago. The woman may herself have been involved in whatever has been allowed to lie dormant for years. How and why the younger man came to be involved, it's too early for me to hazard a guess, but there will be something that connects them."

"Thanks," said McLennan. "So, you think Speke Hill is connected to the killings?"

"No, I didn't say that exactly. What I did say is there is something at Speke Hill, or an event at Speke Hill that connects the victims. That's not quite the same thing."

"Er, right, thanks," said Derek, still a little unsure of exactly what Bland was inferring.

"Finally," said Bland, "it's likely that the male drives a car. He'd need to be mobile in order to track and locate his victims. Mark Proctor had a car and it's missing. Our man could have arranged an accident or immobilised Proctor's car and then ferried him to the murder scene in his own vehicle, which might turn out to be a treasure trove of forensic and trace evidence if we can locate it."

Ross took control of the meeting again.

"Right you lot. You've heard what Doctor Bland has had to say. It may not be much at this point but it does give us some pointers to be going on with. Last chance for final questions, anyone?"

"Sir, one for the doctor, erm, Christine," said Sam Gable.

"Go ahead, Sam."

"Well, Christine says we're looking for a younger man and an older woman, but my question is, just how young is the man supposed to be? Are we looking for a teenager, a man in his twenties, thirties or what?"

Christine Bland was quick to reply.

"These murders have been carried out in a cold and clinical manner, which suggests a high level of sophistication and intelligence. They were obviously well planned and executed, so my belief is that we're looking for someone in his early to late thirties, physically fit, his partner probably being in her later forties or fifties. It wouldn't surprise me if she has some degree of influence over him, in that he perhaps sees her as either a mother figure or maybe even a surrogate for someone who has undergone a trauma that he associates with these men. We have to consider the fact that the woman may herself be a victim of an experience connected to the two victims."

"Thank you," said Gable.

Derek McLennan now added another question.

"Yes, Derek?" Ross said, becoming a little impatient to be moving on.

"Do you think the killers are finished? I mean, are the two victims so far the extent of their 'mission', as they see it?"

This time, Ross provided the answer.

"Doctor Bland and I discussed this at length yesterday. It's hard to anticipate what they intend from now on. It may be that Remington and Proctor were the only targets, or, they may be lying low, waiting to strike again. If one or both of them have any ideas of the way the police work, they'll know we usually scale down an investigation after a period of time if we have nothing to show for our efforts. They may be waiting for that moment to arrive, after which they could crawl out of the woodwork and strike again. Right, anything else?"

"Just one thing, sir," said Paul Ferris, who went on to say, "I was wondering if there might be some significance in the fact that Matthew Remington was killed in St. Matthew's churchyard and Mark Proctor in St. Mark's?"

"May I answer that one, Inspector?" Bland asked.

Ross nodded.

"We don't know, D.C. Ferris. It might be planned, it could be coincidence. I hate to say it, but unless we get another murder, there just isn't enough at this point to indicate anything other than the fact the churches concerned may have simply been convenient for the killers. Or, they're using the names to throw us a red herring, something to make us look for a connection that doesn't exist."

"Now that's bloody clever," said Ferris.

"That's what I meant about sophistication," Bland replied.

"Right you are, everyone," Ross said, bring the meeting to a close. "We've got work to do. Derek, I want you and Sam on Remington. I know we've checked him out already, but we need more, and concentrate on his early life. Let's look for some connection or crossover with Mark Proctor. I'm going to Speke Hill with Izzie and Doctor Bland. Sam, you'll need to postpone taking Christine to talk to Dr. Nugent until later."

Sam Gable nodded, as did Christine Bland, both in agreement with Ross.

" Everything we've learned so far tells us that Mark Proctor was Mr. Squeaky Clean, little orphan boy made good. Well, it's plain to see that someone thought otherwise. While we're gone, let's hope his car turns up. Tony," he said, turning to D.C Curtis, "get on to Traffic Division. Make them understand I want a priority on locating that Subaru."

"Okay sir," Curtis replied.

"And you Paul," he said to Ferris, "start going through those computer records of yours or whatever it is you do. Look for anything to do with Speke Hill that might tell us what may have taken place there during Remington and Proctor's youth."

"I'm on it sir," Ferris confirmed.

"Okay everyone. What are we waiting for?"

There followed a scraping of chairs on the floor as everyone rose to go about their allotted tasks, a hubbub of voices accompanying the departure of the murder team as Ross led Drake and Bland out of the building to the car park, ready to begin their investigation into Speke Hill.

Chapter 18

St Luke's

Iris Redding had done the priests proud. Breakfast had been a wonderful concoction of bacon, sausages, fried eggs, tomatoes and hash browns, sufficient, both priests agreed, to feed the two of them and probably half the church choir too. Mrs. Redding, her face bright and cheerful, simply ordered the Fathers to eat as much as they wanted. She'd make up some sandwiches for her husband from the leftovers. Tom Redding would soon be arriving to tend to the gardens and trim the grass around the graves in the churchyard, and bacon and sausage sandwiches would suit him down to the ground for a lunchtime snack.

After she'd cleared away the breakfast pots, she dusted the living room, vacuumed the carpets and then left the priests with a cup of coffee and the morning newspapers as she went about the business of cleaning the rest of the house.

"We'd be lost without that woman," Byrne observed after hearing the dulcet tones of her footsteps as she made her way upstairs and out of their hearing.

"We would indeed, Father," Willis agreed. "Not only that, but she probably thinks we'd starve too, if she didn't ply us with mountains of food every morning for breakfast."

Both men laughed, the pair in relaxed mood, enjoying a rare quiet morning with no services to conduct and no pressing engagements until the afternoon.

"Can I ask you something, Father Byrne?" Willis asked, the question coming at Byrne completely unexpectedly.

"But of course, Father," Byrne replied.

"You've been having the nightmares again, haven't you? I'm concerned for you Father. They're coming frequently aren't they? You'll never tell me what they are about, but they disturb you greatly, that much I do know."

Gerald Byrne didn't reply at once. He hadn't been aware that his continued nightmares were becoming a regular disturbance to the other priest's sleep.

"I'm sorry, David. I really am. I assure you there's nothing for you to worry about, though I'm upset if I'm causing you loss of sleep as a result of the dreams."

"But, Father, they're not just dreams, are they? I've heard some of the things you shout in your sleep. You seem to be describing some terrible event from your past. Forgive me for intruding, but on the couple of occasions when I've gone in to attend to you, you have indeed sounded quite terrified at what you were seeing in your mind."

"David, listen to me please. When you've been in the priesthood as long as I have, been to some of the countries I've been to, and witnessed man's inhumanity to man to the degree that I have, then you might just begin to understand that the human mind is like a great repository of memories, not all of them good ones, and that sometimes, the only way the mind can deal with those memories is to replay them in a man's dreams, for I believe if we did not dream of such things and bring them to mind in such a way, those memories just might become all consuming. In his wisdom, our Good Lord allows us to relive them in a way that makes us realise they were once real, not to be forgotten, but not to be confined to the deepest recesses of the mind, where they may fester and turn us bitter and twisted. I have walked in places in this world, David, where God was truly forsaken by those who inhabited such lands and where the sights would truly have given you nightmares had you seen them."

David Willis heard the older priest's words, all of which made sense, so why, he wondered, didn't he wholeheartedly believe Gerald Byrne? Not wanting to press the matter, however, he merely replied,

"I understand Father, I think, but if such things are troubling you, do you not think it wise to seek help, perhaps a talk with the bishop, or maybe even medical help if the dreams are causing you such mental anguish?"

"I'm fine, David, really. I appreciate your concern, honestly, I do, but there's nothing for you to worry about. I pray to the Lord every day for his help in reconciling what I've seen with the words of our Father in Heaven. Perhaps you'll join me in prayer right now and then we can move on with our day."

Byrne had cleverly backed the younger priest into a corner. Unable to refuse his offer to join him in prayer, Willis felt obliged to let the matter drop, for now.

After ten minutes of prayer, a short silence followed between the two men, broken by Gerald Byrne.

"And how is your work going David? You devote much of your time to the sick and the needy of the parish. I feel remiss at times for not joining you for an occasional morning as you do your rounds. I know you must find it hard sometimes, being up early and out before the crows have taken their breakfasts."

"Oh, it's all going well, Father, and I know you have enough to do here without having to join me out there. I enjoy what I do, and feel I'm achieving a great deal."

"Well, there you are then, David. We're both happy, aren't we?"

"Yes, Father Byrne," Willis replied. "I suppose we are."

"Well then, let's have no more talk of dreams, nightmares or what-ever. I must go and begin work on preparing my next sermon. You, I take it, have places to go and people to see, so I'll see you at lunchtime, when Mrs. Redding will, I'm sure, make certain we don't feel the pangs of hunger during our afternoon's labours."

Byrne rose from his chair, placing the newspaper he'd been reading on the coffee table in front of him, and strode from the room. David Willis watched him go and picked up the paper he'd been reading. It lay open at the latest report on 'The Churchyard Murders' as they'd been dubbed by the local press. Father Byrne had discussed the killings at length with Willis the previous evening, and appeared to be very interested in the subject of the murders, so it seemed to David Willis.

Chapter 19

Orphans & Demons

The journey from headquarters to Speke Hill would, under normal circumstances, take no more than fifteen minutes, but the traffic was heavy all over the city, thanks to the sudden descent of thick fog, that had made its way inexorably inland from the Irish Sea, enveloping the city in the muffled calm generated by a thick old-fashioned pea-souper.

Izzie Drake behind the wheel, the Mondeo almost seemed to groan at the forced lack of speed as the fog presented motorists with an almost impenetrable grey cloud-like barrier. Small golden-yellow haloes appeared around each of the normally bright street lights, adding a surreal feel to the vista that presented itself to those brave or foolhardy enough to attempt to drive in such weather conditions.

Ross felt an almost imperceptible increase in speed as the unmarked police vehicle began to close the distance between it and the car in front, an old Ford Fiesta that even in the thick fog appeared to be well past its best, with rust and scratches to the paintwork evident to Ross's keen eyes. He knew Izzie was growing impatient and even though his trusted sergeant had passed the police force's own advanced driving course, clearing her to participate in high-speed car chases if necessary, he didn't fancy their chances if she got too close and the old Fiesta suddenly slammed on the anchors.

"Izzie?"

"Sir?"

Please get us there intact. You can't even tell if that old bucket in front of us has got working brake lights. Before you know it we could be wrapped round his rear bumper."

"I know, sorry, sir, it's just so bloody frustrating, crawling along like this. We should have been there by now."

"It's the same for everyone, Izzie, and let's not give our guest in the back heart failure while we're at it."

"Oh, don't worry about me," Christine Bland piped up from the back seat. "I'm keeping my eyes shut, so I won't know anything until we get there or hit the car in front."

Ross and Drake both broke into spontaneous laughter, relieving the tension and boredom of the snail's pace journey. Ross's mobile began ringing, the unmistakable sound of the theme from The Great Escape emanating from the depths of his jacket pocket. He quickly fished around the pocket, retrieving it just before it switched to voicemail. The screen identified the caller as Paul Ferris.

"Paul, hello, I take it this is important? We're stuck in traffic in this bloody fog. Not even got to Speke Hill yet."

"Yes sir, I think you'll consider it very important."

"Well, don't keep me in suspense, Detective Constable. Let's have it."

"The car's turned up, sir, Proctor's Subaru, and we have two suspects in custody, and listen to this, they're a man and a woman."

Forgetting for a moment that Christine was in the back seat, Ross exclaimed, "Fucking hell, Paul. That was quick."

Remembering Christine he turned and quickly said sorry but she waved his apology away and he asked Ferris for the details.

"The car was found in Southport, sir, parked on the promenade, in plain view for the entire world to see. Two enterprising traffic cops were making a routine sweep of the seafront and thankfully they'd had the foresight and intelligence to read their alerts and bulletins and recognised the car as being sought in connection with the murders here in Liverpool. Seems they kept an eye on the vehicle under orders from their sergeant back at Southport Nick, and while they waited for the plain clothes guys to turn up, a man and woman came sauntering along the sea front carrying fish and chips and got into the car. Not wanting to risk them driving away and losing them, the two constables left their patrol car where they'd parked up to watch the Subaru, and quietly approached the vehicle and took the pair inside totally by surprise. They had the cuffs on them before you could say 'Cod 'n Chips twice please', apparently. That's the way it was related to me not more than five minutes ago by Sergeant Reeves in Southport."

"I presume we're getting them back to Liverpool post-haste?"

"We are, sir. I let D.C.I Porteous know of course and he grabbed Tony Curtis and seconded our old mate Nick Dodds who was walking past his office at the time to drive up and bring them back for interview."

"We have names yet, Paul?"

"No, sir, not yet. Anything special you want us to do with them if they arrive before you and Sergeant Drake return?"

"Just put them in separate interview rooms with a uniformed constable to watch over them. We should be back in a couple of hours, if we ever get to Speke Hill in this bloody fog. It'll give them both time to stew and they should be ripe for questioning when we get back."

"Right sir, good luck up at the school. Hope you find something that might help us nail these two, that's if they're our killers of course."

Drake and Bland had heard Ross's end of the conversation and he quickly filled them in on Ferris's input.

"Seems too easy, sir," said Drake.

"I agree," said Christine Bland. "So far your killers have shown resourcefulness, care and meticulous planning. It doesn't seem plausible that they'd slip up so blatantly as this."

"I tend to agree also," said Ross, "but the pair in Southport were found with Proctor's car, so they are involved in some way, but we won't know anything more until we question them."

"Well, anyway, we're here at last, sir," said Drake with relief as she turned off the road and through the entrance gates to Speke Hill, gravel crunching under the tyres as they motored up the sweeping drive, through the arch of trees until the main buildings hove into view.

The fog had lifted slightly, enough to give them a decent view of the gothic-style buildings as they pulled into the parking area in front of the largest, central building, a large sign outside listing the various departments inside, including Administration and most importantly, Visitor Reception.

"Creepy," said Drake as she looked up at the old Victorian walls, and the crenulated roof, giving the place the look of a typical haunted mansion, she thought.

"Very Gothic," Christine Bland agreed.

"Still looks like an asylum to me," Ross commented as he led the way through the main entrance doors.

Inside, they followed an arrow on the wall that led to reception, where a cheerful young woman reacted with surprise when they identified themselves and asked to see the Chief Administrator or Headmaster, whoever was available. Five minutes later a rather severe looking woman, no more than five feet three in height, but well proportioned and in good physical shape, wearing a plain grey skirt suit, her hair, greying at the ends tied in a bun at the back, arrived and introduced herself as Vera Manvers, the School Secretary. As soon as Ross informed her of the reason for their visit she led them to her office where she asked them to sit down while she contacted Charles Hopkirk, the Chief Care Officer, and Alan Machin, the Headmaster, as she assumed they'd need to speak to both men.

A short time later, Vera answered the phone on her desk, listened for a minute, then replied, "Right away, Charles," and turned to the detectives and the profiler.

"Mr. Hopkirk has got Mr. Machin with him in his office, Inspector. If you'll come with me I'll take you there now. It's a terrible business, isn't it? Such a shame about poor Mr. Proctor, and him being such a popular teacher too."

Ross thought it odd that she hadn't spoken a word to them until that point, but put it down to her rather abrasive and uncooperative demeanour, despite her efforts to appear affable. He was a good judge of people, usually and he simply couldn't find himself liking Vera Manvers.

"Thank you, Mrs. Manvers," Ross replied, "and yes, a very nasty business indeed. You knew the dead man of course, so we may need to speak to you too after we've spoken to the Headmaster and Mr. Hopkirk."

"I'll be here in my office, if you need me, Inspector, and it's Ms Manvers, actually."

She emphasised the *Ms*, as though Ross had insulted her by inferring she was married.

That's it, she's probably a closet lesbian, hates all men, Ross thought, as he moved to follow her.

"Right, my apologies, Ms Manvers."

She led them from her office, along a short corridor where she knocked and walked straight into the larger and airy office of Charles Hopkirk. The Chief Care Officer and the Headmaster were both standing waiting to greet them and after a round of introductions and hand shaking, they all sat, chairs having been provided to accommodate everyone.

"So, Inspector, we've been expecting you, of course, haven't we, Alan?"

"Indeed," the headmaster replied. "As soon as we heard about poor Mark, it was only a matter of time before you arrived, wasn't it?"

"Yes," said Ross. "How did you hear about Mr. Proctor, by the way?"

He knew the press hadn't released the name of the second victim as yet so it would be interesting to know where the school had got their information from.

"We had a call from poor Melanie Proctor, Mark's wife, Inspector. She was beside herself as you can imagine. She'd contacted us on the morning after his last day at school, telling us he hadn't come home. It was Alan, Mr. Machin, who advised her to go to the police, wasn't it, Alan?" said Hopkirk.

"Yes, I did. It was totally out of character for Mark to simply disappear, Inspector. He was devoted to Melanie and I was sure he must have been in an accident or something. He'd never have made her worry like that, not deliberately"

"Right, okay," Ross was thinking as he replied. He needed to move as swiftly as possible into the youth of Proctor and Remington but wanted the two men to feel at their ease first. Truth be told, Ross felt rather intimidated by the old asylum, despite its current mode of use. The sooner he could get back to headquarters the better.

"Well, gentlemen," he began, "I need to ask a few questions. I'll try not to take up too much of your time, but it's important you tell me all you know about Mark Proctor. How long had he worked here as a teacher?"

"About five years," Machin replied. "He was recently appointed as head of the P.E. Department as a reward for his hard work with the pupils. He was a popular and efficient teacher."

"And did that popularity extend to both the boys and girls he taught?"

"Yes, of course. What an odd question, Inspector."

"I just want to learn as much as I can about the man, that's all, Mr. Machin. That means asking some questions you may find strange, but I assure you they're all relevant. Did you ever feel there was any animosity shown towards him by any other of the staff members?"

"Never," said Machin. "Like I said, he was a popular teacher."

Ross looked at Drake, a signal for her to enter into the interview. She didn't hesitate, sticking to their pre-arranged plan.

"Mr. Hopkirk, as you are responsible for maintaining all the records of Speke Hill as I understand it, I believe that Mark Proctor was an orphan himself and actually lived here and attended the school?"

"Well, yes, that's quite correct, Sergeant. Mark was very proud of that fact, having been a student here and ending up as head of department."

"And is it also correct that at the same time as Mark was at school and living here, you also had a pupil by the name of Matthew Remington?"

"I don't know, I'd have to check the records. The name sounds familiar though."

"Matthew Remington was the first murder victim, Mr. Hopkirk. His body was found in the churchyard of St. Matthew's church."

"Oh, God," Hopkirk exclaimed. "And you think there may be some connection between the two men?"

"Yes, I do, sir. How long would it take for you to check your old records and confirm that both men were in residence and in education here at the same time?"

"Oh, well, the old archives are still on hard copy. They are planned to be put onto computer but we've never got round to it, yet."

"How long, Mr. Hopkirk, please?"

"If I enlist the help of Vera, our secretary, I may be able to find what you need by tomorrow at the latest, Inspector. I do have other work I have to do, you know."

"This is a murder investigation, sir," Drake stepped in quickly. "I think that's slightly more important than the mundane everyday task of running the orphanage, don't you?"

"Well, yes, of course, I only meant... well, yes, I'll give it top priority."

"One more question, gentlemen," Ross added. "In the last few weeks or say, the last three months, have you employed any new members of staff; teachers, orphanage carers, even gardeners or odd job people, anyone at all?"

"No, nobody," said Hopkirk. "Oh well, not unless you count the new chaplain."

"You have a new chaplain?" Ross's interest was immediately engaged. Anything connected to the church had to be of significance.

"Yes," said Hopkirk. "You know we were once a wholly run Catholic Church endeavour?"

Ross nodded in the affirmative.

"Well in those days the orphanage and school were both run by the church, most of the teachers were priests and the school's church of worship was St. Luke's down the road at Woolton. After the local authority assumed control of Speke Hill we maintained the link with

St. Luke's and the parish priest became traditionally the chaplain to the school and orphanage. Just a few months ago the previous priest passed away and was replaced by Father Byrne. He's not employed by us of course, but he's the only newcomer to the routine of Speke Hill in recent times. That's was another happy coincidence for us, because it turned out that Gerald Byrne was also a Speke Hill 'old boy' and attended here at the same time as Mark."

"He did?" said Ross, almost incredulously.

"Oh yes, and in fact they remembered each other well, and Mark showed Father Byrne around when he first came to see me, just to show off our modern facilities etc. Things have changed considerably since he was here as a boy."

By now, Andy Ross's senses were on high alert. A brief glance at his two companions and the looks on their faces told him they shared his thoughts. This was too much of a coincidence. A new priest arrives on the scene, an ex-Speke Hill resident and scholar and within weeks two of his former peers are found horrible murdered.

"Mr. Hopkirk, Mr. Machin, I appreciate the fact that these men were all here many years before your time at Speke Hill, but it may be there is some connection, a thread of circumstances that may point to the motive for these brutal murders. I hope I can count on your discretion to say nothing of this matter outside these four walls, and certainly not a word to Father Byrne until we've had a chance to talk to him."

"You can't seriously imagine Father Byrne has anything to do with these terrible murders," a shocked looking Alan Machin said in reply.

"I'm not saying he's directly involved, Mr. Machin," Ross replied, "but it does appear he may have known both victims when they were all boys together and he may be able to give us important information relating to events at Speke Hill during those days of their youth."

"Ah, of course. I see what you mean," Machin said with a hint of relief in his voice. "As a matter of fact, Father Byrne isn't due to visit us in the next couple of days anyway, is he, Charles?" he delivered the question to Hopkirk.

"That's right, Alan. We won't see him to speak to until you've had a chance to speak to Father Byrne, Inspector."

"Good, thank you. We won't keep you any longer for now, gentlemen, but we will have a quick word with Ms Manvers on the way out if you don't mind."

"Feel free Inspector," said Hopkirk. "We're happy to help in any way we can, if it will help bring Mark's killer to justice."

Machin agreed and Ross, Drake and Bland took their leave of the two men and stopped at the office of Vera Manvers on their way out.

"Hello again," the school secretary said as Ross led the way through her door, the three investigators standing in line before her like three naughty schoolchildren, Ross felt.

"Ms Manvers, Mr. Hopkirk will be enlisting your help in a search of the school archives later, but in the meantime, I just want to ask you if you personally know of anyone, either staff or pupils, who may have had any reason, no matter how trivial you may have thought, to feel a sense of grievance or ill-will against Mark Proctor?"

Vera Manvers was silent for a few seconds as she appeared to be delving into her own personal memory archives. Just when Ross began to think she'd forgotten they were waiting for her response, she seemed to return to the present and finally replied to his question.

"To be perfectly frank with you, Inspector, I knew very little about Mark Proctor, apart from his reputation within the school, which was of a very high standard. I met him socially twice, I think, at staff functions, when he was accompanied by his wife of course. I have very little day to day contact with the school itself or the orphanage. My role, as you can see, is purely an administrative one. I make it my business never to listen to rumours, or unsubstantiated facts that may sometimes be bandied around the staff room."

"So, are you saying there were rumours, Ms Manvers?"

"No, I'm not saying that at all. Just that if there were, I wouldn't have listened to them."

Ross felt the woman was being evasive, but he wanted desperately to return to headquarters and speak to the man and woman they had in custody there. Ms Vera Manvers and her rumours could wait for a little while.

"I see. Well, thank you, Ms Manvers. Just so you have advance notice, a couple of my detectives will also be arriving later and they will want to speak in turn to all the teaching and care staff, and any ancillary workers who may be present today. If they have to, they'll return tomorrow to complete the interviews."

"Very well, I'll make sure they have a suitable room allocated where they can speak to the staff, Inspector. I'm sure everyone will want to help find Mr. Proctor's killer."

* * *

"Bloody irritating woman, that Ms Manvers," he said to his two companions as Drake drove them back towards headquarters in bright sunshine, the fog having lifted during their time at Speke Hill.

"My thoughts, exactly," Drake concurred, "almost as if she knew something, but wasn't prepared to divulge it for some reason."

"I though they were all rather elusive and hardly totally forthcoming," Bland added. "I felt they weren't exactly lying, but were perhaps being a little economical with the information they were prepared to give us."

"I agree," said Ross. "Maybe they're being defensive of the establishment and its reputation but that doesn't help when we have a couple of killers running around out there. And there's this Father Byrne. We need to talk to him, Izzie. If we have time, I want to visit him later today."

"I'm with you, sir, whatever you decide."

"I just have a feeling we're on the cusp of discovering something, but whatever it is, I can almost feel a wall being thrown up to keep us out. Does that make sense to you, Doctor Bland?"

"Actually, it does, Inspector. I know my job is simply to provide you with a profile but I must admit my instincts all tell me the same as yours. Someone knows something, but they just aren't telling."

"Well, we're here now. Let's go see what Southport have dug up for us, and before we speak to them, I want you to arrange for Ferris and Gable to go out to Speke Hill, Izzie. Sam's good with women and Ferris has a certain instinct, as well as an understanding of the way such places operate I think."

"Right, sir," said Drake as she parked the Mondeo and switched the engine off.

As he marched ahead into the building, Ross couldn't wait to begin interviewing the two suspects apprehended in possession of Proctor's car.

Chapter 20

"Billy Ruffian"

Pausing only long enough to grab a quick coffee and an update from D.C. Ferris, Ross and Drake prepared to interview the couple found in possession of Mark Proctor's silver Subaru. Ferris had made sure the couple had been kept apart in separate interview rooms as instructed, and informed Ross of the names they'd provided, Archie Pitt, and Carrie Evans, aged twenty-six and twenty-two respectively. Neither one had requested or been offered legal representation. After all, they hadn't been charged with anything as yet, and had been told that for the moment they were 'assisting with inquiries'. Ross felt instinctively that this young couple were not the killers, but the fact they'd been in possession of Proctor's car put them, quite possibly, at the scene of the victim's abduction, and maybe even made them witnesses to what had taken place on the night of the teacher's disappearance.

Ross and Drake spent a few minutes peering at the pair through the one way mirrors that gave them views into both interview rooms from the viewing area that served to separate the rooms. Christine Bland and D.C.I. Porteous were with them and would observe the interviews from there. Ross decided to take the young man, with Ferris as back-up, Drake would interview the woman, with Nick Dodds, who'd helped collect the couple from Southport as her number two, the other team members being out and about carrying out their own allocated inquiries. Dodds had worked with the team before and was well respected by Ross and the others, and was only too pleased to help out.

"Archie Pitt, that your real name?" Ross asked the scruffy twenty-something young man sitting opposite him.

"Aye, course it is. Why should you think otherwise?"

"Archie, that's a Scottish name."

"So, me Dad liked the name. Told me he named me after a character in that old war film, *The Great Escape*."

"Ah, right, *Archibald 'Archie' Ives*, known as *The Mole*, I believe," said Ross. I rather like that film too. The name suits you. You look like a little mole to me. Now, Archie, are you going to tell me how you came to be caught in possession of a car that belonged to a man who was murdered in a particularly nasty fashion? Just what part did you and your girlfriend have to play in all this?"

Archie Pitt's face fell at the mention of the word 'murder'.

"Whoa, hold your horses there, Mr. Policeman. I ain't had nothin' to do with no murder, like, you know?"

"That's just it, Archie, I don't know. You tell me. I want to know exactly how you came to be driving that Subaru, where and when you found it and why you took it."

"Okay, okay, as long as you know we didn't do no murder, you know?"

"So talk to me."

* * *

"I've only known him a couple of weeks," Carrie Evans bleated in a rather irritating high-pitched voice. "We met up one night in town in a club and sort of got along, like, you know?"

"So tell me about the car, Carrie," said Drake.

"Yeah, right. Well, we was in the Billy Ruffian that night, early doors you know? Archie said it was a good place to score."

"What was it you were after, Carrie, cocaine, heroin?"

"God no, nothing like that. I'm not into the hard stuff, just a bit of grass, you know?"

"Okay, calm down, Carrie and tell me the whole story."

Behind the mirror, Bland looked questioningly at D.C.I. Porteous, and asked, "Billy Ruffian?"

"A pub near the old Clarence Graving Dock, used to be popular with seamen. Its real name is *The Belerophon*, named after one of Nelson's warships at the Battle of Trafalgar. The pub sign shows the old ship, all guns blazing, quite impressive."

"I see, thanks for the history lesson," Bland replied, smiling as they turned back to the interviews in progress.

"Archie saw the guy he was looking for, and went to talk to him, while I sat at the table next to the window."

"Who was this man, Carrie? Do you have a name for me?"

"Shit, I don't know. I'd only been in there once, the week before with Archie. I don't know the name of his supplier if that's what you want?"

"I'm not interested in a bit of cannabis, Carrie. I just want someone who can confirm your story, someone who can make me believe you're not involved in two murders."

"Murders? I'm not into anything like that, honest, and I'm telling the truth. I don't know who the man was. You've got to believe me."

"What did he look like, then? Describe him to me."

"I only saw him from the back, while Archie talked to him at the bar. He was just some scally, thin, with long black hair and he was wearing an old donkey jacket, black with leather across the shoulders, you know what I mean?"

"Yes, I know what a donkey jacket looks like, Carrie. Anything else, jeans, trousers?"

"Jeans, I think."

* * *

"What's his name, Archie?" Ross asked as Archie Pitt told a similar story in the next room.

"Er, I don't know."

"Yes, you do. You don't expect me to believe you regularly buy cannabis from a man and don't even know his first name."

"It's Mac, and honest, Inspector, that's the only name I've ever known him by. Everyone just knows him as Mac."

That, at least, was believable.

"So you bought your drugs, then what?"

"I bought us a drink, a pint for me and a gin and tonic for Carrie, then went and sat back down with her."

"Where were you sitting?

"Next to the window that looked out on to the car park. That's when I saw the car."

Now he had Ross's attention. By careful questioning, Ross had brought Archie round to what he really wanted to know. Now, perhaps Archie would reveal something of real relevance to the case.

"Go on, Archie. I'm listening."

* * *

"Archie saw this car pull up," Carrie Evans said. "It was a silver one. He said the guy who got out of it was a pillock because he didn't lock it. He could tell he said, 'cause the idiot just got out and walked away without pointing the keys at it, you know, like, to lock it. Archie said we'd leave it a few minutes and if the guy didn't come back, we could maybe take it and go for a ride."

* * *

"This man, Archie. Did he come into the pub?"

"No, that was the weird thing, like. He just got out of the car and walked away. Then, I saw him standing by the side of the main road, like he was waiting for someone. Another car pulled up and he looked around as if he was looking to see if he was being watched, then jumped into the car and it sort of sped off. I knew he'd left the Subaru unlocked so me and Carrie finished our drinks, and walked out, casual, like, and I checked no one was watching and told her to get in. I, er, well, sort of hot wired it and we were away before you knew it."

"Done it before, have you, Archie, car theft?"

"Yeah, alright, once or twice, but you said…"

"I know, just tell me the truth, Archie."

"That's about it, really. I had a few quid in me pocket, you know, so I said to Carrie it'd be nice to go to the seaside for a day or two. Less chance of the car being spotted too, I thought, so I drove to Southport and that's where we stayed until those two coppers picked us up."

"Did you get a good look at the man who left the car in the pub car park?"

"Well, no, I didn't. When he got out of the car, he had his back to us, and didn't even turn round to look at the pub. He was tallish, maybe five foot nine or ten, had a dark blue hoody on with the hood up and it was pulled tight if you ask me so it covered a lot of his head and face. He had gloves on too, black ones if it helps."

"Could you tell if he was black or white?"

"No, not that I was taking notice. I was more interested in the car."

* * *

"What about the car that picked him up, Carrie?" Drake asked. "Do you know what kind of car it was?"

"It was red, I think," Carrie replied. "I don't know nothin' about cars."

"What about the driver. Could you see if it was a man or a woman?"

"Too far away to tell," said the girl. "Soon as he got in they were away like the wind. We went out, got in the car and Archie did something to it and it started and he drove us to Southport for a little holiday, he said."

* * *

"Come on, Archie, you've nicked cars before so you must know what type of car picked him up." Ross was hoping for a real clue, depending on Archie Pitt's answer."

"Look, Inspector, I'd smoked a couple of joints that afternoon, and I was kinda focussed on the Subaru, so I wasn't paying much attention to the friggin' car that picked the jerk up."

"Think, Archie, come on, for God's sake man, you must have seen it for at least a few seconds."

Archie Pitt closed his eyes, trying to recall those few seconds when the driver of the Subaru climbed into the other car. He shook his head and replied,

"I'm real sorry, honest, but I just don't know. It was red, I think, that bright pillar box red, you know, the bloody default colour the dealers offer to everyone when they can't supply the colour of choice to customers. Fuck me, Inspector, every bloody car maker on the planet makes cars that colour. But listen, I think I remember it was a hatchback, not too big, maybe a Ford or Vauxhall, or then again it could have been a Honda or even a Citroen. I just don't know. It's not like I thought I'd ever have to bloody well remember the damn car is it?"

Archie threw his hands up in a gesture of despair and somehow, Ross felt he'd got all he was going to get from the young cannabis smoking car thief.

* * *

Izzie Drake passed a box of tissues across to Carrie Evans, as the young woman sat quietly sobbing. Carrie had finally broken down when Drake told her the potential trouble she could be in, and was now in fear of having to tell her parents about the mess she'd got herself into. Unlike Archie Pitt, who appeared to live on his wits and rented a poky little flat in one of the city's few remaining high rise blocks, Carrie lived in Huyton in a modern three bedroom house with her stockbroker father, stay-at-home mum, and younger brother, all of whom would be in shock at the trouble the young rebel of the family had got herself into.

"You're going to have to face up to it, Carrie. You'll probably end up in court over this little mess so your parents are bound to find out. Best to tell them now and get it over with. You might find they'll forgive you and stand by you, but my advice would be to dump your asshole loser of a boyfriend before you tell them," Izzie Drake advised.

"They'll go ballistic when they know about the drugs," the girl cried into a tissue.

"Can't help you there, Carrie," Drake continued, but maybe you'll see this as a lesson and stay away from cannabis or any drugs in future. I don't care what scallys like Archie Pitt and his kind tell you, there's no such thing as a safe drug, Carrie. Even long term use of cannabis can harm your brain, believe me."

* * *

"What's going to happen to me now, then?" Archie Pitt asked Andy Ross.

"You're going into a nice warm cell for a little while until we check out your story, Archie. If you're lucky, you'll be charged with taking away a vehicle without consent, and with being in possession of a controlled substance. Bit stupid of you to be caught with that cannabis in your pocket wasn't it old son?"

"Yeah, but I thought you said you'd turn a blind eye if I helped you?"

"And that's what I'm doing, Archie. If I wanted to really drop you in it, I'd send a team down to the Beleraphon and raid the place. I bet we'll find more than just your mate Mac dealing in that place, and they'd all be really interested to know who tipped us off about them doing business there, don't you? So I'm turning a blind eye on this one occasion, but don't be surprised if a couple of plain clothes coppers drop in there one night soon and find a couple of dealers at work, know what I mean, Archie?"

Archie Pitt nodded slowly.

"You're telling me stay away from the place, right?"

"Sounds like a good idea to me, Archie. Oh, and one other thing."

"What?"

"Our boys are going over the Subaru even now, as we speak and if they find any more drugs in there, enough to suggest to me you're dealing as well as using…"

"They won't, I'm not, I told you, I just smoke a bit of dope now and then."

"Now and then? You've admitted you were half stoned when you stole the car, Archie. How responsible was that, eh? You could have knocked a child down, caused a serious accident, anything. Driving under the influence of drugs is as bad as drunk driving as far as I'm concerned so you'd better hope our paths don't cross again in the near future. Take him away, Paul, lock him up and give our friend here a chance to think of the error of his ways until we've checked the car out."

"Right sir," said Paul Ferris as he placed a hand on Archie's shoulder and the young man rose to his feet. "Come on sunshine, let's get you settled. You never know, we might even treat you to nice cup of tea."

"Yeah, can't wait. I'm bloody ecstatic," Pitt quipped, trying to sound tough.

"Oh, get him out of here, Paul," said Ross as the pair exited the room, followed a few seconds later by Ross who instead of taking the same route, stopped and entered the viewing room where Porteous and Bland were watching Izzie Drake bringing her interview with Carrie Evans to a close.

* * *

"Well, that was almost a total waste of time," Ross blasted the words out, frustration in his voice. "They're not our killers, not that I thought they would be. Whoever killed Remington and Proctor had more brains in their little fingers than our friend Archie bloody Pitt. He doesn't have the brains or the sophistication to have planned something like this. No, he's just a thieving little scally who saw a chance of a free ride to the seaside with his girlfriend and grabbed it with both hands. We'll show Proctor's photo around in *The Belerophon* but it's likely the murderer just picked it as a random location to dump the car."

"It certainly wasn't as productive as we'd hoped, Andy," Porteous agreed.

"No sir, it bloody well wasn't."

"But we know the accomplice drives a red hatchback, at least," Christine Bland added, trying to sound positive."

"Yes, but have you any idea how many red hatchbacks there are on the roads of Liverpool and the surrounding area? Probably around two thousand at a guess," said Ross, "and bloody Archie in there couldn't even tell his Fords from his Nissans, he was so toked up at the time. And, the red car could have been nicked like the Subaru, so we're really no further forward, unless there's any trace evidence in the car."

"Miles Booker is working on it himself," Porteous informed him. "If there's anything to find, he'll find it."

Ross turned to look through the one way mirror as Izzie was closing her interview with Carrie Evans.

"Anything from the girl?"

"Useless," said Porteous. "She saw even less than Pitt. She's more worried about what her parents are going to say when they find out about her being picked up by the police."

"I wonder why neither of them asked for a solicitor," said Bland

"They weren't under caution yet and were simply helping with enquiries," said Ross. "Once we finish the forensic examination of the car, we'll have them in again, caution them and offer them legal representation. Then we'll take formal statements from them and they'll be charged and released on police bail. When we catch our killers, and we *are* going to catch these murderous bastards, I'll want them both to give witness statements, no matter how vague they may seem, so I want them in the system where we can find them at the right time."

"What now, then, Andy?" Porteous asked.

"First, I want to talk to this Father Byrne, the ex-Speke Hill pupil who recently became Parish Priest at St. Luke's, Woolton, and then when I get the reports from the interviews with the staff at Speke Hill, we're going to have to go back there and dig deeper. Whatever triggered this killing spree, I'm certain it has its roots in something that happened there in the past."

"I agree," Christine concurred. "From a profiling point of view, I have to say that there is usually a trigger to these types of killings, something that activates a long dead, or dormant memory. The F.B.I. profilers call it a 'stresser,' but I prefer trigger. I'd like to visit Father Byrne with you if you don't mind. My own gut feeling is that the arrival of this man, another Speke Hill old boy, may have provided the trigger for these killers to start their murders. It's almost too coincidental that he arrived back in the area just before the killing began."

"You're welcome to join me," said Ross, "but there's another option you haven't considered here."

"Which is?"

"Well, as you just said, he arrived here just before the killings started, so we also have to take into consideration that this Father Byrne could be one of our murderers."

"Oh, shit," she replied, quickly throwing a hand over her mouth, just as the door opened to admit Izzie Drake, young Carrie Fisher being escorted to the cells by Nick Dodds.

"Have I missed something?" Drake asked, seeing the shocked look on Christine's face.

"Only that your boss just hypothesized that one of the killers could be a bloody Roman Catholic Priest," Porteous said, with an almost comical grin on his face.

"It couldn't be, surely," said Bland.

"Why not?" said Ross. "Stranger things have happened. There've been numerous murderous doctors over the years, so why not a priest?"

"Even so," Bland remonstrated with him. "It's a big stretch to think a Catholic Priest could have done this."

"Not if he's lost his marbles," Izzie pointed out. "And don't forget, the Inquisition was wholly run and executed by the Catholic Church. They killed thousands in the name of God in the Middle Ages."

"True," Christine agreed. "I suppose in my job I shouldn't exclude any possibilities, though I still think it's unlikely."

"We'll get a better idea when we speak to him," Ross went on. "Let's go home, get some rest and turn off for a few hours. We'll hold the morning briefing as usual tomorrow, catch up with the rest of the team and then head for St. Luke's and see what we can make of Father Gerald Byrne."

Ross spent five minutes tidying his desk, rose from behind his desk and was about to head off for home when the telephone on his desk rang. Debating whether to ignore it and walk away, he thought better of it and reached across to answer the offending, jangling instrument.

"Andy Ross, you old reprobate, how are you?" came the hale and hearty voice of his old friend and former partner, now Detective Inspector Oscar Agostini.

The two men had worked together some years before as sergeants, and had become firm friends, though Agostini's promotion had taken him a little out of town and he now worked out of the police station at Church road in Sefton, serving the town of Formby. Six feet tall, his dark brown wavy hair a giveaway to his Italian ancestry, Agostini had always been something of a magnet for members of the opposite sex and Ross had been surprised but delighted when his friend announced his intention to marry, and had been best man at Oscar's marriage to Fern, some ten years previously.

"Oscar! I'm harassed, hungry and in a hurry to go home. Apart from that, I'm fine. How's yourself, and the beautiful Fern?"

"Ah, nothing's changed then eh? I'm okay my friend, Fern too, and she sends her love, but listen, we're not exactly a million miles away and I still keep up with the news there in big-city-land. I think we may have a case here that somehow connects to those churchyard murders of yours we keep hearing about."

"Go on, Oscar, I'm all ears."

"Right. A few days ago, we attended a suicide by drowning off Formby Dunes, a young girl, only seventeen, called Lisa Kelly."

"Yes, I saw the news of that one, tragic by the sounds of it."

"Yes it was, poor kid was obviously seriously depressed. But here's the thing, Andy. She had one of those new-fangled mobile phones with a mini-recording device built in to it. Her Mum said it was her pride and joy, that phone. She'd saved up for it from her wages from the day she started working at Woolworths on South Road in Waterloo. Anyway, it turns out Lisa left a kind of suicide note cum confession on her phone, Andy, and it mentions one of your victims."

Agostini had Ross's full attention by this point.

"I'm intrigued Oscar, please go on, mate."

"Sure, so, it seems young Lisa was a confirmed member of the Catholic faith, and as a result of events in the last year, she was so wracked with guilt that the poor kid ended up topping herself. On the recording she mentioned being raped, and then finding she was pregnant a short time later. Her mother was supportive of her, don't get me wrong, but there was so much religious feeling in that house, Andy, that when she decided to have a termination, her mother was supportive but horrified at the 'sin' involved in going so strongly against the church's teachings. Lisa had gone ahead with the abortion anyway, but since then, the girl had grown progressively more and more depressed, and found she couldn't live with what she'd done in 'killing her baby' as she put it. For God's sake, Andy, I'm a Catholic, but I'd like to think I wouldn't pour all that religious fervour and guilt onto a child of mine if she was in that situation. Sorry, I'm digressing. Anyway, on the tape she says she wished she'd reported that man Remington when he'd raped her. Seems her Mum talked her out of going to the police at the time because of the 'shame' she thought it would bring on the family, for fuck's sake."

"My God, Oscar. What kind of Mother would do that? Didn't she want to see her kid's rapist locked up and put away?"

"I know, Andy. It fucking beggars belief doesn't it? Anyway, she'd read about the murder in the papers and once you'd released his name she knew it was the man who'd ruined her life, and in her mind, he'd cheated justice. There was no way she could ever absolve herself from what he'd done to her, as she put it."

"Hang on Oscar. How did she know her rapist was Matthew Remington? Wasn't he masked or anything when he raped her?"

"Oh, it's worse than that, my friend. Seems he'd known the family for years and she thought she'd be okay when she bumped into him in town after work one evening, and he offered to walk her to the bus station."

"Bloody Hell, Oscar. Didn't her mother warn her to stay away from him?"

Agostini seemed to hesitate and take a deep breath at the other end of the phone.

"You won't believe this, Andy, but her mother, good Catholic that she is, told her that Remington had done wrong in the past, but had paid his debt to society, and because he'd apparently repented his sins, God would have forgiven him and he was entitled to begin a new life, without his past sins being held against him."

"Jesus, Mary and Joseph!" Ross exclaimed, disbelief clear in his voice. "How bloody naïve can that woman be? Look, Oscar, I know you're Catholic, my friend, but surely not everyone is as gullible as this woman appears to have been."

"She damn well knows it now Andy. In fact she's now on the world's biggest guilt trip. Seems she was always telling Lisa her skirts were too short, her make-up too thick, all that kind of stuff, but then allowed her to think a man like that was reformed because she'd met him at church one day soon after his release and he'd told her that whole crock of shit about repentance."

"Remington went to church?"

"For a short time, apparently. Long enough to pick out his next target if you ask me."

A thought occurred to Andy Ross, another possible connection?

"Oscar, did the mother tell you what church she attends?"

"Yes, The Church of St. John the Baptist. It's only about half a mile from her home, but that's all Remington needed to push young Lisa into an alleyway and do the business with her, leaving her bleeding, crying and bloody pregnant."

"I just don't understand why the bloody mother didn't report it. I mean, her own daughter had been raped, for fuck's sake, Oscar, and she rationalised it by saying it would bring shame on the family? That's not good religion, mate, that's fucking crazy, religious fanaticism maybe, but not religious realism."

"I know, mate, and she knows it now it's cost her a daughter. Anyway, I hope the intel helps, old buddy."

"It might, Oscar, thanks a lot. It gives me another avenue to explore for sure. And now, I'm going home to my gorgeous wife, where I expect a hot meal, a couple of hours vegetating in front of the telly, then bed, and who knows what might happen?"

"Dirty bugger," Agostini laughed. "And give the beautiful Maria a kiss from me while you're at it."

"You should be so lucky, Agostini." Now it was Ross who laughed and the two men said their goodbyes and for the second time in the last half hour, Andy Ross rose from his desk, this time managing to make it out of his office and the building and was soon on his way home to Maria.

Chapter 21

Goodnight Sweetheart

"You haven't heard a word I've said, Andy Ross." Maria said, as they sat across from each other at the dining table, supposedly enjoying the beef bourguignon she'd prepared for the two of them.

"Eh, what, oh, sorry darling. What were you saying?"

"Only that Alice and Ray have invited us over for dinner next Saturday night. Alice was on the phone today, telling me Ray's a lot better since his heart bypass."

"That's good to hear. I'm sorry if I'm a little pre-occupied this evening."

"A little? Andy, I've known you long enough to know when a case is really getting to you, and this one is, isn't it?"

"Big time, Maria. I don't know why, but I feel as if I'm on the cusp of discovering something vital, but I just can't put my finger on it. After talking to Oscar earlier, I'm sure something he said triggered something in my brain, but whatever it was refused to surface properly. It was nothing concrete, just a hint of something that was there, and then it was gone, if you know what I mean."

"I think I do. Like when something's on the tip of your tongue and then simply disappears, but in this case, it wasn't a word, but a thought."

"Yes, that's it exactly. Not only that, but I can't understand the mentality of that girl's mother."

He'd talked to Maria as she'd prepared dinner and brought her up to date on the case. His wife had tried, unsuccessfully to get him to talk about something else, but it was evident to Maria that her husband was totally immersed in his need to apprehend the killers of the two men.

"You've been in the job long enough by now to know you can't argue with the religious fervour that drives some people, Andy. The mother was probably brought up in a family where everything revolved around the church and God. Old-fashioned hellfire and damnation stuff, every small transgression treated like a major sin, you know the type."

"Yes, mores the pity," he agreed. "Anyway, dinner's great, thanks, and you can phone Alice in the morning and tell her we'll be glad to go for dinner."

After dinner, Andy and Maria curled up together on the sofa, and watched Andy's favourite movie, *Independence Day*, Maria having bought him the DVD for his birthday. Maria always enjoyed watching it with her husband who she thought would have made a good stand-in for the actor playing the President of the USA, whose name she could never remember.

Before they knew it, eleven o'clock had arrived and Andy locked up the house while Maria went up stairs to get ready for bed. Andy's mind had at last relaxed and when he walked in to the bedroom to find Maria sitting on the bed, wearing a very short, very sheer pink nightie, her legs crossed suggestively, his eyes lit up. With a gleam in her eye, a smile on her face and affecting her best 'vamp' voice, his wife said, huskily, "Well, hello there, big boy. Wanna play?"

This time, he didn't fall asleep!

* * *

Peter Foster lay on his back, smoking a cigarette as a naked Izzie Drake lay beside him, twirling the hairs on his chest between her fingers.

"That was amazing," Izzie gasped as she attempted to bring her breathing back to normal after a highly passionate session of lovemaking.

"You were great," Peter said, turning to look at her with a satisfied smile on his face.

"I wish we could do this every night, Peter," Izzie said, dreamily.

"Well, there's one way we could do it every night, mornings too if you wanted to," he replied.

Izzie sat up straight and looked him in the eye.

"Peter Foster, you bad, bad boy. Are you asking me, a police sergeant of all people, to move in with you and live in sin?"

"No." was all he said and fell silent.

"What then? What exactly do you mean?"

Peter stubbed out his cigarette in the large glass ashtray on top of the bedside cabinet and quietly opened the top drawer of his bedside cabinet, removing a small, blue velvet box. He slowly turned towards Izzie, whose eyes began to glisten with tears of emotion as he opened the box to reveal a sparkling diamond solitaire ring."

"Marry me, Izzie, please."

"Oh God, Peter. Are you serious?"

"Deadly, if you'll excuse the word, considering my job," he replied, slipping the ring slowly onto the third finger of her left hand. It was a perfect fit.

"How did you know my size?"

"I guessed."

"Wow."

"Well?"

"Eh?"

"What's your answer you daft girl?"

Izzie fell silent, looked Peter Foster in the eyes, and then, after keeping him waiting for an agonising fifteen seconds, she threw her hands round his neck, kissed him passionately on the lips, whispered the one word, "Yes," and lay back, pulling Peter on top of her as they took up from where they'd left off half an hour ago.

Chapter 22

A Question of Faith

A few minutes after Andy Ross had climbed out of bed, feeling great after his night of unbridled passion with Maria, the telephone rang. Surprised to hear the voice of D.C.I. Porteous so early in the morning, Andy nevertheless came instantly alert as his boss asked him to arrive a quarter of an hour early and meet him in his office before commencing the morning briefing with the team. All would be explained when he got there, Porteous informed him.

Intrigued, Ross quickly showered and dressed and popped a couple of slices of bread in the toaster as he made coffee for himself and Maria, who arrived in the kitchen as the kettle boiled.

"Who was that on the phone?" she asked, smiling at Ross, her eyes a little bleary from lack of sleep.

"The boss. He wants to see me before the briefing."

"Did he say why?"

"Nope, all very mysterious if you ask me. I tried not to wake you, but failed by the look of it. You look tired, darling."

"Hardly surprising is it? You wore me out last night, Mr. Super Stud," she laughed and Ross grinned back at her.

"Your fault," he laughed in return, as the toast popped up. "You shouldn't have worn that incredibly sexy little number should you? But I'm bloody glad you did."

Maria giggled, grabbing the two rounds of toast, buttering them and placing them on a plate on the table for him, placing two more slices in the toaster for herself.

"Ha, it didn't stay on very long once you got going, did it, you sex maniac?"

"Yes, well, if I'm not totally knackered tonight, how do you fancy a rematch?"

"Now, that sounds like an offer a girl can't possibly turn down," she said as Ross hurriedly swallowed the last piece of toast and grabbed his jacket from the back of the chair where he'd left it the previous night. A quick kiss, and Ross was out the door, climbing into his car and on his way to work.

* * *

"You're not serious, sir, surely?" Ross asked as he sat across from Harry Porteous in the D.C.I's office, the door closed to prevent anyone hearing their conversation.

"But I am, Andy," Porteous insisted. "I'm taking early retirement and I'll be leaving at the end of the month. That's why I'd really like to finish on a high and get this bloody churchyard case closed with a couple of arrests before I go."

"May I ask why you're retiring, sir. I mean, you're still relatively young?"

"Exactly, Andy, and that's one compelling reason to go now, while I'm young enough to enjoy life with Sarah. And no, before you ask, she hasn't pressured me into it. I've been a copper for over thirty years, Andy, and I'll get a full pension and we can enjoy some quality years together, maybe do a round the world cruise or two, who knows"

"I take it Jake and Laura are happy for you too?"

Porteous's two children were both grown up and married, Jake, the eldest, now a successful architect, and Laura was happily married to an airline pilot, had two children of her own, and lived down south, not far from Heathrow airport, where Geoff, her husband was based.

"They're delighted for us both, Andy. Geoff thought it was about time I treated his Mum to some good times, and Laura says it might mean we'll see more of the grandkids, and can go and visit her down in Hounslow more often, stay a while from time to time and so on."

"Well," Ross sighed, "I guess we'd better pull out all the stops and catch these murderous bastards for you, sir, hadn't we?"

"Yes, please," Porteous smiled. "There's one other thing, Andy, a small matter of my replacement."

Ross's stomach lurched, knowing Porteous might want him to accept a promotion and take over his job when he departed.

"Sir, I hope you don't want me to take over from you. I know I've passed the exams and everything, but you know as well as I do that I'm not cut out to direct investigations from behind a desk. I'm a field investigator, always have been and always will be."

"I thought you'd say that, and I admit I tend to agree with you. You'd be like a fish out of water stuck in this office most of the day, every day, but I want you to know the promotion and the job's yours if you want it. The Chief Super has agreed to it if you decide that way but he also knows how you'd feel and to be honest you'd be a loss to the team if we took you out of the field of everyday investigative work. Thing is, if you do turn the promotion down, it might be a long time, if ever, before you get another chance at senior rank."

"I don't mind, sir. Maria already earns more than me as a G.P. and we're not exactly hard-up. She knows I'd never want to be a desk jockey as well, so she won't mind me turning the job down."

"Well, that's that, then. You'd better get off and get on with the briefing. We've got two killers to catch. My replacement will be announced in due course, but I'll make sure you're informed of the appointment before anyone else knows. I'm sure once the jungle drums start spreading the news of my imminent departure the chief will receive more than one or two calls with suitable, and maybe unsuitable candidates putting themselves forward for my job. You can inform the team but please ask them not to broadcast it too far and wide just yet."

A handshake later and Ross exited the room, arriving in the squad's conference room just as the last of his team, in this case, D.C. Curtis was entering the room, the young detective holding the door open for Ross.

"Morning sir."

"Morning Tony."

Within five minutes, Ross had informed the team about Porteous's impending retirement, ending with the news that the Chief Superintendent wanted the D.C.I.'s replacement in place at least a week before his departure to give the new man a settling in period, working together with Porteous, so they should expect an announcement at any time on the name of their new boss.

Ross allowed a further ten minutes for the rest of the team to update him with mostly negative progress reports, before he informed them of the phone call from D.I Agostini the previous afternoon.

"Bloody hell, sir," Izzie Drake said. "That throws a new light on everything, surely."

"It must do," Paul Ferris agreed. "It could mean the case has nothing to do with the past, or with Speke Hill, but could be rooted right here in the present."

"Possibly," said Ross, "but this Kelly girl was raped by Remington, not by Proctor. We have no evidence as yet to give us a concrete link between the two men, yet something has to put them in the frame together for something, sometime. We have to look at another possibility too. If Remington raped Lisa Kelly, it's highly likely he raped or assaulted others too. We all know a lot of women refuse to report rape or other sexual assaults for a variety of reasons, one of which we've seen in the Kelly case, with all too tragic results. I also want us to look into rapes and assaults that have been reported but remain unsolved for, say, the last three years, to begin with, and while we're at it, let's look a lot deeper into Mark Proctor's life. Izzie and I are going to talk with Father Byrne this morning. Christine, please join us. I'd like your thoughts on the good Father. The rest of you, get to it, people. Tony, take Sam and pay a visit to *The Belerophon*. Knock the landlord up out of bed if you have to. Show him the photo of Proctor, maybe also the one of Remington. Let's see if either man used the pub regularly or at least any time recently, assuming the landlord takes notice of who's drinking in his pub."

"But isn't it more likely the killers chose the pub sir, rather than it being a hang out for the victims?" Curtis asked.

"Yes, it is, Tony," Ross replied, "but we're clutching at straws a little. It may be our killers first encountered one or both of the dead men in *The Belerophon* and identified them as targets from there. We have to explore all possibilities."

"Understood, sir."

"Good. As interviews with the staff at Speke Hill produced nothing we have to assume if anything linked the dead men it was either something that happened there a long time ago, which is where Father Gerald Byrne could be helpful, or as we now suspect, something much more current in time, so we need to look very deeply into every and I mean *every*, aspect of these men's lives."

"Any good talking to the mother of the dead girl, sir?" Derek McLennan asked.

"Maybe, Derek. Go and see her. I wouldn't trust myself near that woman right now. I hate to say it but she's right, her daughter would probably be alive today if she'd handled things differently. Show her Proctor's photo as well. See if you get a reaction."

"Right sir," said McLennan, pleased to have his suggestion acted upon.

"While you're at it, see if there's anyone at the Church of St. John the Baptist near her home. Remington went there a few times apparently. The priest there might remember him, and Derek?"

"I know sir, show him the photo of Mark Proctor, too."

"Good man, you're learning." Ross smiled at the young detective.

* * *

"Are you alright sir?" Izzie asked Ross as they drove across town en-route to St. Luke's to speak to Gerald Byrne. "You're very quiet. Is it D.C.I. Porteous?"

"No, Izzie, nothing like that. I've had something eating away at the back of my mind since I talked with D.I. Agostini yesterday. Something, a buried thought almost broke through as he said something, I don't know what, but it came and went before my conscious mind could grasp it."

"I might be able to help with that," said Christine Bland from her seat in the back of the car."

"Really?" Ross asked. "How?"

"It's a technique for helping witnesses remember long buried thoughts. The Americans have used it with some success. I studied the method while I was at Quantico. Maybe we can try when we get back to your office later. We need peace and quiet and no distractions, hardly the thing we can do in a moving car."

"I'll think about it, thanks," said Ross as Drake slowed the car down as she pulled up outside St. Luke's Church.

* * *

The two detectives, plus Christie Bland, had been greeted like old friends by the redoubtable Mrs. Redding and were shown into the sitting room and invited to sit. Ross and Drake took up positions on one of the two large, comfortable sofas in the room, the profiler taking up one of the two velour upholstered armchairs. Mrs. Redding scurried away to summon Father Byrne, who, she informed the inspector, was taking a breath of fresh air in the garden. Before the priest arrived, Ross spoke quietly to Izzie Drake.

"Usual strategy, Izzie, OK?"

"OK sir."

In reply to Bland's quizzical look, Ross explained.

"We each take a different tack. I go one way, and Izzie will step in with questions that deviate from the main point. It tends to throw a suspect off and often leads to them slipping up."

"So Father Byrne is a suspect?" Bland asked.

"Only until we can definitely eliminate him, Christine. Your opinions on him may help us in that respect, which is why I wanted you along today. He's closely connected with the victims, albeit historically, and the orphanage, and he arrived on the scene just a short time before the murders began."

Byrne joined them a couple of minutes later and, introductions over, took a seat in the remaining armchair.

Ross was impressed by the physical appearance and overall demeanour of the priest, who certainly looked as if he could handle himself in a bar-room brawl if needs be. The man exuded an overall sense of athleticism, perfect for hauling a body up and suspend it from an angel memorial, the inspector thought.

"So, how can I help you, Detective Inspector?" Byrne addressed his question directly to Ross, who appreciated the fact that Byrne used his correct title. So many people simply called him 'inspector' and he hadn't the heart to correct them most of the time.

"I'm sure you're aware of the recent murders that have taken place in two local churchyards?"

"Only too aware, Detective Inspector. Horrific, truly horrific."

"The thing is, I've been made aware by the staff at Speke Hill that you were actually acquainted with both victims."

"Ah, I see. Yes, Inspector, I knew Mark Proctor, quite well at one time, but the first victim... er?"

"Matthew Remington, Father."

"Yes, right, thank you. You must understand, Detective Inspector Ross, that at the time I was at Speke Hill as a boy there were probably around a thousand children resident and being educated there. I'm perhaps exaggerating slightly, but it was certainly well over five hundred, I'm sure. I'm not sure how well you've been informed on the set-up back then, but the boys were of course segregated from the girls in respect of their living accommodation, and we were further split up into various dormitories usually up to thirty boys per dorm. We would all have known the boys in our own dormitory rather well as we lived with them on a day to day basis, but, unless our paths crossed during lessons at school, or if we played together in one of the various school sports teams, we could go through our entire time at Speke Hill without making the acquaintance of some of the boys or girls who lived separately from our own dorm, which in many ways was like our own private world within the orphanage."

"So you're saying you didn't know Matthew Remington at all, Father?"

"To be honest, Inspector, what I'm saying is I don't remember a boy of that name. Our paths may have crossed but I know for sure he wasn't in my dorm and I don't remember him from any sports teams. I was quite good at various sports in those days, played football for the school, rugby too."

"Would a photo help, Father?" Izzie Drake asked. "We had a couple of detectives over there to talk to the staff about Mark Proctor and Miss Manvers loaned these to us," she said, opening a large brown envelope and withdrawing a small handful of black and white photographs, each one a different year photograph of boys and girls, all posed in what Ross now assumed to be individual dormitory groups.

"Ah, yes, the redoubtable Miss Manvers," Byrne replied, smiling knowingly at the sergeant. "I hope she was helpful, Sergeant. I shouldn't say this, but that lady is a bit of a dragon at times."

Drake smiled back at the priest, warming to the man.

"We've noticed, Father, yes. Now, please take a look at these for me."

"Perhaps if you could point out the boy you're referring to, it might be helpful, or I could sit here all day and not realise I'm looking at him."

Ross, agreeing that was a fair point if Byrne was being truthful, nodded at Drake, and she leaned across and pointed a finger at a thin and gangling boy, aged about twelve or thirteen, who stood at the end of the tiered ranks of boys in the picture. The photographer had arranged the boys, smallest in front, tallest at the back, with the medium height lads in the centre row, with Remington and another taller boy acting as 'book ends' at each end.

"That's the young Matthew Remington, Father," said Drake. "Ring any bells?"

Byrne studied the photograph intently for a while. His brow furrowed as he allowed his mind to drift back in time, recognition slowly beginning to dawn as he peered at the boy in the picture.

"That's Plug," he suddenly said, his brain eventually plucking the name from his memories of the past.

"Plug?" Ross asked

"As in the Bash Street Kids, Inspector, in the comic, *The Beano.*"

"Yes, I remember it," Ross nodded his head, as he reached across, took the photo from Byrne and glanced at it.

"Oh, I see what you mean," he smiled at the priest. The young Matthew Remington did bear an uncanny and unfortunate resemblance to the character in *The Beano.*

"So you did know him, Father?" Drake now asked.

"Well, yes and no, Sergeant. He wasn't a friend or anything like that, and he tended to be the butt of quite a few jokes and taunts because of his looks. It wasn't his fault of course, but, well, boys will be boys, and especially back then, when there was less, shall we say, tolerance, he got a lot of grief because of his teeth especially. I can only assume he eventually had them fixed when he grew up."

"Yes, he must have done," Drake agreed. "They definitely weren't as bad as they were back then, anyway. So, what exactly was your relationship with him, Father?"

"I didn't have a relationship with him, Sergeant. I suppose all the lads knew him as Plug of course, and we all indulged in our own fair share of teasing him, I'm ashamed to say. He most definitely wasn't in any of my classes, or sports teams. I do recall he wasn't too bright, and I was in the top stream for most subjects, so our paths wouldn't have crossed much. You must understand I was just a child, not a priest at that time, no different to any other boy of my age really, so might easily have been involved in a bit of name-calling and so on, but I never really knew him, and wouldn't have known him at all if you hadn't shown me that photograph. I'm not even sure if I would have known his real first name in those days, let alone his surname. He was just Plug to me. I do seem to recall him being something of a troublemaker, a bit like Mark Proctor. I think every dorm had one or two boys like that."

"Proctor was a troublemaker?" Ross asked. "So far everyone has told us what a great teacher he was and that he was a really lovely man."

"People change, Inspector. When I came back to Speke Hill, Mark volunteered to show me around, showing off all the new stuff they'd incorporated over the years. We swapped a few stories from our time as kids there, and I think I only saw him a couple of times in passing during my occasional visits after that first day. As a child, Mark Proctor was a bit of a bully to be honest and would often hang around with the older boys, and got involved in a few scrapes in his time. He was a useful junior boxer but as he grew older he started to put on weight in the wrong places, lost his fitness and ended up having to quit the ring. I'm not surprised nobody told you or your detectives about him. You have to remember that all of today's staff have only been there a few years at most. They wouldn't have known Mark's record as a child unless they'd deliberately looked up his records. I'd have thought Miss Manvers and Charles Hopkirk and probably the headmaster would know though. Surely they'd have checked back on his time at Speke Hill before he was accepted on to the teaching staff."

"Yes, you'd think so, wouldn't you?" Ross mused. "I wonder why nobody mentioned it."

"Respect for the deceased? Not wanting to sully his name because of some childhood misdemeanours?"

"You're probably right Father, thank you."

Ross decided to take a chance and think out of the box for a minute.

"Father, I'm sure you heard about a young girl's suicide at Formby soon after Matthew Remington's death?"

"I saw something in *The Echo*, yes, such a tragedy. It didn't say much really."

"Show Father Byrne the photo, please Izzie."

"Oh, no," Byrne exclaimed as he looked at the photograph of Lisa Kelly.

"So, you did know her?"

"Yes, that's Kelly. She started coming here not long after I arrived. She told me she wasn't happy attending her Mother's church any longer. I never knew her surname. The newspaper didn't identify her and I'd no reason to think it was poor Kelly. That poor dear child."

"Her real name was Lisa Kelly, Father. She obviously kept her real name from you. She was raped by Matthew Remington, found she was pregnant afterwards and then had a termination. She simply couldn't live with the feeling she'd committed some terrible sin and became deeply depressed. You know the rest."

"That's just terrible news. I now realise I only took the poor girl's confession that very morning, not that I knew it was her when I read about the suicide of course."

"I'm afraid the mother didn't help the situation" Ross said rather accusingly.

"I'm guessing from your attitude she was something of what we might call a religious zealot?"

"Exactly. She made her own daughter feel dirty, rammed it home to her she was an unworthy sinner and had the nerve to say that because Remington had started going to her church and had repented his sins, he should be forgiven, and Lisa just couldn't handle it."

Byrne looked genuinely horrified at Ross's short summary of Lisa Kelly's last days on earth.

"I'm only guessing, but from the way you tell it, I assume Remington wasn't prosecuted for his attack on Kelly, sorry, I mean Lisa?"

"That's right Father. Her mother virtually accused her of inviting the rape by wearing short skirts and provocative make-up. I suspect Remington may have got away with more than just the rape of Lisa Kelly."

"Oh, in the name of all that's Holy. She was little more than a child, experimenting with her own feelings of growing up. I can see why she left her church and came here. She must have been looking for help. I just wish she'd trusted me enough to tell me about it. I may have been able to help her."

"Without judging her, Father?"

"I don't judge anyone, Inspector," Byrne stated firmly, having now dropped the 'Detective Inspector' and reverting to the usual shortened version most people used when speaking to Ross. "That's a privilege reserved for our Lord in Heaven. I promise you, I'd have done all I could to help the poor girl, and I'm saddened that I will never have that opportunity. I don't mean to pry, Inspector, but if it's not confidential information, may I ask what church she originally attended?"

Ross saw no harm arising from giving Byrne the answer.

"It was The Church of St. John the Baptist."

"Ah, that would be Father Joe, real name Father Giuseppe Albani. I've met him a few times since I arrived, at the regular monthly meeting held at the Bishop's Palace. I know now why the mother was so committed to the old-time faith. Although many of us in the Catholic church have embraced a certain degree of liberalism in the last few years, I'm afraid Father Joe is very much of the old school. His way could almost be described as being deeply entrenched in Catholic fundamentalism. Sin is sin, and redemption can only be achieved by total acceptance of the literal word of The Bible."

"And you don't believe in the literal word?"

"We live in a world where we are all, priests included, allowed to question certain things in the good book, Inspector. Perhaps the hottest potato at present is the subject of the Creation. Do we accept it as being literally as told in Genesis, or is it in fact a wonderful but stylised rendition of the story of how our world began?"

"And the Catholic Church is actually debating the subject?"

"Indeed it is."

Ross found this all very interesting but he realised the conversation had drifted off course and he heeded to return to the reason for being here.

"Tell me Father Byrne, do you feel that all is well at Speke Hill?"

"How do you mean, Inspector?"

"Look, cards on the table, Father. You're new in terms of how long you've been there as a priest. Has anything struck you as odd, or has anyone behaved in a way that has given you any cause for concern on any of your visits?"

Byrne looked shocked at the question.

"Well, no, I can't say it has, Inspector. Everyone has been quite normal as far as I've been able to discern, but then I don't spend much time there, I hope you realise that."

Ross found himself unable to really voice his thoughts without revealing exactly what was on his mind. He tried another approach.

"Father, when you were boys, do you recall whether Remington and Proctor were ever involved in any sort of trouble?"

"What kind of trouble?"

"The kind of trouble that might cause someone to harbour a grudge over the years, something bad enough to cause someone to want to murder both men."

"Oh," said the priest.

Ross's instincts sensed that Byrne might know more then he was saying.

"Father Byrne, please, if you know something that could be relevant to these killings, I need to know about it."

Rather then reply to Ross, Byrne turned to look at Christine Bland.

"Doctor Bland," he said, hesitancy in his voice. "You're a profiler, but also, due to your title, I assume you're a doctor of psychology or similar, am I correct?"

"Yes, Father, I hold doctorates in both Clinical Psychology and Criminal Psychology."

"Look, this is difficult and I'm not sure how to say this without sounding ridiculous, but lately I've been having a recurring dream."

"Please, go on, Father."

"I had a sister, Angela. We were at Speke Hill together. She was older than me, and lived in the girl's home, obviously but we were still close. Angela died at the age of twenty-three, running away from a man who had tried to assault her, much in the way Matthew Remington assaulted his victims."

"He tried to rape her, in other words?"

"Yes, that's right. The thing is, Angela got away from her attacker but as she ran away, she ran into the street and was hit by a car. It wasn't the driver's fault. He didn't have time to react as she appeared in front of his car."

"I'm so sorry, Father, that must have been awful for you."

"It was, Doctor. I was at the seminary by then, training for the priesthood and for a time, I admit to questioning my faith, and wondered if I'd ever make a good priest, but that's irrelevant now. The thing is, the dream that's kept me awake for so many nights is a warped, surreal nightmare. I'm a boy again, it's the night after Sports Day, and I'm wakened by a scream. Next thing I know, I'm outside the building on the grass and I can see Angela being held down by Mark Proctor and three other boys. Mark is on top of Angela, trying to force her legs apart. I was too young to understand what rape was at that time, Doctor, so I didn't really understand what was happening, but knew it was something bad. Angela is screaming, and yet there's not a sound coming from any of the boys, or from me, like I'm somewhere else, looking on but not being a part of what's taking place. I try to get closer, but something is stopping me and then, just before I wake up screaming myself, one of the other boys turns and grins at me. Until this morning, I didn't know who that boy was, but since the sergeant showed me that photograph, I now know that boy was Matthew Remington."

As Byrne paused, Ross asked,

"Father Byrne, are you telling us that Mark Proctor and Matthew Remington raped your sister?"

"No, no, not at all, please hear me out. You see, they were the same age as me, and I certainly wasn't sexually mature at that age, so I doubt they were. And believe me, if anything even remotely resembling a sexual assault had taken place on Angela at Speke Hill, she'd have told me and the staff, and anyway, she was quite capable of taking care of herself and would have put up one heck of a fight against four boys so much younger than herself. My point is this, Doctor," Byrne again turned to look almost pleadingly at Christine Bland, "no such thing ever happened, and yet the dream is so real. I apparently scream so loudly that it wakes young Father Willis up and a couple of times he's come into my bedroom to make sure I'm alright."

"Who's Father Willis?" Drake asked.

"Oh, sorry, he's my assistant, my deputy priest. He lives here too. You're not Catholic, any of you?"

They all shook their heads.

"Well, in the Church of England, I think you'd call him a rector, you know, he assists the priest in services, and helps with community work and the general running of the church. He's out doing visits to the sick right now as a matter of fact."

"I see. Thank you for the explanation, Father. Please go on."

"Yes, of course," Byrne appeared lost in thought for a moment or two. "Doctor Bland, the thing that's been torturing me at night and increasingly in the daytime too, as a result of the dream is, could I, as a young boy, have seen something that didn't register logically in my mind and then blocked it out for years?"

"Yes, it is" said Bland. "You were young, and it's quite possible you saw something, maybe only a second or two of whatever was happening, and your mind then either ignored it as irrelevant to your young mind's way of thinking, or you knew it was bad, and your mind blanked it out, as you've suggested. Something must have happened in recent weeks or months to trigger the old memories and the dream has been your mind's way of processing the information by mixing it up with the facts surrounding Angela's tragic death."

"I see, thank you. I thought I was going crazy."

"Far from it, Father. Such events are quite normal, I assure you, and happen more frequently than you imagine."

The wild theory that had sprung into Ross's mind earlier now seemed less fanciful to him.

"Now, that's the kind of trouble I was talking about. It's possible Remington and Proctor were involved in some kind of assault or deviant behaviour as youngsters, maybe in their teens and you saw or heard something, as Doctor Bland suggests. If that's the truth, I want to know why there's no record of it at Speke Hill, or if there is, why nobody there mentioned it when we talked to the Headmaster, Chief Carer and that irritating school secretary."

"I can't help you there, Inspector," said Byrne.

"No, but there might be a way to help you remember the facts, the truth about what you saw as a child," Christine Bland said suddenly.

"There is?" Byrne asked.

"If you're willing, I could organise a session of hypnotism. If you're suffering from a form of retrograde amnesia caused by a mental trauma as a child, it's possible we can unlock those memories under carefully controlled conditions."

"Hypnosis? I'm not sure, Doctor."

"It may help us both, Father, by revealing to the inspector something that could help his case, and in your own case, it may help put an end to the dreams."

Byrne thought long and hard before replying.

"I'm a man of God, Doctor," he said. "I can't say I'm comfortable with this. Please can I think about it?"

"Yes, Father." It was Ross who answered. "But please don't think for too long. We've got two murderers to catch."

"I'll be quick, I promise you, Inspector."

"Then I think we're done for now, thank you Father," said Ross, who rose from his chair.

Drake and Bland took his movement as a signal for them to follow his lead and were soon out the door and on their way back to headquarters with the priest's promise to give them an answer later the same day on Bland's hypnotism proposal.

Ross remained relatively quiet on the journey as his latest theory formulated in his mind, becoming more tangible by the second.

Chapter 23

Brenda

Helmdale Lodge Psychiatric Nursing Home stood in its own extensive grounds, on the outskirts of the seaside resort of Rhyl in the county of Denbighshire in North Wales, some forty three miles from Liverpool. A private facility, the Lodge was a small and self-contained unit, with views over the Irish Sea, that catered for no more than thirty patients at any given time, most of them on a long-term basis.

A hundred years ago, Helmdale would perhaps have been described as a private mental asylum, but modern day enlightenment had removed such stigma from the treatment of mental illness and there was nothing of the Speke Hill style Victorian Gothic about its appearance, or in the way its inmates were treated; private rooms with television, comfortable beds and furnishings replacing such Victorian niceties as rubber coshes, water cannon, straight jackets and padded walls.

Built a mere thirty years previously, Helmdale appeared no different to the majority of onlookers than any run-of-the mill residential care home, with the obvious exception of a tall, eight feet high fence that encircled the entire property, complete with closed circuit television cameras mounted at strategic points on the fence, giving staff a constant video stream of the Lodge's perimeter.

Not that anyone had ever attempted to escape from the home. With all the patients being private, only those regarded as 'non-risk' patients were admitted to Helmdale Lodge. Fees were usually paid for by family members grateful to find a place where their mentally disturbed loved ones could be cared for in a pleasant and non-institutionalised environment. Everything about Helmdale Lodge was designed to make patients feel at home and comfortable and the doctors and nursing staff employed by the home's owners were of the highest calibre imaginable. Even the general care workers and ancillary staff were carefully selected, ensuring a sense of harmony prevailed at all times within the walls of the unit.

* * *

The man slowly pushed the wheelchair along the smooth black tarmac path that wound its way through a pretty, tree-lined avenue of poplars and firs, all kept neatly trimmed and at a height that wouldn't cut off the sunshine from those who felt like the walk that led to the extensive gardens beyond the trees. Here, the path opened up to reveal well-lawned, perfectly mown areas to both sides, and as the man arrived at the gleaming, silver painted ornate double gates that opened into the garden, his female companion walked ahead of him to open the gates, closing them after he'd wheeled his charge into the garden area.

The woman in the wheelchair stared straight ahead. If she saw the profusion of summer blooms that nodded their heads in the soft sea breeze that wafted through the garden, she made no acknowledgement of the fact. Peonies, Roses, Gladioli, Sweet Williams and so many more cast their heady scents into the air, in particular a bower of climbing roses in alternate red and yellow gave the garden the appearance of a place of peace and tranquillity, occasionally enhanced by the buzzing of a visiting bee, gathering nectar at its leisure, to the accompanying twittering of small birds, seeking seeds from various hanging feeders strategically placed so residents could watch the sparrows, greenfinches and other wild birds that regularly visited the garden.

"It's so beautiful here, isn't it, Brenda?" the woman asked, not expecting nor receiving an answer from the occupant of the chair, some ten years younger than herself, though the years spent locked away in her own mind, never mind behind the tall fences of the home had not been kind to her. A casual observer might have put them at the same age, such were the ravages of body and soul that time had wreaked on the younger woman.

It was important to try and engage in conversation with her sister, though, so the staff had always told her, and she never gave up hope that one day Brenda just might show some sign of recognition, might remember who she was and the life they'd once enjoyed as sisters.

"Look at those roses, they're so pretty. You always loved roses didn't you? You knew most of their names too. I just liked to look at them, but you were cleverer then me and used to tell me all about them."

She pointed at one particular hybrid tea rose bush as the little trio slowly passed it by, the smoothly oiled wheels of the chair virtually silent as they rolled along the smooth tarmac path.

"I do know that one, though, Bren. It's called Blue Moon isn't it? You used to tell me it wasn't really blue, more a sort of pale mauve really, but it was the nearest that growers had ever come to growing a real blue rose. I've never forgotten that."

"You know she's never going to answer us, don't you?" the man finally spoke as he carefully, lovingly, used his fingertips to push a lock of hair away from the patient's face, where it had been blown by the wind, slightly obscuring her view of the garden. Whether she acknowledged them or not, he did nevertheless feel, or rather hoped that she knew where she was, and could see and perhaps deep down in her subconscious mind, still take some pleasure from her surroundings.

"You never know. They said there's always a chance she might just snap out of it one day. Something might just shock her back to reality. We can't give up hope."

"That was over fifteen years ago. For crying out loud, you have to be realistic. Yes, there may have been a chance she'd suddenly snap out of it back then, maybe in the first year or two, but I've long ago accepted reality, even if you haven't. This is Brenda, as she is today, and will be every day for the rest of her life."

As he spoke, tears ran down his face, and he knelt down in front of the woman in the wheelchair, his hands gently stroking her hair and then tenderly touching her cheek as his body shook with emotion.

"Oh my darling, Bren," he sobbed. "You're still as beautiful to me as you were back then. I've never stopped loving you, and never will. If only we'd married as we planned. We'd at least have had some time together, time to love each other before... before..."

The words dried up, choked by his emotions and the woman in the chair continued sitting there, her face a blank canvas, devoid of emotion, as he poured his heart out knelt there on the hard tarmac, surrounded by the beauty of the garden and with sunshine pouring down on them, with a warmth he couldn't even be sure she could feel any more.

A hand on his shoulder snatched him back to reality.

"We should be getting back," said his companion. "You know they don't like her being out too long."

"We've only been here for ten minutes, at least let her have a little more time in the garden before we go."

"Okay," she replied. "You see, you do hold out hope, don't you? You might not admit it, but you do still hope she'll come back to us."

"Don't be fooled by my tears. Oh, yes, they're real alright, but like I said, I'm a realist. I know she's never coming back to us and that's exactly why we're doing what we're doing, isn't it? It's time they paid the price for their actions, and we're the ones to exact that payment, that retribution from them."

The woman took a step or two back from the wheelchair, as if not wanting the other woman to hear her words.

"So, when do we start again?"

"Soon, number three returns from holiday in a day or two and I want him to establish his routine again before we strike. I don't want to get caught out by him making changes to his previous routine after the holiday. Let's be sure he's sticking to everything as before."

"Alright, though I can't wait to finish what we've started. I must say, my nerves were on edge when the police were crawling all over the school and orphanage the other day. I thought they could see right through me, and knew exactly what I was thinking."

"Of course you did. That's only natural, but you have to stay strong, remember they have no real idea what it's all about. They have no way of connecting us together and are probably still working on all sorts of wrong theories, connected with religion, the Catholic Church versus the Church of England. Using a Catholic and a Protestant churchyard for the first two should act as a good smokescreen. As long as they keep working the religious angle they'll never work out what we're really doing."

"You're sure about that?"

"Yes, of course. Trust me. We've waited all this time. I'm not going to allow the prospect of vengeance slip by now we've started."

He turned to the woman in the wheelchair once again, this time taking her left hand in his own.

"Brenda, beautiful, gentle Brenda, you'd never hurt a fly would you? Those bastards did this to you, and now, at last, they're going to pay the price. I know you don't know what I'm talking about, but in God's name, the others will suffer as the first two did before we've finished with them."

He stared into her face, her eyes, eyes that once sparkled with the love and energy of life, but now stared out blankly at the world, stripped of every sign of emotion and feeling. A single tear now ran from his right eye, down his cheek and dripped on to their joined hands. He slowly drew his hand back and took a handkerchief from his trouser pocket, using it to gently wipe Brenda's hand.

"I think it's time," he said, and slowly he turned the wheelchair around and began a slow walk back though the garden, out of the decorative gates, retracing their path through the tree-lined arbour, returning Brenda to her room some ten minutes later.

"How was she today?" asked a nurse, as the pair walked along the corridor towards reception after getting Brenda settled comfortably in the armchair in her room before leaving her.

"Oh, you know, the same as always," the man said.

"I thought maybe she might give us a sign today," the woman added. "You know, like the doctor said, one day, if we hope and pray?"

"Yes, of course," said the nurse, whose name badge identified her as Registered Psychiatric Nurse Paula Dale. "You should never give up hope."

"I won't," said the woman. "Is Doctor Feldman here today? I'd like a word with him if at all possible."

"Oh, no, I'm sorry. Dr. Feldman is consulting at the Royal today," said Paula Dale, referring to the Royal Alexandra Hospital in Rhyl. "He'll be there until around four o'clock but he will be checking in here afterwards. He always comes back here before going home, to check on his patients after a day at the Royal. If you like, you could come back a little later. I'm sure he'd be happy to talk with you about Brenda."

The man reached out and placed a restraining hand on her arm. He spoke quietly but firmly as he addressed the nurse.

"I don't think we can hang around that long, but thank you Nurse Dale. Perhaps you can tell Doctor Feldman we were here today, and we'll try and catch him next week?"

"Oh, right, I see. Yes, I'll do that."

"It's time we were going now. Thanks again for all you're doing for Brenda."

"You're welcome, I'm sure," Paula Dale replied as the man turned and began to walk away towards the exit doors. The woman appeared to hesitate for a second or two, as though unable or unwilling to leave her sister, until the man looked around, saw her lagging behind, and called to her.

"Vera, are you coming? *Vera...*

Chapter 24

Mykonos

The sun was just reaching its zenith on the tiny Greek island of Mykonos, one of the brightest jewels in the Aegean Sea. Poolside speakers at the small but well-appointed Hotel Sunbird played a continuous loop of music, alternating between traditional Greek and the ubiquitous and at times annoying Europop sounds. For those relaxing on the hotel's sun-loungers, strategically placed around all four sides of the pool, the hotel owners thankfully kept the volume at a manageable level, so it was never overly intrusive.

Back home in Liverpool, where it would just be approaching nine a.m. the temperature was a comfortable sixty degrees Fahrenheit, but on the sun-drenched island the mercury had just passed eighty five degrees and was steadily rising. The island itself seemed to bask in the sunshine, it's white-walled houses, set against the backdrop of surprisingly lush and verdant trees, shrubs and olive groves reflecting the glare of the sun and appearing as tiny, pristine jewels to anyone approaching the island from the stunningly azure blue waters of the Aegean. The little island's idyllic charm was disturbed only by the influx of summer visitors who might provide a good source of income for the locals, but whose presence was still resented by a few.

The ever popular *Cotton Eye Joe* by Swedish group Rednex, had just begun a new round of Europop emanating from the speakers as one guest tried his best to ignore the sound of his mobile phone, which began to ring from its place in his poolside bag, containing the phone, his cigarettes and lighter, and just in case he ever got the opportunity to use it, his personal CD player and a small selection of discs he'd brought from home to keep him entertained. So far, he'd only used it while lounging on the beach, no chance of being able to hear anything properly over the constant throb from the hotel's sound system.

The ubiquitous sound of the Nokia ringtone finally died away and the man closed his eyes and let his mind take him back to the previous night. One of hotel's young maids had succumbed to three days of careful 'grooming' and an offer of one hundred dollars in American Express travellers cheques and joined him in his room late at night, where she participated in what he described to her as his 'rape fantasy', nothing nasty he'd said, and he'd kept to this promise, for the most part. He smiled to himself at the still fresh memory of seeing the girl, hands tied to the metal bed-head, her ankles secured to the legs of the bed, her legs spread invitingly. Her only complaint had come when he'd begun to take photographs of her in her spread-eagled position. Whether she thought he'd show them around at the hotel and that word would reach her parents of what she'd done, he didn't know, but her shouts had become dangerously loud and he'd given her a quick slap across the face, the only thing that marred the evening. He'd taken the girl three times and then released her from her bonds, apologised for the slap, not wanting to draw attention to himself in the last days of his holiday and handed her an extra fifty dollars in travellers cheques to ensure her silence. In truth, he shouldn't have done it, and should have simply concentrated on improving his tan and enjoying the last couple of days of his time on the island, but his sexual urges had got the better of him. In the end, no harm had been done, he decided, and turned his attention to trying to decide what to have for lunch. The Sunbird's poolside bar did a mean cheeseburger with fresh salad, and just as he was about to rise from his lounger and look for a waiter to call and order his burger, the phone in his bag began ringing once again. Irritated, but deciding he should answer it in case the caller kept up a barrage of calls through the day; he reached into his bag, pulling the phone out just in time, before it rang off automatically. With little or no time to look at the number of the incoming call, he pressed the green button to accept the call.

"Hello?" he said.

"It's me," an instantly recognisable voice came though the phone's speaker.

"I can hear that," he replied, anger evident in his voice. "What the fuck are you calling me for? I'm on holiday, trying to get some relaxation, and this call will be costing you a bomb."

"Look, I know you are, and I didn't want to spoil your holiday, but there's something you need to know and it can't wait any longer."

"What the hell is it, then? It had better be friggin' important."

"There's no way to put it any other way. Someone's on to us, they know about the club."

"Don't talk soft, man. What the fuck do you mean? Have the bizzies been sniffing around?"

"No, it's not the cops. I almost wish it was."

"Well, what the fuck are you talking about?"

The caller took a deep breath, clearly audible over the phone and then said, his voice dropping to a quieter tone.

"Razor and Mark are dead."

"What?" How the hell...?"

"They've been murdered, man, both of them. Whoever did it slashed their throats and mutilated their bodies, really badly, including sexual mutilation, according to *The Echo*."

He didn't mention the sexual mutilation in detail because the press had been asked not to reveal the exact nature of that side of the killings. The term, 'sexual mutilation' could mean anything and for now, the press were content to use the all-encompassing term that gave their stories on the killings sufficient sensationalism and dramatic effect.

"Fucking hell!" the man on the lounger exclaimed. "Have the bizzies caught the murdering bastard who did it yet?"

"No man, they haven't. Don't you see, whoever did it must know about us? Some bastard's decided to take revenge on us, man. We could be next."

"You need to stop panicking. Their murders might have nothing to do with us. You know as well as I do that they've both got up to enough tricks of their own over the years. Mark was lucky. No one ever fingered him to the cops so how the hell could someone suddenly crawl out of the woodwork and start killing any of us?"

"I don't know, but I'm scared, looking over my shoulder all the time. I'm thinking of leaving town for a while. Maybe for good, you know? Even if I have to live rough, change my name, just do what it takes, like, if it means staying alive. Maybe you should just stay out there in Greece for a while. They can't get to you there."

"Are you totally stupid?" said the man on the lounger, trying to keep his voice as low as possible. "I'm on a fucking package holiday, you moron. I have to leave my hotel in less than two days time and fly home. You can't just extend your stay when you're on a package. And what the hell would I do out here? Do you seriously think I could just hide away on a Greek island for the rest of my life, just in case some nutter comes looking for me? I'll tell you now; it won't pay anyone to try it on with me. I can look after myself. I'll kill any bastard who thinks they can take me down. If you want to run, you run, but don't expect me to do the same. Listen, we'll get together and talk about this when I get back, okay?"

"Yeah, right, okay, if you think that's best."

"I do, and try to stay bloody calm until I get home, and one more thing."

"Yeah, man anything you say."

"Don't ever let me here you mention the club over an open telephone line again, you got that?"

"Yeah, right, sorry man. I was just kinda panicking, you know?"

"The only people who call it that are you, me and the others. It's just our own little in-joke name for it, isn't it?"

"Of course, like I said, I'm sorry."

"Okay. Now, are you going to let me enjoy the last couple of days of my holiday? I'll call you when I get home. Don't worry. We'll get it sorted. No one's going to get you or me, Johnny boy, got that?"

"If you say so," said the worried man back home in Liverpool. "Sorry about spoiling your day. I'd better go. Need to get to work, but I don't feel like going to be honest, you know, just to be on the safe side."

"Go to work, Johnny. It'll look suspicious if you suddenly stop turning up."

"Yeah, right, I suppose so."

"I'm going now, get off to work and stop your worrying."

With that, the man on the sun-lounger pressed the 'end' button on his phone, cutting his friend off. Despite what he'd said to Johnny, the news from home was indeed seriously perturbing. There was no way he was going to derive much enjoyment from the next two days on Mykonos. If indeed someone had uncovered his secret life and embarked on a mission to eliminate the members of his very special, very private and exclusive 'club' he knew there was only one way to stop them. He'd have to identify and eliminate them first.

Chapter 25

A Good News Day

"Come in, Izzie," Ross called from within his office, recognising her distinctive knock on his door.

Izzie Drake walked in and closed the door behind her.

"Something wrong?" he asked her. "What happened to your usual knock and walk right in?"

"Well, it's more personal than business, sir, so I thought it best to wait and see if you were free."

"Oh, for God's sake, Izzie, what is it? You look like a cat on hot bricks, and your face is red as a beetroot. Don't make me guess at whatever it is."

Izzie Drake took a deep breath, and blurted out her news before she changed her mind about telling her boss.

"I'm getting married," she said, "Peter proposed, and I said yes."

"Oh, is that all?" Ross relied with a smile on his face. "I had an idea something like that was coming from the way you've been acting for the last day or two."

"You knew all along then?"

"I'm a detective, remember? I guessed." Ross grinned from ear to ear.

"And here's me, getting all worked up about telling you."

"Why, Izzie? You don't me permission to get married, and Peter's a great guy. Congratulations to you both."

"Thanks, sir, that's a bloody relief," and the two of them laughed together.

"Listen," Ross said. "I'll have a word with Maria and the two of you can come over and we'll have a bit of a celebration dinner for you."

"Wow, yeah, that'd be great sir, thank you."

"Right then, that's sorted. Now, Sergeant, do you think we can get back to the business of catching killers?"

"But of course sir, any time you say," she smiled at her boss, breathing a big sigh of relief at the same time. She didn't know why she'd got so worked up about telling Ross about Peter's proposal. After all, the two of them had worked together long enough for her to have known her boss would be pleased for her. Anyway, it was done now, and he was pleased, she was happy, and it was time to get back to work.

She didn't get off quite so easily however, as Andy Ross began the morning briefing with an announcement of her engagement. Five minutes of celebration followed with one or two ribald comments thrown in for fun.

"Did he propose, before, during or after, Sarge?" Curtis asked, grinning like a Cheshire cat.

"Bollocks, Tony," Izzie laughed, picking up a pencil from the nearest desk and throwing it at the grinning Curtis.

As the laughter and congratulations flowed, Ross felt grateful for the distraction brought about by Drake's news. It had, temporarily at least, given the team a chance to release some of the tension that was gripping them all with each day that passed without an arrest. The door to the conference room opened and D.C.I. Porteous walked in to see the team engaged in their light-hearted banter.

"Am I missing something?" he asked. "I hope this isn't a celebration of me leaving the team, by any chance?"

"Not at all, sir," said Ross. "Sergeant Drake has just announced her engagement.

"Oh, yes, the young man from the mortuary. I'd heard about that. Congratulations, Sergeant."

"Thank you, sir, but, wait a minute. Where did you hear about it?"

"Doctor Nugent at the lab was talking to me yesterday. Seems your young man had already told him the news."

"Is there anyone on the Merseyside Police force who doesn't know about it?" Izzie groaned, still smiling.

"Okay, everyone. That's enough, I think," said Ross. "Can we do something for you sir?" he enquired of the D.C.I.

"Just thought I'd sit in and see where we're at, if that's okay with you," Porteous replied.

"Of course, sir. Take a seat. Right, everyone, let's get to it."

The earlier frivolity quickly forgotten, the small group of detectives took their seats and all attention focussed on D.I. Ross as he cleared his throat and instead of his usual request for updates, which he knew in his heart would all be negatives, he decided on a new tack, having been awake for much of the night, allowing the theory that had been forming in his mind the previous day to percolate and take shape.

With Drake seated to his right and Christine Bland to the left, he began.

"First, I want to say that I know we've all been working bloody hard on this case, with very little to show for it. That's nobody's fault, because the clues just haven't been there, we have no witnesses and so far, we're only guessing at a motive, though we're all pretty much agreed on revenge, some kind of vengeance or retribution as the number one possibility. The question we have to answer is exactly what the killers feel they are avenging."

"It has to be a rape, sir, surely," said Derek McLennan.

"I agree, Derek, but a rape that took place years ago when Remington and Proctor were young men, or one that took place very recently? Also, we have to remember that Mark Proctor had no criminal record, had never been arrested on suspicion of committing any crime whatsoever, and not so much as a parking ticket against his name. I'll come back to him later."

"So, how do we find out which it is, sir?"

"Exactly, Derek, and if we find the answer to that question, we could be one step from identifying the murderers. Doctor Bland's original profile still holds good as far as I'm concerned. We know the type of people we're looking for, but unless we can pin down the crime that links our victims to them, we're still blundering around in the dark."

"So, what do we do next sir?" came a question from Sam Gable.

This was it. Ross prepared to test his theory. He'd outlined it very briefly to Maria over breakfast. His wife, always a willing sounding board for his more outlandish ideas, agreed it had merit and urged him to put it to the team.

"I have an idea, and I want you all to listen very carefully. I've had a theory taking shape in my mind over the last two days, and it's time you all heard it, so here goes.

Let's assume for one minute that this case has its roots in events that took place back in the nineteen-sixties at Speke Hill. Just remember that what I'm about to say is just an idea, a conjecture, a wild speculation on my part of what may have taken place, so bear with me as I outline it to you, and we can discuss it when I've finished.

Matthew Remington, known as 'Plug' apparently because of some resemblance he bore to a character in *The Beano*, a popular kid's comic of the day for those who don't know it, was obviously not the best looking kid on the block. Mark Proctor, however, was good looking, a talented boxer, at least until he passed through puberty and piled a few pounds on, and had a reputation for being a bit of a bully. Knowing how kids minds work, let's suppose young Proctor took Remington under his wing, and young 'Plug' became dependent on Proctor for protection, and in gratitude, became a devoted follower of the better looking and by all accounts, more intelligent boy. As they grow older, Proctor and Remington indulge in typical acts of schoolboy bullying, nothing overtly serious, but then, that word puberty raises its head again.

They begin to experience the beginnings of sexual urges. Whether they managed to experiment with any of the girls at Speke Hill, I can't say, but, and here's a wild card, the priest at St. Luke's in Woolton, Father Gerald Byrne, admits to suffering a recurring nightmare that makes no sense, as though his mind is mixing up a pot-pourri of fact and fiction. In it, he sees Proctor, Remington and two other lads, as yet unknown, attacking his sister, Angela. In this dream he sees Proctor trying to force his sister's legs apart, an obvious reference to sexual assault, but Father Byrne assures us that no such attack took place while he and his sister were at Speke Hill. However, years later, Angela was attacked by persons unknown in an attempted sexual assault, managed to break away from her assailant and in the course of running away, the poor girl ran across a road and into the path of an oncoming car, which knocked her down, the young woman eventually dying from her injuries."

A low buzz of sympathetic noises quickly went round the conference room like a Mexican wave.

"Yes, I know, bloody horrible set of circumstances, I agree, but, that's how it happened. Now, Christine, Doctor Bland, assured Father Byrne that such nightmares are quite common, where fact and fiction become distorted, particularly where childhood memories are concerned. She's offered to try and probe his memories through hypnosis, and just before Sergeant Drake came to see me with her happy news, the good Father called me to say he'd thought it over and he's agreed to allow Doctor Bland one session only in which to try and unlock his memories. The thing is, this dream, nightmare call it what you will is in fact the first suggestion we've had of Mark Proctor being involved in any overtly sexually deviant behaviour, and I think the young Gerald Byrne actually did see or hear something all those years ago, something his mind has blanked out, which has then become entangled with the terrible memories of what happened to his sister. Doctor Bland agrees and hopes to untangle those memories. If we can find one tiny clue as to what took place at Speke Hill, and who the other boys in Byrne's dream are, we may actually and surprisingly have our first tangible clue.

Now, my theory gets a little more outside the box here. Let's suppose that the four boys involved in whatever took place at Speke Hill, assuming Byrne's dream to have its basis in fact, which again, Doctor Bland thinks is highly probable, not only got up to some kind of sexual activity in their teens, but then carried on their aberrant behaviour into adulthood. The four of them remain in touch and go on to carry out a series of rapes and sexual assaults over a period of time. We know Remington was convicted of the rape of Claire Morris, and we've since learned of his unreported attack on the unfortunate Lisa Kelly, so who's to say there weren't more attacks over the years? As for Proctor, Mr. Squeaky Clean is obviously far from that, but we have no evidence to prove it, as yet. I want a full scale probe launched into every aspect of Proctor's life. His wife clearly has no idea what her husband was getting up to, but he must have been going somewhere from time to time and giving her a load of bullshit about what he was up to. Maybe she thought he was doing extra curricular teaching, coaching some fictitious sports team, I don't know. Maybe she thought he was having an affair and didn't dare ask him about it in case she was right and her 'perfect' marriage collapsed like a house of cards around her ears.

Izzie, I want you in charge of a comprehensive probe into Proctor's life, and I mean every aspect of it. Sam," he said, turning to look at D.C. Gable, "you'll work with Sergeant Drake on this, as you at least have a little knowledge of how Speke Hill worked a few years ago through your childhood friends and you worked Vice for a time so you have some idea how the whole sex crime thing works."

"Yes sir," Gable replied.

"Paul," he said next, addressing D.C. Ferris, "I want you to give them all the back-up you can from whatever records you can access on that super computer of yours, and anything Sergeant Drake needs, she gets, understood?"

"No problem, sir."

"Right, now, where was I? Oh yes, back to the subject of Speke Hill. Something is 'off' about that place. I know all the staff there today are new compared to the time period we're looking at, apart from Father Byrne of course, who was there as a boy, but he's only their visiting chaplain, and not there on a full tine basis. The thing is, they have records, and I would have thought they would show up any incidents of potentially serious aberrant behaviour in any of their pupils, even all those years ago, but according to the secretary, there's no mention of anything like that in any school or orphanage records."

"Sir," came an interruption from Derek McLennan.

"Yes, Derek, what is it?"

"Sorry for interrupting, but I can think of two reasons why the secretary came up with nothing."

"Go on, Derek, we're listening."

"Well sir, back in the sixties, the orphanage and the school were still very much under the control of the Catholic Church. I know that the council had assumed overall control of the place, but from what we've discovered so far about the place, it wasn't like any other Council-run home or school I've ever known. Most of the teachers were still Catholic priest and nuns, with a smattering of 'civilian' teaching staff, for want of a better word. The same applies to the actual orphanage where the Church retained most of the control over the place until well into the seventies. Anyway, sir, my point is this: if such incidents took place under the auspices of the Roman Catholic Church, as stupid as it may sound to us today, it's possible the priest in charge of those boys might have known about it and dealt with it internally. We're talking Catholic Church, remember, sir. If the boys were caught and knew they were in a lot of bother, it's possible they admitted their transgressions to the priests and were given the opportunity to repent their sins in return for forgiveness, or, they admitted their crimes under the absolute secrecy of the confessional, in which case the priest who heard their confession could never reveal what he'd heard to another soul."

Ross was impressed by the thought that McLennan had put into his own theory, and said so.

"Well done, Derek, good thinking. The whole sanctity of the confessional could be covering up a multitude of sins here and we can't do a thing about it unless we can find out the truth some other way. I just hope Father Byrne provides us with some names if there really are two more possible rapists out there. Anyway, you said you had a couple of ideas concerning the records?"

"Oh yes, sir. The second idea is that just possibly the bloody secretary is quite simply lying to us."

"You know, Derek, that same thought had struck me too, though I don't know why the woman would want to protect them."

"Ah, but it wouldn't be them she's protecting, Inspector." D.C.I. Porteous rarely spoke at these morning conferences, but for once he decided to add a little input.

"Sir?"

"She sounds like a few women I've come across over the years. Middle-aged spinster, no love life to speak of, married to the job and fiercely loyal to her employers. If she was going through those records and found something she thought might be potentially embarrassing or detrimental to those who pay her wages and give her a focus in her life, I certainly wouldn't put it past a woman like that to lie to protect their name and reputation. Then again, you also have the possibility she's lying to protect the killers themselves due to her having some connection with them. Perhaps she was in love with Mark Proctor, even to the extent of having an affair with him. What you need is a search warrant and or a court order to open up those old records, and I'll see that you get them."

"I see what you mean sir, and thank you. Even the old bat who seems to be jealously guarding those records can't turn us away now. Sounds as if we need to look a little more closely at the secretary. What's her name again, Derek?"

"Manvers, sir, Vera Manvers."

"Right, that's a job for you, please, Derek. Find her home address. Visit her away from school. I'd put money on the fact that her office at Speke Hill is her ultimate comfort zone, a place where she feels in total control. Maybe you turning up on her doorstep will succeed in rattling her cage a bit."

"Right sir, I'll see to it."

Porteous now raised a hand and Ross gave the D.C.I. his full attention.

"You want to say something else, sir?"

"Yes, Andy. Please don't think I'm interfering but let me say this. I've listened to this briefing and I'm impressed by your theory. It has a ring of credibility about it, but as you say, we've no actual evidence yet to even suggest Proctor's involvement in any crimes at all. Can I make a suggestion?"

"Please do, sir. You know I'm always ready to hear your thoughts. You're the boss after all."

"Yes, but we all know who the brains of this squad is, Detective Inspector. Anyway, compliments aside, I think what you're suggesting beneath the thinly veiled exterior of your theory, is that Remington, Proctor and two other, as yet unidentified men met as boys at Speke Hill and grew up to form some hideous gang of rapists, possibly helping each other to target and select their victims, maybe even helping in the actual rapes themselves. I'm going to second D.C. Dodds to the squad again for the duration of this case and he and young Curtis can work on listing every unsolved rape case, and indeed, attempted rapes, for the last twenty years in Liverpool and the surrounding area. Obviously, when such cases occurred they'd normally have been investigated as single cases but suspecting what we do now, we may find that a pattern emerges, something that will link a number of them together and may point us in the direction of these bastards. I think we definitely have a pair of vigilantes at work, and it's almost certain they're reacting to an unsolved case where they feel the rapists got away with it, or perhaps were arrested but never came to trial, another angle we should look at, so we need to work fast to try and bring the other two rapists in to custody before our killers can strike again. We may also find a study of those unsolved cases will identify the vigilantes' motive for this sudden spree of killings."

"Yes, sir, thank you sir," said Ross, impressed by his boss's immediate grasp and acceptance of his theory, and for throwing his weight behind it by the addition of Nick Dodds to the squad for the duration. He felt he needed to add one thing, though.

"Can I suggest that in addition to the unsolved rapes, we also have Dodds and Curtis include unsolved serious sexual assaults for the period, too? We all know there's often a fine dividing line between the two."

"Of course, Andy, you see to it. Now, I'll leave you to it, and good luck everybody."

A short series of "Thank you sirs," emanated from the assembled detectives as D.C.I. Porteous exited the room, closing the door quietly as he left.

"Bloody hell, sir, that was a turn up," said Curtis.

"Yes, it was, rather, Curtis," Ross agreed. "Thankfully the boss agreed with my theory. So, let's get to work. You all know what you need to do, so come on people, let's find ourselves a couple of killers, not to mention a possible pair of serial rapists while we're at it."

The sound of chair legs grating once again on the conference room floor not only put Ross's teeth on edge, but signalled the end of the meeting as everyone set off to work on their allotted tasks. Izzie Drake stopped at Ross's office door on her way to begin the in-depth investigation into the life of Mark Proctor, beginning, she'd decided with a visit to Melanie, his widow, who she knew wouldn't be pleased with the questions she'd already decided needed to be asked. But first, a word with Ross was her priority.

"Sir, a quick word?" She stood framed by the doorway. Ross sat behind his desk, making notes on a pad.

"Go on, Izzie, what is it?"

Drake was grinning as she said, her face deadly serious,

"Well sir, I just wanted to make sure you're going to be alright going out and about in the big wide world without me there by your side, holding your hand, so to speak."

Thankfully, Izzie possessed good reactions, as she just managed to dodge the folded-up copy of the previous night's *Echo* that sailed across the office in her direction.

She was already halfway across the squad room laughing to herself as Ross's voice boomed out of his office and followed her to the door,

"I'll see you later, *Sergeant* Clarissa Drake..."

Chapter 26

Too Good to be True

"I don't know what you're getting at. I've already told you, Mark was just a lovely man. Ask anyone. They'll all tell you the same."

Melanie Proctor had been surprised to see the two detectives standing on her front doorstep when she answered the ringing of the doorbell. After recovering her composure she then asked Drake if she'd come with news regarding the capture of her husband's killers. She'd then found herself being interrogated on the most intimate details of her life with Mark and was becoming more upset by the minute, but Izzie wasn't about to give up on her line of questioning.

"Melanie, I'm sorry, but I just don't believe you. You're basically asking us to believe that Mark went to work in the morning, came home in the afternoon and never went out at all, even at weekends. That's just too far-fetched for anyone to believe."

"Well, you know, he did go out sometimes, just not very often."

"That's better. Now we're getting somewhere. So, come on, Melanie, where did he go on these rare occasions?"

"I'm not really sure."

Sam Gable joined in the questioning. It was time for 'good cop, bad cop' with Gable assuming the good cop role.

"Listen, please Melanie. We know you're grieving for Mark. He was your husband and you loved him, but we are trying to find out who killed him, and stop them before they do anything like this to someone else's husband. Whatever Mark may have done isn't going to hurt him now, is it?"

"I suppose not," Melanie agreed with a degree of hesitation in her voice.

"Listen, Melanie, we're not accusing you of anything. If Mark did have any secrets from you, it's hardly your fault is it? But if he was up to anything that wasn't strictly legal, it could have provided the motive for someone to have killed him, do you see?"

"He played poker," Melanie just blurted out, without replying directly to Gable's question.

"Poker?" Gable asked. "Who with, and where and how often?"

"I honestly don't know," Melanie sniffed as she began to cry, quietly. "He went out once, sometimes twice a week to meet his friends. He said they met at a pub in Crosby, I don't know the name. In the early days, I asked him who his friends were, but he just said they were some old school mates, and the only name I ever heard was one time when he answered the phone and he mentioned the name Johnny. I think that was probably one of his poker playing pals because once I overheard him say something about having a 'full house' next time. That's a poker term, isn't it?"

"Yes, it is," Gable agreed, but thought it could also have been some kind of private code for something entirely different. "And you say you don't know the name of the pub where they met? You never heard any mention of the name, ever?"

"No, sorry, I've no idea."

"Didn't you think it strange, Melanie, that your husband never told you where he was going or exactly who he'd be with?" Izzie Drake asked her. "What if there'd been some sort of emergency at home? How would you have been able to reach him? That really wasn't very thoughtful of him was it?"

Melanie Proctor's sobs had turned to serious tears now and Sam Gable reached across to the coffee table and passed the box of tissues that stood there to the weeping woman.

"Melanie, please be open with us. Nothing's going to bring him back is it? We need to know everything about Mark's life if we're to put a stop to these killings and find whoever did this to him. You don't really think he was playing poker do you?"

Sam Gable had spent three years working vice before joining Ross's team. She'd seen plenty of prostitutes who'd been subjected to vicious assaults and rape, and she couldn't help but feel a certain degree of empathy for Melanie Proctor. Somehow, the woman presented a similar vulnerability as those girls, trapped in a situation they had no control over, and having no one to turn to when things went bad.

Melanie slowly regained control of herself, and as she brought the tears to a halt, she looked up at Sam, and shook her head.

"I thought he was seeing someone else," she said. "I loved him, but there was a too good to be true element about Mark. Do you know, he even went out on a Saturday morning to do the weekly shopping at the supermarket? I wanted to go with him but he always said I worked hard enough all week in the home and deserved to put my feet up for a couple of hours at the weekend. But he was gone too long. I would have done the shopping in about an hour at most, but he'd take at least two hours, sometimes longer. He'd joke about it if I asked him why he'd been so long and say he had a lousy sense of direction in supermarkets and ended up going down the same aisle time and again, and that he couldn't find certain things but he went every week so he should have known where most things were shouldn't he?"

Izzie understood the woman now. She must have spent years in denial, suspecting her husband of having an affair but believing excuse after excuse from him because she didn't want to believe him capable of such a thing. In fact, Izzie was now fairly certain he'd been guilty of so much more then marital infidelity.

"Listen, Melanie, I can't go into details with you at this time, but we don't believe Mark was having an affair."

The woman looked at Izzie Drake, and as their eyes met and locked, realisation dawned on Melanie Proctor.

"You think he did something bad, Sergeant Drake, don't you?

What is it you think he did when he was supposed to be playing poker with his mates?"

"I'm sorry, I'm not at liberty to tell you, as I said earlier, but we do need to find his killers and you can help by telling us everything you can about Mark, right back to the time you first met him."

Melanie had passed the point of no return. Her desire to protect the outward appearance of a happy marriage and a loving husband crumbled to nothing as she took another tissue from the box, blew her nose and placed the crumpled tissue in the pocket of her jeans, and with a steel-like resolve said,

"Tell me what you want to know."

Chapter 27

Under the influence

Gerald Byrne looked slightly incongruous as Ross greeted him in his office. Having agreed to the suggestion by Christine Bland, he was dressed casually, as she'd suggested, in a simple t-shirt emblazoned with the words, *Jesus Loves You* in bright red against a black background, a pair of blue denim jeans and black trainers that made him look anything but a Catholic priest. Ross led him to the office of D.C.I. Porteous, who had given up the use of his own inner sanctum when Bland had expressed a need for somewhere private and relatively comfortable in which to carry out the session. The profiler had asked that she be allowed a few minutes in private to prepare Byrne and to 'put him under' and Ross reluctantly agreed to wait outside the door, having wanted to see exactly how Bland achieved the act of hypnotising her subject.

"You can come in now, Inspector," she said as she opened the door ten minutes after she and Byrne had disappeared into Porteous's office. Ross found what followed engrossing. Unlike various TV dramatisations, Gerald Byrne didn't regress to talking in a childish voice or give any outward indication he was under hypnosis at all. However, what he revealed was illuminating to the detective. First of all, Christine Bland asked him to recall his days as a junior in the Lower School at Speke Hill. Most of the information that came from the priest was routine and irrelevant but certain passages of his memories struck a chord with Andy Ross.

"Nineteen sixty-four? Oh yes, the year of the Moors Murders, Hindley and Brady. We were being constantly reminded of the dangers to children at morning assembly in school and during services in the chapel. At first the children were reported as missing and the bodies weren't found until later, upon Saddleworth Moor.

Father Mullaney was especially concerned that those children who were allowed out of the grounds to go to the local shops or on Saturday trips to town were chaperoned at all times. There were always a couple of adults, usually priests or nuns to accompany the children, but if a couple of kids wanted to visit a store to buy something with their pocket money, well, the adults couldn't be everywhere at once, so it was made a new rule that we could only be apart from the grown-ups for a maximum of twenty minutes and there had to be at least four children together, two Uppers and two Lowers, so that the older boys or girls could take care of the young ones. That was around the time poor Keith Bennett went missing. Of course, nobody knew he was a victim of Hindley and Brady until they confessed to his killing in the nineteen eighties. The poor boy's body has never been found, you know, even after so many years."

"Do you remember Matthew Remington and Mark Proctor being together on any of those trips to town, Gerald?"

"Oh yes, they were usually together from when we got off the bus until we returned to Speke Hill."

"And they had two older boys with them if they went off on their own, away from the adult staff?"

"Yes, that's right."

"The older boys, Gerald, do you remember their names?"

"No, sorry, I don't."

Damn, Ross thought. He now had an idea that the two boys who took Remington and Proctor under their protection all those years ago could well be the two senior members of whatever weird, perverted association that eventually led to them eventually becoming serial rapists, if his theory held up.

Christine Bland, however, carried on, unfazed by Byrne's inability at this stage to identify the two elder boys.

"Tell me about Angela, Gerald. How did she feel about the awful case of the missing children?"

"Angela was three years older than me, of course so she probably understood a lot more than me about it. She didn't say much about it, as far as I remember, except to say that the children who'd gone missing were all from around Manchester and she didn't think we were in real danger in Liverpool. I remember the two of us going into a record shop, with two older girls. Angela bought *Have I The Right* by the Honeycombs. They were her favourite group at the time. She loved the fact they had a girl drummer and said one day she wanted to be just like Honey Lantree and play the drums in a pop group. It was just a childish dream, of course. I think I wanted to be like Billy J Kramer when I was seven years old. The girls in Angela's dorm had saved their pocket money for ages and clubbed together to buy a second-hand Dansette record player at the market in town. Sister Thomasina was the nun in charge of their dorm and was a dab hand at fixing things, and she made sure the record player worked properly for the girls. Anyway, a loft of the older boys were jealous because at that time, I think only one of the Upper boy's dorms had a record player, so sometimes, in the evening, a group of boys could be seen gathered on the grass outside Angela's dorm. The girls would place the record player as near to an open window as they could, and play the latest records for the boys to listen to. Funny really, when you think about it, all those lads jigging about on the grass and the girls dancing to the music inside the dorm."

"And did Angela ever have any problems with the boys at that time, Gerald? You know, did she ever tell you about any of them bothering her or making unwanted suggestions to her about doing things she knew were wrong or indecent?"

"No."

"So, you never heard Angela screaming in the night, or found her being pinned down on the grass by Matthew Remington, Plug you called him, and Mark Proctor?"

"Oh no, nothing like that."

Convinced by now that nothing untoward had taken place in the time frame suggested by Byrne's nightmare, he used hand signals to indicate to Christine Bland, urging her to move forward in time. She now asked Byrne to fast forward to his teenage years. She asked him the same question regarding any form of assault on Angela.

This time, the answer varied slightly.

"Nothing ever happened to Angela, no."

Something in those words alerted both Bland and Ross's instincts. Both profiler and detective knew from the way Gerald Byrne spoke of nothing happening to Angela, that he was in effect saying 'but' as though somewhere in his mind lurked a memory of an incident relating to another girl, one that had become subconsciously entangled in his mind along with other recollections of his sister to form the basis for his current nightmares.

"Did something bad happen to another girl, Gerald? One of Angela's friends perhaps? Try and think. Let your mind take you back, you saw something, didn't you, or maybe it was Angela who saw it and told you, her little brother, all about it?"

Christine Bland waited, as the priest drifted away once again on a tide of buried memories, and all she, and Andy Ross could do, was wait to see where, and at what point in time Byrne's mental rewind stopped. Gerald's breathing intensified for a few seconds and then very slowly returned to what appeared to be a normal rhythm. His eyes, previously cast downwards, now shone brightly as he appeared to be focussing on something, an event from the past?

"What is it Gerald? Where are you? What do you see?"

Without hesitation, Byrne replied to Christine Bland's questions.

"I was walking across to the girl's dormitories. I'd arranged to meet Angela after tea, just to go for a walk around the grounds. We often did that, so we could talk in peace and privacy. Before I got there, where

Angela would be waiting outside as usual, Father Rooney called to me from the doorway to the Admin block as I passed it."

"Okay Gerald, that's good. Describe what happened next. How old were you at this time?"

"Not sure, but I remember we all loved a song that was in the charts that year. It was called *Nobody's Child* and was about a blind orphan boy who nobody wanted to adopt. All us kids thought it was kind of like us being stuck here in Speke Hill. I must have been about twelve, thirteen perhaps. There was another song I liked, *Bad Moon Rising*."

Ross knew that one. *Creedence Clearwater Revival* was one of his favourite groups from the sixties, having discovered them much later, when he was in his own teens, having heard the song when it was featured during a very scary werewolf transformation scene in the film *American Werewolf in London*. It would be easy to pinpoint the exact year Byrne was talking about as long as he was talking about the time both songs were current in the U.K charts.

"Alright, Gerald. So, Father Rooney called to you. What happened next?"

Now it was as though Byrne had slipped through a time warp in to the past as he relived the next few minutes of his youth.

* * *

"Gerald Byrne, please, wait a moment," the voice of Father Rooney halted the young Gerald in his tracks. He turned to see the priest calling to him from the Administration Building.

"Hello Father," he called in return.

Father Rooney walked down the three shallow steps from the building entrance to the path and approached Byrne who waited for the priest to catch him up.

Slightly out of breath, Father Rooney smiled as he stopped in front of the young lad.

"Thanks for waiting, Gerald," he said. "How would you like to earn yourself a shilling?"

"A shilling, Father? All for me?"

"All for you, Gerald, and just for doing me a small favour."

"Okay, Father. What do I have to do?"

"Nothing arduous young Gerald. I collected the first fifteen rugby kits from the laundry today and dropped them off at the pavilion, ready for tomorrow's match with The Blue Coat School. I've a meeting to go to later and I just realised I must have left my motorcycle gauntlets in the pavilion. I have some important marking to do and can't spare the time to run down there right now. Would you be a good boy and run down and get them for me and bring them back here?"

"I was just going to meet my sister, Father."

"That's alright, go and meet her and she can keep you company. Tell her there's sixpence in it for her too. That won't interrupt your plans too much will it?"

"Oh no, Father. We just meet and go for walks around the grounds some evenings, that's all. We can easily go down to the sports field and the pavilion to get your gloves."

Rooney smiled.

"Gauntlets, Gerald. They're called gauntlets. You know what they look like, don't you?"

"I think so, Father, big black things with like, kind of flap things that stick out and cover your wrists when you're riding your motor bike?"

"Yes, I suppose that's a decent enough description, young Gerald. At least you know what you're looking for. They should be in the changing room where I unpacked the clean shirts and hung them up on the team hooks ready for the tomorrow. Here's the key to the pavilion." Father Rooney tossed the key to young Gerry Byrne who deftly caught it in his right hand.

"Okay, Father," Byrne said to the motorcycling priest, probably his favourite among the ecclesiastical members of staff at Speke Hill. Father Rooney, probably because of his love of motorcycling, seemed more 'with it' than the other priests and nuns, Gerald thought.

Leaving Father Rooney to return to his marking, Byrne skipped off happily to meet Angela who was waiting patiently outside her dormitory building, one of two large buildings allocated to the girls of Speke Hill. She was sitting on the grass, her knees tucked beneath her as she waited, a small book in her hand.

"What kept you?" she asked as Gerald arrived, slightly breathless from running the last few yards.

"Father Rooney," he replied, and explained Rooney's request to his sister.

"Okay, come on then," said Angela, holding a hand up so her brother could help her to her feet."

"What's the book?" Byrne asked his sister as they walked. She handed it to him.

"*The Observer's Book of Birds*," he read from the cover.

"I borrowed it from Maggie Miller," Angela said. "I love birds, Gerry, and thought it might be nice if I could identify them when I see them. We might see some down on the sports field, looking for worms and things."

"But we only get sparrows and blackbirds round here, Angie."

"Don't be daft. I've seen greenfinches, robins and lots of birds I don't know the names of."

"Oh well, if it makes you happy, that's okay."

It was quite a walk from the accommodation block to the far side of the sports field, where the grandly named 'pavilion' stood. It was a small, wooden building, with two cramped changing rooms for opposing teams, whether it be for cricket, football, rugby or whatever, and a small central area where a small refreshment table could be set up when entertaining visiting teams from other schools as would be the case the following day. Though the school had considered installing showers for the players the cost of installing the necessary plumbing had been prohibitive and so the pavilion retained a rather dated air, with its overhanging roof that provided cover over the small raised outside wooden terrace and steps that led down to the field.

As brother and sister drew closer, Angela suddenly spotted a flurry of avian activity in the bushes that formed the border between the playing field and the adjoining field belonging to a local farmer and currently lying fallow.

"Oh, Gerry, look," she enthused. "Maybe there are some birds I haven't seen before. Do you mind if I go and creep up quietly and see what they are while you go in and get the Father's things?"

"Go ahead, Angie," Byrne replied. "I'll only be a minute though, so don't go far."

"Okay, I'm only going over there," she pointed.

"Angela quickly skipped away, book in hand, and Gerry Byrne strode up the steps, unlocked the door and entered the pavilion. He moved automatically into the changing room to the left, knowing it was used as the 'home' changing room. Sure enough, as soon as he walked in he saw Father Rooney's gauntlets where he'd left them on one of the wooden bench seats that ran along the wall under the hooks that held each freshly ironed rugby kit, ready for the Upper's big match the next day.

As he was about to turn and leave, a noise from somewhere behind the pavilion reached his ears. Instinct told him it was the sound of someone, a girl, in some distress.

Louder, male voices could be heard, too, and Gerry Byrne, sensing something wasn't quite right about what he was hearing, padded almost on tiptoe to the small window, covered by steel mesh, that was fitted high up into the outside wall of the home changing room. Not being very tall, Gerry had to stand on the wooden bench seat and even then, reach up on tiptoes to gain a very restricted view of what was happening behind the pavilion.

Four boys were out there, on the grass and they had a girl with them. From the sounds the girl was making, she wasn't enjoying or encouraging whatever they were doing.

"Go on Plug, get her skirt off," a voice Byrne didn't recognise ordered as a boy he recognised as Matthew Remington slapped the girl across the face, causing her not to scream but to cry, her tears only serving to fuel the boys' cruelty.

"Shut up, you little bitch or it'll be a punch in the face next time," Remington leered at her, as he tried to force the poor girl's legs apart.

"Oh, move over, Plug, let me have a go at her," said the unmistakable voice of Mark Proctor, much to Gerry Byrne's horror. He couldn't get high enough to see the girl's face, so he wasn't able to see who it was the boys had pinned down on the ground, but whoever it was, it was plainly obvious that what the boys were doing to her was very wrong. Gerry Byrne, still innocent in the ways of the world was in a quandary. He didn't know who the other boys were, but something in their voices told him they were older than Plug and Mark. He knew he had to do something to stop them from hurting the girl, but what could he, one young lad do against four of them, without probably getting badly hurt himself if they retaliated against any attempt he made to help her? He didn't have time to run back to Father Rooney and he suddenly thought of Angela. What would happen if she walked in to the situation now, and saw and heard what was happening? Dare he risk his sister being caught by the older boys and suffering the same fate as the girl on the grass?

"Please don't do this," the girl pleaded.

"Shut it, bitch," one of the older boys snapped at her. "For God's sake, Mark, if you can't the fucking skirt off, just lift it up and get on with it."

"She's struggling too much," said Proctor.

"So fucking slap her again," said the unknown voice.

As Gerry Byrne tried to think of a way to help the girl without ending up being beaten or worse by the four thugs outside the pavilion, fate, or maybe the God he would end up serving through the church, took a hand in proceedings.

Some four hundred yards away, Angela was scurrying about under a clump of trees and bushes, seeking bird life, when she inadvertently disturbed a family of crows, roosting peacefully in one of the trees. The birds took to the air in a flurry of flapping wings, accompanied by a cacophony of screeching bird calls, and by chance flew directly in the direction of the ongoing assault, flying directly over the scene, forcing the girl's assailants to suddenly look up in surprise. Simultaneously, a man walking his dog in the fallow field just beyond the boundary of the school playing field began calling his dog, which had run off in pursuit of the birds that had caught his attention with their flapping and screeching. The dog found a small hole in the boundary fence and slithered through into the school field, and within seconds the four boys were surprised to see a muscular, black Doberman pinscher bounding across the field in their direction. The dog's owner's face appeared at the fence as he shouted, "Paddy, where are you boy?"

"Bloody hell, lads, fucking leave her and leg it, quickly; don't you dare say a word, bitch or we'll be back," said one of the older boys, and in less than a second the four boys abandoned the attack on the girl and ran off in the opposite direction to the dog's approach. Luckily for them, the dog stopped as it reached the distressed, crying girl, and began licking her face affectionately. From his position at the window, Byrne was able to witness the arrival of the man who had climbed the fence to follow his runaway dog.

The man quickly ascertained that the girl was alright and amazingly accepted her claim that she'd fallen and hurt herself. *Didn't he hear her screams?* The thought ran through Gerry Byrne's mind. He seemed more concerned about his dog, Paddy, who's back bore a long, angry looking red scratch where he'd cut it as he'd wriggled under the seven foot high chain metal fence between the playing field and the narrow path that ran along the side of the adjoining farmer's field.

Feeling it was safe to exit his hiding place in the changing room, Gerry stepped out and quickly ran round to the rear of the wooden structure to where the man was on his knees, his attention seemingly divided between the girl on the ground and Paddy the dog. When she saw him approaching, at first the girl's eyes registered fear, obviously thinking he was one of her attackers, perhaps returning to ensure her silence, but then she seemed to realise he was a newcomer to the scene.

"Are you okay?" Gerry asked the girl, who looked up at him as though he were a being from another planet.

"Seems the young lady fell down and hurt herself," the man said to Gerry before the girl had a chance to reply, and at that moment, Angela arrived, and took one look at the girl and somehow, in the way that only a female possibly could, she seemed to know exactly what had happened.

"What the heck's going on?" she asked.

Gerry looked at his sister, as if to say, *"don't say anything until he's gone."*

As if on cue, satisfied that the girl was safe in the hands of her two 'friends' as he called them, the man clipped Paddy's lead to his collar and left the scene, leaving Gerry and Angela to attend to the girl.

"Right, is someone going to tell me what happened here?" Angela asked again.

"Four boys tried to do things to her," Gerry said. "I could hear them and see some of it through the little window in the changing room, but I didn't know what to do to help her."

"Is that right?" Angela asked the girl, taking hold of one trembling hand.

"Yes," the girl said, trying hard not to burst into tears.

"What's your name?" Angela asked her.

"Elizabeth Dunne," she replied. "They call me Lizzie."

"You're not from Speke Hill, Lizzie, are you?"

"No, I met this boy, and arranged to meet him here, and he sneaked me in through the gate at the far end of the path along the field. I thought he fancied me, you know, and he was good looking and a bit older than me so I was flattered when he asked me to meet him. Anyway, when we got here, he changed completely, and there were three other boys waiting behind the building, and they tried to…to…you know?"

"Bastards," said Angela through clenched teeth.

"What was this lad's name, Lizzie, and where did you meet him?"

"He called himself Johnny, and I met him in a coffee bar in town last Saturday."

"Did you see him, Gerry?" Angela asked her brother.

"Not properly, no," Byrne replied. "But I know who two of them were."

"Who were they, Gerry?"

"Mark Proctor and Plug, you know, Remington?"

"Bloody hell."

Gerry had never heard his sister swear before, and the vehemence in her voice took him by surprise.

"We've got to tell someone," Angela quickly decided.

"Oh please, I don't want to get into trouble," Lizzie pleaded. "If my parents find out I've been hanging around with boys they'll kill me."

"But, they tried to rape you, Lizzie. That's what happened, isn't it?" said Angela, far more forcefully than Gerry would have thought possible at her age.

"Yes, but they didn't actually do it in the end, did they?" said Lizzie.

Ten minutes of discussion ended when Angela told Gerry he'd better take Father Rooney's gauntlets to him and think of an excuse for being late, while she walked Angela safely out of the grounds. Unfortunately for the little group, Father Rooney, worried at Gerry's long absence, appeared at that very moment, and unused to lying to a priest, the children soon revealed all to the shocked looking Father.

Lizzie refused point blank however, to reveal her surname or her address to Rooney, insisting she wanted to forget the whole episode. Knowing he couldn't force the girl to talk to him, Father Rooney stood silently for a minute as he tried to decide his next course of action. Reaching his decision, he ordered Angela and Gerry to go about their business as though nothing had happened.

"Carry on with your walk, as you normally would, and I'll walk young Lizzie here safely out of school grounds. As for the boys responsible for this appalling act of savagery, you leave them to me. I don't want you two involved, do you understand?"

"But Father," an incensed Angela said, "we don't even know who the other boys are, and they're just going to get away with it, aren't they?"

"No, they most certainly are not, Angela, and as for the other two boys, I can promise you that Proctor and Remington will reveal all to me. I'll make sure of it. But listen, if they know you two have talked to me and are involved in me finding out what's taken place here today, they could make things very difficult for you both for the remainder of your time at Speke Hill, do you understand that?"

Gerry and Angela simultaneously chorused "Yes, Father."

Angela then asked, "But how will you say you found out, Father?"

"Oh, you leave that to me, Angela. For one thing, I can say I came here to get my forgotten gauntlets and found this young girl, and she told me what had taken place. I can assure you they'll be terrified at the prospect of what may happen to them next, and they know she heard the names, Mark and Plug, and Johnny, so it won't seem too strange to them that I was able to identify them. Now, do as I've told you while I see Lizzie off the premises."

Feeling shaken and a little unsure of themselves, Angela and Gerry nevertheless did as Father Rooney asked and went back to their walk, though neither found any pleasure in their remaining time together. Gerry noticed that, despite her earlier enthusiasm, Angela never looked at *The Observer's Book of Birds* once during the rest of their walk. Brother and sister hugged each other as they parted a while later at the entrance to Angela's dormitory, having promised each other never to mention what had happened in front of a living soul, as long as they had to live at Speke Hill, trusting Father Rooney to make sure the guilty boys were punished.

* * *

Andy Ross now felt he had not only the explanation for Father Gerald Byrne's rather mixed-up nightmare, but more importantly, confirmation of what he guessed had been the beginning of an evil partnership of four young men who would go on to commit further acts of evil as they achieved maturity. Now, if only Christine Bland could extract the names of the two older boys from the depths of Gerald Byrne's memory. She now tried to do just that.

"Tell me please, Gerald, what happened after that evening. Did you hear what happened to the boys who'd perpetrated the attack?"

"We never heard a word. Father Rooney called me aside one day and told me the matter had been dealt with privately, *within the orphanage* as he put it. Though we'd promised never to talk about it, Angela and I discussed it years later when we'd both left the orphanage and our promise no longer held firm. We both agreed there had to have been some kind of cover-up. Speke Hill had closed ranks to protect its own. Maybe they did punish the boys in some way, but it was never made public, as far as we knew."

"And do you recall the names of those other boys, Gerald, the older ones who seemed to be egging on the two younger ones?"

"I only know one of them was called Johnny, because I heard the other older boy say his name one time. I never saw his face because if I had done, I might have seen him with the other boy in the following days and been able to find out the other boy's name, but it never happened."

Christine Bland drew the session to a close and told the priest, "I'm going to count to five, now, Gerald. When I reach five, you'll wake up and your mind will recall what you've told me, not as a nightmare, but as a distant memory from long ago, and it will no longer disturb you. You were a child when what you've told me took place and you will no longer carry the burden of what you saw all those years ago"

Ross said to her, before she began counting, "don't they usually tell people they *won't* remember what they've revealed under hypnosis?"

"This isn't a stage act or a movie, Inspector. This is supposed to be a cathartic process for Father Byrne, a way to help him put the past to bed, so to speak, to banish the nightmare. He can only do that if he remembers the truth about the past, and not some twisted subconscious version of reality."

"I think I understand, and thank you for doing this."

"It's time to bring him back," she said as she slowly began counting to five.

Chapter 28

Back to 'Billy Ruffian

Randolph Newman stood head and shoulders above Detective Constable 'Tony' Curtis. At six foot four inches, he was a good six inches taller than Curtis, and his black, tightly curled hair, dark good looks that betrayed his Caribbean heritage and powerful physique had the effect of intimidating the young D.C. before they'd exchanged a word. Newman hadn't exactly looked pleased when Curtis kept up an incessant knocking on the front doors of *The Belerophon* at nine thirty in the morning. As landlord of the pub, he'd fallen into bed some time after one a.m. after closing the pub, making sure all was secure, and balancing the day's takings before locking them in the safe. He'd been in the cellar, changing a barrel of lager when the knocking began and made sure he finished the task in hand before climbing the stairs, crossing the floor of the pub and opening one of the double doors, just a crack, to identify the cause of the disturbance to his morning.

"Yes?" he snapped at the sight of the young man in blue jeans and a leather jacket standing at his door.

Curtis, forced to look up to face the man directly, took one look at Newman and gulped internally, before pulling his warrant card from the inside pocket of his jacket and holding it up for the landlord to examine.

"Police," he announced. "Detective Constable Curtis, Merseyside Police. I'd like a word, sir, if I may?"

"Humph," Newman shrugged. "I hardly thought you'd be from the Met, would you?"

Curtis looked a little nonplussed by the remark.

"Oh, never mind. Come on in, Detective. I was just about to put the kettle on. Tea or coffee?"

"Er, right, thank you, sir. Coffee for me please."

Five minutes later the two men faced each other across a well used wooden topped table in the lounge bar of the pub.

"How long have you been the landlord here, Mr. Newman?"

"Oh, must be around ten years now, since I left the Royal Navy."

"I see, so you'd remember most of the regulars over that period?"

"Well, maybe not all, but most of them, sure," Newman replied. "What's this all about, Constable?"

Curtis quickly filled Newman in on the reason for his visit and then reached into the inside pocket of his leather jacket a removed photographs of both Matthew Remington and Mark Proctor. The landlord gazed at them for a few seconds, and then nodded.

"Yes, I've seen them in here a few times. Two of the four apostles."

"Eh? What do you mean, Mr. Newman?"

"The four apostles is what I called them, 'cos of their names, right?"

"I'm sorry, I'm not with you."

"When we was very little kids, Constable, me and me brothers, well, our Mam taught us this simple little bedtime prayer. It went like this. *Matthew, Mark, Luke and John, Bless the bed that I lie on. God bless Mam and Dad, Samuel, Levi, and Gary.* Of course, me brothers would insert my name instead of their own, but we could also add anyone else we wanted to the prayer, like grandparents, friends, cousins here and in Jamaica and so on. It was just easy for a little child to remember you see, based on the four gospels of the New Testament, the books of Matthew, Mark, Luke and John, so when these four fellas stars coming in here, and I gradually overheard their names, I thought of them as being all saints' names, like the four apostles of my childish prayer, and I always thought of 'em that way, whenever I saw 'em in here."

Curtis was elated. They had a name for the fourth man. Though saint was the last name he'd apply to the men Newman just described."

"I heard about the murders on Radio Merseyside and on Mersey Radio. One of them said that one of the dead men had a record of serious sexual offences but they didn't give any details."

"We believe all four men were involved in a number of offences, Mr. Newman, but I can't go into details, I'm afraid."

"I understand, Constable," Newman replied. "Need to know basis and all that, eh?"

"Exactly," said Curtis. "You'd have come across stuff like that in the Navy, I suppose."

"All the time. You can count on me to keep my mouth shut. I won't even tell my wife why you were here. She's upstairs and will be wondering where her cup of tea is," he grinned. "I'll tell her you came about a fracas in the vicinity or something and asked if we'd heard anything."

"Mr. Newman, you don't know how helpful you've been. One last thing, did you ever overhear any of them mention any surnames?"

"No, sorry Constable. It weren't even very often I overheard a first name. It probably took me three months of them coming in here before I gave 'em the four apostles name, it took that long to hear all their names."

"How about hearing any of their conversations?"

"I'm a good landlord, Constable Curtis. That means I stay out of the faces and the business of my regulars. It wouldn't do to be eavesdropping on conversations, especially in an area like this, if you know what I mean."

"I see, yes, I get your point, but that's still great. How long have they been coming in to the pub, can you remember?"

"Oh, I'd say at least for the last four or five years. They'd sit at a corner table in the bar. I'll show you their regular spot when we go through there again on your way out. If that table was taken they'd sometimes come in the lounge bar and take pot luck on a table."

Curtis was delighted with the result of his interview with the land-lord of *The Belerophon* and felt sure D.I. Ross would be, too. He thanked Newman who duly showed him where the four men usually sat in the bar, and then duly departed and made his way back to headquarters, a sense of satisfaction overtaking his earlier trepidation at the sight of the very tall, heavily built ex-seaman, now the jolly 'mine host' of *The Belerophon*. Curtis made a mental note to try not to judge people quite so quickly based on nothing but their appearance. The tall and power-ful Jamaican-born former seaman had just taught the young detective an important lesson that would serve him well in future investiga-tions.

Chapter 29

A Woman of Many Faces

Having spent most of the day in the office with Nick Dodds, pulling the required records of past rape, attempted rape and serious sexual cases as Ross had requested, Derek McLennan looked at his watch, stood up from his computer screen and stretched to loosen the stiff and aching muscles in his back and neck.

"Had enough, Derek?" Dodds asked as Derek almost slumped into his chair again.

"For now, yes. Listen, Nick, school's out now. Why don't we nip down to the canteen, grab a sandwich and give the Manvers woman time to get home? I pulled her address earlier, and it'll only take about twenty minutes to get there, traffic permitting. I don't think the boss will mind if you join me in going along to talk to her and two heads is better than one anytime. You might think of something I don't while interviewing her, unless you want to just head off home. It's been a long day, after all."

"What's to go home for?" Dodds replied. Since his divorce a few months earlier, Nick had left the marital home and now lived in a small rented flat above a Chinese restaurant in the city centre, not far from work. His evenings tended to be, long, lonely and monotonous, so he was in no hurry to finish work for the day.

* * *

Vera Manvers stepped from the shower, dried her body and then padded barefoot into her bedroom, where she quickly blow-dried her hair, and allowed it to fall into its natural wavy shoulder-length tresses. After sitting before her dressing table and applying her make-up, she dressed in a pair of comfortable, slim-fitting black slacks, topped with a lightweight cream coloured polo-neck sweater, then sat back on her dressing table stool to admire the transformation. She smiled at her reflection in the mirror, knowing that the staff at Speke Hill would be hard-pressed to recognise the attractive, well manicured woman who stared back at her from the mirror from the dowdy spinster who arrived at work with hair tied in a bun, dressed in sensible skirts and blouses or sweaters depending on the weather with her low heeled, sensible shoes, and pale, make-up free face.

She thought how surprised they'd be if they could see the real woman in her off duty garb, the above the knee skirts showing off a well formed pair of legs, her high heels and general appearance taking at least ten years off her apparent age.

Vera Manvers was in fact much younger than she appeared to her colleagues at work. Even her name was a fabrication. Some five years earlier she'd scoured local churchyards, slowly building a list of names of children, mostly babies, who'd died in the first few months of life. With the help of her partner, she'd gradually completed extensive checks on her final short list of four names, finally selecting the one with not one single living relative, and therefore no chance of her new identity being accidentally revealed by some suspicious cousin, grandparent or whatever. Vera Manvers, who had died at the age of just two months in a tragic house fire, along with her parents and two siblings had been tailor-made for her plans. From there, it had been a simple matter of obtaining a copy of the dead child's birth certificate and, through the contacts her partner had established, obtaining enough fake documentation to quickly establish herself in her new identity. To ensure she would be able to continue to work legally and receive any state benefits she was entitled to, she quit her previous job, changed her name by Deed Poll to Vera Manvers, dropped out of circulation for nearly a year, and then returned to every day life in her new guise, ready to avenge her sister. Vera's plan for revenge had built up over a number of years, and she and Brenda's still devoted fiancé had decided the time was ripe for their plans to be put into fruition when 'number three' on their list rose to the verge of success in his chosen profession, one that would be a gross travesty in light of his 'other life' activities. He would be the next to feel the wrath of vengeance and by the time they got to him, he'd know the true meaning of fear, because by then he would know they were coming for him. They'd wanted to save him till last but circumstances had altered things drastically and they needed to move him up the list.

Her sister had retained just enough of her wits and sanity to tell her the details of her attack before the full horror of what had befallen her had sent her into the state of semi-catatonia she now lived in. The next thing 'Vera' and Brenda's fiancé had done had been to follow their target for months, with Vera gradually finding a talent for disguise, being able to change her appearance almost at will, able to watch the man who'd been the prime mover in the attack on her sister with almost total impunity. Brenda had known the man slightly, but couldn't tell Vera much about the other three men who'd gang raped her as she and her so-called 'friend' Matthew Remington, had walked home from a date.

Her surveillance of Matthew Remington, beginning from the time of his release from prison had instantly enabled her to identify Mark Proctor as another of the men involved. Using her new found skill as a mistress of disguise, she'd 'accidentally' bumped into the repulsive Remington in a pub one night and plied him with enough drink to discover he'd been brought up at Speke Hill Orphanage, a link to Mark Proctor who she'd learned was a teacher at the school there. It now became a possibility that all four of Brenda's assailants had a connection to Speke Hill, but the problem was, how could she and Brenda's fiancé confirm their suspicions? The answer soon presented itself. Brenda's fiancé had visited Speke Hill under the guise of a visiting child care official and discovered that the school secretary was on the verge of retirement. Now there only remained the problem of guaranteeing Vera got the job.

They soon found that Charles Hopkirk, who would be responsible for interviewing and hiring the new secretary was something of a ladies man, who enjoyed trawling the city's clubs on Friday and Saturday nights, often managing to fall into bed with numerous one-night stands, probably all the worse for drink and or recreational drugs. Wearing a blonde wig, party clothes and heavily made up, a totally changed Vera, going under the name of 'Poppy Gillespie' followed Hopkirk to the Red Pelican club one night, waiting until he'd drunk enough to be slightly inebriated before making her move.

Later that night, lying on her back with Hopkirk grunting above her, she'd pushed aside her revulsion long enough to get him to tell her about the vacancy at his workplace. Saying she had a friend who'd love to work at the orphanage, she'd allowed him to use her body again and promised to meet him the following week if he'd agree to consider her friend for the job.

Five days later, 'Vera' arrived at Speke Hill for an interview and was promptly hired by Charles Hopkirk. He never once suspected that the prim and proper, dowdy spinster with a rather 'plummy'accent sitting across from him at the interview was the sexy and very gorgeous 'Poppy' he'd met at the club.

The following Saturday night, 'Poppy' had met Hopkirk again as arranged. She needed to be certain he wasn't about to go back on their deal and found herself once again in his bed, promising herself this would be the last time. As he groaned and grunted his satisfaction for the last time, she lay back, thinking she'd never have to do this again, after he'd told her how impressed he'd been with her 'friend' Vera Manvers.

She was in! As much as it had disgusted her to virtually prostitute herself in such a way, she considered that opening her legs for Charles Hopkirk had been nothing more than a means to an end, a giant step in the quest for revenge for her sister's life having been effectively ended by Remington, Proctor and two more, as yet unidentified men. At least she was on the pill and there was no chance of Hopkirk's seed producing anything more than a short inconvenience as she washed herself in the bathroom after what would be her last 'date' with the odious little man.

In the coming days, as Vera settled into her new job, Charles Hopkirk, puzzled that he hadn't seen Poppy in the club as usual, asked her 'friend' Vera if she was alright.

When she informed Hopkirk that 'Poppy' had developed a rather nasty sexually transmitted disease and had retired from the social scene while undergoing treatment at the local STD clinic, the look on his face had been pure gold for Vera. He visibly paled and began to sweat as Vera informed him she was sure Poppy would look him up as soon as she was cured and 'back on the scene' ready to go clubbing again.

"Are you alright, Mr. Hopkirk?" she'd asked, trying so hard to maintain a sweet and innocent demeanour. "You look a little pale."

"Oh, yes, of course, Vera, thank you. Please tell Poppy I'll look forward to seeing her soon," said Hopkirk, deciding there and then to never set foot in the Red Pelican again. The next few weeks and months would be a continual source of worry for him as he checked and re-checked himself for any sign of scabs or lesions that might indicate him having contracted some dreaded sexual disease.

Let the fat bastard suffer, Vera thought as she revelled in his misery.

It took her quite a while in her new position to systematically scour the old records of Speke Hill in her search for any connections between Remington, Proctor and any other boys who may have been involved in any kind of illegal activity, either individually or as a group.

She'd only conducted her search a small piece at a time, not wanting to draw attention to the fact she was searching past records of the school and orphanage, none of which bore any reference to her current employment so it took a little longer than she'd at first anticipated.

Boys being boys, there had been a number of instances of lads from Speke Hill having been in trouble at various times, mostly for trivial and non-criminal offences.

Eventually, her senses were alerted by a sealed envelope that carried the pencilled names, now a little faded, of Proctor, Remington and two others she'd never heard of before. With a shaking hand, she took her letter opener and without further hesitation, sliced the envelope open. She'd hit pay dirt! The whole incident relating to the attempted assault on the girl behind the pavilion was revealed to her, and now, at long last, she felt able to prepare, along with Brenda's fiancé, to exact revenge for her sister's treatment at the hands of the monsters who defiled her for life and so it began.

* * *

Her thoughts were suddenly interrupted by an unexpected knocking on her front door. Annoyed, as she rarely had visitors of any description, and certainly not unannounced ones, Vera walked to the door, pulled it open, expecting to find a couple of Jehovah's Witnesses or perhaps a double glazing salesman at her door and was instead surprised to find two police detectives, warrant cards already held up on display, standing on her doorstep.

"Miss Vera Manvers?" the older of the two detectives asked.

Struggling, and just managing to maintain her composure, Vera replied, "It's *Ms* Manvers, if you don't mind."

"Right, okay, Ms. Manvers," said Nick Dodds. "Can we come in please?"

"What's this about?" Vera asked.

"Just a few more questions about Speke Hill," Derek McLennan said in response to her question.

"Well, yes, I suppose so, but I hope this won't take long, I have to go out soon."

"I can see that," McLennan replied. His look at his fellow detective said it all. They'd both expected a dowdy spinsterish woman in her fifties to answer the door. Instead, they were both a little taken aback to see the very attractive, well dressed woman standing before them, who couldn't have been more than forty-five at the outside.

They followed Vera into her tidy living room, and seated themselves in opposite armchairs. Vera sat on the sofa, and the act of crossing her legs made her already short skirt ride up, revealing even more of her well tanned and shapely legs.

"Well?" she asked, aware that the two men were staring at her, particularly her legs.

Derek McLennan spoke first.

"Ms. Manvers…"

"Oh, do call me Vera, dearie," she interrupted, almost coquettishly. She'd decided the best way to deal with the two young detectives was to try and thrown them off guard a little and so far she felt it was working.

"Okay, Vera," McLennan went on, "we need to inquire a little more into the subject of the records of Speke Hill, going back to the fifties and sixties."

"Yes? What about them? How can I help you?"

Nick Dodds joined the questioning.

"Our colleagues previously visited you at work, Vera, looking for information relating to both Matthew Remington and Mark Proctor."

"Yes, that's correct."

"You're aware that we're involved in the investigation into their murders, Vera?"

"Yes of course I know. I did what I could to help the police, but the information you were requesting went back to a long time ago and the old paper records are not exactly easily available or necessarily filed in proper date sequence, a failing of the previous person to hold my position, I'm afraid," she replied, attempting to divert any blame or suspicion from herself.

"That's as maybe," McLennan said, "but our boss, D.I. Ross feels you may have been holding something back from us, Vera."

Vera looked shocked. In truth, she was afraid they may be onto her, but McLennan's next words gave her cause for hope.

"He thinks you may be going out of your way to protect Remington and Proctor by withholding information about them that might assist us in our inquiries into their murders."

Emboldened, Vera replied, "Now, why on earth would I do such a thing, Detective Constable? In the first place, I never knew Matthew Remington, and I only met Mark Proctor when I went to work at Speke Hill, and that was only a passing working relationship."

McLennan was thrown off kilter by the logic of her answer, and Dodds came to his rescue.

"We think you may be trying to protect the reputation of Speke Hill, Ms. Manvers. If the place has certain skeletons in the cupboard, so to speak, as secretary, you have access to all past records and would be in a position to withhold anything that might throw a bad light on your employers."

Vera relaxed a little at Dodds's words. They actually thought she was trying to protect those vicious perverts. Surely, if that was the case, they had no inkling she was in fact responsible for the murders.

With new confidence born from that thought, she replied to Dodds confidently.

"I can assure you, Constable that I have never tried to withhold any information from the police, certainly nothing that would interfere with your inquiries into the murders of two men, one of whom was a respected teacher at my place of work."

"I hope not," Dodds continued, "because we will be obtaining a court order to grant us access to all of Speke Hill's records, both for the orphanage and the school, and we will without a doubt soon discover if you're being evasive with us."

"I'm sure that won't be necessary," Vera replied. "The headmaster has already given his permission for you to access the records and I provided your people with all the help I could on your previous visit."

"Yes, I'm sure you did," said Derek McLennan, "but you may have overlooked some detail that we may think important, even though you may not have been aware of its significance."

"Of course. I understand," said Vera, a little perturbed again as she thought of the police trawling through the records and finding the envelope containing the details of the four boys who'd attacked the girl behind the pavilion. Would they become suspicious at seeing what should have been a sealed envelope opened as she'd left it? Depending on circumstances, she knew she'd need to access the file room and place the documents in a new sealed envelope as she should have done when she'd found it, only to leave it in her excitement at her discovery of the contents.

McLennan and Dodds, despite sharing a belief that there was something 'off' about Vera Manvers, realised there was little point in pushing the interview any further. Yes, they'd confronted her at home and been very surprised to find her a very different woman from the one they'd expected, but that in itself wasn't reason to be particularly suspicious, but she'd seemed helpful and co-operative. If there was more to Vera Manvers, it would need further background investigation to reveal it. They certainly hadn't been able to ascertain any cause for them to think she was protecting Remington and Proctor, as D.I. Ross suspected.

Chapter 30

At the end of the day

Ross, tired and frustrated, was preparing to leave for the day. With most of the team still out pounding the streets or following up with their allotted lines of inquiry, he knew he'd catch up with everyone in the morning. He had one more thing to do however, before heading off and doing his best to switch off from work for a few hours. He'd acknowledged a phone call from D.C. Curtis a little earlier in which Curtis had given him the fourth name they'd been searching for, but there was little they could do about tracing the mystery man until the morning. A knock on his door heralded the arrival of Press Liaison Officer, George Thompson, who Ross felt might be able to assist in identifying not just the newly mentioned Luke, but also the other elder boy, Johnny.

"You look knackered," Thompson said as he took a seat in the visitor chair opposite Ross's desk. "You should go home, get some rest, carry on with all this in the morning."

"That's a pretty good assessment of my current condition, George," Ross replied with a wry grin. "You should be a detective."

"Ha, ha, very funny, Andy. I think I'll stick to what I do best, thanks. Speaking of which, how can I help you?"

"I have an idea, and you could maybe help us in identifying the two older boys who quite probably instigated everything while the boys were at Speke Hill. I still believe Remington and Proctor were nothing more than followers and the older lads were the ringleaders of this bloody horrendous perverted quartet."

"Okay, what do you want me to do?"

"Can you put out a new press release, George? I want to appeal to the public without them really knowing the extent of the crimes Remington and Proctor were involved in."

"Hang on," said Thompson. "I thought you had no evidence to suggest Proctor committed any crime?"

"We don't as yet, but I'm sure we'll find it, soon enough. Meanwhile, I want to put out a public appeal for anyone who knew Matthew Remington and Mark Proctor during their time at Speke Hill, to com forward with any information they can give us about their childhood. If anyone remembers them well, they might just be able to recall the names of the older lads they were knocking around with in their teens. If we can put surnames to Luke and John, we're well on our way to identifying two more potential victims for our killers. For all we know they're planning to hit one or both of the other men any time now, and I don't want another bloody and gutted corpse on my hands if I can avoid it."

"No problem," Thompson replied. "It's an ingenious idea actually, Andy. I can word it so that readers think they're assisting us in finding the killers, which they are of course, in a way, but mainly, they're helping you to identify two rapists and potential victims for the churchyard killers."

"You've got it, George. Can you do it by tomorrow?"

"Of course. I'll have it ready by the morning briefing for you if that's okay."

"You don't mind? It means I'm asking to stay and work while I'm swanning off home for the evening."

"Don't be silly, Andy. I can compose the new release while I'm sitting watching TV with my wife. She doesn't like me to talk and interrupt her while *Coronation Street's* on the box, anyway."

"You're a star, George. Tell Liz thanks for me for butting in on your evening."

"Thanks for what? I just said, she'll welcome the silence emanating from my armchair, so you're doing her the favour, not the other way round. She should be thanking you for giving her a completely George free half hour while she watches *The Street.*"

Andy Ross laughed, and after Thompson said goodnight and left his office, the D. I. rose from his desk, stretched his tired limbs and was soon following the Press Officer out of the building, looking forward to spending some quality time with Maria.

* * *

A few miles away, on a small estate of industrial units in the Garston area of the city, work had also come to an end for the day. Situated to the south of the city centre, Garston was in the midst of much urban redevelopment, with large areas of its old Victorian terraced housing being redeveloped and improved and modern housing replacing much of the old red brick back-to-backs. The area's claims to fame lay in having been the home at one time of singer Billy Fury and of Ray McFall, owner of the Cavern Club, who first booked *The Beatles.*

Garston also stands as a huge container port, independent of the Port of Liverpool, and is regarded as a separate port altogether. It was close to the container port that the small gathering of units stood not more than a quarter mile from the main complex.

John Selden pulled his rather battered old Audi 100 to a halt in the car park, outside one of the larger units on the estate. Most of the businesses had closed for the day and the only lights visible as evening drew closer and a slight mist crept in from the Mersey, were in the unit whose name was picked out in bright red lettering, against the corrugated grey metal walls of the building.

Selden looked up at the name, *A. J. Devereux & Son, Ships Chandlers, (Wholesale Only),* killed the engine of the Audi, switched off his side-lights and exited the car, being sure to lock it before walking the few yards to the door that was marked 'Office' and knocking firmly, the sound of his knocking seeming to echo and reverberate from within. Second later the door was opened from within and a hand reached through the smallest of gaps and Selden felt himself being pulled bodily into the building. Before he could speak a word, the door slammed shut and a hand reached past him and turned the key in the lock, trapping Selden inside the building.

"Bloody hell, Lucas, you almost scared me to death," he protested when he was released by the grasping hand and turned to see the man he'd been summoned to meet standing before him. Lucas, (Luke) Devereux, the 'son' in the company name, was the sole proprietor of the business. There'd never been an A.J. Devereux of course, the name being nothing more than a fabrication by Lucas aimed at giving his business an air of additional credibility, longevity and respectability. If anyone queried his ancestry, Lucas would play on his true past as an orphan made good, and sentiment always brought understanding at the pretence he'd set up to give his business a family feel to make up for the real family he'd been denied in his youth. Thankfully, there was nothing illegal in adopting such a practice, or his business ploy might have had a detrimental effect on his current plans to enter parliament, as Liverpool's latest political 'whizz-kid' after serving successfully on the local council for the previous five years. As things stood, Devereux had emerged as the narrow favourite to win a seat in parliament at the forthcoming by-election, brought on by the death of the sitting M.P. and now just one week away.

Business was doing well, thanks to his shrewd tactics of dealing wholesale only, and thus being able to order, if necessary, a ship's boiler for delivery direct to the customer, without needing the massive storage space other such businesses might require. His customers ranged from the individual owner of a Fleetwood trawler to a couple of smaller container shipping lines, always on the lookout for a cheap deal or a discount, which Devereux was prepared to give in order to expand future business opportunities. The burgeoning use of the internet for marketing opportunities had also opened up whole new vistas for his business. Things could only get better!

"Come in, sit down and fucking shut up whining," Devereux said, and Selden could smell the unmistakable aroma of whisky on his breath.

"What's wrong, Lucas?" asked an already jittery Selden, who'd been waiting to hear from Devereux since his return from Mykonos.

"Read that," said Devereux, sinking into his leather office chair behind a large and almost barren desk, and passing a small A5 sheet of paper into Selden's hand as he stood next to Devereux's desk.

Selden did as he was bidden and read the few words that had been pasted to the sheet of paper, letters cut from a newspaper like some old style ransom demand in a movie.

YOU WILL NEVER SIT IN PARLIAMENT, LUKE!

"You think this is from the killer, don't you?" Selden asked, his own hand shaking as he held the offending message.

"Of course it is," Devereux replied. "It's fucking obvious isn't it? Only people who knew me as a boy would call me Luke. Everyone calls me by my real first name nowadays. They intend to do away with me before the election, Johnny boy, but I won't just sit back and be an easy target for the murdering bastard."

"When did it arrive?"

"Today, of course, you fucking dimwit. You don't think I'd have sat on it for days without letting you know, do you?"

"But Lucas, It might not be from the killer. Maybe it's from some disgruntled voter or political opponent."

"Oh, for fuck's sake, get real Johnny. I know the police would probably say that if I reported it to them. They'd say politicians are always getting hate mail and stuff like that. If it had said, 'You're next to die' or something like that, they'd perhaps have taken it seriously, but this is just ambiguous enough, at least to the cops, not to constitute what they'd see as a valid threat to my life, but I know it's from whoever killed Matt and Mark, I just know it is."

"So, what can you, we, do?"

"I'm going to hire some muscle, Johnny boy. First thing tomorrow, I'm hiring a couple of bodyguards to be with me twenty four hours a day."

"Yeah, right, but where does that leave me?"

Devereux stood, walked to the small window that overlooked the car park, and turned to face Selden. At six foot three, Devereux stood well clear of Selden's five foot nine, but with Selden seated in the chair, and Devereux's blonde hair, highlighted by the fluorescent lighting in the room adding a rugged Nordic look to the man, he appeared much taller to Selden, far more imposing.

"You, Johnny? You don't think I'd desert my old mate, do you?"

"Er, well, what do you...?"

"You're moving in with me tomorrow, Johnny boy. Whoever this crazy bastard is, he'll find it a damn sight harder to get to either of us if we're both together. He can't get to us while we're at work, we're both businessmen, so if we stick together like glue outside of working hours, we should be safe, and if he dares try to come near either of us, the bodyguards will have him for sure."

"But Lucas, we can't stay together like that for the rest of our lives, man. It's okay for you. You've got people around you all day. As for being businessmen, you've got this place plus your council work. Me? Some businessman, with a massive fleet of two ice cream vans. I don't think *Mr. Speedy Cream* ranks anywhere near your bloody business empire, do you? Plus, I'm on the road nearly all day. I'm fucking easy prey out there on my own. We've got to hope the cops find out who it is and arrests them before he can get to us."

"Johnny, what did I tell you? We can't tell the cops a thing without incriminating ourselves. We have to handle this on our own."

"But, how can we stop whoever it is?"

"By setting a trap and catching the bastard ourselves and then making sure he never lives to tell the tale."

"You mean, kill him?"

"It's kill or be killed now, Johnny. The cops seem to think there might be two killers working together according to the press, so we might have two to dispose of. Look, if you're that nervous, go home now, pack a bag and come back to my place tonight. We'll talk strategy and work out how we're going to sort this out when the bastard decides to make a move. It's bloody obvious he, or they, want to get to me before you, so they can screw up my election campaign."

John Selden felt that Devereux's plan, if it could even be called a plan, had more holes in it than a leaky colander, but for the time being, he could think of nothing better. Lucas had always been the brains of their group, his own work as an ice cream salesman often helping by allowing him to trawl the streets and often identify potential targets for their attacks, but Selden himself had never been a decision maker. That had always been Luke's domain. He knew his limitations, and saw himself as a faithful lieutenant, able to organise the two younger men at Luke's direction as and when they needed to get together for a new 'mission' as Luke always called their attacks on their unsuspecting victims.

* * *

With new-found confidence, Vera Manvers made a phone call, and after five minutes talking to her murderous partner, she felt the thrill and exhilaration of the next kill beginning to course through her veins.

"We need to move quickly, Vera," he said. He'd got used to always addressing her by the Vera Manvers name, giving him less chance of any slip ups if he revealed her true identity. "That bastard, Devereux, he really thinks he's going to win a seat in the House of Commons. If only the people in his party and all his supporters knew what he'd done, they'd want to crucify him. I'd almost like to see him live, go to jail and let the prisoners inside subject him to the type of homosexual gang rape his pretty boy looks would attract, but once they knew he's a multiple rapist, I think they'd just do him in anyway, so I'd rather we had the pleasure of that little task."

"Yes," said Vera, "and anyway, we can still give him a real pain in the arse before we slit his throat, if you know what I mean."

The laughter that erupted from the other end of the line made Vera hold the phone away from her ear for a second until it subsided.

"Why, Vera Manvers," the man said at length, "I do believe you're suggesting a little sadistic pleasure wouldn't go amiss in dealing with Mr. Lucas Devereux.

"How did you guess?" she grinned as she spoke. "Was it something I said?" and the two of them collapsed into a short, joint paroxysm of laughter.

* * *

Neither of them could be bothered to cook, so Andy and Maria Ross settled for a Cantonese banquet meal from their local Chinese Take-away, while Izzie Drake and Peter Foster decided against visiting the cinema to see Toby McGuire starring in Spider Man, and enjoyed an evening of steamy sex at Foster's flat instead.

As the opening credits of *Coronation Street* rolled on the television in the home of P.L.O. George Thompson, his wife's attention riveted to the screen, Thompson instead sat making notes in preparation for his new press release as requested by Ross.

The lights in the office of A. J. Devereux & Son finally went off around the time the credits of *'The Street'* faded and Lucas Devereux stepped from the now darkened building, walking briskly across the car park to the space reserved for his sleek, black, classic, Jaguar XJ6. He'd sent Johnny Selden home a half hour earlier, and arranged to meet up with him at his city flat, overlooking Albert Dock, a little after eight.

With none of the other businesses on the estate working at night, the car park possessed a slightly eerie, ghost-like quality as the mist of another damp evening rolled in from the Irish Sea and up the Mersey Channel. Devereux shivered involuntarily and hurried to his car, which started first time, as always, and he quickly reached behind him and grabbed hold of the seat belt, pulling it forwards and clipping it into place.

As he reached the wide, double-gated entrance to the industrial estate, ready to pull out onto the encircling estate road which then led to the main road out of Garston, he checked in both directions, and seeing the road clear both ways, began to edge out onto the road. It was at that moment that Lucas Devereux felt the force of a rear-end collision that pitched him forward and just as quickly, back again as his seat belt did its job. Cursing, he looked in the rear view mirror, to see the front of a large white van which must have followed him from the car park. The driver, probably half asleep, had shunted his van smack into the gleaming rear of Devereux's pride and joy, and anger overtook his other emotions as he almost flung himself from the car and ran to the rear to assess the damage.

"What the hell were you doing?" he shouted in the direction of the van. "Couldn't you see me right there in front of you?"

Instead of receiving a reply, Devereux instead watched incredulously as the driver's door of the Transit van slowly opened and a pair of very shapely, totally feminine, stockinged legs appeared, followed by the rest of an extremely good looking woman, her blonde hair partially obscuring her face. Devereux's attention was totally fixed on the figure before him as she turned to face him and smiled an enigmatic, knowing smile at the exact instant a man stepped up behind Devereux and the last thing he felt before collapsing to the ground was the short, sharp jab of the hypodermic needle containing a fast acting sedative that was thrust into his neck by the man who'd crept up silently behind him from his hiding place just outside the gates, while his attention was fixed on the legs and the alluring figure of the woman from the van.

Chapter 31

Devereux's Demise

The Stygian blackness that filled the mind of Lucas Devereux slowly gave way to a feeling of general nausea and restricted movement. He felt as if he was in some kind of box, and panic gripped his fevered mind as the thought he might be in a coffin, buried alive, took hold of his thoughts, only to be dispelled a minute or two later as his senses returned sufficiently for him to ascertain that he was tied hand and foot, secured with plastic ties and his eyes, gradually focussing once more, just managed to tell him he was in a darkened room with a concrete floor on which he was lying sideways, on his right, a garage perhaps, or a warehouse of some kind? His mouth felt strange; as though his lips were prised open and he tried, but was unable to speak or scream or do anything but make strange, incoherent noises. He'd been rendered silent by a ball gag.

The realisation suddenly dawned on him that he was naked. Naked and as vulnerable as a new born baby. Waves of panic and nausea again gripped Lucas Devereux as he realised his plans for self-preservation had been laid too late. He had no doubts he was in the hands of the killer or killers of Matthew Remington and Mark Proctor. Struggling as much as he could, he attempted to free himself but quickly realised it was hopeless. Not only were his hands and feet immobilised by the plastic ties, but a long length of something, thin rope he assumed, kept him in a hog-tied position, hand behind him and legs bent backwards at a grossly uncomfortable angle.

Despite the ball gag, Lucas attempted to shout, scream, make any kind of sound to try and call for help, all to no avail. It was useless, hopeless and as the fear of his situation took hold of his almost fully conscious mind, Devereux shivered in trepidation as he thought of the press reports on the deaths of his friends. They hadn't revealed a lot, but what they had been able to report sounded horrific enough. He had to hope his quick wits and silver tongue might still find a way out of this situation. *Money, yes,* he thought. *Maybe I can buy my way out of here.*

A strange sound reached his ears. Though clearing, his mind was still slightly befuddled and he couldn't work out what it was. Then he knew. It could only be the sound of old, rusted iron gates swinging open. The metallic grating was followed by the unmistakable sound of stiletto heels tottering down the series of steps that led to his cold, grim place of incarceration.

What he couldn't see or hear were the soft, almost silent footfalls of the man in rubber boots who followed the woman down the steps. The sound of a switch being thrown followed and the room was bathed in the soft light of a single, low wattage light bulb, suspended from a fitting in the centre of the ceiling.

"Well, hello, pretty boy," the woman spoke mockingly as she walked up to and stood directly over Lucas Devereux, who tried to look up but could do more than stare at her legs and feet, no more than twelve inches from his face.

"Oh, I don't think he looks so pretty now, do you?" said the unknown man whose voice startled Lucas, who had remained unaware of his presence until that moment. "Do you feel like a pretty boy, Luke?"

"Aw, he can't speak," the woman mocked. "He's got a big red ball gag stuck in his mouth, haven't you, Luke?"

"Bet you've used a few of those in the past eh, Lukey baby?" the man added.

Lucas struggled impotently against his bonds, and then, without warning, strong hands grabbed him by the arm and leg and rolled him over. Now, Lucas could see where he was. They had brought him to a crypt, probably underground, judging from the steps, and at least two stone coffins stood before his eyes. The man now cut the rope that joined his arms and legs, and forced him into a sitting position and the fear rose in the naked man again. Resting on one of the coffins was a selection of cutting and sawing tools whose use Lucas could only imagine at, increasing his growing terror.

"We've got such plans for you, Luke," the woman said. "You're going to be so sorry for the things you've done, Lucas. We're going to make sure you go to hell before morning, but in the meantime, you're going to suffer as you've never suffered before."

A gurgling sound came from behind the ball gag, an incoherent mumbling that did no more than produce a stream of spittle that ran down Luke's chin.

"You like causing pain and fear, don't you?" the man asked, not expecting an answer of course. "We're here to show you what it's like to be on the receiving end for a change."

"Oh look, he's wriggling with excitement," Vera said, as he struggled vainly against his bonds.

"You like scaring and raping young girls and women, don't you, you piece of scum? It's your turn now," the man added.

Suddenly, the woman reached into a handbag that stood on the nearest coffin lid and lifted out a small six by four inch photograph of a young woman, little more than a girl, that she held down to Lucas's facial level.

"Remember her?"

He shook his head, vigorously.

"No, you wouldn't would you, you bastard? Too many years ago. How many have there been since then, I wonder? You ruined her life, Lucas bloody Devereux, you and your twisted little cronies. Her name was Brenda Gillespie. You gang raped her, left her for dead and never gave her another thought, you bastards. Well, she's had to live with the results of what you did to her ever since, and so have we. She was, and still is my little sister, and he," she gestured towards the man, who Lucas couldn't see properly because of the cowled hood he wore that hid most of his face, "he was going to marry her, until you bastards caused a total mental breakdown that she's still living with, every day of her fucking life, living like a vegetable in a wheelchair, unable to speak, move or do anything for herself because the horror of what you did simply destroyed her. We're here to exact revenge for my sister, his fiancé, and all the other poor girls you've terrorised over the years."

Devereux knew now that he had no chance of leaving the crypt alive. All his plans, all his dreams for the future were about to end in this cold, dank place, but, he thought, *what horrors are they going to inflict on me before they let me die?*

"Scared, are you, Devereux?" the woman asked, not requiring an answer. "You should be. Remington went quickly, too quickly really, but we hadn't refined our means of disposing of you all at that point. Proctor was a little more fun. We made him wait longer for the final release of death. He screamed his lungs out, but with the gag in place, he couldn't exactly make himself heard. Of course, the papers haven't told the whole story, because the police wouldn't tell them everything. The only thing I found unsatisfying about the two of them was that it's not a lot of fun slicing off a limp, dead penis from a corpse before stuffing it down their throats."

A look of pure terror spread across Lucas Devereux's face, and without warning, he lost control of his bladder, the fear overcoming any hope he had of arresting the flow.

"Oh, what a dirty boy you are, Luke. We'll have to punish you for that as well, won't we? And don't worry, we'll find a way to make your dick stand up before we cut it off, won't we?" she asked the man who stood a few feet behind her, who simply laughed quietly and nodded his head. "Poor Brenda can't control her bladder either. She has to wear a bloody bag to catch it in. Would you like a bag, Luke?" Vera added.

Devereux shook his head vigorously, still making incoherent sounds from behind the gag. The woman stood so close in front of him, he couldn't help looking up and all he could see was her legs, slightly apart, encased in a black mini skirt, and he could see as far as her stocking tops, and he just knew she was deliberately flaunting herself before him. She suddenly walked away and the man took her place, looking down at the shivering man, whose body was now wracked with paroxysms of fear.

"You're nothing but a waste of a heart and soul, Devereux," the man said, with a voice so flat in intonation that Devereux felt his tormentor to be completely devoid of emotion, and he knew that even if he was allowed to speak, no offer of money was likely to sway him or incite him to deviate from his intentions, which Luke knew were simply to cause him as much pain as possible before ending his life.

"I'm going to take great pleasure in watching you die and sending you to Hell, where I hope Satan decides you're too evil even to dwell there, and sends you to purgatory, where what's left of your soul will be tormented by demons for eternity. Come on Vera, we've wasted enough time on this piece of scum. Let's get started."

Lucas Devereux felt himself being lifted up by his wrists and the man suddenly spun him round and then kicked him behind he knees, causing him to pitch forward and land heavily on his knees on the concrete floor.

"In case you're wondering," the man said, his voice still flat and emotionless, you're in a crypt, Lucas, a fitting place for what we intend, don't you think? The inhabitants are long dead and the family who originally owned it have long since died out, so I doubt anyone will mind us using it. If it wasn't for the gag, you could scream the place down and no one would hear you. Do you know how long you've been out? Oh, I forgot, you don't have a watch do you? We removed it with your clothes. Time has no meaning for you any more, apart from the length of time it's going to take for you to die. Clothes, watch, money, all the trappings of wealth, they've all gone now, and you won't be needing them any longer will you?"

Devereux tried his hardest to voice the word, "please" through the gag, but if the man realised what he was saying, he took no notice whatsoever.

"Let's get him up," the man said to Vera, and Devereux couldn't help looking upwards where, to his horror, he saw what had to be a newly added butcher's hook affixed to the ceiling.

The woman joined the man in forcing Devereux to take the few steps that placed him directly under the hook. The man now walked to the side of the room, and took hold of a length of rope which he quickly attached to the butcher's hook by standing on a small, two-step stepladder. Next, a pair of manacles were attached to Devereux's wrists, replacing the plastic cable ties and together, the rope threaded through them, and the man and woman hoisted the bound man up until his feet were barely touching the floor. They were ready to begin.

* * *

Two hours later, the man and woman stepped back to examine their handiwork. Lucas Devereux was still alive, but only just. Thanks to their study of various methods of torture and of prolonging the victim's life during the process, the pair had managed to inflict such pain on the now pitiful man who hung, suspended from the butcher's hook that he had reached a point where death would come as a welcome release to him. But, they hadn't finished with him yet.

His body was bleeding in multiple places, his chest, belly and back a crazy patchwork of numerous knife wounds, all painful but designed to be non-fatal. Most painful by far had been the slicing through of Devereux's Achilles tendons, leaving his feet useless, and unable to ever support his body again, even if given the opportunity. Blood pooled all around his dangling body and his earlier attempts at screaming had reduced to a series of long, pathetic and pitiful sobs, though pity was the last thing on the minds of his tormentors.

"Do you want to know what triggered all this, at this moment in time, Luke?" Vera suddenly asked. Without waiting for an answer she knew he couldn't give, she went on:

"Your mate, Remington. He couldn't stop himself could he? Wouldn't even wait for you to come up with a new target for your perverted lust, would he? When he targeted a young teenage girl who went to a local church, and she ended up having an abortion, then couldn't live with what she'd done, and she killed herself, we decided the time had come to put our plan into operation. We'd wanted to do it for years, but it had always been theoretical, and then we snapped after that young kid died, because of you, Remington and all your kind. When you're gone, it'll be Johnny's turn, but maybe we'll just sit back and watch him fall to pieces with fear, maybe turn himself in to the police to save his miserable hide, but we all know what they'd do to him in prison, don't we? I think it best if we send him on to join you and your mates in hell, don't you?"

"You're wasting your breath," the hooded man said from somewhere to the rear of Devereux. "Let's finish this."

"Right," Vera replied, as she walked across to the stone coffin and through his tear stained eyes Devereux saw her pick up a large, black sex toy. He had an idea what she intended and tried hard to shake his head in panic.

"Rape, Lukey baby, terrible thing, isn't it? Oh, sorry, I forgot, you like raping young girls and women, don't you? Forcing yourself onto them, into them, violating their most private, intimate places. Ever wondered what it feels like to suffer that kind of violation? No? Well, before you die, we want you to know a little of what it fells like."

Panic gripped Lucas Devereux as Vera walked behind him, pulled his buttocks apart and despite the gag, he screamed at last as the sex toy was rammed into him, stretching and tearing as Vera laughed at his agony and torment. The man stood back, watching dispassionately until she'd had enough of the game and walked around to face the man who'd been the prime focus of her hatred for so long.

"Had enough, Luke? I'm getting tired of this now. Oh look, he's got all excited."

Lucas couldn't help it. It had been totally involuntary, but his bleeding, weakened body was actually showing signs of arousal.

"Perfect," said Vera as she moved in closer, a long gleaming surgical knife in her right hand, at the same time as the man moved behind Luke and released the ball gag allowing hours of pent up agony to escape Luke's lips in what became little more than a loud agonised gasp, which grew to a scream once again as Vera took hold of his manhood with one hand and the blade flashed once, emasculating him in one swift brutal slashing movement.

Blood seemed to flow everywhere from the gaping wound, and now, knowing their victim couldn't last much longer, the pair exchanged a look that said the time had come.

Without further hesitation, the hooded man removed another blade from a pocket in his hooded top and grabbed hold of Luke's head, pulling it back sharply, exposing his throat. One slash, and Lucas Devereux saw the blood spurting in a fierce jet from his throat as he gurgled and began to choke on his own life-blood.

Before death took him, however he had just enough life left in him to feel the final cut as his belly was opened up, and Vera herself completed the job of disembowelment.

It was over. Lucas Devereux, parliamentary election candidate, respected local businessman and rapist of at least twenty women had been sent on his final journey to the realm of the damned.

Vera and the hooded man quickly took the body down from the butcher's hook and within half an hour, the remains of Lucas Devereux were in place, draped suggestively, naked, legs apart and bent over a randomly selected tombstone in the graveyard above. Vera herself added the final touch by pushing the amputated penis of her victim into his mouth and forcing it as far as possible into his throat. It was their 'signature' after all.

Chapter 32

A Place to Die

The discovery of the body of Lucas Devereux was made just after seven-thirty a.m. by Tom, the husband of Iris Redding. He'd dropped his wife at the front of the manse before driving around back, parking his car and making his way towards the graveyard's tool shed, where he stored the lawn mower and other tools needed to ensure the grassed areas, graves and pathways of St. Luke's remained as pristine as possible.

Tom Redding had the presence of mind to leave the church grounds for the few minutes it took for him to walk down the lane to the nearest public call box where he dialled 999 and summoned the emergency services. He'd not wanted to upset his wife by announcing his grim discovery and making the emergency call whilst trying to answer the barrage of questions he knew he'd face from Iris and the two priests, Fathers Byrne and Willis.

After entering through the kitchen door, he'd asked his wife to summon the priests and he'd informed them of his discovery. Father Byrne seemed to turn almost parchment-white with shock, though the younger priest, Father Willis, appeared to Tom to be made of sterner stuff, and offered to wait outside with Tom until the police arrived.

As soon as the call was made for the duty medical examiner to attend the scene, Doctor Vicky Strauss faced a minor dilemma. The newest member of Dr. William Nugent's team, twenty-eight year old Vicky was due to finish her tour of duty at eight a.m. Her watch read seven forty, and she knew Nugent would be arriving in the next ten to fifteen minutes and would want to attend the scene, having responded to the earlier churchyard murders, but she was equally aware the police would want an immediate response from their department. Vicky gathered her bag, and on her way out, left a message for Nugent with Peter Foster, who'd just arrived to begin his day shift. She had no doubt Nugent would arrive on the scene within a few minutes of her own arrival, but guessed correctly that a prompt response was not only necessary but vital. As she climbed into her car and pulled away from the car park, she couldn't have been aware just how vital!

Mere minutes after arriving at headquarters, Ross was informed by D.C.I. Porteous of the latest murder. He'd only just reached his office and certainly hadn't been prepared for another gruesome killing to be dropped in his lap this morning.

"St. Luke's, at Woolton?"

Ross could scarcely believe it.

"Exactly," said Porteous. "Home of your friend, Father Gerald Byrne, no less."

"Oh, shit," was all Ross could say, but Porteous wasn't finished.

"It gets worse, Andy. The two uniforms who responded both recognised the victim as soon as they saw him. It's Lucas Devereux."

"The councillor?"

"Councillor and would-be local Member of Parliament. Let's not waste time. I saw Drake getting out of her car from my window. She'll doubtless be here any second. You and she get over there as fast as you can. I'll deal with things here."

"Right sir. The team..."

"I'll see to things here. Who do you want to join you over there?"

"Thanks sir. Send Gable and McLennan. He might throw up but he's a good detective. Any more is useless based on the lack of evidence at previous crime scenes. Can you send Curtis and Dodds to check out

Devereux's home? I remember reading somewhere that he was single and never married."

"I'll see to it, and arrange a few uniforms to join you to conduct house-to-house inquiries and ensure the crime scene remains secure. You do realise this one is going to pull a whole load of heat down on us, don't you, Andy?"

"Yes, sir, but not as much heat as when we reveal Devereux was part of a rape gang who've escaped detection for years. We just found out the first names of the last member yesterday, and we just needed a surname. I think our killers have given it to us. The name we got was Luke, and I'll bet my pension that Lucas Devereux was known as Luke to his pals."

Drake walked in at that moment and before Porteous could say another word, Ross took her by the arm, turned her round and marched her right back out of the squad room.

"Don't ask," he said in reply to her look of shock. "I'll explain on the way."

* * *

Doctor Vicky Strauss had just conducted a preliminary examination of the body. Miles Booker's Crime Scene Unit was on the scene and Andy Ross and Izzie Drake arrived just ahead of the car containing William Nugent and Francis Lees.

The new arrivals quickly made their way to the grave where Devereux's remains were still displayed somewhat lewdly in the position he'd been found by Tom Redding.

"Fucking hell!" Ross was appalled at the sight.

"Look at the number of wounds, sir," Drake said, as yet only able to see the rear of the corpse, and still to be further shocked when she took in the frontal view.

"Inspector Ross," Strauss approached the detectives quickly, "Vicky Strauss, duty Medical Examiner."

"Hello Doctor," Ross replied. "I kind of expected Dr. Nugent to be here, somehow."

"And so I am, Laddie," came a booming voice from behind him, as William Nugent and his assistant Lees came thundering down the path towards them.

"What do we have, Victoria?" said the pathologist, ignoring the detectives at that point.

"Well, Doctor," she began. "The body was clearly dumped here. There's not enough blood present for this to be the site of the murder."

"But hang on," Ross interrupted. "The previous killings all took place in the churchyards."

"Aye, well, Victoria here says otherwise and that'll do for me."

"She's right, sir," said Miles Booker as he joined the small but growing gathering. "He's been carefully placed in that position, quite deliberately, I'd say, to make a point, or to tell us something."

"I'd agree with your last point, definitely, Miles," Ross answered as he moved closer to get a better look at the corpse. Nugent and Strauss closed in on the scene at the same time, while Izzie Drake swerved off to one side to quickly search the immediate surrounding area for any clues or trace evidence.

Despite having been witness to the appalling cruelty inflicted on the previous two victims, Ross couldn't help but feel the killers had taken things a step further with the murder of Lucas Devereux. Even at this early stage, he could see there were differences between this and the previous killings.

This was confirmed soon afterwards when Christine Bland arrived in the company of Sam Gable and Derek McLennan, the profiler having just arrived at headquarters as they were leaving to join Ross and Drake, and thereby hitching a ride to the scene with them.

"I think they're devolving," she said quietly to Ross after taking in the scene, and walking around the body which was still being scrutinised by both pathologists and Miles Booker, the senior Scenes of Crimes officer. They had raised the body sufficiently to make a quick examination of the front of Devereux's remains, and had been horrified at the proliferation of wounds present.

"Devolving?" a puzzled Ross repeated the word.

"Yes, it's a word they use a lot in the States. Basically it means our killers are now so caught up in their bloodlust that they're beginning to take risks, becoming sloppy. Whereas the first two murders gave the impression of meticulous and orderly planning, everything here hints at a level of sadism not displayed in the first two kills, and the complete change in methodology makes me believe they're essentially heading down a path of eventual self-destruction."

"Do you mean you think they're suicidal?"

"No, I'm sorry if I gave that impression. What I meant was they are now not doing things as carefully as before. Look at the facts. Previously, they left no trace evidence, and before you say you haven't found any here yet, I think you will do. The wounds on the body indicate not only a degree of sadism and, dare I say it, torture, over a period of time, and the fact that the murder took place not here in the graveyard, but elsewhere marks a distinct change in their method. There's a glaring indicator here that we're most definitely dealing with two very different personalities."

"Please, go on. What do you mean by that last remark?"

"It's like a pendulum has swung from one side to the other," she said. "Previously, I think the dominant one in this partnership, who I've always believed to be the male, was in charge, keeping them on track according to some well laid plan. This time, I think the woman somehow imposed herself on this murder and wrested control from the man, who was quite probably appalled at the way she carried out Devereux's torture and eventual murder."

"Why would he be appalled?" Ross asked. "He's already killed twice and was obviously intending that Devereux should die anyway."

"Ah yes," said Bland, "but I don't think he intended things to go this far. Did you see the damage around the man's anus?"

"Hard to miss, really," said Ross disgustedly.

"I think you'll find that was done by the woman and that could be their first big mistake."

"How so?" Ross was intrigued now.

"Because I now believe with a degree of certainty that the woman is taking a form of revenge for a very personal reason. Either she, or another female, very close to her, was the victim of an attack by your team of rapists, Inspector. It may be a daughter, a sister, maybe even a mother, but your answer lies in a previous and possibly unprosecuted rape from the past."

"Wow, that's a lot to glean from a quick glance at the scene," said Ross.

"It's my job, remember," Bland replied.

"I hope you're right, about them devolving," said Ross as he heard the voice of Izzie Drake calling to him. Looking up, he saw her standing about thirty yards away, next to an old, grotesque looking mausoleum, a crypt of some kind that looked to be as old as the church itself.

Ross summoned Sam Gable and Derek McLennan to join him. This time, McLennan had managed to control his stomach and felt rather proud of himself for not being sick at the scene.

Izzie Drake, standing close to the old crypt, waited until the three others joined her and then, without wasting a second, pointed to the old padlock on the iron gates to the crypt.

"Sir, you have to look closely, but if you get up close, you can see that this old padlock has been sawn through. It would have needed a damn good hacksaw or something similar to cut through the hasp on the old padlock, and whoever did it needed time to tackle the job. And that's not all," she said, as she bent close to the ground in the slightly overgrown grass that had sprouted up around the walls of the old crypt.

"Oh, my god, is that what I think it is?" Sam Gable asked, turning a little green at the gills as she and the others bent down to examine what Drake had indicated.

"A piece of intestine, I think, yes," said Drake as Ross waved across the graveyard for Miles Booker to join them.

"You might want to bring a couple of your team over here, Miles," said Ross as Booker carried out a tentative examination of the padlock and the small but significant piece of human remains that lay in the grass beside the entrance to the crypt.

The iron gates creaked ominously, like the entrance to the gates of hell, or maybe Castle Dracula, Derek McLennan thought. In the gloom that lay within the entrance to the crypt, Booker turned on a powerful halogen-beamed torch that instantly illuminated their surroundings. Five steps led down into the depths of the crypt, and before taking even one step into the darkness below they all smelled it, the sweet, cloying, coppery smell of blood, and Derek McLennan prayed he wouldn't let himself down by throwing up yet again.

"Oh, shit, in the name of God, look at this place," said Booker as his torch beam swung around the main body of the crypt.

The detectives stood, staring incredulously as the scene played out in the light of the torch, like a surreal and horrific old-fashioned flickering silent movie, although this one was in full colour and accompanied by the stench of death.

"Wait," said Ross as the torchlight indicated a light switch on the wall at the bottom of the old concrete steps. He quickly flicked the switch, and the crypt was illuminated by the glow from the single overhead bulb in addition to the swaying beam of Booker's torch, which he kept switched on in order to highlight the scene as they knew they were literally walking in a sea of evidence.

Derek McLennan threw a hand over his mouth as he gagged at the sight that assaulted their eyes. Ross heard the sounds emanating from Derek's throat and shouted, "Outside, Derek, right now."

McLennan turned and ran up the steps and out into the daylight, where somehow, he managed to control the gag reflex and much to his surprise, his breakfast remained in place in his stomach. Of course, he knew the boss had sent him out not just for his own benefit, but because he feared McLennan would contaminate what was now clearly the scene of Devereux's murder down there in the depths of someone's family mausoleum.

* * *

The floor of the crypt resembled that of a nineteenth century slaughterhouse. The blood from the multiple wounds inflicted on Lucas Devereux's body had stained the concrete floor a deep, dark red. The walls literally dripped with blood spatter, presumably, Ross thought, from the cutting of the man's throat, with a massive stain spreading from a lump of tissue on the floor, a large part of the man's intestines, the rest having been left attached to the corpse. The smell was terrible and it was all those present could do to prevent themselves joining Derek McLennan outside in the fresh air. Ross's eyes, and those of Drake and Booker, were drawn inexorably to the butcher's hook dangling from the ceiling. They could only imagine the suffering that must have been inflicted on Devereux as he hung from that vicious looking hook.

Sam Gable was busily taking notes, writing down the tiniest detail of everything she saw in that terrible place. It came to Ross that the fervent scratching of her pen of the paper on her notepad was probably her way of tuning out a little from the horrific sights and smells of the crypt.

"They didn't find this place by accident," Ross observed, after taking a few seconds to gather his thoughts.

"You're right," said Miles Booker. "That hook wasn't part of the original design of the crypt, that's for sure. It looks new. Someone planned this well. They were ready for him. This was their combined bloody torture and execution chamber."

Booker's two crime scene technicians were by now busily photographing the room from every angle and noting down measurements of every splash of blood, and much more.

"What about the light switch, sir?" said Drake. "Surely crypts weren't built with electric light built-in whenever this one was built."

"Not originally, but the last burial interred in here was fifteen years ago, I looked before we entered," said Booker. "It's possible the family arranged it for some reason. The switch and wiring look old enough."

"But the point remains, someone knew about this place, and I want to know who," said Ross. "I'll leave you and your lads to examine this place while we go and have a word or two with Father Byrne."

"Thanks for nothing," Booker grimaced at Ross.

"Any time, Miles," he smiled a wry smile at the Crime Scenes boss before leading Izzie out of the room of death.

Chapter 33

Overkill

"Something's not right with this one," Ross spoke quietly. "It just doesn't stack up. Don't ask me why, but I think the killers have slipped up and we just need to work out how and where."

"Your instincts are usually on the button, sir," Drake acknowledged. "What are you thinking?"

"So far, the killers have been meticulous in their planning, leaving nothing to chance. This is so sloppy, there's a sense of overkill about it. I think we're going to end up with more clues than we've had previously. It's as if they want to be caught, as if they're challenging us to work it out."

"But if what the landlord at *The Belerophon* told Curtis is correct, there's still the matter of the one called John to account for," said Drake with a slight look of puzzlement on her face.

"Maybe he's not as important to them as Devereux."

"Or maybe they knew Devereux would be harder to get to if he won a seat in parliament," Drake hypothesised.

"A very good point, Izzie," Ross agreed. "Tell you what, Izzie," Ross said in a quick change of mind, "while we go and have another chat with the pathologists up top, send Sam and Derek to begin talking to the priests and Mr. and Mrs. Redding. Make sure they talk to them one at a time. We'll catch up to them as soon as we're finished out here."

Drake left the crypt, leaving Ross, Booker and his technicians in the bone-chilling atmosphere of the murder site.

* * *

"Just awful," Nugent concluded after Ross questioned him and tried to pin him down to a preliminary determination of cause of death.

"You can't be more precise?" Ross pressed the pathologist.

"Inspector, I doubt we'll be able to be more precise even once we get the remains back to the mortuary. The wound to the neck and the one to the abdomen would both have been sufficient to cause almost instantaneous death, and it will be almost impossible to determine which came first."

"Either way, you're looking at two very sick killers," Vicky Strauss added from her place, kneeling on the ground beside the corpse, which had by now been removed from its previous obscenely grotesque position and was now laid respectfully on a black groundsheet, ready to be transferred to a body bag for transportation to the mortuary. Strauss was cataloguing the most serious injuries, as Francis Lees' camera continued to click away in the background as he photographed not only the corpse, but every inch of the scene around the grave where it had been deposited.

"We know that, already, Doctor Strauss," Ross replied, and then asked, "Any particular reason why you should say that, bearing that in mind?"

"Most of the injuries are superficial, designed to cause pain without being lethal," Strauss said. "But, as far as I'm aware, a lot of the injuries inflicted on your previous victims were inflicted post-mortem, right?"

"That's correct. So you're saying there's a significant difference here?"

"I believe so, Inspector. We should be able to determine it for sure at autopsy, and there's one other thing."

"Go on, what it is it?"

William Nugent took up the story from his junior doctor.

"The first two victims, they had their manhood cut off post-mortem before having them stuffed in their mouths. Victoria found something disturbing in this case."

Drake looked horrified as she asked, "You don't mean they…"

"Yes, they did," Nugent replied. "They must have somehow made sure Devereux was sexually turned on before they cut his penis off, Sergeant Drake."

"You can tell that from looking at it?"

"Of course we can. It's still erect, exactly as it was when they sliced it from his living, breathing body."

Drake almost turned green at the pathologist's revelation.

"They really wanted to make the poor bastard suffer, for sure," Ross said.

* * *

Devereux's body had been sealed in a body bag and removed to the mortuary by the time Ross and Drake walked the short distance to the house where Sam Gable and Derek McLennan had begun interviewing Fathers Byrne and Willis and the housekeeper and her husband.

Miles Booker's forensic team were going over the entire scene, above and below ground in a meticulous search for the smallest piece of trace evidence that could assist the investigation, while the uniformed officers promised by D.C.I. Porteous had arrived and been sent to conduct house-to-house inquiries in the area, though Ross held out little hope they'd discover anything of use.

It lurked in the back of Ross's mind that in some way, the killings were inextricably linked either to the recent arrival of Father Gerald Byrne, who never seemed far from the hub of the investigation, or to Byrne's time at Speke Hill so many years before and yet, he found it difficult to believe a direct involvement by Byrne in the horrendous series of murders. Though not an overly religious man, Andy Ross just couldn't imagine Byrne as a killer.

Meanwhile, back at headquarters, based on a vague suspicion voiced to him by Tony Curtis after his and Derek McLennan's interview the previous day, Paul Ferris and his trusty computer were on the verge of the breakthrough Ross had been waiting for. For now though, he was speculating, and it would take a little time to turn that speculation into facts that the inspector could use to his advantage in tracking the killers of three men.

Chapter 34

Beginning of the End

"Are you absolutely sure about this?" D.C. Tony Curtis could hardly contain his excitement as he read the information that Paul Ferris had just printed out.

"Of course I'm sure," Ferris replied. "Looks like you and Derek were bang on in your estimation of the Manvers woman. Nothing about her adds up at all. She's what I'd call a real enigma."

"Great," said Curtis. "This stuff is like dynamite. The boss was wrong about her motives, obviously, but he was right to be suspicious of her. You don't think he'll be mad at me and Derek for proving him wrong do you?"

"Don't be bloody stupid, Tony. If it helps the case move closer to a solution, he'll be over the bloody moon and might even recommend the pair of you for a commendation."

"You think so?"

"Well, that's maybe going a bit too far, but he'll be bloody pleased with you both, that's a certainty."

"Talk me through it one more time, Paul. Save me having to read it all again. Then I'd better call the boss."

Ferris did as Curtis asked.

Meanwhile, Ross had moved on to interviewing the residents at St. Luke's. Gable and McLennan had done well but hadn't got as far as talking to the priests yet. He'd read through Gable's notes following her talk with Iris Redding and McLennan's account of Tom Redding's rendering of his discovery of the body. While husband and wife were helpful and cooperative, neither statement threw much light on the case. Neither of them spent their nights at the manse and could throw no light on how or why Devereux came to be found in the crypt. Tom Redding's statement only contained one piece of useful information. Father Byrne's predecessor, the late Father O'Hanlon, had once informed Tom that he'd installed the lighting in 'the old Greasby crypt' as he'd described it with the permission of the family's executors after the passing of the last member of the family. It appeared the crypt was the oldest of its kind in St. Luke's graveyard, and the best preserved too. With over twenty members of the Greasby family interred there, Father O'Hanlon wanted to carry out a personal investigation into the history of what he'd told Tom were an 'ordinary everyday merchant class' Liverpool family. According to O'Hanlon, the family were pretty much just a step above working class, and by no means wealthy, but their faith in God and the Church had been an example to others over the years. There were many old Latin inscriptions on the walls of the crypt itself as well as on the sides and tops of the stone coffins interred within the underground family vault. With no natural light present down there, O'Hanlon would have struggled, even with a torch, to make out some of the oldest, faded inscriptions, with which he hoped to assemble a chronicle of the family's faith and devotion through the generations. By so doing, he'd informed Tom as the gardener was working the grounds around the crypt one day; he hoped to bring some of the Greasby family values to his current day parishioners and congregation. Sadly, Tom had said in his statement, the old priest died before he could complete his task. At least, Ross thought, the mystery of the electric light in the crypt had been satisfactorily explained.

Ross and Drake were jointly interviewing Father Byrne. The man was a definite enigma. *What the hell is his connection to the murders?* Ross wondered for about the hundredth time.

"Father Byrne, don't you find it rather coincidental that you, or your name at least, appears to rise to the surface every time one of these murders takes place?" Ross asked the priest, whose face betrayed nothing but sadness and shock at what had taken place in his own churchyard, so close to his own home.

"I admit it's all rather suggestive, Inspector Ross, but, truthfully, I cannot say just why these terrible murders have begun since my return to Liverpool, or why I seem to be getting dragged into your investigation somehow. I hope you're not suggesting I may have some connection to these terrible crimes?"

"I'm suggesting nothing, Father, but I'm not a great believer in coincidences, and there do seem to be rather a lot of them springing up around your name, don't you think?"

"I'm sorry, Inspector. In this case I believe the thinking part of it is all down to you. I can offer no satisfactory explanation other than that of the one thing you appear to reject, and that is a terrible liturgy of awful coincidences. I'm shocked and appalled at what's taken place here at St. Luke's. Why my church was chosen, I really don't know."

"Oh, we can at least give you an answer to that one, Father," said Drake.

"You can, Sergeant?"

"Yes. Apparently it may be linked to a prayer."

"A prayer? But in the name of God, how?"

Drake began slowly reciting, "Matthew, Mark, Luke and John..."

Byrne took up the words, "Bless the bed that I lie on. Yes, it's an old, simple children's prayer, but what the heck has it do with these horrendous murders?"

Drake explained how the landlord at *The Belerophon* had used the four apostles names to describe the four men they assumed to be the targets of the killers. That being the case, it seemed logical that in some twisted way, the killers also thought of them in that way and were using churches bearing the men's own names as killing grounds for their victims.

"But, the man out there was Lucas, you said, not Luke," said Byrne.

"But he was apparently known as Luke to his friends, Father," Ross enlightened the priest.

"Oh, I see. So, what happens now, Inspector?"

At that point in the interview, Ross's mobile phone began to ring.

Excusing himself, Ross stood up and walked across to stand near the window, looking out onto the well-tended garden beyond the glass.

"Ross," he said into the phone, irritation in his voice at being interrupted.

"It's Curtis, sir," the voice that spoke replied.

"This had better be important," Ross said.

"Oh, I think it is, sir. It's about the Manvers woman."

"Go on then, Curtis, and make it quick."

"She's a fake sir. Vera Manvers, the real one, died as a baby in a house fire years ago, and she was the only Vera Manvers born in Liverpool in the last hundred years according to Ferris, who's looked it up. Anyway, sir, our Vera Manvers suddenly appeared about five years ago, and Ferris has traced a deed poll document which shows her birth name to have been Ruth Gillespie."

"You've got my full attention, Tony. Keep going, lad."

"Well, sir, I just can't see how she got the job at Speke Hill, because she doesn't appear to have any previous work records that we can locate, even as Ruth Gillespie."

"Okay, Tony, this is all very interesting and I must admit, a little suspicious, but I can sense you're holding something back. You and Derek have managed to connect her to the case, haven't you?"

"To be fair sir, it's more thanks to Paul Ferris's digging around in the records. Fifteen years ago, a young girl by the name of Brenda Gillespie was gang raped while walking home one night with her boyfriend. She was later able to identify the boyfriend as being one of her attackers. His name was Matthew Remington."

"Bloody hell. Go on, Curtis, go on."

"Right sir. The problem arose because she reported the rape, accused Remington, but he produced a string of witnesses that said he was nowhere near the place she was raped that night. He apparently admitted taking her out that night, but said he'd dropped her at home an hour before the attack and at the time she was assaulted, he claimed to have been in a card game with a group of others who all gave him a solid alibi. He alleged she must have been so traumatised by the attack that she got confused and accused him by mistake. The police investigated thoroughly at the time, but there were no witnesses to the rape, no forensics to tie Remington to the attack and no reasons to disbelieve the men who gave him his alibi, even though there's a note on file that the senior investigating officer, a D.I. Spencer, strongly suspected the men who'd provided the alibi, who just happen to have been Mark Proctor, Lucas Devereux and a John Selden could easily have been the other three rapists, but Brenda Gillespie never saw their faces, as the three unknowns wore masks, and before the investigation could be concluded, she suffered a total mental breakdown and had to be admitted to a sanatorium of some kind, a specialist place where they treat long-term patients. The name of the institution isn't mentioned in the report, I'm afraid. I can't say for sure sir, because the case was closed due to lack of evidence, but she's probably still there if she's still alive. The thing is, she had a sister, sir."

"Don't tell me, Tony, let me guess, Ruth Gillespie?"

"Got it in one sir."

Ross fell silent for a second as he quickly processed Curtis's information. If nothing else, he now knew they had the name of one of the killers, and also of John Selden who without a doubt had to be the fourth man on Manvers and her partner's death list.

"Revenge, Tony, that's what this has always been about. I was wrong. I thought she was protecting Proctor and Remington out of some warped sense of loyalty to Speke Hill, but she used the place to access the records and managed to identify the other three rapists. The police at the time of the attack certainly wouldn't have released their names to her, they were in effect nothing more than witnesses to Remington's alibi, so she must have worked out, somehow, that the other rapists would be found amongst Remington's circle of friends. That can't have taken her forever, so she must have waited years before something set her off on the killing spree. Maybe it was her idea to start killing them now, or maybe it was the man's. She turned herself into a private investigator in order to identify and track them down. She didn't want us finding out the names of Devereux and the last man, whoever John is, before she got to them. We have to find this John Selden, and fast."

"Agreed, sir. What about Manvers? Do you want me to pick her up, sir?"

"Yes, I do, but take Paul Ferris with you. Don't forget, there's a man involved in this too. I don't want you walking into a situation where he might be with Manvers and you end up in any danger from the pair of them. God knows what they might do if they feel cornered. Dodds can check out Devereux's house with a couple of uniforms for company. I doubt they'll find anything of value and it's probably locked up but tell him to make a thorough external search and of course, if a door should have been accidentally left unlocked..."

Ross let his last words hang in the air.

Curtis acknowledged his instructions before going to find Nick Dodds to inform him of the change in plans,

"Right, sir. Consider us on our way."

"Curtis," Ross said with caution evident in his voice.

"Sir?"

"Be careful. Listen, take no chances. Go and tell D.C.I. Porteous your findings and ask him to send a couple of patrol cars along as back up when you and Ferris go to make the arrest. Also, with all the pressure we're likely to get on this latest killing, the boss should have no trouble getting a search warrant before you leave. Tell him we need the warrant to cover Vera's home and place of work. The uniforms can help with the search, and I'll ask Miles Booker to get a couple of crime scene techs to meet you at the house. She'll be at work by now I think so go there first and let Booker know when you're heading to the house, so the C.S. guys aren't hanging around waiting for you. I'd rather be with you, but I need to talk to the priests here at St. Luke's first. I'm sending D.C.'s Gable and McLennan to meet you there as well. Don't make a move on Manvers until they get there, understood?"

"Understood sir."

"And Curtis?"

"Yes, sir?"

"Great work lad, you and Ferris."

"Thanks, sir. Don't forget, Derek was with me yesterday too."

"Of course. I'll make sure he's aware of what's happening before he leaves here with Sam. Make sure you do everything by the book when you pick her up, and keep her isolated in an interview room until we can question her."

"Okay and thanks again, sir," said Curtis, ending the call and allowing Ross to turn and fill Izzie Drake in on the call.

Chapter 35

Home from Home?

Detective Constable Nick Dodds, accompanied by two uniformed constables, arrived at the home of Lucas Devereux within an hour of the discovery of the body in the graveyard.

Constables Flynn and Davis were both experienced officers and Dodds felt he could rely on them to back him up in case of unforeseen problems, though he doubted they'd encounter any. He knew the dead man had been single and lived alone, so he expected the search to be nothing more than routine. In the back of his mind, however, lurked the thought that no one had told him where Devereux had been abducted from, so there was a chance he could have been taken from home, in which case, there just might be evidence at the house that would prove important. Having informed Flynn and Davis of such a possibility he decided to take the front door himself, while the two uniforms were sent round to the rear of the house, along the narrow path that ran along one side of the property.

Dodds knocked on the front door, first using his clenched fist and then, receiving no reply, by use of the heavy brass door knocker in the upper centre of the door. Continuing to receive no reply, Dodds tried the brass door handle, situated just above a keyhole. The door was securely locked. Looking up, Dodds saw a small sensor situated in the corner of the door frame, obviously part of Devereux's alarm system.

Any attempt to force entry through the front door would doubtless trigger the alarm. Not knowing if it was a silent or audible alarm, Dodds decided against trying to force an entry, for fear of setting off an incessant loud alarm that might attract any number of inquisitive neighbours.

He moved to one side and, placing his hands either side of his head to obliterate glare and reflection, peered through a large bay window into what appeared to be the lounge of Devereux's home. He could make out a large television set in the far right corner of the room, a leather three-piece suite with chesterfield-style sofa, a glass topped coffee table and a tall, expensive looking hi-fi system in the opposite corner of the room. An ornate fireplace stood out from the chimney breast in between the TV and the hi-fi unit, the mantle-piece bearing a couple of framed photographs and a large anniversary clock, the balls gently twisting back and forth, oblivious of the passage of time. Nothing appeared out of place. If there had been an altercation in the house leading up to Devereux's abduction, he was fairly certain it hadn't taken place in the room he was looking into, unless Devereux had been taken by total surprise, maybe even held at gunpoint before being taken from his home, but that could mean the dead man may have let his killers in through the front door, also leading to the possibility he knew his killers and unsuspectingly let them in to his home. Nobody knew the facts of Devereux's abduction thus far and Dodds' scenario did at least fit the facts as far as he was aware at that point.

Suddenly, however, he was jolted from his thoughts and his viewing through the window by a shout that came from the rear of the house.

"Oy, you, come here you bastard," Constable Flynn shouted, followed by the voice of P.C. Davis as he joined in with a shouted warning. "Coming down the path, Nick."

Dodds quickly took three steps to his left, just in time to see a dishevelled, unkempt looking man running towards him along the path at the side of the house.

"Police, stop!" he shouted, only to be knocked to the ground by the outstretched arm of the man as he bundled his way past and onto the grassed lawn, heading for the front gate, hotly pursued by the two uniformed constables.

"I'm okay, go get him," Dodds called to the two constables as they hesitated, in case he'd been hurt.

Flynn and Davis were younger and fitter than the fleeing man, and before he managed to make it through the front gate, they were on him, an expertly timed rugby tackle by Flynn bringing him down, after which Davis quickly pinned him to the ground, wrenching the man's arms behind him and slapping the handcuffs on his wrists.

Dodds picked himself up, quickly dusted himself down and walked across to where Flynn and Davis had pulled the man to his feet, and now held him by an arm apiece as he glared from one to the other malevolently.

"Right, you," Dodds spoke with authority. "What the fuck are you doing here, on private property? And why did you run away when the constables found you?"

"They took me by surprise," the man replied. "I thought they was goin' to hurt me, like."

"And why would they do that? They're in uniform. Couldn't you see that?"

"I never took the time to stop and look, mate, honest. I was scared and just ran for it."

Dodds turned to P.C. Flynn.

"Where was he, Mike?"

"He was holed up behind the shed, Nick. As we walked round the back, he just legged it before we could say a word. Looked like the hounds of hell were on his tail."

"Right, sunshine," Dodds spoke firmly to the scruffy looking man.

"You'd better tell me what you're so afraid of and why you're hanging around in Mr. Devereux's back garden."

"I was supposed to meet Luke here last night," the man began. "I saw him at his office and he told me to go home, get some things and come and spend the night here with him, but when he never showed up, I was too scared to go home. I hope nothing's happened to him, has it?

He's not been home all night so I ended up sheltering behind the shed where no-one could see me."

Saying nothing about Devereux's murder, Dodds simply replied,

"I see, and just what is it you're so afraid of, Mr...?"

"Selden, John Selden," the man replied, and all became clear to Nick Dodds.

"Right, Mr. Selden," he said, "I think you'd better come along with us. We've some questions for you to answer and once you've warmed up and had a hot cup of tea, you're going to give us some answers, you got that?"

John Selden silently nodded his head, and as he was marched to the patrol car by the two constables, Dodds saw the man's shoulders visibly sag as if his body was acknowledging the fact he'd reached the end of the road.

As they drove back to headquarters, P.C. Davis sitting in the rear of the patrol car with Selden, Nick Dodds knew without a shadow of doubt that D.I. Ross would be eager to question the man who sat, his face a mask of fear in the back seat, staring vacantly at nothing in particular.

Chapter 36

Arrest

As the handcuffs snapped shut on the wrists of John Selden, a few short miles away Tony Curtis and Derek McLennan strode into the office of Vera Manvers at Speke Hill. Both officers did a quick double-take as they tried to reconcile the dowdy, matron-like woman who sat behind the secretary's desk with the vampish and sexually attractive woman they'd spoken to in her home the previous day. This Vera Manvers, with her hair scraped back, wearing a high-neck yellow sweater and long brown skirt and with nothing but a little eye shadow in terms of make-up, and reading glasses hanging from a chain round her neck could have passed as a totally different woman. The two men looked at one another before Vera herself broke the deadlock of silence.

"Good morning, detectives. You look shocked. Is it my appearance? Surely you wouldn't expect me to arrive for work in my 'off duty' clothes would you?" she smiled.

"Ms Manvers, hello," said Curtis. "Yes, I must say you do look rather different."

"Very different, in fact," said McLennan.

"Well, now that my appearance has been sorted out between you, perhaps you can tell me what I can do for you."

"Yes, Ms Manvers, or should we say Miss Ruth Gillespie? You can accompany us to police headquarters where we need to ask you some questions on an extremely serious matter."

Vera's face fell. The shocked look told the two detectives immediately that they were facing a guilty woman. If she could have turned and run away at that moment, they were both certain she would have done just that. Trapped as she was, behind her desk in the small office, there was nowhere to run. Having thought she'd outwitted the two officers the previous day, she now realised she was cornered. Somehow, they'd worked it out, or at least, some of it. She'd need to be very careful, and try to find out just how much they knew.

"Am I under arrest?" Vera asked with a faint tremor in her voice.

"I'm afraid so," said McLennan and D.C. Curtis proceeded to read Vera Manvers/Ruth Gillespie the standard police caution as McLennan helped her to her feet before snapping the handcuffs in place.

As the two men led Vera from the office, Charles Hopkirk stepped from his own office along the corridor and stared aghast at the sight that met his eyes.

"Vera?" he almost choked as he said the word. "What's going on here?"

"Ms. Manvers is accompanying us to police headquarters," McLennan said in response. "We need her to assist us with certain inquiries."

"But really, officers, are the handcuffs really necessary?"

"I'm afraid they are, Mr. Hopkirk. Now, if you'll please step out of the way?" said Curtis, taking a step towards the chief care officer, who reluctantly stepped to one side as the two men escorted his secretary from the building. He would have been less surprised if he'd been able to see through her daily disguise and recognised his one-time lover, Poppy.

In a final gesture before leaving, Curtis turned back to face Charles Hopkirk, showing him the search warrant. "A forensic team will be here soon, Mr. Hopkirk. This warrant grants us access to all the records at Speke Hill, past and present and in particular, Ms. Manvers' office."

"Oh my God, Vera, what have you done?" Hopkirk gasped.

Vera Manvers just stared ahead, blankly, as if she hadn't heard a word he'd said.

Vera remained silent in the car on the way to headquarters, only speaking give her name as Vera Manvers to the desk sergeant as she was booked into the building, before being led to an interview room, where she was asked to sit and wait, under the watchful eye of a uniformed female constable.

Chapter 37

A Question of Alibis

Sitting in the comfortable living room of the manse at St. Luke's, Ross and Drake couldn't be aware of the events that were taking place around the city as their fellow detectives gradually began piecing together the various links that would eventually lead to the final solution of their case.

Father Byrne had been as helpful as he could be, but remained mystified as to the reason the killings seemed to be in some way connected to his arrival back in Liverpool. Neither Ross nor Drake could shake his belief that his presence in the middle of all the mayhem surrounding the murders was nothing but a terrible and unfortunate coincidence, his time at Speke Hill somehow running parallel with whatever was taking place around him. Ross remained convinced in the priest's innocence in the matter, and tended to believe in Byrne's hypothesis. His instincts, usually reliable in such matters, told him the priest was telling the truth. Now, as Byrne left the room, he was replaced by Father David Willis.

Ross and Drake hadn't really had much contact with the younger priest so far, and Ross couldn't help but notice the look of tiredness and dark rings under the eyes of David Willis as he sat down in the chair opposite the inspector.

"A terrible business, Father Willis," Ross began.

"Indeed it is, Inspector," Willis agreed. "I was staggered when Tom Redding came to the door with such awful news."

"Pardon me for saying so, Father, but is everything alright? You look tired."

"Oh, I'm fine, thank you. Sleep is quite elusive sometimes, Inspector. Since Father Byrne began having his nightmares, I must admit I tend to lie awake at night, almost expecting another one to strike him. I've attended to him once or twice when they've occurred in the past. He can get in quite a state with them."

"It's good of you to care so much for his welfare, Father."

"Yes, well, it goes with the calling, Inspector, doesn't it? And Father Byrne is such a nice man, he really is. Did you know he has a bad heart as well?"

"I didn't know that, Father Willis. So you kind of keep a watchful eye on him, is that it?"

"You could say that, yes. I was close to Father O'Hanlon, who Father Byrne replaced and was extremely upset when he passed away. I'd hate to think of something similar happening to Father Byrne. He's still a relatively young man after all."

Ross nodded his understanding before proceeding with his next question.

"Tell me, Father Willis. Were you aware of the fact that an electric light was fitted in the Greasby family crypt some years ago?"

"Of course I was, Inspector," Willis answered without hesitation. "In fact, you'll find most of the members of the congregation were aware of it. Father O'Hanlon had it installed I believe, and often regaled the congregation with little snippets of information he'd either gleaned from the inscriptions in the crypt, or that he'd learned about the Greasby family. He was quite fascinated with their history, though I never really understood why."

"I see, and you were here all night last night, I take it?"

"Yes of course, here in the manse that is, not in the crypt, carrying out heinous crimes against Mr. Devereux."

Father Willis smiled ruefully as he spoke.

"I'm sorry. I didn't mean that to sound facetious, Inspector. It's just that I've never been questioned in connection with a murder before."

"That's alright Father. People do often react in odd ways when asked to provide an alibi for a crime."

"Oh, I see. I am a suspect then, am I?"

"To be honest, everyone is, Father," Izzie Drake replied. "You have to understand we have to look at everyone who was here last night, or who had the means or opportunity to commit the murder."

"Yes, of course. I understand," said Willis.

"Can anyone vouch for the fact you were here all night?" Drake asked.

"Oh dear," Willis said, ruefully. "Well, I didn't think I'd have to account for my movements of course, but, let's see. Mrs. Redding was here until shortly after six-thirty, maybe closer to seven p.m by the time she'd got her coat on and said goodnight. I walked outside with her and saw her into the car when her husband arrived to pick her up. I went back indoors and found Father Byrne asleep in his armchair, so I took the opportunity to take a walk around the parish. I often do that if the weather's fine. I came back and went up to my room, read the Bible for half an hour, took a shower and came downstairs just as Father Byrne was waking up. I didn't think to check the time, but it must have been around eleven p.m. I made us both a mug of cocoa and we went to bed soon afterwards. That's the best I can do, I'm afraid."

"No, that's fine, thank you, Father. We do know it's hard to account for every minute of a day, and especially when you're not expecting to have to account for your time. Too many criminals out-think their situation and have a ready answer for every minute. That's not always the best thing to do."

"Oh, I see, thank you Sergeant."

Ross now asked what he hoped would be his last question, allowing him and Drake to get back to headquarters where it appeared things were moving apace in his absence.

"Do you know a woman by the name of Vera Manvers, Father?"

"The name is rather familiar, Inspector. It's an unusual name, Manvers, isn't it? Of course, she works at Speke Hill. I've met her a couple of times, I think. After Father O'Hanlon passed away, and before Father Byrne arrived, I stood in as chaplain at Speke Hill, a job that goes with the parish of St. Luke's. I'm sure I met her there, not at Sunday services, you understand, but when I had to visit Mr. Hopkirk to arrange to fulfil my temporary duties there."

"I see, well, thank you Father," Ross said, concluding the interview. "If we need to speak to you again, you'll be here?"

"But of course, Inspector Ross. Where else would I be?"

"Where indeed, Father?" said Ross as he and Drake rose to take their leave.

Outside, Miles Booker and his team were still painstakingly going over the scene where the body of Devereux had so recently been displayed, and also the actual murder site, below ground in the Greasby crypt. Booker promised to let Ross know the instant they found anything of interest.

The body of Lucas Devereux had already been removed from the scene and transported to the mortuary, where Doctor William Nugent would already be overseeing the autopsy, aided by Francis Lees and Doctor Vicky Strauss. As the first M.E. on the scene, she would want to be part of the post-mortem team for sure, and Ross knew Nugent well enough to know he'd be encouraging the young pathologist to expand her talents under his watchful gaze.

Izzie Drake was talkative in the car on the way back to headquarters.

"You seemed almost angry back there, sir, talking to the two priests."

"Did I, Izzie? Maybe I was. It's just the whole religious thing."

"How do you mean, sir?"

"Father Byrne and Father Willis, acting all nice and Godly, for want of a better word. They have a man murdered in their own graveyard, in a bloody crypt for heaven's sake, and yes, they're very sorry and it's all so awful, but you just get the impression it's all in day's work for them."

"But it is, isn't it, sir?"

"Is it?"

"Well, yes, especially for Catholics I think. To a Catholic Priest, death is all part of God's great plan, I think. You know, we live, we sin, we go to church, we pray for forgiveness, confess our sins and receive absolution and then the only way we get to Heaven is by giving up our earthly bodies through the medium of death, allowing our souls to rise to Heaven where we supposedly dwell in paradise at the side of God for all eternity."

"Very profound, Sergeant, very profound indeed."

"Well, you did ask, sir," she grinned as she drove into the car park at police headquarters.

"Oh, come on," Ross said, shaking off his maudlin thoughts, "coffee first, then let's go talk to the Manvers woman."

"Right sir. You really think she's a killer?"

"It's certainly stacking up that way, Izzie. From what Curtis told me, she's got a sister somewhere. Let's get Paul Ferris working on locating her fast, unless the Manvers woman tells us right away of course, making things easy for us, but when do they ever do that, eh? And there's still the matter of her accomplice, whoever he is."

"You don't fancy either of the priests for the other killer then sir?"

"Byrne, no, Willis, maybe," he replied.

"Are you being serious?" Drake asked.

"There are holes in his alibi. He could have taken a shower to wash away the blood. He could have slipped something into Byrne's drink at dinner to knock him out for a while, allowing him to slip out and commit the murder, before arriving home in time for bed."

Drake laughed, and after a few seconds pause, Ross joined in.

Five minutes later, Ross and Drake were elated as they were informed by D.C. Dodds that John Selden had literally run into their arms and was also being held in an interview room, waiting to be questioned.

Chapter 38

Breakdown

Ross and Drake studied the woman sitting stoically in Interview Room 1 for almost ten minutes prior to beginning the interview of Vera Manvers. Silent and motionless, she appeared to Ross to resemble one of the giant stone figures he'd seen in TV documentaries of Easter Island. Her face gave nothing away, and he wondered how hard it might prove to break her down and find a way to incite her to talk about the murders he was now almost certain she'd been a party to. More importantly, he needed to try to get Vera to reveal the identity of her partner in crime, who had so far managed to remain anonymous to the investigators, despite Vera's capture.

"She's not moved a muscle since she was placed in there, sir," said P.C. Andrews, one of the two constables who'd taken turns to stand guard over Vera in the interview room, awaiting the arrival of the inspector.

"Looks like she may be a tough nut to crack," Ross said, before an idea struck him.

Turning to Izzie Drake, he said, "Izzie, go and ask Sam Gable to start ringing round all the private sanitoriums in the area. If we can find the one in which one her sister's being cared for, it may give us some leverage."

"Right sir," said Drake, turning to leave the viewing room. Drake also added, "Another thing that's bugged me is where the money has come from to pay for the sister's care. It must cost a fortune to keep someone in one of those places for all those years."

"You're right, of course," Ross agreed. "Perhaps it's not private, after all. It's also been my experience over the years that a lot of people use the term sanitorium as a polite, socially acceptable way to refer to a psychiatric hospital. Tell Sam to check out N.H.S, long term facilities too. Tell her to ignore those designed to house the criminally insane, like Ashworth, and concentrate on what I'd call 'normal' long-term psychiatric hospitals."

"I'll tell her now sir. I agree, they'd hardly keep her in a place like Ashworth," referring to the maximum security facility where people like the notorious Moors Murderer, Ian Brady is held to this day.

Drake was gone and back in two minutes.

"Sam's on it, sir. I told her to come in and tell us if she finds the sister. It could give us some leverage."

"Excellent. Right then, let's go talk to *Ms.* Vera Manvers."

Ten minutes of futile questioning followed. Vera had obviously decided that silence was the best defence against any form of self incrimination. Ross, used to dealing with many hardened criminals over the years, marvelled at her continued stone-faced refusal to utter a single word.

Feeling the time had come to play his trump card, even though Sam Gable hadn't as yet brought them any news relating to Vera's sister, Ross made his big play.

"We know all about Brenda, Vera."

Both Ross and Drake noticed a sudden twitch of the woman's eyebrows. They'd touched a nerve.

"We know you killed them to gain revenge for what they did to Brenda. Most people would have wanted to avenge their sister after what they did to her, but most wouldn't have the courage to see it through as you have. Of course, you needed help, didn't you? We'll find him soon enough, even if you don't tell us his name, Vera."

Vera maintained her silence, but there were visible signs that Ross was reaching her. He noticed a slight tremor in her hands where they rested on the table, and her eyes had taken on a watery appearance, as if she might be on the verge of tears. He could tell it was taking all her self-control to maintain her current level of non-cooperation.

Just when he thought he was going to have to continue to bluff his way through the rest of the story, a knock on the door was followed by the entry of Sam Gable.

"Can I have a word, sir?" she asked, and Ross rose from the table, recording the suspension of the interview on the obligatory tape recorder. He returned a few minutes later, nodded to Drake from a position behind Vera Manvers, out of her line of sight, and proceeded to re-start the recorder, then he sat down again, this time looking at a sheet of A4 paper, handed to him by D.C. Gable.

"That was Detective Constable Gable, Vera. She's just been talking to Senior Psychiatric Nursing Sister Leyburn, one of the supervisors at Helmdale Lodge."

Vera began to fidget in her chair.

"Your sister, Brenda's condition is unchanged. She thought you'd like to know. She was very surprised to hear you're in police custody. Seems she was expecting you to visit Brenda again soon. D.C. Gable pointed out to her that it may be some time before you're able to visit again, and she expressed her sadness at the fact that your sister would be reduced to only one visitor if you were 'tied up' as she diplomatically put it."

Ross fell silent for a few seconds, and Izzie Drake stepped in to the conversation.

"You can't seriously have expected to get away with it, Vera, could you? All your plans, all your meticulous planning, all for what? So you can spend the rest of your life in jail, while your sister sits there in that place, trapped in her own mind, wondering why you never come to see her any more? That's assuming she knows who you are of course."

A sound, more a whisper than anything else, suddenly emanated from the crestfallen woman.

"What was that? I couldn't hear you," said Ross.

"She knows. I said she knows I'm there and who I am. Brenda knows. I don't care what they or David says."

"David? Sister Leyburn mentioned Brenda's fiancé, David. What's his other name, Vera? He's your killing partner isn't he?"

Vera suddenly realised she'd placed David in jeopardy by her outburst, and realised they'd played on her fear of being cut off from Brenda. She fell silent again.

"Come on, Brenda. You know it's all over," Drake spoke quietly, gently, trying to coax Vera to confide in her.

"I can't," Vera sniffed as her eyes slowly filled with tears.

"Can't what, Vera? Tell us his full name? All we have to do is leave a constable at Helmdale Lodge and as soon as he turns up to see Brenda, he'll be arrested. Do you really want your sister to see her fiancé arrested in front of her?"

"Help us now, Vera, while you can. It'll help your defence if we can say you co-operated fully with us," Ross urged her, without revealing to Vera that the nursing sister had already given Sam Gable the name of Brenda's fiancé. He wanted to see if they could break through the cold and impenetrable façade that Manvers had created. The tears forming in her eyes were a sure sign that her resolve was crumbling. He passed the notes from Gable to Drake who quickly read them and saw the name of the fiancé herself, and like Ross, gave nothing away to Vera Manvers. Another knock saw Sam Gable again put her head round the door, and this time, she stepped in to the room and quickly walked across and whispered in Ross's ear before turning and walking out again. Ross knew the figurative noose was now tightening around Vera Manvers' neck.

"D.C. Gable just received word from our forensics team, Vera. They're at your house. They found your white van, parked in your garage. A very interesting collection of items in there, apparently. Bloodied clothes, surgical boots and scrubs, knives, hammers, surgical tools, and a suitcase containing changes of clothes for you and your gentleman friend. I guess you haven't had the time to dispose of the clothes and a rather expensive men's watch yet, have you, Vera? We wondered how the killers came and went so easily when they should have been covered in the blood of their victims. You and he treated it like a bloody day out at the seaside didn't you? You took a change of clothes along with you, carried out the murders, changed in the van and then burned or otherwise disposed of your old clothes and those of your victims. When Mr. Booker, our chief Crime Scenes Officer opened the suitcase containing your clothes, he found something that was a bit of a giveaway, Vera. Can you think what it was?"

"David," she said, softly.

"I know that, Vera. Tell me his other name, please."

"Willis," Vera whispered. "David Willis."

"As in Father David Willis, Vera?" Izzie Drake asked her.

Vera nodded her head.

"For the purpose of the recording, the suspect just nodded her head in response to Sergeant Drake's last question," Ross said, then went on, "Are you confirming that the man who was your partner in the murders of Matthew Remington, Mark Proctor and Lucas Devereux was Father David Willis, of St. Luke's Church, Woolton?"

"Yes," Vera spoke very quietly, just loud enough to be heard and picked up by the recording machine.

That was it. Vera's barriers had been breached and the floodgates open as she opened up and told the whole, sorry story, beginning with the rape of her sister, Brenda Gillespie. Ross's previous, almost jocular theory surrounding the killings proved to be almost one hundred percent accurate. She told how she and David Willis, then a young engineering student, planned and plotted the theoretical killing of those responsible for Brenda's condition. At the time, they'd never dreamed they'd one day put those plans into effect. It was an exercise, a means of playing out their revenge in a hypothetical scenario. She explained that Helmdale Lodge was neither private or NHS funded, but was a charitable institution, set up by a pair of wealthy philanthropists to care for special cases like Brenda's. Donations helped of course, but the wealthy owners were very much involved in the running of the home which provided the best care possible for Brenda and those like her.

Eventually, David Willis, unable to accept the love of any other woman, decided to enter the Catholic Church and was eventually ordained as a priest, whilst still harbouring his devotion to the woman he could never have, and his hatred for those who had ruined her life. He threw himself into his new life, worked hard and supported many good causes in the community. He found some comfort from working as a councillor at a rape crisis centre, where he first met a young girl by the name of Lisa Kelly. He'd introduced Lisa to Vera, who felt sorry for the girl and tried to take her under her protective wing. When she'd informed him of her pregnancy following her rape by Remington, the old anger rose in his mind again and together with Vera, began to actively plan ways to put their long-laid plans into motion. Despite his advice to Lisa not to abort her child, his Catholicism not allowing him to condone such action, she went ahead anyway, only to be consumed by guilt and eventually committing suicide at Formby Dunes.

Willis had placed no blame for her religious transgressions on young Lisa, instead laying culpability squarely on the shoulders of her rapist. The fact that she'd identified Matthew Remington, only for him to escape prosecution due to lack of corroborating evidence was the proverbial straw that broke the camel's back and set Willis and Manvers on their irrevocable course of death and destruction. Willis had indeed used sleeping tablets to ensure the new parish priest, Father Byrne, was safely out of the way on the nights when they needed to be together to carry out the killings. Willis had expressed regret to Manvers as he believed the tablets he'd crushed and administered to Byrne, either in his food or drinks had been the cause of the Father's terrible nightmares, hence his overly solicitous care of the older priest when he was present in the house to care for him after the nightmares. He'd used different medications at different times to experiment in finding an effective way of ensuring Byrne was totally unconscious during the hours he was missing from the manse.

The only regret Vera Manvers expressed was that she and Willis had been exposed before they'd finished their 'work'.

Ross omitted to tell her that John Selden was at that very moment sitting in the next room, relating everything concerning the many years of rape and sexual assault he and the others had been involved in. Derek McLennan and Tony Curtis had purposely not told Selden that the killers of his co-conspirators had been either arrested or identified. His fear of becoming a potential fourth victim of the graveyard killers as they had now become known had encouraged him to tell all. It seemed certain that the information he was providing would help the police to close the cases on a large number of unsolved rapes and sexual assaults. He told the officers that Devereux was the leader of the gang, who expressed his belief that *fear was the key* to their successful litany of crimes. If a woman felt that any one or more of four rapists was likely to come back and do her further harm, it helped to deter them from reporting the crime in the first place, thus many of their crimes would probably never be identified as they'd never been reported. McLennan and Curtis were satisfied however, that they had enough to put Selden away for many years.

At the end of their interview with Vera Manvers, Ross and Drake had her formally charged with the three murders and saw her safely locked up in the headquarters custody suite before heading out once again, this time to bring in Father David Willis.

Chapter 39

Ross and Drake pulled up in the driveway of St. Luke's manse for the second time that day, closely followed by constables Flynn and Davis in their patrol car. Ross stationed the two constables outside the front door to the manse, while he and Drake hoped to make a quiet arrest once they gained entry to the house. Not far away, in the graveyard, Miles Booker's forensic team were continuing their painstaking examination of the crypt and the grave site.

Iris Redding, surprised as she was to see the two detectives again so soon, nevertheless ushered them into the living room where Father Byrne stood up from his armchair where he was reading the newspaper, to greet them.

"Inspector, Sergeant," Byrne said, "is there something else you need from me?"

"It's David Willis we need, Father, as a matter of urgency, I'm afraid."

"You sound troubled, Inspector. When you say, a matter of urgency, what exactly does that signify?"

"Is he here, Father?" Ross spoke bluntly.

"He should be returning any minute now. He's been counselling at the Rape Crisis Centre. Please, can't you tell me what this is about?"

Ross saw no way of sweetening the bad news, and quickly, without going into details, informed the priest that David Willis was wanted for questioning in relation to the three recent murders. Byrne looked aghast as Ross finished delivering the shocking news.

"David? Surely not, inspector. There must be some mistake. Murder? I simply can't believe it."

"We're so sorry, Father," Izzie Drake said, softly, trying to cushion the impact of the news, knowing that Father Byrne had a heart condition and not wanting to exacerbate the problem by maybe inducing a heart attack through the shock. "It's true though. We have his collaborator, Vera Manvers in custody already and she's confessed to the crimes and implicated Father Willis."

Stunned, Gerald Byrne slumped into his armchair. Drake looked at the man and could later swear his face aged ten years in the few seconds it had taken to go from standing to sitting.

"He was even slipping drugs into your food and drink to make sure you were fast sleep so he could sneak out, commit the murders, and be back before you woke up," Ross added.

"Oh, Lord!" Byrne suddenly caught on. "So I'd fall asleep, knowing he was here, and when I woke up, he was still here as far I was concerned, so I became his perfect alibi."

"That's right, Father. The pills he was giving you were quite probably the cause of your nightmares, a side effect of the drugs. He was genuinely concerned about your health, which is why he was so solicitous, coming to your help and checking on you when you woke up screaming. If you'd had a heart attack and been admitted to hospital, they'd have likely found the drugs in your system and he'd have had a hard time explaining how they came to be there."

"Drugging me is one thing, Inspector, but the thought of him, a man of God, sworn to uphold the sanctity of life, being a cold-blooded murderer is simply appalling and I still find it difficult to believe."

Before Ross could say anything more, the living room door flew open as P.C Flynn came hustling into the room, unannounced.

"Sir, it's Willis, he's doing a runner."

"What? Tell me man, quickly."

"He just pulled into the drive, and must have realised the game was up when he saw me and Davis guarding the door. He reversed out, burning rubber I might say and set off in the direction of the city centre."

"Are you cleared for high speed pursuit, Flynn?"

"Yes sir."

"Well, don't just stand there man. Get after him. We'll follow you out. Sorry Father, we must go."

Ross and Drake positively flew out of the house, hot on Flynn's heels. Ross shouted to Flynn as he got into the police Peugeot. "Radio headquarters and report every turn he makes. Did you get his number?"

"No sir, all happened too fast."

"Alright, now go man, quickly. Get on his tail."

"He could be a mile away by now, sir," Drake said as she drove as fast as she could in order to stay on the patrol car's tail.

"It's a straight road into town from here, Izzie, unless he turns into one of the housing estates along the way, and I doubt he's stupid enough to trap himself that way."

A minute later, the patrol car radioed that they had Willis's blue Escort in sight. The old Ford was no match for the almost brand new police patrol car and with Drake keeping close behind the Focus with its lights and siren scything a way through the city traffic they were soon gaining on the fleeing priest, who suddenly threw his car into a hard left turn.

"He's heading south. I think he's going to try to make it to the M62, sir," said Drake.

"He's going nowhere," Ross said determinedly, as he radioed in to headquarters, requesting roadblocks at all strategic entries to the motorway.

"Why is he running, sir? He must know he'll never get away."

"Simple flight or fight response, I suppose, Izzie. He must know we'll get him in the end, but his instincts have taken over."

Just ahead of their car, the patrol car driven by Flynn had closed to within a few yards of Willis's vehicle, all other traffic having pulled over at the sound of the police siren and the sight of the flashing lights.

With abrupt suddenness, another police patrol car shot out of a side road a hundred yards ahead of Willis's car, the driver swinging his car to block the left hand side of the road, narrowing Willis's path of escape and the priest, not used to having to manoeuvre a car at speed, made a vain attempt to swerve past the parked car and swerved head-long onto the pavement, the few watching pedestrians scattering in panic. Willis's face contorted in horror as he realised he was heading straight for a deadly combination of a lamp post that stood immediately next to a bright red Royal Mail pillar box.

He virtually stood on the brakes, and the Escort began to fishtail as he attempted to bring the car to a halt before striking the immovable obstacles. Flynn slowed the patrol car almost to a stop, Drake doing the same with their unmarked car as they watched the scene unfold.

David Willis almost made it back onto the road, but the rear of the car struck the base of the lamp post as he tried to swerve past it and the effect of the collision caused the escort to slew round almost in a full circle, sliding into the road, losing speed, until it virtually floated into a slow collision with one of a number of cars parked at meters on the opposite side of the street.

The police were on him immediately, and after a quick check to ensure he was unhurt, Constable Davis pulled Willis from the car, and Flynn snapped the handcuffs on the would-be escapee. Ross and Drake walked up to where Willis stood between the two uniformed officers and Ross stood face to face with the second of the graveyard killers.

"Did you really think you were going to get away, Father?" he asked.

"No, of course not, Inspector Ross. To be honest, I just panicked when I saw the constables outside the house. I'll not cause you any more trouble, I promise."

"I'm pleased to hear it," said Ross. "You know, you almost got away with it. If Vera hadn't suddenly tossed all your careful planning out of the window and gone crazy with rage, we might never have caught on to you. You were also a bit stupid using your own church to dispose of Devereux."

"Yes, well, I couldn't find another St. Luke's close enough for us to carry out the job and still allow me to get home again in time to create my alibi."

"Why did you do it, Father Willis? Couldn't you and Vera have simply gathered sufficient facts and then presented them to the police so we could have prosecuted them?"

"What? And let them walk away like they did all those years ago, after what they did to Brenda, and again the way Remington got away with raping poor Lisa Kelly? There was no way we were going to trust the police to deal with them, no disrespect to yourself intended, Inspector Ross."

Ross couldn't think of a suitable reply to Willis's statement. In fact, he privately admitted the priest had a point, though he could never openly acknowledge it. Instead, he ordered Flynn and Davis to ferry Willis to headquarters, where he and Drake would conduct their second interview of the day in Interview Room 1.

Over the following two hours, David Willis recounted virtually the identical story to that told earlier by Vera Manvers. Unlike Vera, however, the priest required no persuasion or cajoling to give a full and concise statement of the pair's murderous activities.

Standing in the viewing room, behind the glass of the one-way mirror, Doctor Christine Bland stood with D.C.I. Harry Porteous, listening to the way the priest verbally re-lived the three murders and the long years of planning that had gone into them. Christine felt her profile had been somewhat vindicated, and considered it to have been reasonably accurate, down to the fact that it had taken just one trigger event, the death of Lisa Kelly, to set Manvers and Willis on the eventual path that had led to the deaths of three men. Porteous agreed with her, and despite his many years in the job, he felt a coldness emanating from David Willis he'd never encountered before.

A third person in the viewing room took great interest in David Willis's version of events. He would after all, be replacing Harry Porteous at the end of the month and the forthcoming trials of the two killers would affect what would by then be his squad.

By the time Ross and Drake left David Willis in the care of the custody officer, the pair were both tired and elated at the same time. Stepping into the viewing room, they both looked in surprise at the additional figure in the room.

"Oscar?" said Ross. "Great to see you, but what are you doing here?"

"Perhaps, I'd better answer that," said Porteous. "D.I. Ross, Sergeant Drake, I'd like you to meet my replacement. I'm aware you two know each other quite well," he said to Ross."

"Oscar, you old dark horse," said Ross, grinning. "You got promoted?"

"I did indeed, Andy. I hope my new elevated rank won't stop us working well together, or affect our friendship outside working hours, of course?"

"Of course not...erm, sir."

"Cut out the 'sir', Andy. That'll keep for official or formal moments. We'll work better together if we keep things between us much as they are already."

"That's fine by me, and bloody hell, congratulations," said Ross who turned to Drake and said, "Izzie, meet Detective Chief Inspector Oscar Agostini. We go back a lot of years, and I know you're going to enjoy working with him."

"I'm sure I am, sir. Welcome and congratulations on your promotion sir," she added, speaking to Agostini.

"Thanks," said the new D.C.I. "That was some case you've just concluded. Must have given you a few nightmares along the way?"

"Well, the odd sleepless night, perhaps," said Ross. "The nightmares were reserved for someone else."

At the reference to Father Byrne, both Ross and Drake shared a knowing smile. Agostini noticed it and decided he'd let Andy tell him the full story another time. He could see how tired they both looked.

Christine Bland, having already said her good byes to the rest of the team, now took her leave of Ross and Drake.

"I hope I was some help in the case, Andy," she said, hoping he'd agree at least to some extent.

"Actually, I wasn't sure about you at first," he replied, "but your profile was damned good. It prevented us going off on a tangent and looking at every serial sex offender in Liverpool to begin with. Your profile effectively reduced our suspect pool and by concentrating on the events at Speke Hill and its people, we soon had it narrowed down, though we needed a large slice of luck in the end."

"Aye, well, we all need that luck from time to time, Andy, that's for sure," said Agostini.

"Thank you, Andy," Bland replied. "It's been a pleasure working with you on such an interesting case, you too Izzie," she said as she reached out to shake hands with each in turn.

"Oh, to hell with it," said Ross as he grabbed her by both arms, pulled her close and gave her a great bear hug, before releasing her to the accompanying mirth of the two D.C.I.s.

"Wow, thanks," was all Christine could say as she finally took a deep breath and looked at Andy Ross, surprised at his show of emotion.

"Just promise you won't tell Maria," he laughed at Agostini.

"Oh, I doubt she'd mind anyway, but your secret's safe with me," said the new head of the murder investigation unit.

Ross and Drake stood on the steps of the headquarters building, watching as Christine Bland climbed into her still pristine Vauxhall Carlton and drove away as the first grey wash of evening began to fall over the buildings of their city.

"You tired, sir?" Izzie asked.

"Bloody knackered, Sergeant. How about you?"

"The same. Fancy a pint before we go home?"

"Why, Sergeant Drake. First a hug with the profiler, and now my sergeant wants to buy me drinks. What is the force coming to?"

Izzie smiled, a devilish grin on her face as she said, "Sorry, sir, I never said anything about me paying."

Ross laughed, Izzie laughed, the tension that had built up in the two of them through the long day at last released in a moment of humour and camaraderie.

* * *

"What do you think will happen to them?" Maria Ross asked her husband as they lay in bed together later that night.

"It'll be up to the courts, of course," Andy replied, "but I can see David Willis going away for a very long time. I was surprised how cold and dispassionate he was about the whole affair when we interviewed him this afternoon. He displayed no emotion at all. I think any emotions he did possess probably died when Brenda, his fiancée was left a physical and mental cripple for the rest of her life. His own life, his hopes and dreams for their future together all died at the same time. I very much doubt whether, if she were able, Brenda Gillespie would recognise the David Willis of today. He's certainly not the man she fell in love, of that, I'm sure."

"And what about her, the woman?"

Andy Ross lay quietly thinking for a few seconds before replying.

"I'm not sure about her, Maria. She's something of an enigma, even now. She was prepared to sleep with any man she met if she felt it was necessary in the scheme of her plans to eliminate the four men. She could change her appearance like a bloody chameleon. Charles Hopkirk at Speke Hill slept with her as Poppy, but then never suspected Vera was the same woman. That was one of the most effective deceptions I've ever come across. There's a certain something, call it a madness of sorts about that woman. I don't think she'll be seeing the light of day for a long time either, but whether she'll end up in prison or a secure psychiatric unit, I just don't know."

"Well, you've done your part, darling. Come on, put the light out and let's get some sleep. You need it, and that's the doctor's orders," she said, reaching over to kiss him softly on the lips.

Just as he put the light out, Andy Ross stroked his wife's warm, bare thigh, and said, very quietly, "Oh, I forgot to tell you, I hugged a profiler today, my darling."

"Mmm, that was nice for you. Now go to sleep Andy, it's late."

* * *

Around the time Andy and Maria Ross fell asleep, wrapped in each others arms, Izzie Drake lay in the arms of her fiancé, Peter Foster.

"Wow," she gasped. "I thought I'd be too tired for that, tonight."

"So did I to be honest," Peter smiled languidly at her. "Must have been the wine and Indian takeaway that did it," he joked.

"Whatever it was, I'm glad about it. You make me feel so good, Peter."

He reached across, turned her face towards him and kissed her passionately.

"Are you glad that case is over?" he asked.

"You bet I am," Izzie replied. "So much blood and two real whackos at the end of it. A good result"

"Yes, but you know, a lot of people might say they did the world a favour, Izzie."

"Peter, we can never condone vigilante justice, no matter what the circumstances."

"Oh, come on, Izzie, they've rid the world of three scumbags, from what you've told me. Even if they'd been caught and jailed they'd probably have been released to do it again in a few years."

"I know, Peter, and a lot of people would agree with you, but my job is to uphold the law, and that's what I do every day, to the best of my ability and the same goes for all the team. I daresay a few of them have had similar thoughts during this case, but, like I said, we have a job to do and we just get on with it."

"I know, and I'm proud of you, really. I just wonder sometimes..."

"Yeah, we all do, Peter. Now, come and give me a kiss and then, I need some sleep."

Peter Foster grinned a devilish grin.

"Sleep? Really?"

"Really."

Epilogue

The first of the graveyard killers to come to trial, some six months later, was David Willis. Stripped of the priesthood by the Vatican, he was described by the judge as, "One of the coldest, most calculating killers ever to stand before me. You planned these murders with malice aforethought and executed your victims in the most callous, painful and brutal manner imaginable. You have since shown no remorse for your crimes and it is the duty of this court to sentence you to life imprisonment, with a recommendation that you serve a minimum of twenty years."

Due to the fact that he'd been responsible for 'disposing' of three sex offenders, always hated by other inmates, the 'graveyard killer' became something of a celebrity among his fellow inmates. Though no longer an ordained priest, David Willis found himself in demand by many inmates who had 'found' religion whilst under lock and key, and soon made himself useful to the prison authorities by organising Bible classes for those who showed interest. Prison, it seemed, had given Willis a new lease on life.

Two months later, Vera Manvers stood trial, but escaped prison when she was found incapable of pleading, her mental health having deteriorated during her time on remand. She was now a shadow of the woman who had cold-heartedly joined in the torture and executions of their victims and her eyes displayed a haunted, other-worldly look. She was sentenced to be detained 'at her Majesty's pleasure' in a secure psychiatric hospital, and the likelihood is that she will never be released.

John Selden, having confessed to over twenty counts of rape, received a twenty year prison sentence, but, only six months into his sentence, despite being held on the isolation wing of the prison for his own protection, he was attacked and knifed to death in the showers. The 'four apostles' had all met their deaths through violence, as Willis and Manvers originally intended.

Much to everyone's surprise a relationship grew between Melanie Proctor and Charles Hopkirk, and rumour has it that wedding bells are in the air.

Brenda Gillespie, oblivious to the fate, or existence of her sister or former fiancé, continues to live her life in peace and quiet at Helmdale Lodge, where she is visited weekly by Father Gerald Byrne, who took it upon himself to take over the pastoral care of the innocent victim whose brutalisation had started the whole train of events that led to so much violence and death. Father Byrne no longer has nightmares.

About the Author

Brian L Porter is an award-winning author, whose books have also regularly topped the Amazon Best Selling charts. Writing as Brian, he has won a Best Author Award, and his thrillers have picked up Best Thriller and Best Mystery Awards.

Writing as Harry Porter his children's books have achieved three bestselling rankings on Amazon in the USA and UK.

In addition, his third incarnation as romantic poet Juan Pablo Jalisco has brought international recognition with his collected works, *Of Aztecs and Conquistadors* topping the bestselling charts in the USA, UK and Canada.

Brian lives with his wife, children and a wonderful pack of ten rescued dogs.

He is also the in-house screenwriter for ThunderBall Films, (L.A.), for whom he is also a co-producer on a number of their current movie projects.

A Mersey Killing, the first of the Mersey Mystery series has already been optioned for movie adaptation, in addition to his other novels, all of which have been signed by ThunderBall Films in a movie franchise deal.

Look out the next three books in the Mersey Mysteries series. *A Mersey Maiden, A Mersey Mariner* and *A Mersey Ferry Tale* will be coming soon.

Dear reader,

Thank you for taking time to read *All Saints, Murder on the Mersey.* If you enjoyed it, please consider telling your friends or posting a short review. Word of mouth is an author's best friend and much appreciated.